band of brothers

ERNEST FRANKEL

the macmillan company   new york   1958

for Louise

BAND OF BROTHERS
A Novel of the U.S. Marines in the Korean War

ERNEST FRANKEL

Band of Brothers, originally published in 1958 by the MacMillan Company, New York, is part of the UNCOMMON VALOR REPRINT SERIES.

Printed in the United States of America

UNCOMMON VALOR SERIES EDITION
May 2023

ISBN: 9781951682811

We few, we happy few, we band of brothers;
For he today that sheds his blood with me
Shall be my brother...
—*Henry V*

The epic battle of the First Marine Division in Korea is part of history. In this book the larger units involved, the tactics they employed, their route of march and the pattern of their deployment have not been disguised. But the Able Company of this story never existed. Though many men did serve in similar companies and fought in similar engagements, though 20,000 marines did battle the sixty miles to the sea, the characters depicted in this novel live only in the imagination of the author.

1

The marines lay on the cold ground at the crest of the ridge, their eyes fixed on the silent village below. Only the fitful wind moved across the Korean landscape. Only the nervous stirrings, the hoarse whispers of the men broke the eerie stillness of noon. The patrol had come three miles into the ominous quiet of enemy territory.

A hundred yards away, squatting in the russet valley, were rows of thatched huts. On either side were rice paddies. Then a crumbling stone wall. Farther, the jagged ramparts of the mountains. Beyond, Manchuria.

A marine held one hand over his mouth to muffle the sound of his voice. "Think we'll go down?"

He was answered with a shrug.

Tipping back his camouflaged helmet, he rested his sweating forehead against the smooth, cool stock of his rifle. "Feel rotten ... pooped."

"You're shook," the BARman beside him said.

"You're not?" He moved closer. "Three months out of P.I. and you're a real old salt!"

"Beat your gums!"

The rifleman turned away, peered through the rear sight of his weapon and swung it slowly across the front. "I'll make out," he muttered.

The BARman grinned, and nudged his friend. "You and the captain," he whispered. "Real gung-ho gyrenes—" He stopped in mid-sentence and frantically signaled for silence. There was movement in the scrub growth to their rear. Both men whipped around, thrusting their weapons before them. "Watch it," the BARman breathed. "Christ! Watch it ..."

First Sergeant Wally Goober crashed through the underbrush. "You stupid knuckleheads," he said, his shrill voice muted, his jowls quivering. "You ever point a weapon at me again, I'll have you rota tin' on the end of it!" He jerked his head toward the village. "See anythin' down there?"

"Nothing," the rifleman said.

"Well, keep lookin'. And clear those pieces before you shoot somebody." He crawled away into the brush. Hearing voices before him, he guided on the sound. *All this damn' whisperin'. All this snoopin' and poopin' on your belly. What a crock!* The voices were clearer now. He could see the men twenty yards below him, in the caked mud of a drainage ditch. Corporal Mel Firesteen sat on his helmet; and Monk Nelson was propped against his radio.

"Musta seen half the doctors in Pittsburgh," Firesteen said, his cherub's face furrowed in concentration. "Wife and me figure I got booted in the family jewels playin' football, so maybe it's my fault we can't connect. So they put me on wheat germ and hormones ..." Goober slipped down in the concealment of the underbrush and lay with his back on a mat of pine needles. Reaching into his helmet liner, he took his cigarettes from beneath the webbing, lit one and puffed, closing his eyes, half hearing the murmur of conversation,

"You was too anxious," Nelson said. "Gotta relax. Like I said, we couldn't do no good either. Then we adopt our girl. Bango! Six months later, I got one in the oven ..."

Goober inhaled, released the smoke slowly and waved his meaty hand to dispel it in the wind. *Better finish the rounds and get back to playin' nursie.* He allowed himself two minutes. Then, taking another long drag, he ground out the cigarette, shook the tobacco loose, rolled the paper in a ball and tossed it away.

"I was gettin' a razzin' from her family," Firesteen was saying. "Then we find out it's not me. They start workin' on my wife. I'm tellin' you, the poor kid, she was a nervous wreck with oil in the tubes and injections and shots of this pregnant-horse urine—I should drop dead, I'm not givin' you the straight scoop—maybe it was sheep. But with seven days left till I had to ship out, I clue you, I had my work cut out for me."

"Knock it off!" Goober came into the open and slid down to them. "You're supposed to be watchin' the front."

"So all right, I'm watchin'," Firesteen said. "I been watchin' for half an hour and whisperin' and makin' like a mole. When the hell we gonna secure the butts?"

"When the captain makes up his mind," Goober said.

Nelson turned a cleaning patch in the chamber of his carbine. "He still losin' his cookies?"

"Give him time," Firesteen said. "He's just a couple days off the boat. He'll get squared away, and God forbid, he's liable to turn out a hard-chargin' marine."

Goober spat. "He wouldn't make a wart on a good marine's can! What frosts me is, we already got the best skipper in the division—as good a marine as ever took a dump behind a pair of boondockers—and they gotta send us a pogue to put over him."

"Seems like a good egg," Nelson said. "I was gassin' with him back at the C.P. Wanted to know 'bout my family, where I'm from..."

"When the brass starts actin' buddy-buddy," Firesteen said, "stand by for a ram!"

"Looks like a recruitin' poster," Goober said, scowling. "A Hollywood marine if I ever saw one." He had a mental image of the captain, in dress blues, with rugged features and grim smile, swinging on an A-frame sign before the post office back home in Matoon, Illinois. But at the same time, he felt guilty. Shouldn't run down superiors to the troops. Disloyal. Louse yourself up. Louse up your outfit.

Nelson suddenly dropped flat on his stomach and waved the others to silence. "Thought I saw somethin' ... like a shadow ... movin.'"

Goober and Firesteen slipped down beside him, and together they stared at the village. "You're clutched up," Goober said. "I don't see a thing."

"I coulda swore ..." Nelson hunched his shoulders and sat up again. "Right near those huts in front."

"You gotta stop drinkin' that gook likker," said Firesteen.

"Well," Goober said, pushing himself up, "keep on—"

"Watchin,'" Firesteen cut in. "Watchin' and waitin' and whisperin' ..."

Goober climbed back into the scrub growth, crawled to the reverse slope and stood erect. Then he made his way toward the flank.

Fifty yards away, a sentry eased up on his elbows and lit a cigarette. "Why doesn't he pull us out of here?" he whispered to the man beside him. "We might be sitting in the middle of a whole army ... one pooped-out squad."

"You seen any slopeheads?"

"Everybody knows they've been pouring in. There's probably a pot full of them in that creepy village. We keep screwing around, he's going to get us clobbered."

The other marine yawned, tapping his knuckles against his teeth. "At least he don't act like he's shot in the ass with The Corps, like Anderson. And that suits this boy fine. Might not volunteer us for every damn' cruddy detail—"

"Stow it! Goober!"

The first sergeant was lumbering toward them, crouched low, his belly bobbing over the top of his pistol belt. "You people quit your yackin,'" he said. "And duck that butt. You hear anybody say the smoking lamp was lit?"

"Jezuz, Top!"

"Captain's orders."

The marine pinched off the cigarette with gloved fingers and put it behind his ear. "Nuts. He's as fouled-up as a Chink fire drill!"

"Shut your hole," Goober whispered harshly. "You sound off about the captain again, I'll have you on report!"

He left them and followed a wooded path down the side of the ridge.

"Reckon ole Top is takin' off, goin' over the hill!"

Goober dropped to his knees. He recognized the voice, knew that he had passed the position, but couldn't spot his men.

"You're it, Top," the voice taunted.

"All right, Justus, you wise bastard ..."

"If'n I was a goonie, you'd be buzzard bait by now," the voice said. Then a foot was wagged above the brush.

Goober pushed through the woven net of branches. "That's right. Play grabass! I told you to watch the village."

Lochran Justus rolled over lazily, hands behind his cropped blond head. "Nothin' down there but the stink, Top. Garlic and pee and the honey pits."

Jesus Sanchez squatted beside Goober. "You want us to go down and take a look?"

"That's up to the captain."

"Wish he'd get on the ball. Don't feature choppin' back through them boondocks at night," Justus said.

"You guys are his runners. Why don't you tell him you got a problem?" Goober turned his back on them and plodded up the path.

Justus rubbed his beardless chin. "That cap'n's liable to get on the panic button. All mornin' he's been fidgety as a nigger in new shoes."

"You wasn't no loose goose when you first come here." Sanchez got up and slung his rifle.

"Goober's got no use fer him. You can tell."

"Aw, Lock, Goober's so busy kissin' Anderson's tail he don't see nothin' but brown."

"Bet a coon dog 'gainst a corncob the skipper never acted like this feller. Not his first day, not ever."

"He's not skipper no more," Sanchez said. The voice was husky, pitched low. "Anderson's just exec now."

"Where you goin'?"

"Down to take a look. Always find things in them villages."

"Goin' by yerself?"

"No. You're going with me."

"The hell you say!"

"We'll be back in ten."

"Not Ma Justus' boy Lock."

"Chicken!"

"Keerect!"

"Yeller!"

"You sure got me pegged."

"There's a jar of sick-bay alky in my pack at the C.P. You come, you can have half."

"Hope to die?"

"Yeah."

Lock picked up his rifle. "Buddy-roe, you talked me into it." He followed, watching Sanchez move slowly down the hillside. Glides like a mountain critter, he thought. Real quiet and graceful-like.

They worked their way, picking their concealment, first through a grove of elms, then behind a stone wall, and down a creek bed. Sanchez scouted the first hut with Lock covering him.

"Hot damn!" Sanchez pointed to a Mauser, its blue steel shining at the bottom of a manure tank. He motioned for Lock to join him. "Just luck I saw it, Lock. I'm gonna get it outta there."

Lock stared at him, then leaned over the hole. "You mean yer gonna stick yer paw in that honey pit?"

"I can wash my hand, but maybe I'll never find another pistol like that one." He put down his rifle. "Grab my feet while I reach for it." Lock held his shoes as he swung perilously over the hole, just out of reach of the Mauser. "Don't jerk, dammit!"

"Down a little," Sanchez said.

Lock leaned forward. "Watch it. Yer boondockers are loose."

The stench was bringing tears to Sanchez's eyes. "You drop me, I'll feed your dingus to the gooney birds!"

Something prodded Lock in the back. He tightened his grip, then turned. Two enemy soldiers were standing behind him, their rifles leveled. He could not speak. He threw his hands up.

There was an angry shriek, spitting, cursing from the offal pit. "You ... You ... wedge-assed hillbilly ..." Sanchez sputtered, screamed. "I'll kill you when I get outta here!"

The enemy soldiers were giggling. One of them, a hulking, broad-chested man, motioned for Lock to get his companion out. But the marine could hardly move. He kept watching the enemy, sure they would shoot at any moment. The big soldier grunted, pointed impatiently. Lock reached down. "We got company," he whispered.

But Sanchez was still yelling. "I'm gonna soak you in here—head down—

overnight!"

"Hope to die, we got company." Then, urgently, Lock croaked, "Gooks! Gooks!" Grasping the grimy hand, he pulled him from the pit.

Sanchez was crusted, smeared. "Holy Mary, Mother of God ..." he mumbled as he faced the enemy.

2

Captain Bill Patrick got to his knees and carefully, noiselessly, parted one twisted branch, and then another. He looked down at the village again. Somewhere. The enemy was somewhere. Maybe even watching him now.

Then a gleam of light flashed below. His heart quickened painfully. He caught his breath. Tense, eyes fastened on the spot, he waited. —For the glint of a rifle. Or a bayonet. Or a belt buckle. But, though he stared until his sight blurred and his cramped body ached, he could detect no movement. No sound. Nothing.

He let each branch slip into place, still watching until his view was obscured. Then he leaned back against the trunk of a stunted poplar. It was damp, cool. But he was sweating. He removed his helmet and rubbed the back of his head against the bark.

Fifty days. He had come halfway around the world in that time. September: Overnight from Washington to California. (The farewell party that escorted him to the airport ... and no chance to be alone for a final moment with Ann ... and the drunken rendition of the Marines' Hymn ... and: "It's all over, Pat. MacArthur's got them runnin', too late for you to be a hero.") October: Day-and-night retraining at Camp Pendleton, refresher courses in tactics and weapons, field problems. ("You gentlemen in the Reserve have four years to catch up on, and not even four weeks to do it.") And now it was November: ("See from your jacket you've had no combat experience, but I'm going to try you with a company ...") So here I am, he thought.

Fifty days from an office in D.C. Exposed to the enemy for the first time. And I'm ... edgy. He breathed deeply, as if that might dislodge the lump in his chest. Hell, let's face it, Pat. You're scared. Plain scared ...

He could hear First Sergeant Goober coming back. Sitting up quickly, he put his helmet on and busied himself with his map.

Goober lowered his ponderous bulk beside the captain. Twigs snapped beneath him and his canteen rattled. "Checked every hole. Nobody's seen a thing. Gave the squad leader the word to get his people together on the reverse slope." He looked at his watch. 'Take about fifteen minutes. We'll go down and scout the place."

"No need to go down if there's nothing there."

"Captain, we're supposed to scout that village." Goober opened a can of ham and lima beans. "That's what we came out for."

Pat hesitated, apparently preoccupied with folding his map and slipping it into the case. "We were just told to find out if there are troops down there."

"Well, how the ... How we gonna know if we don't look?" Goober wiped the white grease from the rim of the can, and began to spoon the cold food into his mouth.

Pat gulped for air and, turning away, fought back a rising tide of nausea. He parted the branches again and glanced at the village. God! Don't let me be sick, he thought. Don't let me be sick! In that instant there was movement below. His eyes caught it, would not let his mind reject it.

"Lieutenant Anderson meant for us to go down ..."

Pat signaled for quiet. He saw Goober's mouth churning, beans dribbling on his chin. "Come here! Something down there. Between those huts on the right. A man ... looked like a man!"

Goober crawled beside him. Wiping his mouth on his sleeve, he said, "See you forgot your field glasses." Then he scanned the village. He did it methodically, his eyes examining the foreground, searching from side to side, moving higher, appraising detail, estimating ranges. He did it as he had been taught—from the manual, The Book. "I don't make out anything." He sucked at his teeth. "Probably some scared gooks ... or your imagination. But we oughta go see."

"And maybe run into a whole nest of the enemy?"

Goober picked up his ration. "Hell, Captain, you said you saw ..."

Pat averted his eyes. "I didn't actually see a man. It was more like ... well, maybe a shadow ... He felt that he was being propelled on an uncharted course. "We'd better call company."

Goober chewed thoughtfully. He knew what The Book said; and as long as you followed The Book you were damn' well covered. Your mission—that's what counted—more than anything else. More than yourself. More than your men. "Who you got to ask, Captain?"

Pat flushed. It was his command, his decision. "I mean we've got to tell Lieutenant Anderson what we're going to do. In case ... if we ... if I decide to do something, and things ... go wrong." Goober didn't like the idea. Using the radio might give away the position. The Book said ... He pulled the roll of fat beneath his chin. "Can't reach the C.P. There's too many big hills between us and company."

So soon, Pat was thinking, to run into the enemy so soon! There'd been no contact for over a week. The battalion commander had told him that. Everyone had said so. The North Koreans were running, hiding. The war was practically over. And now, two days after his arrival, they were talking of a new war and a new enemy. To take so few men down there—too big a risk. Too far from help. They were one squad; and somewhere before them, behind them even, around them perhaps, was a hidden army. "I don't want to commit this outfit against God knows what," he said at last.

"We'll send a fire team down, Captain. Let the four of them scout it out; and we'll follow behind, cover them." Goober spoke dispassionately, as if the issue were settled.

In the turmoil of his thoughts, Pat sought some defense for his position. "They're liable to be all over us before we can ..."

The first sergeant scowled, his eyes and his thick lips barely visible in the folds and creases of his face. Skipper told me to play nursemaid, he was thinking. But I've had it. "I'll take them down myself, Captain." Pat turned on him. The sting of the words was unmistakable. There was contempt in them. "If anybody goes down there, I'll take them," he said, too loud. Already he regretted the revealing anger.

Goober sensed his agitation. Got to watch it, he mused. Green bastard came out on this to prove something. To himself or the troops or maybe to the skipper. He smiled. It was the kind of smile given in response to a photographer's request. "Whatever you say, sir. You asked me. I told you what I thought, what The Book says. But if that's the way you want it, that's the way it's gonna be."

Stupid to have come out on a squad patrol in the first place, Pat thought. But he had felt compelled to do it. Illogically, in defiance of his executive officer's urging and common practice and good sense, he had insisted. Now he reasoned he should have remained at the command post instead, gotten to know his men and his officers, become familiar with the terrain.

"Top?" The squad leader, out of breath, came running up. "Got everybody standin' by—except the captain's runners. Can't find them two guys."

"I told you exactly ..."

"Yeah, and I looked. And I saw where they been crapped out. But they wasn't there."

"What do you mean, they're not there?" Pat asked, alarmed.

"It's that damn' spic Sanchez," Goober said. "Souvenir crazy. Musta gone below.

Idiot!" There was a long, silent moment while Goober looked at Pat. Then: "Well, Captain, what's the word? How you gonna have it?"

The scouting fire team moved with practiced skill from cover to cover. Pat left the concealment of the trees, ran after them, and rolled into a ditch beside a rutted path.

Corporal Mel Firesteen stood over him. "Looks like we'd see them if they was down here."

"What do you think we ought to do?" Pat asked, getting up.

"I don't know, Captain," Firesteen said, fingering the birthmark on his cheek.

Suddenly Pat dropped to the earth again, his long body pressed to the damp ground, his lean face etched with tension. He pointed. "That hut closest to us ... about forty yards ... the one by itself, away from the others. Something moved!"

"Looks like a door swingin'," Firesteen said. He had thrown himself beside the captain, not knowing what to expect. Now he got up. "Just the wind rockin' ..."

"Get down!" Pat whispered, pulling at Firesteen's trouser leg. Then, seeing that the other men in the fire team seemed amused by his posture, by the urgency in his voice, he rolled over. With deliberate nonchalance, he stood. For an instant he imagined his six-foot silhouette moving across the sights of a hidden enemy rifle. Then, girding himself, he purposely turned his back on the possibility of danger. He took out his canteen, tried the bitter-tasting water, and managed to get a little down. When he glanced up, he caught the others studying him.

"Guess we better look that hut over," Firesteen said, breaking the silence.

Pat nodded, not even sure what the corporal had said, thinking only that there wasn't really enough wind to swing a door.

"You people cover me," Firesteen said to his men. "Get that BAR up where it can fire." He left the ditch and ran in a half-crouch, weaving toward the hut.

Pat felt he should have made the first move, should have faced the danger before one of his men. But he hadn't decided on his action when the corporal was already on his way. He watched, mouth dry, pulses beating in his temples, as Firesteen slid along the wall on the blind side. A grenade ... he ought to have a grenade to throw in the window or door. Years before, in Quantico it was, there'd been a mock village ... and a hoarse-voiced lieutenant whose arm was in a sling ... Pat bit his lips. Should have been sure the fire team had grenades. How could he run a company of two hundred and fifty if he couldn't take care of four men?

Firesteen was still moving. He thrust his head and weapon through the window. The hut was empty. He motioned to the others to join him.

Pat moved up with them, feeling reprieved for the moment. "Ought to have grenades," he told Firesteen.

"We're gonna have to try every hut. In case they came down here and got coldcocked."

Fifty yards to the rear, Goober watched from the shelter of a boulder. See what he's gonna do now, he thought. Had to push him. Wouldn't have come down if those stupid kids hadn't gone skylarking.

Pat moved to the corner of the deserted dwelling. Cautiously, he looked down the opening between huts. The next one was a hundred yards across open ground. He had to go this time, he reasoned. He felt a strange sense of detachment, as if he were standing aside, watching someone else, interpreting someone else's emotions, evaluating someone else's behavior, passing judgment on someone else's weakness. And he recognized foreboding. And indecision. He had known them before. But now it was different. There would be no second chances here. A single moment of carelessness, one heedless step ...

His head ached. He felt a spasm in his stomach. He was weak.

Sanchez held his breath, trying to slow the wild beating of his heart. He knew the old feeling of being cornered, trapped, of waiting for the blow to come. Limping, he feigned pain in his leg, forcing the enemy to push him along. Must stall. Once we clear the village, there'll be no chance. He bent over his ankle, hoping to draw the enemy close enough to tackle. But the soldier, wary of deception and repelled by the odor, kept his distance.

A green fly settled on Lock's cheek. He contorted his face, shook his head, trying to dislodge it. He pushed out his lower lip, blew. But with his arms raised he was helpless. He swore. The smaller enemy soldier watched, fascinated. Then, cupping his pudgy hand, he trapped the fly against Lock's face, and captured it. For a moment he held his closed fist to his ear, listening to the buzzing. At last he released the fly and watched it as it droned away. "B-B-Buzz," he said, pointing at Lock. "B-B-Buzz."

Lock made faces, snorted through his nose, exaggerated his bowlegged walk, encouraging the laughter of his captors.

"Knock it off," Sanchez said. "You want their buddies to come help'em?"

"Ponyo, y'smell like a two-seater privy in July," Lock said.

"Drop dead!"

"Don't go temptin' fate!" Lock, his composure regained, sang out as they neared the low stone wall that ran along the far boundary of the village:

"When I give you the word,
You get the big bastard, pal.
B-B-Buzz boy is littler,
And is just right for me!"

Sanchez tensed. His man, staying clear of the smell, was ambling along on his right.

Lock was singing again:

"When you hear the last good ole

Semper Fi, we'll have to knock
These fellers on their hineys!"
The other soldier was watching Lock, mouthing his little joke. "B-B-Buzz ...
Buzz ..."
Lock winked ingratiatingly at him. "You're gonna get yours, you stutterin'
slopehead sonovabitch." He laughed. "Semper Fi," he said, showing the enemy
the traditional gesture of clenched fist with raised index finger. Then he bawled
the song:
" 'For marines all stand together,
And shout their battle cry:
Semper Fi! Semper Fi! Semper *Fi!*' "
Jesus Sanchez drove his shoulders into the stomach of the man who walked
beside him. Before the soldier could react, Sanchez had his throat, his fingers
tightening while the enemy's arms flailed wildly.
Lock swung both fists. He had caught his man by surprise, and now straddled
him. His foe got his arms around the marine's head, and began to squeeze, cutting
off circulation. Lock screamed as teeth dug into his shoulder and drew blood.
The other soldier managed to grasp Sanchez's soggy dungaree collar. Sanchez
felt his finger being pressed back. The pain was excruciating. He let go of the
man's throat, and was pulled down toward him until the stench of his clothing
mingled with the vile odor of the soldier's breath. The enemy began to rock him,
trying to turn him over, to fight off the seeking hands. Sanchez was thrown aside.
The enemy drew a knife from the back of his belt, and dived. Rolling away,
Sanchez waited a split second, brought his foot up, and smashed the groin. The
man howled in agony. Sanchez grabbed the wrist that held the weapon, twisted
while his left fist pounded the Adam's apple. The knife dropped. "Now who's got
it?" Sanchez roared. His fingers pinched off the windpipe. The eyes before him
widened, bulged. Then, quickly, silently, efficiently, Jesus Sanchez cut the man's
throat. He got up, breathing hard, ready to help Lock.
Before he could intervene, the other enemy freed himself, snatched the two
loaded rifles, and dashed over the wall. He was hidden from them by the last of
the huts. The marines grabbed their weapons, then remembered they had been
stripped of ammunition. They huddled against a sagging hovel, listening intently.
The enemy was armed. He knew they could not fire.
"Let's haul ass," Sanchez whispered, still sucking for breath.
"We're dead pigeons we try to cross all that open ground." Lock mopped his
sweating face with his hand. "Prob'ly have his whole damn' army out shootin' at
us. Besides, that stutterin' bastard bit me."
"Mine stunk," Sanchez said, holding his knife at the ready.
"You don't smell like no perfume factory yerself."

Sanchez crawled to the corpse and retrieved the watch the dead man had taken from him. "My sister give it to me," he told Lock. So much misery had come from that watch; and still he treasured it.

They heard the sound of the enemy again. He was apparently scaling the wall, coming back. They got set to rush him. It was their only chance, and a slight one. Then there was a scuffle, a fleshy thud. The two men crept cautiously toward the sound.

Pat was standing there, looking at the stock of the carbine he had borrowed. It dripped blood. The other men in the fire team appeared, running.

"Man, Cap'n, you sure did clobber him," Lock said, digging his shoe into the side of the half-conscious enemy.

Corporal Firesteen was standing beside Pat. "I kid you not, Captain Patrick, you scared hell outta me, goin' all the way down here by yourself."

Pat didn't speak. He had walked the path clutched by fear, unable to think of anything except reaching the end of it. Now he leaned against the stone wall, gasping for breath, as if he had run all the way.

"You hear Lock singin'?" Sanchez asked.

"Damn' well shoulda," Lock said. "I was makin' more noise than a tethered stallion at matin' time!"

Firesteen laughed. "We heard you. That's when the captain took off." He frowned and backed away from Sanchez. "Whew! You stink, friendo!"

"Like a dead goat," Lock said. "Gonna name you 'Goat,'" he taunted.

"I'm a live goat!" Sanchez bent over the battered enemy and took the Mauser from his pocket. "This is what I come for. We can shove now."

Goober came running up, his men spread before him. He stood for a moment, trying to catch his breath. "We better get the hell outta here"

"Take him back," Pat said, pointing to the enemy.

"All right, Sanchez and Justus. You knuckleheads found him, you carry him," Goober said. He ignored their groans. "Skipper's gonna chew you out when we get back."

I'm the skipper, Pat thought dully. Not Anderson. Must talk to Goober. But he knew even then that he would not. He told himself he didn't care.

"Now take and stretch a poncho over your rifles and lug him out. The rest of you people, move. On the double!" Goober jogged to the head of the column and waited impatiently, his gaze combing the hills beyond the village.

Monk Nelson shifted the weight of his radio. He tapped the captain's shoulder. "You okay, sir?"

Pat nodded. "Okay," he said, steadying himself.

Lock and Sanchez lifted the wounded prisoner and joined the column as the men moved off. "Shoulda seen how Sanchez carved that goonie," Lock said. "The

Chink got one whiff of him and passed out cold. Then ole Goat just sat on him and sliced away ..."

Pat was straggling behind. The laughter and loud conversation came back to him. Have to get them quiet, he thought.

"Yours nearly creamed you," Sanchez was saying. "If you'da finished him, we wouldn't be haulin' him back four damn' miles."

"Started to," Pat heard Lock say. "Then I figgered maybe the skipper'd want me to take him alive fer questionin.'"

There were catcalls from the others as they trudged out of the village and started to climb.

The skipper ... the skipper ... Pat was hurrying, trying to catch the column. Belong in front, he thought. Goober was up there, shaking his fist at them now, motioning for silence. Out of breath, Pat began to trot along, passing Sanchez and Lock. Catch the front ... ought to be up front ...

"Ooooh, Goat!" Lock sang out. "Y'smell like a Honolulu chippie after a Satiddy-night shore leave!"

Laughter.

"Knock it off!" Pat called to him. "All of you! Didn't you get the word? You want to advertise we're here?" He started past the sullen faces, barely hearing the grumbling. He felt a stitch of pain in his side. He could run no longer. As he slowed to a walk, the column began to pass him again. Thank God it's over, he thought. Thank God. He sighed, swallowed. He saw the blood on the lacing of his combat boots, the spattered design on his trousers, the vivid pattern congealing in the lines and creases of his palms. He felt lightheaded. Hunger and nausea gnawed at him. He bent over and retched violently.

Goober, setting the pace at the head of the squad, turned and looked back. "Hell with him," he muttered. "Hell with him. I'm all outta sugar tits ..."

3

Four men sat before the mouth of a shallow cave in the bright moonlight that night. They were in the center of the company command post, sheltered by a dangling boulder and by the horseshoe of the surrounding ridge.

Pat was exhausted. Still listening to the interrogation, he pulled the hood of his parka over his helmet, walked past his executive officer, the interpreter, and the prisoner, and sat across from them in the lee of a rock, out of the bleak wind.

Above them three rifle platoons spread a protective arc across five hundred yards. There marines took turns in the snug warmth of sleeping bags, cursed the dampness and the cold, listened eagerly to conflicting rumors, enhanced them, reshaped them as they whispered along the line.

"What's the skinnay?" Monk Nelson asked Firesteen.

"Kid you not, Monk. We're in for trouble. That's the word Goober's passin.'"

"Ah-hh, Goober!"

Below, the mortar section bedded in defilade. They listened to Lock Justus tell—another time—of the day's patrol: "You pisstube operators miss all the rough details. Right, Goat?" Of the new captain: "Got shook from creamin' the gook, and dragged his butt at the rear." Of the prisoner: "Hope to die, he's a Chink. And that's straight poop."

Clustered in groups, a few yards from the cavern's mouth, were radiomen, runners, demolition teams, drivers, and corpsmen. They lay on the dank, numbing ground, trying to overhear the insistent questions they could not understand, the halting answers in a strange tongue, the cryptic translation.

Many of them had been with the Marine Brigade, fought on the Pusan Perimeter, landed at Inchon, driven through Seoul, battled north from Wonsan.

And yet, until now, they had never been face to face with the enemy. The enemy had been a bloated, decaying corpse. The enemy had been a crafty, fearless, unpredictable shadow on the skyline, behind a rocky crag, among the trees, off in the distance. Now he was but a few feet away; and they saw, with a vague sense of disappointment, that he was slight, helpless, and bewildered.

"All right, you people, shove!" First Sergeant Goober forced the men aside and found a place closest to the group before the cave. "Get back where you belong," he whispered to Huckabee, a Negro corpsman who held a seat of vantage on a rock.

"I was here first."

"R-H-I-P," Goober said. "Move!"

Huckabee stared at him a moment, then got up. Goober took his seat. Turning to the men behind them, Huckabee tugged his trousers down around his hips and pushed out his stomach. "All right, you people," he said, impersonating Goober's stance and shrill voice. "Shove! I got to get up there where I can get my licks in." Hushed laughter.

"You sucking for a bruise, you chancre mechanic?" Goober whispered angrily.

Huckabee's keen, intelligent face relaxed into a vacant stare. His shoulders slumped into a caricature of dejection. His eyes half-closed, his head bent forward, he said: "Naw, suh, bossman Legree. I is jes a po' nigger that ain't meant no wrong." Laughter. And Huckabee walked away.

"Knock off that grabass!" It was Lieutenant Anderson, the executive officer. There was immediate silence.

Skipper ought to be wearing his gloves, Goober thought. Damn' cold. He debated whether or not to interrupt him and offer his own. But he hesitated, afraid he might be rebuffed publicly.

Pat tossed an unfinished can of chicken and vegetables into a pile of rubble. Uncomfortable, he loosened the cord about his waist, slipped off his pistol belt, and held it in his lap. He had left his cigarettes in the cave. Quietly, he went for them.

Lieutenant Anderson leaned against the company jeep, his squat frame exposed to the full sweep of the wind. His fierce green eyes, set in a flat, red-bearded face, shone like those of a cat, a lithe, powerful cat. He was sure he had been right all along. But being right, he thought, might be small consolation. Suddenly impatient, he slammed a small, furry paw against the back of the seat, and padded across to the prisoner. When he spoke, his thin lips barely moved. "Tell him I'm gonna ream him from anus to appetite if he doesn't remember damn' quick."

Won Kook Choy; the South Korean assigned as company interpreter, sat cross-legged, a blanket about his frail shoulders. His slender fingers pinched the bridge of his straight, sharp nose. He yawned. Then, slapping the enemy's face with his gloved hand, he repeated his question.

The prisoner looked furtively at Choy. His head throbbed. Again he tried to answer. His mind phrased his reply. The words puffed up his cheeks. He strained to force them out, to work his tongue. He was trembling—with the exertion of speaking, with pain and with fear. Choy slapped him again.

Pat, returning from the cave, saw the blow, saw the soldier stare dumbly ahead, as if he had not felt it. He studied the enemy, the caked blood on the bandage about his head, the dull cow eyes, the unattended sore on his neck, the unwashed stench, the stuttering voice, the dirty padded cotton uniform, the flimsy rubber and canvas shoes. He pitied him.

Another slap. No answer.

"Well?" Anderson demanded.

Choy shook his head. "I think he does not know the name of any other units. He is only a private soldier in the Seventy-ninth Chinese Division."

"Ask him what kind of transport they used. Ask him when they crossed the Yalu."

Choy phrased the questions. The prisoner stuttered his reply. "He says there were many camels and oxen and horses on the march. He says they crossed the river ten days ago."

Pat offered Anderson a cigarette, but the lieutenant waved it off.

"Get back in the cave, you want to light up." He waited while Pat stuffed the package in his pocket and sat down. Then, turning to Choy, he said, "How many divisions? Ask him that."

"I asked. He does not know."

Anderson bent over the prisoner and smashed a fist into his ear. "Ask him again."

The Chinese slumped wearily. His chin rested on his chest. Choy lifted the face and repeated the question. The answer came faster this time. "He does not know."

"I mean business, you stupid bastard!" Anderson crouched beside the enemy, as if ready to pounce. "You better think!" Drawing back his boot, he drove it into the prisoner's stomach.

Pat was on his feet. "Lieutenant! Cut that out."

Anderson looked at him, amazed. When he spoke, his voice was tinged with impatience, as if he were explaining to a difficult child. "They're animals. They don't understand anything else."

"He has rights ..."

"What do you think they do to our people?" Anderson tugged at the mane of red on his chest, trying to control the anger in his voice. "Listen, Captain, this is important. We haven't seen a Chink since we clobbered them at Sudong. That was the 124th. This one's in the Seventy-ninth. The mountains are probably crawling with them." Bending over the enemy who lay writhing on the ground, Pat looked up at his exec. "He's half dead," he said softly, aware that the men were watching them.

"We been trying to convince the brass in Japan that the Chinks are all the way in this war." The tone was hard now, without deference. "And they've been hoping they're volunteers. Volunteers my ass!"

Pat knew he had to stop the exchange. He had the words ready— "That's enough, Lieutenant!"—but he didn't speak them. He should, he told himself. It was bad enough to argue before the men, but to be bested before them by a subordinate was still worse. And yet, when he looked up at the wiry, tough-fibered man, saw the passion and anger in his eyes, he could not use the easy weapon of seniority. "There are other ways of getting information," he said, lowering his voice. "What ways, dammit? What ways have you been using?"

The point was made, Pat thought. Captain, I am. But a boot. Unaware. Inexperienced. 'You're not accomplishing anything by mauling him," he said, nodding at the prostrate enemy.

"I'm not through!" Anderson advanced a step and stood over Pat and the prisoner. His teeth were clenched and his stubby fingers clawed at his chin. "1'm not through," he repeated.

"We better send him back to Battalion," Pat said.

"Battalion?" Anderson shook his head, and bent down to speak in Pat's face. "And Battalion will send him to Regiment," he said, his voice tight with anger. "And Regiment will send him to Division. And Division ..."

"Let's let it go at that," Pat said, knowing there could be no backing down now.

"This isn't the first prisoner I've ever seen. I know how to handle them. Just take my word for it, will you?"

There was a soft murmur from the men. Pat could hear it swelling. "Lieutenant, I think—"

"Think? Goddammit, you just don't know!" Anderson caught himself, stopping the outburst as if a hand had been clapped to his mouth. He sighed heavily, expelling a cloud of frosty breath. "Captain, for Christ's sweet sake, move and let me get on with this."

Pat felt his heart pounding in his chest, the muscles constricting in his throat. He stood up, a full head taller than Anderson. Controlling the quaver that threatened to blur his voice, he said clearly, distinctly, so he might be heard beyond the circle at the cave's mouth, "That will be all, Lieutenant!" Then, avoiding the stare of fury, he turned, and called for a corpsman.

Huckabee responded, dropped to his knees and began to loosen the prisoner's belt. "Move him over there," Pat said, indicating a spot sheltered by rocks and tangled brush. "See if you can do something for him."

Anderson followed Pat, and started to speak, but something in the captain's glance changed his mind. He called Goober. The first sergeant lumbered over, his full-moon face twisted in a frown. "Wally, set up a watch on the Chink. Radiomen and company runners. We'll have to turn him over to Battalion in the morning." He knelt before the cave and crawled inside.

Pat watched him go, wondering if he had made a mistake, if—after all—his executive officer was right.

Choy broke in on his thought. "In the rear they will be gentle. They will give him cigarettes and hot coffee and promises. And they will learn nothing."

"I didn't ask you for a briefing," Pat said, snapping at him. Then, moderating the heat of his reply, "He's a prisoner. You can't beat him to death."

"No. It is against the law." It was a quiet observation, with no hint of disrespect. Choy put his blanket under his arm, and walked away.

Pat began to pick up the prisoner's belongings. It was something to do while he gathered his thoughts, while he decided how to deal with the lieutenant. A mess can. Four morphine syrettes, apparently captured from American stocks. A white powder. A bag of rice. A pay book. A Communist fund record. Two condoms. A rifle—a roughly machined Japanese model. A few cloves of garlic. He put the articles in a poncho, and carried it to Choy who was filling his canteen from an expeditionary can on the side of the jeep.

"Better see this stuff goes down with him in the morning." The interpreter inclined his cropped head, acknowledging the order. "You look at that kid, in that sleazy uniform, and this junk, and the cheap rifle ... pitiful, isn't it? Like an army of another century."

"Because you have trucks instead of camels and oxen? Because your rifles have smooth barrels? Because your men eat fine food and could—if they wanted— make out the words in a newspaper?" Choy grunted, tightening the cap on his canteen. "Your George Washington had a ragged army of dissidents, a poor supply system, little or no money, shabby equipment. And he also fought the wealthiest nation on earth." The bony face turned up. The lips were pursed as if he would continue. He smiled faintly. "Good night, Captain Patrick."

Pat watched him part the undergrowth and disappear. What brought that speech on? And what bred the bitterness in the articulate, waspish little man? He walked to the edge of the area and stood beside Huckabee as he worked over the prisoner. "He all right?"

"Just scared more than anything else." The Negro paused in thought as he felt the enemy's ribs. "Bruised up some."

"Maybe he could use some chow." The sergeant who ran the mortar section had come up. Pat recognized the equine shape of the balding head, the buck teeth, the meaty jaws, the acne-pocked cheeks. "Want me to give him some chow, Huck?"

'You can try, Horse." Huckabee pulled back his patient's eyelids, and examined the pupils. "He'll be okay, Captain."

A small Korean boy who looked no more than fourteen came up to Pat and stood respectfully until he was noticed. He wore a cut-down marine utility uniform and a black cap. "Raundry, sho-nuff?"

"What?"

The face wrinkled in a shy smile. "Raundry," he repeated, rubbing his knuckles against his chest. "Have for wash me, honey?"

"I see him around all the time," Pat said. "What does he want?" The Horse was opening a can of rations. "Does laundry. Cooks sometimes."

Huckabee helped the prisoner sit up. "Been with us since Wonsan, sir."

"What's he trying to say?"

"They've been teachin' him English," The Horse said. He wiped his spoon on his parka and handed the can and the utensil to the Chinese. "Don't know much more than 'laundry' and 'wash,' but Lock Justus got him to sayin' 'honey' and 'sure enough' because he's a South Korean. We call him 'You-all.' "

Rubbing his hand over the black fuzz on the youngster's head, Pat said, "Thanks, You-all. But I haven't anything for you." He shook his head; and the boy ran off. "You're Huckabee, aren't you?" Pat asked the corpsman.

"Yes, sir."

"I know the sergeant here, but I hadn't gotten around to meeting you." Pat held out his hand. Huckabee started to take it, hesitated, removed his glove, and grasped the hand firmly. Then he bent over the enemy again. The Horse held the man's arm, and Huckabee jabbed a morphine syrette and squeezed the tube.

"I've been checking the records," Pat said. "Seems you're senior man, Huckabee. So you stay with the C.P. from now on. You'll run the corpsmen for me."

Huckabee had stretched a tom canvas over his patient. He looked up. "Sir, if you don't mind, I just as well stay where I am."

"Don't you think you can do the job?" Pat asked, surprised.

"It's not that. I ... there are six other corpsmen with the company, sir. I'd just as soon let one of them do it."

The Horse had gotten up. "Huck here is an awful good man, sir."

Pat smiled. "When a sailor gets any praise from a marine, he must be good. Move your gear down in the morning. I'll tell the first sergeant."

"Good night, sir," The Horse said.

When Pat was out of earshot, Huckabee said, "Why'd you have to sound off like that?"

"What's wrong with you, Huck? He's givin' you a good shake."

"I don't want to be bossin' those others around."

"You're a First Class. The others are H. A. Deuce. You rate it." "Forget it, will you? Just forget it." Huckabee began to put his pack together. Somehow, he thought, he would get out of it.

Pat walked back to the cave. He could postpone it no longer, he had decided. He would have to make it clear to Anderson and to Goober, to all of them, that he was running the company. Right now.

As he ducked before the entrance, he remembered his pistol belt. He had left it on the ground by the rock. He found it. But the holster was empty. He retraced his steps, searching for the pistol, but could not find it. Must be inside, he thought. Slinging the belt and holster over his shoulder, he crawled into the cave.

4

First Lieutenant Joe Anderson sat beside a blue flame which burned fitfully between two stones. He was leaning back against the sloping sides of the cavern, heating his food. His hair awry, his beard wild and shining in the half-light, his lips puckered in contemplation, he looked like an Old Testament prophet. Like a youthful Jeremiah, Pat thought.

"I left my pistol in here."

Anderson stirred his can of frankfurters and beans with a knife. "Left it?"

"It's here someplace." Pat pulled his sleeping bag aside, moved his map case and his pack. "I came in for some cigarettes, must have put it down..." He stopped, posed on his knees, trying to recall his movements. "I was feeling a little rocky," he mumbled. "And I loosened my parka ... took off my belt ... and then I came in here for the cigarettes ..." His voice trailed off as he searched the floor of the cave.

Anderson tasted his beans, sucking them off the blade. "Sure it's not outside?"

"I wouldn't have left it," Pat said. He was getting alarmed. "Maybe for just a couple of minutes... but I must have taken it with me..."

"Probably one of the men picked it up," Anderson said. "They'd steal MacArthur's sunglasses if they had a chance." His fine white teeth showed in the brush of red whiskers. "Might have been Sanchez. He's our souvenir hunter. Can strip a body before it hits the deck. Come to think of it, he presented me with this knife tonight, maybe as insurance against getting caught with your .45. We'll have a shakedown in the morning, get it back."

A great joke on the green captain, Pat thought. He recognized the knife now. The same blade had slit the Chinese soldier's throat.

Anderson pointed to coffee bubbling over the flame.

"No, thanks." The confrontation Pat had planned was suddenly ridiculous. It was impossible to talk now of command when he was guilty of a marine's worst sin—not taking care of his weapon. Besides, he thought, although Anderson was out of line, he needed the man. He acknowledged that. All he wanted was to come out of it all whole and alive, to get back to his job and Ann and the future. Since he was not yet equal to the task, Anderson could guide him. The battalion commander had told him: "Andy's a hard-charger. A little reckless— sometimes acts like he's a squad leader. But he's a great one to have around in a fight." Everything Pat had seen since assured him it must be true. Hard, gruff, easily angered, Anderson was, nevertheless, a rarity.

"Think I'll try that coffee after all," Pat said. He took it and blew at the steaming can. He wondered how old the man was, what lay under the bearded disguise. Must be about five years older than I am, he reasoned. Thirty-two, thirty-three. He sipped the coffee. "About the prisoner," he said. "What did the Old Man say when you called?"

"Skinhead was at regimental C.P. I got the Two. And he was excited about us grabbing one." Anderson dipped into the can and ate again from the blade. "A little scuttlebutt, too. Seems General Smith's been fighting orders from topside that want us to spread out more, envelop the enemy."

"But if the Chinese are really in this thing ..."

"Sure, you know that. And I know it. And every marine and dogface around here knows it. But MacArthur never got the poop. The desk commandos tell him what they think he wants to hear: 'The war is over. Doug's done it again! All hail!'
"

Pat took a swallow of coffee. "Pushing the division in an attack to envelop the enemy is like telling you and me to surround the Notre Dame ball club."

"I kid you not, we ought to be pulling in, getting ready for them if they link up." Anderson wiped the knife on his trousers. "Hellfire, we're already spread out too much. No protection on our flanks, an impossible supply line. Least that might happen is that the North Koreans'll regroup, hit our separated outfits and give us a hard time. The worst, the Chinks'll come in strong, cut between our units and clobber us one at a time."

Pat started to question him, but Anderson held up his hand while he lighted a cigar. "Just look at the map, Captain. Here." He put his knife between them on the ground. "This is the Yalu," he said, running his finger across the sharp edge. "My side's Manchuria. Your side's Korea." He broke a biscuit, chewed a piece, and placed the other half a few inches below the knife. "This is the Choisin Reservoir." Picking out six beans from his dinner, he spaced some of them beside the biscuit reservoir. "These are the battalions of the Fifth and Seventh Marines.

Right? We're here—this bean on the southwest shore, between Yudam-ni and Hagaru. Now, below us, you put in the First Marines." Pat placed beans along a line a few inches away. "Okay. Plenty of space between them. They're trying to keep the MSR open so we'll continue to be supplied." Anderson leaned back and indicated the bean-knife-biscuit relief. "Look at it. An invitation to be picked off."

"I was talking to an Army major the other day—just before Skinhead sent me up here. And they're really out on a limb." Pat swept the remains of the beans and the biscuit into the fire. "They've got troops above us on the reservoir."

Anderson picked his teeth with the knife. "And if the crap hits the fan, they'll probably get splattered first."

"Now we wait and see," Pat said gravely. For a moment he considered, then decided that he would be frank, show the man he was being honest. "I'm going to depend a lot on your help. I've never had a command larger than a platoon before. I joined the Fifth after Iwo was secured, went with them to Japan for occupation duty ... and then I got out."

Anderson sucked at the cigar and lighted it again. "Captain, there are people running armies out here that never commanded more than a staff section or an orderly. So don't let it bother you."

Pat smiled. "Didn't mean to bark at you like I did a while ago."

"You pack the gear. You're the captain." He placed the empty can between his palms and crushed it flat. "I've been chewed out before."

"I didn't chew you. I just felt ..."

"More coffee, Captain Patrick?"

Pat shook his head. "Look, we're going to be together for a long time. How about making it Tat?"

Anderson wiped a hand across his mouth, brushing crumbs from his beard. He drew deeply on the cigar and blew a screen of smoke toward the rocky overhead. "Sure."

He had figured Patrick the wrong way. He had been certain he wouldn't speak up before the troops. His kind always observed the rules; and the rules forbade it. Anderson had expected him to be petulant, though, to remind him subtly but unmistakably of his rank, even to get him transferred from the company that he had trained and led and tempered. Instead, Patrick was being honest, admitting he was inexperienced. Give him credit for that, Anderson thought. He's got the railroad tracks on his collar. But he knows the company is mine.

There were obvious things about Patrick: The way he spoke, softly, with overtones of what sounded like Harvard. The way he carried himself, erect, shoulders back as if he were too conscious of his handsome body. The way he dealt with subordinates, as if orders were requests, as if compliance was an expected favor. These things Anderson had translated into an appraisal of the captain. Patrick, he had decided, was a rich man's son, over-educated, over-polished, who had never worked a day in his life, knew how to get what he wanted by exerting charm, and was essentially a weak, though pleasant, fellow.

Now Anderson considered that he might have misjudged in some particulars. Jess had teased him about the way he made snap judgments of people, the way he responded to them without trying to understand them. The thought of her knifed his consciousness. He felt physical hurt, the sharp pain of guilt as she invaded his mind again. The million sights and sounds and odors of their life together swarmed in his memory. How little it took to evoke the image of her!

He could visualize the corner bedroom, cramped with used furniture and the steamer trunk they never managed to get unpacked ... And the window beside the bed from which they could see the strands of jeweled light looping gracefully above the bridge, the tinsel flow and movement on the waterfront, the palette of red-green-blue-yellow reflections across San Francisco Bay ... And there was the stain on the ceiling where the paper was blistered ... and the flaking plaster... He remembered coating his hand with baby oil, and rubbing her swollen belly, feeling the hardness there, putting his cheek against it, watching, awed, as the mysterious living thing inside rippled the surface. "He's going to be big, not sawed-off like his old man. And powerful. Look how he moves! And handsome, because you're his mother..."

And Jess, laughing, pulled his ears until he slipped up beside her. "That's the way you are about people—even little people who haven't been born yet." Then she had bitten his chin. "You can't figure out everything there is to know about someone by the way they stand or shake hands or hold a cigarette or get a chair for a lady ... or kick their mommie's stomach. Don't make up your mind about people that way. I want you to empathize—there's a five-dollar word!" And her laughter again. And then, growling in her neck, kissing her fiercely, and feeling her teeth on his lip, "If you weren't in such a lopsided condition, I'd empathize you like you've never been empathized before!" And that mischief, that promise in her eyes, and her whispering, "Come, let's look out the window ..."

He had thought he knew all about her, thought he had memorized every mood and shade and quirk. But he had not. And he had destroyed the one high moment in his life. Suddenly he realized that the captain was extending his hand. He could not gauge how long he had been sitting that way.

"You hear something?" Pat asked.

"No." He took the smooth, tapered hand into his callused one and pumped it. "Next time you eat me out, you might call me 'Andy.' "

"Andy Anderson. Swede?"

"The name's really 'Joe.' But probably I'm a Swede 'way back. You're a Mick, huh?"

"No." Pat grinned, recalling the story as his father had told it. "My dad was a Welshman," he said. "Came to the States with a foot-long name. When he got ready to marry my mother—a farm girl from Crab Orchard, Kentucky—her folks wouldn't hear of her going off with some foreigner. He worked for a contracting outfit, Patterson and Rickey. Well, not wanting to favor either of them, he made a Solomon's decision, and came up with Pat-Rick. Armed with a sainted name, he wooed, won, and rode off with the farmer's daughter."

In the next moment, in the time it took him to light a match, snuff it out, and take a first long puff at a cigarette, Pat's mind was crowded with remembered times and scenes and faces. There was the brown-faded picture in the wedding album, a burly red-faced man, tie askew, standing beside a fragile, slim woman with deep-set eyes ... And he could visualize massive hands, with wiry black hair below the knuckles, holding a plumb line, sliding a level. "Now you try it. You can learn, son. Why, when I was your age, ten years old ..." And there was the tall presence behind him, the reassuring grip on his belt, as he walked a steel girder twenty feet up. "Don't look down, son. And stop shaking. I got you." And the sound of hearty laughter, "Ought to fan your seat for you. Sneaking off from your mother and that revival meeting! Well, sit down and have some milk and don't listen to the cuss words!" (The rough good-natured talk of construction workers. The smell of the beer-wet counter and chili and hamburgers and onions and black coffee.) Then, years later, the angry face, stubbled with whiskers, eyes aflame with fury ... "No goons can tell me how long I can work or how much I can do! When they come back, they'll find out. Take this pick handle, Pat—you and me, son— we'll knock some brains in!" (And they had. And were arrested. And his mother wept over his proud, bruised face.) And finally ... that strong, powerful body, now broken, now lying crumpled below a web of scaffolding, and Pat's own voice saying, "My fault. I called him down. If I hadn't of called him down ..."

Andy was laughing. "I coulda swore you were upper-crust Boston Irish."

Choy slipped into the cave. "You did not say what time you wish the prisoner to go down in the morning."

"Soon as it gets light enough to see the road," Andy said.

"I will be back in the afternoon." Choy slipped out as quietly as he had entered.

"Strange character," Pat said.

Andy nodded. "You don't know the half of it. Doesn't miss a chance to lecture on the U.S. and the downfall of democracy—about which he doesn't know his ass from a hole in the ground." He lighted his cigar again. "Good interpreter, though. Knows three Chink dialects, Korean, English, high-school French, even some German."

"He's already made me a little speech." Pat took off his gloves and began to massage his hands. "Think one of us ought to go with the prisoner, too? Huckabee says he'll be all right by that time."

"You can't hurt them easy. I never saw a soft, flabby one yet."

"By the way, I told Huckabee to move his gear down. Let him take over as chief corpsman."

Andy rubbed his knuckles over his beard. "Better hold off on that. Makes a touchy situation."

"He didn't want it," Pat said. "But it's only fair."

"Listen, Pat. I don't give a rat's tit that he's black. But he's a clown. You can't count on a clown. If he was white, nobody'd like taking orders from him. But black—you're looking for trouble."

"I don't think there'll be any."

"No sense in stirring up something. We're not social workers or chaplains. We got a company to run. All we've got to do is be sure we run a tight ship no matter what."

"I must have put him on the spot."

"Sure. Huckabee's all right. He does his job and doesn't push himself. He's not the kind that sends off a letter to his congressman or the NAACP every time some knucklehead calls him a coon."

Goober crawled in. "Gonna sack out, Skipper. Anything you want me to do first?"

"One thing," Andy said. "Tell the captain who you recommend as chief corpsman."

The first sergeant sat on his haunches. "Haven't checked since we lost that swabbie with the crud." Smoothing his jowls, he thought about it. It was obvious that the skipper had somebody in mind. He didn't want to blunder. Always best to stick with The Book. "Think Huckabee's the only First Class we got, sir."

"Would it make any difference to you if your company commander was black?" Andy asked. "The truth." '

Goober watched Anderson for some clue, saw that the captain was also waiting for his reply. He couldn't fathom what the point was, what the skipper wanted him to say. The answer was too obvious. "When you sign up," he said, hesitating, "you take an oath to obey all officers over you, no matter who."

Andy was nodding. "Wally read the manual in boot camp and hasn't bothered to think since."

It seemed to Pat that Goober winced. His face was a blank now.

He was resting on his hands and knees. Pat had a nearly overpowering desire to pound his back, to say something that might relieve him. At least he could help him retreat. "Thanks, Top. Just wanted your advice. You can hit the sack now."

Goober began to back out. Miserable, his anger was directed at himself for having failed the skipper, and at the captain—"Just wanted your advice"—the damn' sarcastic ...

"You lost me an argument," Andy called after him. "Next time we pitch a liberty, you buy the beer."

"Sure, Skipper," the first sergeant said gratefully. "The beer's on me."

When he had gone, Andy leaned back and began to pull off his boots. "One thing you want to learn, Pat. Know your people. They've all got their weaknesses. Even a big dependable slob like Goober's got his blind spots...

5

The prisoner watched the Fat One come out of the cave. He wondered at the perversity of the Americans. The Tall One had clubbed him, and then had his wound dressed, had allowed him to be beaten, and then had protected him from the Wild Red One with the bearded face. He had been slapped, cursed, threatened by the Korean who spoke his dialect. Then he had been fed by the Ugly One, tended by the Black One whose palms were pink.

Kao Teh, sixteen years old, born in Tsingtao, China, afflicted Number Two son of a consumptive fruit peddler, private soldier in the Seventy-ninth Chinese Division, the Twenty-seventh CCF Corps, thought on this. And his mind, doped with drugs and fear, could frame but one answer. He was being preserved for torture. The Yellowlegs, marines of the United States, he had been told, were recruited from jails and insane asylums. They had proved themselves as rapers of their mothers, murderers of their fathers. They were men who killed with lust, for joy. They would cut a thousand wounds, and while his life ran out as sand between the fingers they would slash away his manhood, as a pig is slashed.

Now the Fat One with the voice of a woman stood beside him. "All right, Monk. You got one more hour to go. Justus'll relieve you. Then you start the jeep, let it warm up good so it won't freeze, and you can get some sack time. Meanwhile, this yellow bastard bats his eyes, you bat his face in."

The Bald One waited until they were alone. Then he poured water in his cup, and offered it. Afraid to refuse, Kao Teh sipped, watching his guard over the rim. He returned it. "You ... be ... okay," the marine said slowly. "You ... be ... okay," he repeated, making circles of his fingers. He smiled at his success. And, because his delight was funny, Kao Teh smiled, too. The marine laughed and backed off. Twenty feet away, he sat down and leaned against the rocks.

They are strange, the prisoner thought. His guard seemed simple, And yet he was a marine, a butcher. The Americans were a puzzle. He had seen them before. "Welcome U.S. Troops" the signs had said. And all of Tsingtao had lined the harbor and the roads. Flags had waved and the bursts of firecrackers had been lost in the sounds of cheering. While other children had run in gangs, begging gifts from the marines, following them to their billets, he had watched from a distance. He could not speak so fast, nor think so fast. So, as always, he had been alone with the girl-child Shu Lee who would not laugh at him or hide from him or beat him.

Together they had watched as the Japanese from the great houses were whipped in the streets. (One had no trousers on and wept like an amah while the people carried away furniture and silks from his home.) They had seen Japanese girls dragged from their brothels, spat upon as they deserved to be, reviled by those they had mocked.

And then the odd, the inscrutable marines had chased their Chinese allies from the doors of their common enemies, had guarded the houses of the Japanese women.

There had been other things, too. His brother had become Number One Boy for marines. They had given him rich food and U.S. money and strong cigarettes, and once, a great can of berry jam which his father had sold for 8100 CNC. Yet later, when he had asked but a little thing, a tip from the laundryman, they learned of it, and were angry. They had cast him out as if he were a leper or had plague or a curse on his tongue.

What kind of men were these to give away things of such value, and then deprive a man of cumshaw?

The Americans had brought more to his city. They had brought higher prices to the poor and wealth to the merchants who moved into the houses of the Japanese. The marines did not know how to bargain. They had paid the first price. And yet, he and Shu Lee had seen a curio stall in the bazaar smashed, its goods strewn in the litter, because the shopkeeper had sold soapstone for jade.

How unpredictable! They had thrown their money before them like crazed men. Then they had unleashed fury when they discovered their own stupidity. Strange, Kao Teh decided wearily. A puzzle. A wise man could not solve it.

He slept, and woke suddenly, feeling cold. The Bald One was standing nearby, his rifle weaving before him. "Who goes there? Give me the password."

Kao Teh lay still, sensing another presence close by. He was nearly certain there had been footsteps in the rocks and brush behind him. He strained to hear. Silence. The marine approached and stood a few feet away. "Anybody there?" he called. Then he backed up and sat down again.

Pulling the canvas higher over his body, Kao Teh warmed his hands between his legs. It seemed that he had heard a word spoken, a word in his own tongue. He dismissed the thought. The damp-smelling earth, the soft moan of the wind, the rough cover gave him a sense of familiar comfort. He might have been on the earthen floor of the common room while his father, weak and choking on his own blood, was but a breath away, and Shu Lee lay at his back.

After the marines sailed away, after the Generalissimo's troops fled, the Liberation Army entered the city. Again there were signs in the streets. Again the people cheered and the firecrackers sputtered and gangs of children ran with the soldiers. Again the Evil Ones who had grown fat on the poor were pulled from the fine houses.

His brother joined the new army and was given warm clothes and rice. The father was dead. Kao Teh was alone on the earthen floor with the child. And he knew it was his duty, as the remaining son, to return his father's bones to Tientsin. There his parent had been born. There he should rest.

Kao Teh walked through the province of Shantung, shivering in the fields at night, Shu Lee by his side. The brown paper parcel containing his father's bones lay at their feet. The child coughed and pleaded for food. And he made her huddle about his back for warmth, and sleep, her fingers cold against his neck. They were alone. But it was good, he thought. He would return to Tsingtao having traveled the great distance; and men could no longer laugh at one who had seen much more than they, who had made a difficult journey on such a mission.

Many days later, in the province of Hopeh, their long walk ended. They rested on black moss beneath the great bridge in Tientsin, listening to the rumble of charcoal-burning trucks and trolleys above them, watching the yellow lanterns on the junks as they swayed in the river below. "When it is light we will find the place for the bones of our father. I will work. And we will have food." The child, exhausted, trusting, had believed him.

When they awoke, the parcel was gone, stolen by a luckless thief seeking food or clothing. Kao Teh left the child beneath the bridge and went to the police to plead for the return of his package. The police were of the new order. Unlike those he had known, they asked no cumshaw. They listened. They called him comrade. They asked many questions and demanded a travel permit he did not have. They grew impatient with his stammered explanations, his tortured speech, and beat him with a stick. When at last he was freed, two days had passed. He returned to the bridge. But Shu Lee was gone. This time he did not ask the help of the police. Alone he searched the junks. He wandered the streets calling her. But she did not answer. Drowned, perhaps. Kidnapped to be maimed, then sold as a beggar-child.

Kao Teh felt now the hurt he had known months before. He had failed in his duty as a son. Shu Lee he had failed, too. And today he had failed as a soldier. He heard a noise in the underbrush behind him.

The Bald One heard it, too. He was up again, his eyes staring into the darkness, his shoulders hunched over, his breath coming in short, whistling gasps, his rifle held before him. But he saw nothing. Grumbling, he poked speculatively in the bushes. He licked his chapped lips, looked at Kao Teh, apparently asleep. "Poor slob," he said to the night. "Poor slob ..."

Kao Teh watched as his guard sat down again. Someone, he knew, was close by. In the scrub elms and birch behind him, he could hear uneven breathing. He was afraid. Cold metal brushed his neck. He nearly cried out. Then he heard the pad of retreating feet. He inched back, let his shoulders lie against the metal object. He moved to one side, slid it under the canvas, fingered it. A pistol!

"Hey, Monk?"

Nelson whirled, snapping the safety off his rifle as he turned. "Oh! Mel. Don't come up behind a guy like that."

"Sorry." Firesteen glanced at the prisoner. "Dead to the world, huh?"

"Sure. Figures he's got it made. He's out of it."

The corporal sat down. "Thought I'd crawl under a poncho and finish a letter. Came down to borrow your flashlight."

"Lost it to Lock. Bet me my rifle'd freeze up last night and his wouldn't. He was right. Had to heat mine over a fire to thaw it. That hillbilly had all the oil off his, dry as a bone; worked fine."

"Always got an angle," Firesteen said.

"You wanna write your letter, he'll let you use the flashlight."

"Don't wanna ask him. He's been ridin' me anyhow. 'If the Marine Corps wanted you to have a wife, they'd have issued you one'—that's what he told me this morning. Offered to lay me even money—either way—on if I'm gonna have a baby."

"We get mail, you'll find out."

Rubbing his thumb against the birthmark on his cheek, Firesteen was silent, thinking. "Guess I talk too much about this kid business," he said.

"Stop messin' with your face."

"What?"

"Your face. You're always pullin' on that thing on your cheek. Could give you cancer."

"Where'd you get a idea like that?" Disturbed, Firesteen peered at him, awaiting his answer.

"My wife said it one time, I think. I'm not sure."

"Ah-hh!" Firesteen smiled. "Wish that was all my worries." But he decided to ask Huckabee about that cancer business. "With all I been through, this not knowin' is the worst. No mail in three weeks. I got a idea when Ruth's supposed to ..." He sought a delicate word. "Well, she was due last week. So it's all settled now. Either we're pregnant or we're not."

"When Grace don't write, I don't worry. Like she always says, no news is good news." Monk leaned forward, listening. The prisoner was stirring under his cover. "Chink's tossin' around. Drug must be wearin' off."

Twenty feet away, Kao Teh watched them. He could not solve the mystery of the pistol. Another trick of the Americans? From whom had it come? Fear tugged him in opposite directions. If he used the » weapon, what chance would he have to escape? There were two of them now. How far would he get? If he thrust the pistol back through the bushes, what fate but torture awaited him? Slowly, painstakingly, he began to work out a plan.

"Sure I understand how you feel, Mel." Monk pulled back the hood of his parka and put his helmet on again. "I wouldn't take nothin' for my kids." Removing his wallet, he offered it to Firesteen. "I show you?"

The corporal had examined the snapshots twice before, but he took them. The first was of a plain, stout woman in nurse's uniform, standing by an old-model Chevrolet. The second was of Monk in blue coveralls, a fat, crying baby in his lap, his arm around a pretty, wistful-looking little girl. "Nice," Firesteen said. "Real nice." Then, feeling that he had somehow failed Monk, that he had to match the older man's interest and sympathy, he looked a little longer. "Yeah, that's what I call a real fine family," he said. "Beautiful little girl you got." Nelson took the pictures and held them close to his face, letting the moonlight strike them. "She's our first. Adopted, you know. Don't think we should tell her ever. But Grace says a stitch in time saves nine. We oughta explain it so maybe some stupid kid don't do it first." He looked at his wife's snapshot again. "It's funny, Mel; when you been livin' with somebody ten years you oughta be able to remember her face." He shrugged. "I can remember the way she talks, and how ... at night, she has a kinda starched-sheet smell ... and even her expression when I'm telling a joke to somebody that she's heard a dozen times before ... but I sometimes can't remember how she looks ... really looks. Not like the picture. You get what I mean?"

"Sure," Firesteen said. "It's like in your mind she starts looking like the picture, instead of the picture looking like her ..."

"Well, sorta that." Monk grinned. "Grace's got all kindsa funny ideas about raising kids. Like she tells them the medical names for things, says them right out, so the kids don't think they're dirty." He chuckled softly. " 'Umbilicus,' she'd correct me. 'Not belly button.' "

"Ruth's always telling me about my grammar, but not in front of people. You know. Later. She had two years' college."

"Grace's a R.N., registered nurse," Monk said. "Wasn't for that, we'd be in rough shape now." He felt in his pocket and brought out two pieces of hard candy. "Pogie bait?" Firesteen thanked him and! took one. "Things happen sometimes, Mel, you figure it's awful. Then you see it's for the best. Like because we didn't have no kids right off, Grace finished nursing school and I went through radio repair on the GI bill. Got a job with a good outfit. They give me a month's pay when I left. Every month, like clockwork, the boss writes me a letter. Used to think ... say, I'm talkin' a mile a minute..."

"Naw, I'm interested. I've thought about that, too, about things happenin' for the best and you don't realize it at the time."

"I was gonna say, I used to think I got to have a business of my own, but I seen friends got their own places. Like Grace says, they're always robbin' Peter to pay Paul. Rather not have their headaches." "Right." Firesteen drank from his canteen and gargled the sweet taste from his mouth. "Ruth and me argue about that— not real fightin', you know. But sometimes she gets pretty hot about it—'cause she says I ought to go in for myself. I figure I get a good line to take on the road— something with a brand name—I'm better off. I been selling men's shoes, cheap stuff. Can't count on repeat customers. Never any better than your last trip. But when I get out, I'm gonna shop around, find me something like Arrow shirts or like that."

"Havin' your own business sounds good," Nelson said. "But it's no picnic."

"That's exactly what I tell Ruth. I've seen her brother-in-law. Name's Herman and he's an awful nice guy, really means well, but he's got a business drives him crazy. Ladies' underwear, dresses, things like that. You go visit, all he talks about is this sale and that customer and a two-ninety-eight slip and a forty-nine-cent pair panties ... And worries! He's got nothin' but bills."

"There's a war or somethin', a little guy in business can make a buck," Monk said. "Otherwise, he stays in hot water. Me, I figure when I put in thirty years, I take my retirement from the shop plus my social security and Grace's endowment, we can live like human beings. Nobody's an old man when he's sixty-five any more. Like Grace says, you take care of yourself, you stay sound as a dollar."

"Lousy break, you gettin' called. At least with me, I didn't have kids to leave."

"Ah, I asked for it. Was pickin' up some extra dough going to drills once a week. When the war come along, bango!" The prisoner was moaning. Nelson glanced at him. "Skipper really booted him in the gut," he said.

"I better go," Firesteen said. "Skipper catches me talkin' with a sentry..."

"Stick around. We keep it low, nobody'll bother." He looked at his watch. "I got another twenty minutes till Lock relieves me. Then I'll warm up the jeep, and we can go down to the mortars. Horse's got a place we can heat some joe."

Firesteen leaned back, resting his head on his hands. "Okay." Neither of them spoke for a few minutes. "Someday I'm gonna have to tell my kid what we went through getting him here," the corporal said. "You don't realize how much your folks do to take care of you, bring you up. You could never pay them back."

"People always says how kids owe their people. I don't feel like that," Monk said. "With kids, I mean, your whole life's different." The tip of his nose dripped, and he wiped it on his glove. "It's like when you come home at night and you look in the room at them. And how they smell and they're asleep and their hair's curled up damp on their necks, and ..." He shrugged. "All the time you get paid back double for what you do for them. Don't take much to give them a real charge either. Like you maybe bring home something for a dime, they go crazy for it ... And the funny things kids do..."

"My sister Gert got a boy, six years old, a real wild one. We call him the vildachaiah." Firesteen smiled. "Means like wild Indian," he said. "Last year, it was on Chanukah—"

"That's your Christmas, huh?"

"Comes the same time about. Anyway, I said, what you want your Uncle Melvin to get you, Daryl—isn't that a hell of a name? My sister's supposed to name him for my father David, he should rest in peace. She comes up with Daryl! Anyway, the kid wants to see a television show. I got a friend always gets me tickets. So me and Ruth and the kid go. The MC comes through the audience giving out prizes and stops at Daryl. Tell me, sonny, are you a good boy?' And the kid says, 'Mostly I am.' And the MC says to him, 'You ever do anything bad, Daryl?' And the kid says, 'Well ... one time I farted!' I'm telling you, I couldn't help howlin'. Ruth coulda gone through the floor!"

Monk was shaking with laughter, tears streaming down his face. "Honest?" He struggled to hold it back, and then was convulsed again. "What they come up with!"

Kao Teh listened to the laughter. He groaned, louder so that he might be heard. There were still two. But he had to take the chance, he had decided. His grip tightened on the pistol beneath the canvas; he moaned again.

"Gotta take a look at the Chink," Monk said. "Poor bastard must be startin' to hurt."

"I'll go warm up the jeep for you," Firesteen said. "Meet me there when Lock comes."

Holding his rifle before him, Monk Nelson approached Kao Teh. The prisoner was clutching his throat, groaning. The marine came closer. "Better sleep," he said to the Chinese, putting his cheek on his shoulder to illustrate. The prisoner groaned again, turned, rolled his head on the ground. Nelson debated whether or not to call Huckabee, and decided to let the corpsman sleep. He began to back away. Another groan. After all, Monk thought, the guy's human. Holding his rifle between his knees, he unsnapped his canteen cover, shook the icy water into his cup, and offered it. In his last conscious moment, he saw the pistol, saw the flash of fire.

Firesteen reached the spot as Kao Teh started into the brush. The Chinese took only a few steps before the corporal put four bullets in his chest. When Pat and Andy raced up, the whole command post was awake. Firesteen, crying bitterly, was still firing into the lifeless body.

Huckabee pulled him away, then dropped to his knees beside Monk Nelson. Pat put his ear to the dead man's chest and felt for the pulse on his neck, knowing there would be none.

Andy stood in the crowd above him. "Here," he said. "I found your .45 "

6

During the next week the company stood poised, in readiness, waiting.

But there was no contact with the enemy, no order for attack, no preparation for withdrawal. The battle was against the piercing winds that blew down across the mountains from Manchuria, drove the thermometer to eighteen below zero, slowed movement, dulled reaction.

They kept vigil across the silent front. They patrolled the rugged hills, the deserted villages, the tortuous roads that led nowhere. They huddled around the blazing stoves of warming-tents, arguing practical questions: the best way to thaw rations or heat coffee or oil a weapon or force an entrenching tool into the frozen earth.

The company officers stood around a fire in the command post, burrowing into the hoods of their parkas and stamping their feet to keep them warm. Pat had grown a black, scraggly beard. He had wrapped his throat with a white towel. He carried his .45 in a shoulder holster. "Battalion's had a warning order," he said. "We're going to move. And soon—"

Andy broke in. "We talked to Skinhead. He couldn't say much in the clear. But he's coming up. Something hot's on. I gathered that."

Pat kicked a smoking ember into the flames. "We need information. The Chinese are coming across the Yalu like a dose of salts"—it was Andy's phrase—"but we can't seem to find any concentration of them."

You-all, the South Korean handyman, offered coffee. "Plenny hot. You want, honey?"

Pat took it, motioning for the boy to fill the other cups. "Looks like I've got myself an orderly," he said.

Second Lieutenant Harry Allison, a slim young man of twenty-two, called to the exec. "Better rub your nose. It's getting white."

"Thanks."

"Better rub yours, Stringbean. It's getting brown!" Second Lieutenant Charles Cagel laughed, and the others joined in. "Old Beanpole's bucking for first looie!"

Allison pushed back the blond cowlick that hung over his eyes. "As I explained, Captain, we went over three miles today. And, as usual, nothing to report. A fire burning in the hills. A few Koreans in a village. Choy talked to them."

Pat looked for the interpreter and saw him below with The Horse, cleaning his carbine. He called him; and the Korean joined the group at the fire. "Any information from the villagers today?" Pat said.

"Nothing of consequence." Choy tried to seat the bolt in his weapon. "The Chinese are in the hills. There are many of them. They will drive the Americans out. The usual thing."

"Where in the hills? Did you ask?" Andy took the carbine from Choy, slipped the bolt in place and handed the weapon back.

"Thank you." The interpreter took a printed sheet from his pocket and gave it to Andy. The drawing showed a UN soldier raping a Korean woman while her child lay in a pool of blood at her feet. It was passed around. "You can not expect the people to give information," Choy said.

"Why the hell not? The gooks don't believe that kind of jazz, do they?" Lieutenant Cagle said.

"Mr. Cagle," Choy said, his brows raised, deep lines showing on his forehead, "we should not delude ourselves there is respect for Americans. It would be as foolish as to say there is respect on your > part for these people you call gooks."

"Just a way of talking," Lieutenant Pappas said quietly. He was a young man, but his dark, triangular face was furrowed, an old, wise face on a youthful body. He spoke slowly. "You know we don't mean anything by it."

"Of course not," Choy said. "It is normal to assume superiority toward backward peasants who have no motion pictures or plumbing or automobiles—"

"Let's get on with this," Pat said.

"Of course," Choy said, smiling thinly. "I only hoped to make clear that these people are willing to believe what they are told."

"Like our stabbing babies and raping women?" Pat said.

"The women? I think it must have happened. The babies? I have seen more subtle things, not that." He paused, as if his mind had wandered to a remembered scene. "But the people who are told these things, who see these pictures, who are bombed from their homes— they are not so logical, you see."

"We're not in Korea to protect our own marbles," Cagle said.

"I suggest you think on that a bit, Mr. Cagle."

Lieutenant Cagle stepped in front of the Korean. He was a small man, no taller than Choy. In contrast to the others, he was clean shaven, his crew-cut black hair neatly trimmed, his boots shined. He glared at the interpreter. "I'm starting to wonder whose side you're on!" Pat's thoughts had been phrased by the lieutenant, but the argument was getting out of hand. "All right," he said. "That's enough." Choy spoke over him. "So you will no longer wonder, Mr. Cagle, I tell you I am on the side of Korea. And I remind you that America preferred to trust the enemy's promise not to attack us. For this reason, I am here and you are here. I, to protect Korea. You, to protect your country."

Cagel pushed a finger into Choy's chest. "Now listen, goddammit! If we hadn't gotten here, Rhee and you and the rest of South Korea would've been taken over by the goonies."

"Knock it off, Chuck!" Andy said. He turned to Choy. "I don't want to hear any more lectures from you. Just remember you're working for the U.S. government. You can hate the boss's guts if you like, but as long as you're taking his dough, keep your mouth shut."

"It should be possible to examine realities. I was told I am here to acquaint you with them. The reality is that the average Korean sees little or no difference between you and the Chinese. They have been fed propaganda—even as you have been. And they believe it. Even as you believe yours. They will give us no information because they do not know who will be master tomorrow, and they do not care enough to risk their lives. This is fact. Unpleasant, as most truth is, but fact. Is this so hard to accept, to understand?"

Sensing the man's sincerity, Pat wanted to end the conversation on a different tone. But he could not risk taking sides against his officers. "All right, Choy. If you haven't anything else, you can secure." He tried to make his voice as hard as Andy's. The Korean nodded and returned to the mortar section.

"He pisses me off," Cagle said.

"It's his country," Pappas said. "He's watching it get ripped apart."

"We've had three other interpreters before him. They were pleasant, decent guys who didn't go around cussing us. Did their jobs and kept quiet," Cagle said.

Andy pulled on his gloves. "You mean they kept their opinions to themselves. You never knew what the devil they were thinking."

"Choy gets on my nerves too," Allison said. "Maybe because we expect him to conform to the movie version of the smiling, bowing, humble Oriental. But there's always some truth under what he says; and he does know the Chinese and his own people. I think he's just trying to explain them to us; and he's pretty blunt about it."

Cagle knocked on Allison's helmet. "Stringbean, may I say that you do conform to the movie version of the clean-cut, wide-eyed, true-blue Annapolis product?"

He laughed. "And I'm proud of the education I helped buy you."

Pat was squatting on the ground. "Let's get back to this." He traced a finger over the outlined positions on the map at his feet. "The goonies are all around us, just waiting for the right time and the right place. And we can't find them ..."

"What we need to do is hit them now, get them off balance before they move in on us," Andy said.

"What we need is a prisoner." Cagle blew a smoke ring and punctured it with his finger, apparently oblivious to the edge of irony in his remark, to the silence that greeted it. Innocently, he glanced up and watched the faces around him. All of them were aware, thinking.

Pat had thought of little else, been aware of little else in the six days that had passed since Monk Nelson's death. He was responsible, he had told the battalion commander. Skinhead had agreed and had read him off as if he were a boot. Pat had been over the ground, walked every step he had covered that night. He couldn't understand how his weapon had got into the prisoner's hands. The Chinese had never been close to it. He couldn't have concealed it when Huckabee was working on him, when The Horse was feeding him. He had to get it later. But how? Guilt badgered him, invading his sleep. But it was more than his guilt, more than the look Goober had given him that night, more than the distrust he thought he read in the faces of his men, more than Andy's refusal to discuss it. It was suspicion that grew and unnerved him. Someone had given that weapon to the prisoner, he was convinced. And that man was still in the area, still able to act.

"I'll take the patrol today if it's okay," George Pappas said.

"I'm taking it, George. From your platoon," Andy said. Pat looked up quickly. Assigning patrols was his job. Andy had not discussed it with him.

"But it's my turn," Pappas said.

"But me no buts. How am I gonna get that Congressional sitting on my duff in the C.P.?" Andy pointed to the map. "Already got my route marked, both ways."

"You two can fight it out," Cagle said. "As for me, I'm for packing my gear and going back to edifying the American girl—selling depilatories, girdles, and deodorants for Batten, Barton, Durstine and Osborn. It's too cold here. It's unsanitary. The food is bad. And I need a woman, a luscious, skin-you-love-to-touch, glorified-by-Lustre-Creme, Mum-armpitted, un-briarpatch-legged American broad! Gentlemen, Charles L. Cagle didn't join The Corps for this."

"Chuck hasn't been the same since he left his mama-san in Kobe," Andy said.

They talked about their short stay in Japan, the places they had been, the marines—now dead—they had known. Pat interrupted. "You ever get to Osaka? There was a terrific club there when I was on occupation duty ..." But they didn't know Osaka. They resumed their conversation, and Pat waited for a lull in the talk. "Guess that's all I have. Everybody get your areas policed for Skinhead's visit. Be ready to move if we get word. Be sure your weapons are in good shape. And keep a tight check on ammo. We've expended damn' little, and yet we keep issuing it. Either they're leaving it around or getting rid of weight on patrol. Let's see ... Frostbite. Four men at Battalion aid. Watch it."

The officers began to gather their things. "There's an M-1 and a carbine reported missing," Andy said. "Next man who loses a weapon is going to get racked—by me personally. You can pass that on, too." He pulled off the red flannel sock he wore around his neck, then rewound it. "Stand by a minute, Chuck."

"Okay."

"Those four frostbite cases. All yours. From now on in, you have any others I want to know why."

"I told them to massage one another's feet—"

"I don't give a rat's tit if you rubbed them yourself. If this keeps up, it's gonna be your ass."

"Yes, sir."

Andy clouted Cagle on the back, nearly toppling him. "Well, don't stand there like you just got an ice-water enema. Get the hell outta here."

"I'll get on it, Andy." Calling to the others, Cagle climbed the embankment and started up the ridge.

"Good people," Andy said. "But you got to prod them—all of them. Got to drive them. They're as good as you make them."

"They're awfully young," Pat said.

"Old enough. Pappas picked up a Navy Cross at Inchon. Cagle's a big talker, doesn't know when to shut up sometimes, but nothing excites him. Never loses his head."

"Didn't sound like that with Choy."

"Aw, that. Nothing."

"What about Allison?"

"Stringbean's just six months out of Annapolis—only regular officer in the company. But a good man with the troops, and a damn' genius with a pisstube. We'll switch him to the mortars over The Horse when we get in some replacements, move Pappas back to the machine guns, but keep the sections attached to the rifle platoons. One of these days, we might even get the F.O. we rate."

"We'll see."

First Sergeant Goober walked up to the fire. "Skipper, I got two men want to talk to you. Justus and Sanchez."

"What is it?" Pat said.

"For the lieutenant," Goober said.

The two men were standing behind him. Sanchez was loaded with gear. Slung across his shoulders, stuffed in his pockets, hanging from his belt were a Mauser, a Czech rifle, a saber, a North Korean flag, Communist literature, a burp gun, a Chinese bugle, a Russian pistol. Justus carried both their rifles.

"What you selling, Sanchez?" Andy asked.

"Well, sir, I been thinkin' ... that ... well, Lock and me been thinkin' ..."

"He wants to donate his souvenirs," Lock said.

"Yeah, I'm gonna donate 'em."

"Why you getting so generous?" Andy said.

"Well, Skipper, Goat was thinkin—"

"I asked him"

The Puerto Rican readjusted his load. "Y'see, we was talkin' and we thought it might be a good idea to trade some of my gear for booze—"

Lock thrust himself forward, "—for some good chow. You see, Skipper, it's Thanksgivin' today." He gave due reverence to the word. "Thanksgiving" he said again. "There's some doggies down the road a piece that'd be glad to fix us up with chow, good chow, in swap fer this here gear Goat's got no use fer."

Pat scratched the black bristle of his beard. "We're going to get a Thanksgiving dinner sent up from Battalion. Truck will bring up the works this afternoon. Candy. Nuts. Turkey."

"We wasn't thinkin' 'bout pogie bait or turkey.. "

"No, sir, we wasn't," Sanchez said.

Andy took a cigar stub from his pocket and brushed it off. "Just what were you thinking about?"

Lock struck a match and held it for Andy. "Man to man, Skipper, we been thinkin' wouldn't it be nice to have maybe a few cans of brew —or somethin' like that."

"Something like that? What would you say was something like brew, Captain?"

"What I want to know is who's going to do all this high-powered trading," Pat said.

"Lock thought maybe we—"

Lock jabbed a fist in Sanchez's side. "Gettin' a feller to volunteer fer somethin' like this'd be hard as sewin' buttons on a burp, sir. Goat and me know'd you'd be all fer it, so we're willin' to take on the detail."

"Justus, damn your hide, you're wasting your time in The Corps," Andy said. "You ought to get out, go back with Lieutenant Cagle and give your all for Batten, Barton, and so forth."

Lock pressed his advantage. "Couldn't see that, sir. Why'd I work fer them fellers when I can spend thirty years in The Corps, workin' fer people like you?"

He glanced at Pat and, without hesitating, reinforced his position. "And like the cap'n here."

Both officers laughed. "You trying to snow me?" Andy asked.

"No, sir! Hope to die. You never knowed me to blow smoke up nobody."

"Well... what you say, Captain?" It was the first time Andy had point-blank left a decision to him.

Pat considered it. "Normally, it would be all right, men. I think it's decent of you to volunteer. But chow is coming up. And we've got to be ready in case we get orders for a move ..." He watched the expressions of dismay cross their faces. Why couldn't Andy have disposed of it? Why leave the dirty detail to me? "I'm sorry," he said. "That's it," Andy said.

The two men stood there, uncertain whether to press further or not. "You got the word. Shove off," Goober said, pushing them ahead. "I coulda fixed it myself with the skipper," he muttered. "You had to drag the captain into the act."

"Carry some of this stuff," Sanchez growled at his friend, forcing the saber, the bugle, and the burp gun on Lock. "Your damn' ideas. What a crock!" They both walked away, grumbling.

"Wait a minute!" Pat was striding after them. They turned. He handed them two bottles of whisky. "Brought these out in my seabag. Haven't had a chance to touch it." They stared at him. "Probably be good for bargaining. No sense giving away all your gear."

"We can go?" Lock asked.

"You'll have to be back before dark."

"Yes, sir."

"The jeep's going in. Better run if you're going to catch them." "Aye, aye, sir!"

"Well, just don't stand there like—like you had an ice-water enema. Get the hell out of here!"

Pat and Andy watched the two marines run across the area and stop the jeep as it began to pull out. The Horse, Huckabee, and Firesteen were aboard. "You buggers squeeze in front," they heard Lock say. "What'd I tell you? You stick with ole Lock, you travel first class." Andy stood beside Pat as the jeep rocked out of the field, down to the narrow road. "You got the map?"

"No."

"Thought you picked it up."

Pat returned to the fire. "You had it right here."

"I'll be damned!" Andy was puzzled. "Maybe Chuck took it. I'll check."

"Yes, you better." Somehow Pat knew the map would not be found —as the M-1 and the carbine had not been found, as the ammunition had disappeared.

The jeep below them dropped to the road. "Some combination you got there," Andy said. "Wheels. Booze. An odd-ball swabbie and four thieving marines."

"Wouldn't you have let them go?"

"Hell, no."

"But the way you were joking with them, the way you talked, I thought ..."

"I'll tell you something, Pat. I always keep in mind I'm the doctor. The troops are patients." His smile was faintly mocking. "You ever know a doctor who wasn't a sleekly patronizing bastard deep down?"

"You can't generalize ..."

"Granted the exceptions." He grunted and walked with Pat toward the cave. "Doctor knows best. That's why he lets the patient and the relatives stay dumb and happy. He uses the old bedside manner, holds the patient's hand, says, 'What a gorgeous gown you're wearing!' or, 'What sexy pajamas!' But underneath, he's a cold tool. He tells only what he thinks the patient needs to know. The patient's a body. He smells it, prods it, takes its temperature, and checks its bowels. The patient is dull. Only the condition is interesting. He cures the condition, and incidentally the patient. He fails to cure the condition, the patient dies. Too bad!" He cleared his throat. "Too damn' bad! Do an autopsy."

Pat was staring at him, aware that something more lay beneath the words. "Okay. You don't like doctors."

Laughing, Andy stooped to enter the cave. "Like them? I model myself after them. I don't get fouled up in cheap emotions." Standing again, he faced Pat. "Like putting a screwball in charge of corpsmen because he happens to be a darkie and senior man." He shook his head. "I don't get involved with my patients as people. I remember I know what's best for them better than they do. I jolly them along, give them a good time, am a good egg. But I don't forget."

"There's been no trouble with Huckabee. He's doing all right. No one even seemed to notice."

"You've got a lot to learn, Pat." Andy bent to the cave entrance again and went inside.

Pat heard a jeep grinding up the rutted path from the road. It was the battalion commander; and he went down to meet him. "Good afternoon, sir."

The lieutenant colonel returned the greeting and the salute, unfolded his long legs and swung them over the side. He was a tall, pink-faced man, no more than forty, whose uniform, too short and too big, hung loosely on his gaunt frame. "This weather," he muttered, his pipe jouncing in his mouth as he spoke. " 'In the cold of far-off northern lands, and in sunny tropic scenes ...'" He shivered. "I prefer an honest case of malaria."

"Eighteen below today," Pat said.

Skinhead removed his helmet, exposing his shiny, bullet-smooth head long enough to slip on a woolen cap. "See if you can find us some coffee, will you, please?" He blew his nose and coughed. "And let's get out of this wind, Pat. Where we can talk. We've found our Chinese. And I've got a job for you."

7

The Horse slowed the jeep as they neared a road junction. "Well, there's no mail. And I've got the mortar tube I come for. And Huck's got his gear. Where to now?"

"Let's just hold onto the whisky to celebrate if I get word my baby's on the way."

"Wanna bet?" Lock laughed. "You ain't got confidence in yer-self."

"Don't bet him, Mel. If he put money on his makin' general, there'd be four stars on his shoulders by night." Sanchez piled his souvenirs around him and put the bottles between his feet.

"I know where we can do business with that booze," Huckabee said.

"Forget the we, Sambo. I promoted this deal," Lock said.

"That's a funny guy," Sanchez said.

"Who?"

"The captain. Funny."

"Yeah. You catch that, too?" Lock held to the front seat as The Horse braked the jeep. "Him with that phony beard and the rag 'round his neck and the .45 under his arm, tryin' to make like the skipper."

"Seems to me he's okay," The Horse said.

"He's all right," Huckabee said. "Considerin' he's a marine."

"If he was a marine," Firesteen said, "Monk wouldn't be stone cold now."

"I mean, first he says no dice, then he hands us all this joy juice."

The jeep hit a pothole, and Sanchez felt for the bottles. "Take it easy, Horse." He lifted one gingerly and held it in his lap. "Can't make out why he did it."

"Bet the skipper give him the word," Lock said. "He don't go to the head less'n the skipper tells him it's okay."

"Well, make up your minds," The Horse said. "Where to?"

"I've got the skinnay on the doggies," Huckabee told them. "There's this supply dump down the road that's got vodka and beer. Told me at Battalion aid these army people sent down to this distillery at Hungnam, pulled up water trailers and filled them like at a gas pump. They've got it piled in five-gallon cans. And there's a mile-high stack of beer, too."

"Tell you what," Sanchez said. "Lock and Huck can use the captain's stuff to keep the doggies busy tradin' for beer. Meantime, Horse and Mel and me'll borrow some of that vodka."

Lock reached for the whisky. "Pull up, Horse. We're gonna finish us a bottle of this here booze and figger out the tactics ..."

While the others piled out of the jeep, Huckabee took Sanchez's Chinese bugle and sounded "Attack."

"It's this way, Gyrene. If General Almond, his holiness, hisself asked me, I'd tell him the same thing. We don't issue beer without orders." The handsome sergeant lit a cigarette and flipped the match at Lock's feet.

A soldier with a blanket around his shoulders stood beside him. "Hell, we ain't got beer. Wish we did."

The sergeant smiled. "No use trying to fool a gyrene, Marty. Some people got a nose for women, some for chow. With bellhops, they can smell a brew ten miles away." He grinned at Lock. "I thought Harry Truman had you guys doing police duty back in the States. You over the hill?"

In other circumstances, a briefer, less pungent discourse would have resulted in battle. But Lock checked himself. There were six soldiers in the area—all of whom were muscular specimens and apparently spoiling for something to kill the boredom. "Look, friend, we been on the lines for a hell of a while. We're gonna be jumpin' off soon, goin' God knows where. We figgered nobody gives a hoot 'bout us not havin' anythin' to celebrate Thanksgivin' with. Then I said, 'Our buddies in the Army'll give us a break.' We're dependin' on you, fellers."

"I'm just bleeding for you, Blondy. How come you're telling us your troubles? Why don't you tell them to Pearson or Winchell so you'll get headlines?"

Beyond the group gathered around him, Lock caught a glimpse of Mel Firesteen, fifty yards away, slipping around the cache of vodka with a five-gallon expeditionary can in each hand. "I'm not askin' no handout," Lock told the soldier. "I got stuff to trade."

"What you got?"

"How many cases of beer for a fifth of good booze?"

"If you had it, and if it was stateside stuff, maybe five cases."

"What?" Lock took the bottle from his parka. As the soldiers crowded in, he saw Sanchez slipping under the tarpaulin that covered the vodka cans. "This here would cost you twenty-five bucks if'n you bought it from a buzzboy," Lock said.

"And it ain't gook gall, either."

"Well, maybe I'll let you have seven cases for it—if it's any good."

"I got two bottles." There was a distinct crash from the vicinity of the vodka dump. Lock winced. "I need twenty cases, enough fer two cans apiece fer my outfit."

The soldiers had turned toward the sound and stood uncertainly, listening.

"How about it?" Lock said.

"Okay," the sergeant said reluctantly. "I'll give you ten cases per bottle, if it's real stateside stuff."

"You can take my word fer it."

"I wouldn't take the word of a seagoing cop if he said Jane Russell had boobs!"

Ripping the seal with a flourish, Lock opened the bottle, and held it out. "Try a sip."

"Mm-mm. I don't know." The sergeant gulped again, then handed it to his friend. "See what you think, Marty."

The second soldier took a long drink. "Not bad." He passed it to the next man. "Put your lip around that."

The soldier let the bottle gurgle, cutting it to less than half. Two more tried it. "Man alive, I never seen nobody drink like that," Lock said. "This stuff'll knock you on yer hiney. Better go easy on it."

The sergeant had the bottle again. "We're not candy-assed gyrenes. We're soldiers." He turned the bottle up and let the rest of the liquor drain into his mouth. He shook the last drops on his tongue, savoring it, and handed the empty to Lock. "Okay, Gyrene. You got a deal. You put up two bottles, we'll give you twenty cases."

Lock had endured all the insults he could take. But he swallowed and smiled as he saw The Horse clear the area with his load, and disappear into the woods. "I'll go get the other bottle. You can have yer Yobos start stackin' the stuff."

"What you mean other bottle?"

"You already drunk one."

"Hell, Gyrene, that was a sample. That was for tasting. Don't think you're going to pull some damn' gloryboy trick on me. Two bottles, twenty cases. One bottle, ten cases."

"Why, you dirty sonova ..." The soldiers moved in around Lock, and he reined his temper. "Okay," he said. "I'll go get it."

While Lock conferred with Huckabee at the jeep, The Horse, Firesteen, and Sanchez loaded sixty gallons of eight-day-old vodka, and covered it with ponchos. Huckabee filled the empty whisky bottle with diarrhea medicine and watered it to obtain the right color. Then, with all plans made, Lock returned to make his deal with the Army.

It had started to snow. Light flurries blew across the area. The soldiers were laughing when he walked up. They quieted down and let the sergeant speak. "Okay, let's have it."

"Like hell!" Lock hugged the bottle beneath his parka. "When I get my ten cases of brew, you get the booze. Put it out here in front of me."

"You talk mighty tough for a bowlegged stub. Supposing we just decided to take that bottle away from you?"

"Supposin' I clue you, doggie," Lock snarled. He withdrew his bottle, holding it like a club, and planted his feet squarely. "Supposin' I couldn't bust yer jaw fer you—which I can. And supposin' I couldn't crack a few skulls on yer buddies—which I can. And supposin' I'd come back in a little bit with a couple ponyos of mine, and stuff about ten cases of beer cans up each an' every hiney!"

"Listen to the gyrene!" the sergeant said, laughing.

"Try me!" Lock said. Then, hearing an approaching vehicle, he suddenly grabbed his stomach. "Oh! I'm sick. Sick!" He fell to the ground and began to thrash about, groaning.

The jeep tore into the clearing. Huckabee jumped out. "Thank goodness I found him!" he announced dramatically.

The soldiers were gathered around the prostrate marine. "What's wrong?" the sergeant asked.

"Man," Huckabee said, loosening Lock's parka, "you are the luckiest dog soldiers! I musta got here just in time—before he sold you the stuff."

"What's wrong with it?" one of the soldiers said.

Lock rolled on the ground, still howling, holding the pit of his stomach.

"Help me," Huckabee said. "I got to give him the antidote before it's too late."

"Antidote!" the sergeant shouted. "That stuff ... poison? It was sealed."

Huckabee held out the bottle of diarrhea mixture. "Smell it," he said, "but don't get it too close to the mucous membranes; liable to injure 'em."

"Jezuz!"

"Sonovabitch marine!" the sergeant said. "You can't trust the dirty ... Did you smell the stuff before?" he asked one of the other soldiers.

"Just drank it."

Huckabee placed a crumbled aspirin on Lock's tongue and forced him to swallow it with water. "He'll be all right, I think. Usually takes a couple hours before the pains get too bad."

"We drank that stuff," the sergeant said, excited.

Huckabee shook his head dolefully. "No!"

"You feel all right?" the sergeant asked the others.

"I dunno. Feel sorta funny, I guess."

"I got a headache," another said.

Huckabee nodded gravely. "That's the symptoms. Funny feeling. Headache. A sorta burnin' in the stomach."

"Yeah. I got a burning in the stomach," the sergeant said.

"Probably the carbolic acid startin' to work," Huckabee explained.

"Give us the antidote. Quick!" the sergeant said.

"Not that easy," Huckabee said. "Help me get him in my jeep." Dumbly, the soldiers rushed Lock to the seat.

"C'mon. You gotta give us the stuff!"

"I'm all out of antidote," Huckabee said, clucking sympathetically. "That boy been peddlin' that poison all over the place. I been anti-dotin' for miles, just followin' him. Thanks be we don't have any deaths." He paused, meaningfully. "Yet."

The sergeant tugged at Huckabee's arm. "Where can we get it?"

"About two miles from here there's an aid station with plenty of this special antidote. But I'd need somethin' to trade them for it. Say about twenty-five cases ..."

"Get that stuff on there!" the sergeant yelled to the Korean laborers. Unaware of what was beneath the ponchos, they began to stack cartons over the stolen vodka. The soldiers helped them.

"Tell you what you better do for now," Huckabee said. "Better try to keep that stuff from reachin' the prostate. Once there ..." He snapped his fingers in a gesture of hopelessness. "Well, you've had your last erection!" There was a chorus of protest and moans. "Don't want to take a chance on that. I don't think you had enough to ... kill you ... but there's also the chance of fecalemia developin' ..." They rushed after him. "Hurry, please. Hurry!" one of the men pleaded. "You sure we'll be all right?"

"Get on your hands and knees. That'll keep it from runnin' down." They complied. "That's right. Now cough. Cough as hard as you can." He wiped the thin haze of snow from the windshield and started the engine. "Harder. Cough harder."

The soldiers moved about on all fours, coughing to keep the poison from reaching the seat of their manhood. "What's fecalemia?" the sergeant, suddenly suspicious, yelled to Huckabee.

"Crap in yer blood!" Lock was standing in the jeep. He watched the amazed soldiers on hands and knees, puzzled, but still coughing. "That's great," he yelled. "Bark, you doggies. Bark!"

Huckabee gunned the motor, and the jeep and its load bounced crazily across the area, out to the road, and away.

8

At dusk the mountains, cloaked in snow, crouched like giant polar bears on the horizon. Half the company waited, shivering in their foxholes, watching the desolate valley before them. The others huddled in the protection of the horseshoe ridge, ignoring the icy blasts of wind and the constant flurries of snow. They stuffed themselves with turkey and slabs of cranberry sauce, sweet potatoes and green peas, corn, candy, and mince pie. They sang unending verses of the company song, made up new ones, told involved lies about their uneventful pasts, bragged of their passion and their prowess.

Lock sat on a throne constructed of the cardboard cases he had obtained that afternoon. "Listen up, you people," he called to the marines gathered in the area. "I think we got the first four lines worked out." Huckabee played the melody on Sanchez's bugle. Lock sang off key:

"Oh, the Army had a chow dump.

It was loaded up with brew.

And the Army had some vodka,

Just as pure as mountain dew."

Acknowledging the applause, Lock held his clenched hands over his head. "I sure like that mountain-dew line. It's plumb beautiful."

"You shoulda seen them doggies!" Huckabee, who sat like a court jester at Lock's feet, got down on all fours, crawled and barked. Laughter.

"That sergeant was sure he'd go through life with a danglin' dingus," Lock said. "And Firesteen can tell you that's pure hell!"

"Aw, beat your gums. Beat 'em!" Firesteen said.

Sanchez was sitting beside The Horse on the stacked cans of vodka. "Let's tap the brew," he said.

"Take it easy, ponyo. Yer as anxious as a bitch in heat." Lock patted the case beneath him. "We're waitin' for the skipper to come down."

"What's keeping him?"

"Readying the order for tomorrow." Goober cleared away the crust of snow and stretched out on the cases beside Lock.

"What's the hot poop, Wally? Where we goin'?" Lock said. "Don't you Wally me, Justus. Nobody but the skipper calls me 'Wally.' " Goober glared at him. "We're gonna set up an outpost."

"Any scuttlebutt on the Chinks?" The Horse asked.

"Maybe they're there. Maybe they're not."

"Anybody know somethin' rhymes with 'well?' " Huckabee said. "Hell."

"Yell."

"Who's got the attack tomorrow?" Firesteen asked.

Goober took off a shoe and sock and began to rub his ham-like foot. "Allison and Cagle. Pappas' platoon's in support."

"Hot damn! 'Way back. That's for me," Firesteen said.

"You're a hell of a marine!" Goober said.

"I take my turn up front two outta every three goes. I'm no C.P. pogue. How about you?"

The first sergeant banged his shoe on the carton. "Don't get salty with me. I've surveyed more seabags than you have skivvie drawers. I got more time in the pay line than you got in The Corps!"

"You ever think about gettin' knocked off, Top?" Huckabee asked, hoping to divert him.

"Everybody does." Goober pulled a dry sock on his foot and continued the massage, still staring at Firesteen.

"Damn' if I see the sense in takin' off yer boondockers to warm yer feet," Lock said.

"I think about it—gettin' killed—I mean," The Horse said. "You, Goat?"

Sanchez shook his head. "What's to think? You get it, that's it. That's all she wrote."

Huckabee blew the first mournful notes of the funeral march.

"Knock it off," Goober said. "When you're dead, you're dead like this turkey."

"I don't believe that," The Horse said.

"Goober's an atheist," Firesteen said.

"You can't even spell it," Goober told him. "How about you, Goat? What's your angle?"

"Not that," Sanchez said.

Goober laughed. "Well, you I can understand. You're Catholic. You believe what they tell you."

"I was," Sanchez said, suddenly somber. "But it's not for me." The shadow of memory darkened his mind for the moment, then he brushed it away. "Nobody tells me what I got to believe."

"I think it's all up to the Lord Jesus," Huckabee said.

"I don't think about it," Lock told them. "At home folks say the time you better worry 'bout dyin' is when you hear a screech owl or a whippoorwill call three times of an evenin'. I heared a bird callin' a while ago. Now, I ain't superstitious, but, dammit, it's queer to find a bird out in this freezin' cold, huh? Just to be on the safe side, I stuck my knife in wood, like yer supposed to."

Goober pinched the wattles beneath his chin. "Everybody's got his own kind of gobbledygook."

"Best way to get it is think about it," Sanchez said.

"You ask any guy in this lash-up if he's going to get it, he'll say, 'Hell, no.' But somebody always does. You jump off in the morning, don't you start wondering?" Goober lowered his voice. "You think will you brush your teeth again? Eat chow again? And then you get closer, and you start thinking will you make it to that ditch or that rock? And will you take another breath or will some slopehead hit you right between the eyes ..."

"Aw, bull!" Firesteen climbed up beside Sanchez and The Horse. "Anybody did that much thinkin', he'd deserve to get creamed."

"You talk real tough," Goober said. "But you think about it. And the idea of goin' to Heaven doesn't appeal to you."

"This talk don't appeal to me," Lock said. "Let's talk about somethin' else, somethin' serious—like nooky." He waited out the laughter. "Only one thing I like better than talkin' 'bout it!"

"All I want is for it to be ninety degrees warmer," Huckabee said.

"This weather's bad for my complexion." Laughter. "I'm turnin' white." Laughter. "Give me a rhyme for booze."

"Snooze," Lock said.

"Blues," The Horse said, watching Huckabee.

"Jews," Firesteen offered.

"Mel, yer a pistol," Lock said.

Pfc. Demette, Monk Nelson's replacement as radioman, eased himself down beside Goober. "I ever tell you about the old-maid doctor I used to shack up with in Newport News?"

"Only twice this week," Lock said.

"Trouble with her," Demette said, ignoring him, "was, it was like going to bed in a clinic. Always asking questions. One night she took my blood pressure before and after. That queered me."

"I'm with you," Lock said.

Sanchez hooted at him. "Not you. You guys hear about Lock in Wilmington on liberty from Lejeune? All of us chipped in so he could lose his cherry. Had a pot raised to find a bowlegged, pleasure-bent chippie. Well, we got him up in the hotel ..."

"We called this cocabola," Lock said. " 'Hear this town's closed up,' I say. And he says, 'Yah suh, bossman, was until jes now when you all done called me!' "

"What's a cocabola?" Demette asked.

"Nigger," Lock said.

The Horse, frowning, caught his eye and nodded toward Huckabee. The Corpsman was pounding the bugle in his palm aimlessly. "There a rhyme for liquor?"

"Try 'stick her.' "

Sanchez returned to his story. "This colored man, real nice guy who treated us good, gets Lock a doll. He was so scared, he chickened out..."

"Aw, dry up. I had more by accident than you ever got on purpose. I had more—"

"Come off it already," The Horse said. "There's plenty of decent girls in the world, you know."

"Quiet!" Lock said. "Horse is gonna tell us about the nice girls. The good girls let you and the nice girls help you!"

The Horse ran his tongue over his buck teeth. "I was in Norfolk two years ago, doin' duty at the brig in Portsmouth." His wide mouth hung open as he thought about it. "There was this lady in a pet store I met. And we went over to the beach and walked out on the pier. Fished one whole Sunday."

"Did you get it?" Goober said.

"She was a nice girl."

"Nuts," Goober said. "There's not one of them worth the powder it'd take to blow her to hell!"

Firesteen held up his printed menu. "One of you save me yours. I gotta send one to my wife; and I want one for my mother."

"You're off your rocker. You'll give them the idea you got a plank," Goober said.

"I don't want my wife to worry any more than she has to."

"She's probably like all the rest, Firesteen. Probably in a nice warm sack with some hundred-bucks-a-week civilian right now," Goober said. "I don't like that kind of talk."

"So?"

"So knock it off!"

"Blow it out your butt!"

Firesteen stood menacingly before the reclining first sergeant. "You don't talk like that about my wife."

Goober stood. "I could make a bloody mess out of you, buster."

"I'm not afraid of you."

"Yeah," Lock said. "You fellers fight."

"I could. But I could also get a court for grab-assing with a subordinate. That's you, Corporal. Subordinate. And don't you forget it." He spat in the snow. "Women are good for two things—screwing and making coffee." He turned his back and walked away.

In the cave at the command post, Pat prepared his first combat order while Andy studied the map. Choy crouched against the jagged wall, examining a sketch of the objective.

Rubbing his numb fingers together to restore circulation, Pat picked up his pencil again. "According to the school solution, when you select initial objectives or zones of action you get your platoon commanders where they can see the terrain."

"That comes under 'exigencies of battle,' " Andy said. He glanced at Pat's notes. "Scheme of maneuver looks okay."

"Well, thank God we won't have the enemy to contend with."

Pat scratched a doodle of a Chinese helmet on the margin of his paper, realized what he had done, and erased it. "Well, do you think we will?"

"Will what?" Andy said.

"The enemy," Pat said impatiently. "You think we'll have them..."

"Never know."

"But what do you think?"

"I don't." Andy laughed.

"What the hell is so funny?"

Andy picked a shred of turkey from his teeth with a fingernail. "Simmer down, Pat. Save your worrying. Never do today what you're sure to do tomorrow." He laughed again, and picked up the map.

Must be written all over my face, Pat told himself. All right. I'll take it as it comes. No use inventing problems. But there is a chance ... Andy thinks there's a chance ...

"Skinhead said the Chinks are on the eastern shore of the reservoir," Pat said. "They couldn't ..." He leaned over the map and measured the distances. "That would put them at least twelve miles from our objective."

"That was this afternoon," Andy said. "They could hole up until dark—as they usually do—and march an outfit all night. It's the highest point in this area. They might try for it."

"But twelve miles! And at night ... They couldn't make it. Could they, Choy?"

"To underestimate the enemy is dangerous. I think there is only a slight chance they will attempt it. But the distance is not at all impossible. They could occupy the ground before daybreak."

"I guess it's possible "

Choy pointed to the map. "I see you found it, Lieutenant Anderson."

"No. Just disappeared. That's the captain's."

Pat had considered the possibility of meeting opposition on the objective and had allowed for it as an enemy capability, but he had not accepted it as more than that. "I don't think they can move that fast," he said. But he was no longer so sure.

"You don't know them." Andy bit off the end of a cigar and lighted it. 'They're a rugged bunch."

"Captain Patrick, the Chinese soldier is handicapped by many things. But he is led by clever officers who have been constantly at war and in privation for many years. He is more rigidly disciplined. He can outmarch and outlast your men."

Pat was annoyed. He had asked the man's advice, and now found that he resented it. Not the essence, but the undertones. "They can't do anything our people can't do."

"Do you think your people, who are even now moaning about the cold, could march twelve miles tonight, carrying all their equipment? Do you think they could last indefinitely on rice and dried peas? Do you think they could stay alive in a padded cotton uniform and tennis shoes when they complain in their excellent pile-lined coats and sturdy boots? Do you think they would go into battle unarmed, but ready to pick up the weapon of the first man who dropped, or to seize one from the enemy?"

"Nobody's asking them to," Pat said. "American soldiers always manage to give a good account of themselves—against supermen of East or West." He didn't want to argue, but some compulsion drove him. There was something nearly gleeful in Choy's constant harping on American deficiencies.

"You were not at the Naktong, Captain. You were not on the Kum River line or at Taejon or Taegu. You did not see what I saw, Captain. American soldiers threw down their weapons and ran."

"Those Army troops were sacrificed," Pat said. "They weren't ready for combat, but they held out until help could come. They're responsible for us being here at all."

Choy spoke as if with regret. "They were your first line of defense." Andy moved around beside Pat. "Thanks for the history notes, Choy. Now shove off. We've got work to do."

"Tell me," the Korean said softly. "Why is it you can not accept the truth, and so, knowing, be stronger? My country is now all but unified. The Chinese will go to any lengths to prevent a great Communist defeat, a great victory for the West. I wish only to make you understand this. All life, I have found, is pretense. But it should not be so here."

Andy yawned. "No more of that tonight, Choy. How about making yourself useful? Tell Goober to call the platoon commanders. I want them down at 1900 to receive their orders." The interpreter inclined his head and began to back out. "And have You-all bring us some joe."

When he had gone, Pat took up his sketch again and checked it against his plan. He handed the order to Andy. "Is there anything I haven't thought of?"

"Sure. Lots of things," Andy said.

Pat snatched the sheet from him and glanced down it quickly. "What did I leave out?" he demanded. "Where is it wrong?" His words echoed in the confines of the cave; and he lowered his voice, making a conscious effort to speak calmly, slowly. "Show me. Go on. Show me."

Andy took his time in replying. He puffed his cigar and the smoke, released gradually, hung in his fiery beard. "Pat, if leading a company meant making out an order, any fairly intelligent schoolboy could do it. It's what you do when you get out there and things start to happen that counts."

"You think we're going to run into the Chinks, don't you?"

"I told you. I don't think anything. What I'm getting at is that I know some officers who can draw up a hell of a good plan for an amphibious landing, but couldn't lead a fire team to the head." He tugged at his socks and tightened the laces on his boots. "Maybe you can do both."

'When things start to happen,' Pat thought, I'll be just like anyone else. But if tomorrow everything goes smoothly, and I get the feel ... After tomorrow, it'll be easier.

Andy reached over and took the sketch. "Looks just like the area," he said. "Where'd you learn to draw like that?"

Pat caught the last few words. "Oh, in a way it's my business."

"You an artist, for chrisakes?"

"An architect."

"I'll be damned! I figured you for a lawyer or maybe a teacher." He turned the sketch toward the light of the Coleman lantern. "That's the way it looks, all right. You work on buildings? Anything I'd know?"

The only building of any size he had designed was a modern school. It had been entered in the competition that won him the Architectural Prize. But it was never built. "I haven't been at it long," Pat said. "Until recently, I was doing store buildings, Army barracks, and a lot of cheap housing developments. You know, bulldoze a dump, lay slabs, use concrete block. Change the entry. Move the carport from one side to the other. Use a gable over a door. Use redbrick trim. Use yellowbrick. And in the end they all look the same, and the builder sells them to somebody who wants to exist until he can afford more than the nothing-down-forever-to-pay kind of thing. Pretty dismal."

"I lived in one of those GI slums for about six months when I was managing a drive-in theater outside of Phoenix. Swore I'd kill the guy who put it together if I ever ran into him."

"Nobody's proud of that kind of development. Not the architect or the builder or the owner. But there's a market." Pat realized he hadn't even thought of home or his work for the past week. There had been too much else to distract him. "I do have a building that'll be going up soon. Something I'm going to be proud of. It's a hotel. They're going to build it on a thousand-yard strip of beach in Miami." Andy was lost in his own thoughts for a moment. "That where you work?"

"Offices are in Washington. But we've had jobs all over." He grinned. "Except Phoenix. Not guilty there."

"That's something! I know the beach. Used to work in a hotel on Ocean Drive, ten, twelve years ago when that was the swanky section. That's what sent me into The Corps the first time. A little misunderstanding with an elevator girl I caught sleeping around ... and then I tied on a real toot and slugged it out in the lobby with the superintendent of service. Spent two days sobering up in the Dade County jail. That's when I joined up and took the first train to Parris Island. From Paradise to Hell overnight." He scratched the mane of hair at his neck. "Hated it at first, but when it came time for discharge I didn't want to get out."

"Why didn't you stay?"

"Tried to. But I had a field commission, no college. They wouldn't have me as a regular officer. So I went back to the great wide world." "That when you went in the theater business?"

"No. Later. Long time after that. Thought about going to school on the GI bill at first—but I'd won two thousand bucks at craps coming back from China. So I went on a kick." He smiled, shaking his head. "Wound up broke in Atlantic City. Went to work as a shill for an auction house."

"What were you doing when you got called back in?"

"They didn't call me. I volunteered." Andy appeared to be thinking. Pat watched him stroke his beard, and nod. There was something black, something weighted with pain within the man, he felt.

"Was selling insurance then," Andy said. "Cheap burial insurance. Collect every week. Mostly foreigners, darkies." He paused again, laughed; and the laughter sounded strained, too hearty. "I'm the only Reserve in the division—and that's over half of it—that'll admit he wasn't making ten thousand a year on the outside.

That's why I'm gonna win me a Congressional." He pounded his fist into his hand. "It'll solve my problem. I'll go home a hero, and get me a berth as vice-president-with-medals of some company that does business with the government!"

Choy was in the entrance of the cave. "I have found the first sergeant," he said. "It is done."

"Thanks," Pat said. The interpreter disappeared. "There goes a humorless, cynical, bitter ... Wonder what's behind it."

"You want to know what's behind anybody, you got to figure out what his bitch is. With him, I don't know." Andy wiped a shred of tobacco from his lips. "But he's right about at least one thing. We're not fighting pushovers, Pat. We're up against a tough, disciplined army. You're liable to find it out when we hit that ridge in the morn-

9

Later that evening Pat issued his order. His officers listened, taking scribbled notes, while he oriented them. "We got word too late to let you see the ground, but I had a look at it, Andy had a patrol in the area earlier, and Skinhead went over it by helicopter." He pointed to the map and the sketch. "Our objective is this nobby ridge." They inched forward and examined the drawing.

Andy, on his knees behind Pat, leaned over and ran a blunt finger along the contours of the ridgcline. "Nothing on this slope for cover," he said. "A few boulders, maybe. But that's all. We'll move right down the corridor here." He traced the area. "And then up on the ridge.

Don't know what'll be there tomorrow, but I saw nothing this afternoon; and Skinhead couldn't see any enemy activity from his whirly-bird."

"Wait until I finish," Pat said. He had worked out his plan carefully, in detail, as if he were submitting an examination paper in OCS.

A five-paragraph combat order: Enemy situation. Friendly situation.

Mission. Line of departure. Time of attack. Mission of subordinate units. Supply. Aid station. C.P. location. Communications. "Best way to visualize the terrain is to hold your right hand straight out in front of you, palm down. Go ahead. Do it." He had rehearsed the procedure, rejecting four other similes. "Okay. Now tuck your thumb and make a fist. Imagine we're now at the elbow. And our objective is the fist, a ridge with a gradual slope that's topped by two knobs— your first and second knuckles."

"Good picture," Andy said.

"The enemy was spotted by Marine air this afternoon in two areas and in large numbers. They appeared to be using roads moving toward us, but at a distance of twelve miles."

"The division is tightening up," Andy said. "Has been for the past few days—which is something to be thankful for."

"Our company is going to occupy and defend this position." Pat checked the map. "The line of departure is here—at the head of the valley, or the elbow. We jump off at 0600. Here's our plan of attack: Stringbean, you take the first platoon down the arm here to the wrist. At that point ..."

"There's a dry creek bed there." Andy referred them to the drawing, and there was a long pause while they folded their maps.

Pat waited impatiently. He was already keyed up with nervousness and anticipation; and the delay annoyed him. "All right. You deploy your people there. On order, you'll continue the attack with your objective the highest knob—or first knuckle."

Andy pointed to the sketch. "I want you to take advantage of that lone cover in case we've got to call in artillery. Actually, this whole thinking's probably be a simple march—but we're going at it like there'll be opposition."

"Let me finish, will you, Andy?" For an instant, because Pat was bothered by the repeated interruptions, his temper flared. "Dammit, I'm trying to ..." He waited deliberately as his executive officer leaned back. "Chuck, you'll move your outfit down the valley on the right of Stringbean, maintaining visual contact. You'll also deploy in the creek bed and await the signal from me. Your sector will be the entire area to the right of and including the saddle—or the space between the first and second knuckles."

Cagle winked at Allison. "You see, Stringbean? They picked a man's lash-up to do a man's job."

Allison smiled. "I'll bet you some of Justus's beer we'll secure our ground before you take yours."

Pat quieted them. "George, you're in support." Pappas nodded. "You'll move at the rear of the C.P. Keep in contact. Machine guns remain attached." He peered into the darkness. "Horse?"

"Here, sir."

"Mortars follow the third platoon. Prepare to fire on call."

"Aye, aye, sir."

"You people remember, this is the same kind of thing we've done a dozen times before," Andy said.

"I'll be to the rear and between the leading platoons," Pat said. "And the headquarters section will displace from the line of departure and join me when the forward elements reach the objective. Andy will be with them."

"Now wait a minute! I've got to be up with you!"

"No need for it, Andy."

The others exchanged glances. Whether it was surprise or uneasiness, Pat could not tell. But he was determined to keep Andy back during the assault. It was the only way, he felt, that he could break into the closed fraternity, the only way to expunge the mistakes he had made and assert his independence of his exec.

"We can leave the company gear with Goober," Andy said. "I'll go back and lead them forward as soon as—"

"Hell, Andy, you're going to get that Congressional, all right. But give somebody else a chance." The others laughed.

When the order was completed and the cave cleared, Andy nibbled out his cigar and put the stub in his pocket. "I don't want to stay back minding the store tomorrow. I've tried to explain."

"Don't you trust me?" Pat asked.

"You want the truth, I don't figure you're ready yet. Okay. I'm a lieutenant, talking to a captain. You asked me." As he spoke, he tapped his fists together, punctuating with the hollow clack of his knuckles. "It's not you. Nobody without experience could be ready. It's like a game in a way. Sure, you can memorize the rules, but you really don't know what goes until you've played awhile."

Reminded again, brought back to it again, Pat had a sensation of being winded, of needing air. "You won't be far away," he said quietly.

Justus, Sanchez, and The Horse were waiting outside. "We been standin' by fer you to open the brew, Skipper," Lock said.

Andy punched his arm lightly. "Okay. I'll bar tend." They walked off together.

The Horse stood there. "Why don't you come on too, Captain?" Sanchez had started to leave. He came back. "You can put out the vodka, sir." Pat hesitated. "C'mon, hell, wouldn't be no beer without your booze. Besides, you let us go."

"Sure," The Horse said.

"Okay. I'll be assistant bartender."

When Andy appeared, Lock gave the signal, and Huckabee sounded Adjutant's Call on the Chinese bugle. The marines stood at mock attention. "At ease!" Andy grinned. "Thanks for the salute, Huckabee. When it warms up, I'm gonna get you the biggest watermelon in Korea." Laughter. The corpsman grinned, rolled his eyes and rubbed his stomach. "Want everybody to toast Huckabee," Andy said. "He's really white clean through!" Laughter.

"Hurray fer The Horse's buddy," Lock yelled.

"Hurray fer The Horse's ass," Demette shouted. Laughter. Huckabee drifted back to the fringe of the crowd. Andy cleared the snow from the first case, ripped it open and reached inside. "Well, I'll be damned!"

"What's up, Skipper?" Lock asked.

Andy waved him away, laughing. He reached into the second box, pulled out a small container, and finally exploded in mirth. "You've been had, Justus. The biggest snow-job artist in the First Mar Div, and you've been had!" He tore open the carton and scattered its contents to the crowd of upturned, puzzled faces.

"Tootsie Rolls!"

"Justus, you outsmarted yourself," Andy said.

"Those dogfaces, those cheatin', no-good, thievin' ..."

When the uproar had slackened to a grumble, Andy called to Pat. "Want to try the vodka, Captain?"

"Half a cup per man," Pat said. There were groans and protests. "We're going to save enough to use in our heavy machine guns and the jeep—as antifreeze. Justus, you're the man who suggested it." Lock, stunned by the Army's duplicity, sat atop his mountain of Tootsie Rolls. "You wanna get me lynched, Cap'n?"

The Horse caught sight of Huckabee. The corpsman had withdrawn from the others and was standing alone, watching soberly. The Horse walked over to him. "You ask for it," he said, shaking a finger at him. "All the time you ask for it."

"What're you talkin' about?"

"You know what I'm talkin' about. You act like a jerk whenever there's a bunch around. Always makin' a jackass outta yourself." Huckabee shrugged. "Just havin' some fun."

"You're like somebody else. You even look different," The Horse said. He sat beside him on a rock. Minutes passed and neither spoke. "With me you can be serious sometimes," The Horse said at last. "And we can talk about things. What you're gonna do. Your folks. People. Lotsa things. But soon's you get with a crowd you go haywire ... you act ..."

"Get off my back," Huckabee said, muttering, the words hardly intelligible.

Sanchez came up to them. "I meant to tell you, Huck. You want the bugle, you can have it."

"I'll pay you."

"Naw. Maybe you'll find somethin' I want. Hell, I can't blow it anyway."

"Thanks, Goat."

Firesteen called to them. "You guys come on. Let's get our share of the vodka."

The line moved past Pat, and he filled the last of the canteen cups. Then he clinked his cup with Huckabee, The Horse, Firesteen, and Sanchez. The vodka was bitter, tasting of metal. He surreptitiously poured the drink on the ground behind them. The men caught him, laughed, and grimly downed their own.

"Hey, Skipper," Demette yelled. "How 'bout singin' that verse you know about the chaplain?"

There were shouts of encouragement. Andy held up his hands, dried the vodka from his whiskers, and began to sing in a husky, brawling voice:

" 'A young lady was in trouble,
Told the chaplain of her plight.
Her circumference was double,
Because she slipped one night!
The padre asked the gen'rul,
To find the guilty guy.
The gen'rul told the padre that
He would—in a pig's eye!' "

They all joined in the chorus:

" 'For marines all stand together,
And shout their battle cry:
Semper Fi! Semper Fi! Semper Fi!' "

Fifty yards away a lone figure knelt in the company ammunition dump, listening to the singing. Then he picked up two boxes of flares and worked his way through the C.P. area. Making a wide detour, he slipped into a ditch within the position of one of the front-line platoons. Waiting there, he heard another man challenged.

"Halt and give the password."

The marine standing a few yards from the ditch stopped short. He was one of the veterans of the company, claiming the distinction—at thirty-two—of being the oldest Pfc. in Korea. "Hold it! Don't shoot. Been takin' a leak."

"Gimme the password."

"I'm Torrance. First Platoon. Ask anybody."

The replacement who challenged him clicked off the safety on his rifle. "You better gimme the password."

"You trigger-happy boot, I'm a marine. I ferget the damn' password. You fire, I'll brain you."

Lieutenant Allison came up beside the quivering sentry. "Come on in slowly," he told Torrance.

The aging Pfc. walked into the position. "That dumb jerk was gonna shoot me. And I'm due to be rotated home!"

"In the future you learn the password. And relieve yourself in your hole."

"Yes, sir."

"Password is 'rye,' " he whispered. "Countersign is 'whisky.' "

"Yes, sir."

When it grew quiet again, the figure in the ditch crawled forward, skirted the sentry, Torrance, and the lieutenant, and finally stole out toward the hills and the enemy.

10

The valley, shimmering in the early sun, stretched white and silent before them. The ridge sloped gracefully, its symmetry unmarred by hut or road or terrace, its twin peaks regal in ermine snow, standing against the cyclorama of morning. Porcelain hillside. Ice-blue sky. Amber sun. The crystal gleam of naked rock. The scene looked still, elegant, as unreal as a painting on a Christmas card.

Into the picture, on either side, files moved. Plodding, ungainly figures in green followed their leaders, the mingling of their breath puffing wispy clouds above them. The sounds were the crunch of boots against softening snow, hoarse commands, the wheezing cough of a chalk-faced BARman from Colorado, the muttered oath of Jesus Sanchez as he stumbled, the metallic voice of the radio.

Pat: "Able One. This is Able Six. Over."

Allison: "Able Six. This is Able One. Over."

Pat: "Send out a fresh fire team on your flank, Stringbean. Your people are slowing down."

On the right and seventy-five yards ahead, Pat could see Cagle's platoon. The men were bunching. He called the platoon commander. "Maintain interval, Chuck."

"Wilco. Out."

The word was passed. The formation spread. Pat had a feeling of exhilaration. He was surprised and comforted by the ease with which his orders were followed. Tightening the towel-scarf about his neck, he increased his pace.

Between the two knuckles of the fist-like ridge, a Chinese officer lay, his field glasses trained on the advancing marines. He pointed out the flank patrols, the columns on left and right, the command group; and he spoke to another officer beside him. Then his gaze dropped to the dry creek bed—the wrist at the end of the valley's arm. He found it on the American map before him. He spoke again, this time into a field phone. Then he crawled back to the reverse slope, and gave orders. His battalion moved into position. He saw his mortars being manhandled, aiming stakes being set up. He placed machine guns to sweep grazing fire across the slope below. At last, he lit a cigarette—a Camel—and sat back to wait.

From a hillock—the elbow where the march began—Andy watched the platoons pushing ahead. He handed his field glasses to Choy and checked his watch. It was 0800. Everything had gone perfectly. In another fifteen minutes the forward elements would reach the base of the objective. He chewed his dead cigar. A little slow getting started. A little too cautious, he thought. But the control was good.

Lock and Sanchez walked on either side of Pat down the center of the valley. Huckabee and Demette, the radioman, followed. Lock's feet were leaden with cold as he lifted them in his bowlegged stride. Absently, he offered a Tootsie Roll to his friend.

Sanchez moved rhythmically and without effort through the half-foot of snow, his husky shoulders hunched forward, eyes searching the ridge and the flanks, as if for prey. "Not for me," he said.

Pat, too, refused. His mind was elsewhere. The objective was within effective range of sixty millimeter mortars. In a combat situation, he thought, it would be wise to set them up now, in defilade, so they might support the attack. He marveled at the way the lectures he had heard, the problems he had run, the demonstrations he had watched, weeks or even years before, now seemed to fall in place, taking on new clarity and meaning. He felt especially alert and confident.

"Didn't get no breakfast," Lock was saying. He removed a glove and worked his fingers. Then he tightened the hood of his parka so that only his eyes were exposed. "Cold as a gravedigger's ass. Rations all froze stiff. Goat and me ate these Tootsie Rolls this mornin'. Don't think nobody had a decent chow."

Pat made a mental note to get hot food up when they secured the objective. The cold was already taking a toll. Huckabee had tagged five men with frostbitten feet and hands that morning, and sent them to the rear. Warming-tents would have to be set up right away, too. Glancing behind, Pat saw George Pappas leading his platoon. Beyond was the mortar section, the men slogging along under the weight of ammunition, tubes, and baseplates. He took the small radio from Lock, called The Horse, and ordered him to set up in a slightly defiladed area on the left of the line of march. Might as well do this thing right, he mused. As Andy had said, it was a game. You learned by playing.

Andy paced the narrow trench he had worn through the snow. November twenty-fifth. Today would have been their anniversary, their sixth. The thought of Jess returned to bum in his memory.

There was the first anniversary: The small, bare house in a maze of small, bare houses. Phoenix on the skyline. Midnight supper. Cooking-sherry for a toast. His gift, the practical one she had demanded. Her head wrapped swami-fashion in a dish towel, she conducted the ceremony, pronouncing gibberish over the brass bowl. And he burned twenty-seven dollars and eighteen cents' worth of receipted bills. Twenty-seven dollars and eighteen cents ... and eighteen cents.

And the second anniversary: A mustard-colored boardinghouse outside Tucson. A new job. Selling cemetery lots in a memorial-garden promotion. Two hundred dollars the first week. Nothing the second. Forty-five the third. And then he borrowed advances for a month. Jess went to work in a five-and-ten.

He was in bed in the darkness, hearing her humming as she washed her one good slip. He cursed himself, cursed whatever drove him to leave a steady job and chase rainbows. Only that evening the fat old man with a wart on his nose, who ran the place, had stopped her on the steps. And, standing behind the door, Andy had heard her say, "Of course. My husband will take care of it." When she came in, she had given him her salary. So he could be the one who paid. Lying there on the bed, he said aloud, "I'm just no damn' good." And, as he knew she would, she came to him. And, as he knew she would, she said: "Don't keep saying that. It's the only thing you ever tell me that I'll never believe."

He watched her. Ignoring the slightly crooked nose, the coarseness of hair, he saw only the tender face, the jewel of a mouth, her good, clean radiance. And he marveled that she, knowing him, could still love him. Later, she turned on the lamp beside the bed, and stood there nude, on her tiptoes, her nipples rouged. "Too broke for an expensive present, darling," she said, smiling. "The lipstick idea I got from reading *The Chinese Room.* But the blue ribbon's a touch of my own ..."

The third anniversary: The hospital chapel in San Francisco. He sat there alone. For the first time in his life, he cried. Never before. Not even when his mother's body was lifted from the street in Cincinnati. ("Hey! Take the kid away ..." "Pull down her dress!" "I seen it. She walked right in front of the bus, like she was drunk..."Take the kid away, will ya?")

Not when he left the first foster home for a second one. ("You got no idea what I been through with him ...") And a third. ("Another five a week. It's not too much to ask——") And a fourth. And a fifth.

But in the darkened chapel, he wept and he prayed. He promised whatever God there was that he would make Jess stop work, that he would take a comfortable job at a comfortable salary and stay put, that he would attend church, that he would never ask for anything from Him again. "Just this. Never asked anything. The baby's dead. Save her. Just this." She had fed his famished heart with love. He could envisage nothing without her. "Please, God. Please ... just this ... just this ..."

The fourth anniversary: Their first serious argument. She was pregnant again. "But darling, I feel fine. It's different this time."

And the doctor agreed. "No reason why she shouldn't have a perfectly normal delivery. The miscarriage was undoubtedly due to excessive work, a rundown condition, possibly injury to the fetus ..."

But he would not risk her again. He saw the doctor himself. "It's impossible unless two physicians agree that it's necessary. And it surely isn't." An hour later he was led to the door. "You're wrong, Mr. Anderson. But if you're set on it, I'd suggest you try Cuba. There'd be proper hospital care. Competent doctors ..."

No money for Cuba. He took an extra job at night as a teamster for the *Call-Bulletin*. But time was running out. They talked of little else. Finally, she relented. "I would advise you strongly against it," the man who called himself a doctor said. "It is late—so more difficult. And it will be expensive." He was a pleasant, white-haired old man who looked like the pictures in a retirement ad. "That will be three hundred and fifty dollars—in advance."

Andy borrowed a hundred from a loan company, held out eighty from his week's insurance collections, and got the rest from his night supervisor. The next morning they kept her appointment. Two days later, he was back in the same hospital, in the same chapel ... "Skipper?"

Andy wrenched himself from his reverie, and turned to Goober. "Yeah?"

"Why doesn't he push them, Skipper? They're draggin' ass." Looking at the valley before him, Andy saw the three paths converging on the ridge. "Suppose we let him run the outfit," he said irritably.

"Yes, sir." Goober flopped down. "Want me to get you a cup of joe?" Andy didn't answer. "You cold, Skipper?" Andy shook his head. "Why didn't you go with them? No sense you being—"

"Knock it off, goddammit!" He saw You-all loping across from the old position. "Where the hell you been?" he asked when the youngster climbed up to them.

"Get lose, honey."

"What's he saying, Choy?"

The interpreter spoke to the South Korean boy, then translated. "He says he was asleep. He could not find us, got lost."

"He's freezing. Tell him to cover up with some blankets. Wally, see the kid gets something dry to put on."

"I think, Lieutenant Anderson, it would be wise to be rid of this boy," Choy said. "He does no good."

"He's gotten to be a butler for the captain," Goober said.

"For Christ's sweet sake, get off my back, both of you! If it's not one damn' thing, it's another." Andy put his glasses up again and studied the columns as they moved within a hundred yards of the creek bed. Goober, surprised at his vehemence, was still watching him. "Wally, do what I told you, dammit!"

Five hundred yards away, Pat saw his leading platoons pull in their flank security and move into the winding, rugged cut at the base of the ridge. He motioned to the radioman, and while the marine knelt he called the battalion commander on the 300 radio. His plan had functioned smoothly, and he gave too long and detailed an account of it.

But he wanted to resolve any doubts Skinhead might have had about his leadership. He wanted to make it clear that he was in command.

Allison and Cagle checked in. The platoons stood ready for the long climb to the crest of the objective. Pat gave the order; and all along the creek bed the men clambered up and began the advance.

Thump-thump-thump. The sound was like a rubber mallet on a tire rim; the sound was like a mortar shell, impaled for an instant on a firing pin, then shuttling from the tube. Pat did not notice it. Then angry flashes burst like pockmarks across the face of the ridge, and rock and mud splattered the sterile snow. He fell to the ground, aware that Sanchez was beneath him.

Rackarackaracka. The hollow croup of enemy machine guns sounded now, joined by the ping and whine of small-arms fire that erupted from the crest and swept into the broken lines of marines. The men who had fallen when the mortars came in now rushed back to the promising safety of the creek bed. But two limp green bundles lay un-moving in the snow. Again the *thump-thump-thump.* Again the flashes, the crackling explosions. The clipped voices of machine guns. Shouts. A single scream.

The platoons were disorganized. Men scrambled for the limited safety of the few rocks or burrowed into the snow as if it would protect them. Beneath the scattered boulders that hung over the ditch, men crowded, groping away from the pounding fists that battered at them, from the bullets that thrummed overhead.

The radio in Lock's hands called insistently. "Able Six. Able Six. This is Able One. Over. Able Six. Come in Able Six ..."

Pat rolled aside. He could not think. His mind was knotted with fear. He saw Sanchez crouch beside him, expectant, saw Huckabee staring at him, saw the radio operator, his bulky 300 strapped to his back, still prostrate. 'The Chinese must have ..." Pat cleared his throat. "Choy said they could ..." he began, irrelevantly.

Their eyes had not left his face. They were waiting—as more than two hundred other men in that valley waited—expecting no more from him than an order, no less than ultimate safety. In that moment he understood what all commanders come to know when circumstance endows them with absolute power. He fought to submerge every impulse within him that made him only mortal.

"Able Six. Able Six! ..."

The mortars came in with timed regularity, with accuracy, laying across the entire front. A cluster struck within Allison's position. Others burst just behind Cagle's platoon. The enemy, seeing the confusion below, herded the marines into the creek bed and pinned them there. Pat counted to himself. One ... two ... three ... four ... five. Once more the mortars dropped in, repeating their pattern. Must do something. Right away. One ... two ... three ... four ... five. He was hypnotized into counting the blows. Must be observed fire. And heavy mortars. Close in. His men were in a chute—like animals— being smashed down in turn by the slaughterer's hammer. All madness and chaos. And it was he who was expected to restore sanity and order. He considered sending for Andy. He would know what to do, what chances could be taken. Then he thrust the thought from him. It was his decision to make, his command, his company. He drove himself to think: *Make an estimate of the situation. Decide on a course of action. Reject all others. Make a decision. Follow it aggressively.* He actually visualized the boldface lines on the pages of the manual on offensive combat. He actually saw the scarred face of a forgotten instructor. He willed strength into his voice. "Let me have that radio, Justus." He stood, knowing that he was needlessly exposing himself, but determined to make the gesture. "This is Able Six," he said carefully. "Over."

Allison reported. "Little cover here. Small arms pinning us down. Two dead. Four wounded. Need ..." The voice disappeared with the roar of an explosion.

"Able One! Able One! Do you read me? Able One!" There was no answer from Allison.

Andy listened to the exchange on his 536 radio, and watched the mortars lace the area to his front. "Got to move them through it," he said.

"What the hell's he waitin' for? Those goonies been sittin' there all this time, watchin.'" Goober turned up the volume on the receiver. Lock was trying to contact Able One.

"If they'd move through, close with the Chinks, they'd be okay. They're registered on that creek bed now. And we're sitting there, getting clobbered." Andy spat his cigar butt into the snow and kicked at it. "It's just as safe to go through when you're being hit." He took out another cigar. "Got to get out of there. Got to get some covering fire on the crest, and move up. Got to get some counter-battery on those damn' mortars."

"You want to talk to him, Skipper?"

Andy walked away as if he had not heard. He wanted to go forward, see the situation, give orders. But he held himself back. The bursts of snow and rock were repeating. "Ferchrisakes, move through!" he shouted, as if they could hear his voice.

"Why don't you talk to the captain?"

Andy looked nervously at his watch. "It's 0822, just been two minutes or so. Takes time." Then, impatiently: "The Horse's all set up. They're probably standing by until our mortars can knock off the small arms."

The next minute seemed incredibly long. Goober sat there, pulling at his jowls. Choy watched the explosions. The rest of the C.P. group gathered around the radio, listening to Lock's futile calls to Able One. Andy lifted his face from his hands. "What's wrong with Chuck and Stringbean?" he asked, half to himself. "They ought to know what to do. Somebody got to draw them a picture?"

"It's up to the captain, Skipper. Maybe somebody ought to draw one for him."

"Shut up!"

"Yes, sir."

11

Pat fought for control of himself and of his company. He must not make a mistake. Men must not die because of his error. He tried to plot his moves, to shape out the contours of a plan, testing each idea against its possible failure, each action against an alternative.

"Able Six. This is Able Five. Over." It was Andy's voice. "What's holding you up?"

Pat knew that every other radio on the net was tuned to that conversation, that his platoon commanders, other units of the battalion, were all monitoring the action. And so when he spoke he addressed them all, not Andy alone. "We're ready to go."

"I'm squared away back here. I'm coming up," Andy said.

So simple to say, "Okay." Nothing wrong with the exec coming forward. Pat found himself replying, "Not necessary."

"Have The Horse start—" Andy began.

Pat cut in on the transmission. "Busy, Able Five. Please get off the net. Out." His mind raced now. He ordered his mortars to fire on the crest, hoping to knock out the enemy personnel or at least keep them down when his men left the creek bed. He learned from Cagle that Allison's radio was destroyed but that Stringbean was all right. He directed The Horse to send ammo carriers to evacuate the wounded as soon as the platoons moved out, to send others to the rear for more ammunition. He had George Pappas' platoon stand by, had George send his radio to Allison. He called his forward units and issued his order. They stood ready to jump off, awaiting the concentration from the mortars that would soften up the position, and the white phosphorus that would screen their advance.

He got Andy on the radio. "I'm moving up with the C.P. to Allison's position. We'll evacuate casualties to this point. Huckabee will take charge here. You move them to Battalion aid." The enemy mortars started pounding again.

"I'm coming up," Andy said.

For a moment, Pat hesitated. Then he said: "You have your job. Do it. Out." The company mortars were firing their first answer to the enemy. Pat could see the puffs of snow and earth beating across the crest of the ridge. He looked at his watch, and was shocked by the realization that only six minutes had passed since the enemy first appeared.

"Okay, you three." He pointed to Lock, Sanchez, and the radioman. "We're going up. We'll leap frog across. I'll go first. You follow." They nodded. Pat seated the revolver in his shoulder holster. "Keep your head down, Huckabee." He ran from the sheltered C.P. toward the beleaguered outfit seventy-five yards away. An enemy rifleman spotted him, began chasing him, leading him across the snow.

He fell headlong, and lay exposed. His throat was dry; his breath came in short gasps. Memory jogged him mercifully, pushing aside his fear. He had neglected to call Battalion for air or artillery to search out the mortars. He had to get to the 300 radio. A bullet struck inches from his face. His body quivered. He heard Sanchez's voice.

"Shag, Captain! Get cover," Sanchez shouted from a ditch a few yards to the rear. Then, to Lock beside him: "Fire at the ridge. Try to give him some help."

"I don't see nobody up there."

Pat could see nothing on the ridge either. He noted a dip in the ground to his front, a crater, within twenty-five yards of his destination. Gathering his strength, he overcame the palsy of his limbs, stood, and raced for cover. Weaving on jointless, boneless legs, pursued by fire, he slipped, sprawled. His chest heaved; and from somewhere, somewhere close by, he heard a dreadful animal noise. Amazed, he knew he had uttered that sound. He was gasping, drawing breath from deep within himself.

He struggled to his knees, still sucking for air, aware of bruised arms, a throbbing leg. *Rackarackaracka*. Roll. Jesus, God ... roll ... roll... He made the crater, fell into it, huddled there, his face against the snow, his body drawn up in a tight ball. The machine gun, undeterred by the marine shelling, chipped at the ledge above him.

The wild volley from Sanchez and Lock began again. Pat could hear their clips ejected. Then the radioman, lumbering ponderously under his heavy load, slogged from cover. Pat, urged to his feet by Sanchez's yells, stood at the same time, dividing the attention of the enemy, and staggered toward the promising safety of the creek bed. He was not aware of the bullet that ripped his sleeve as he tumbled into the position.

He sat up, trying to regain his breath, to order his mind. He took inventory of the ravaged platoon around him. The enemy mortars crashed intermittently; but only a few Chinese riflemen braved the marine shells and continued to fire. Allison had reorganized in the lull. His men crouched in a line, facing the enemy, awaiting the signal to attack. Pat was uncertain whether to call in the white phosphorus from his mortars or wait until he could contact Battalion and get aid in seeking out the Chinese guns. *Decide on a course of action. Reject all others.* Stick with it. Don't change now, he told himself. Stick with it ...

A marine sat beside him, the one the men called "Pappy." His face was contorted in savage pain, and his hands clasped his stomach. Pat spoke to him. "We'll get you out of here." There was no answer. The man was dead; and the sliver of steel that pierced him was shining in the sunlight, projecting between his fingers from a raw, naked wound. The grimace, frozen already into immobility, was lewd, indecent. Pat felt pity and revulsion. He didn't want to touch the man. He forced himself, rolling him over to hide the mockery of that face.

Lock and Sanchez dropped beside him. "Hope to die, I was shook," Lock said. "Feel like I got a belly full of green persimmons."

Sanchez started to cross himself, and stopped, reflecting on the impulse that had moved him. "Damn' goonies can't shoot. Didn't hit nobody."

"Where's the radioman?" Pat asked. "Got to call Battalion."

Lock pointed to a hump of ground twenty yards away. An antenna jutted behind it. "He's pooped, butt's draggin', carryin' all that gear. Gettin' rest."

Pat still could not get his breath. It was as if a great weight rested on his heart and lungs. "Not shooting any more. Need that radio. Got to get planes or big guns to knock out mortars." Another shell landed in Cagle's platoon area, only fifty yards away. And another. And another. Pat wobbled to his feet and called to the radioman. "Come in. On the double!"

The marine heard him, got to his knees with the bulky set on his back, stood, stepped around the shelter and started toward them. *Rackarackaracka.* Only one burst from the enemy, but it sliced through the man. He buckled and fell over.

"God. Dear God!" Pat shouted it, incredulous. Then, without willing it, he was over the bank, running, stumbling toward the marine who lay in the snow. *Rackarackaracka.* The enemy beat a pattern around him. Pat rushed on, oblivious to all but a single urgency, to get to the man, to find him no more than hurt. He had given the order. He had made him leave cover and step into a blast from the enemy. He reached the body that was bent over like an ostrich, tried to lift him. The radio held him like an anchor. Pat dragged him back to the cover from which he had ordered him, unbuckled the heavy set, pulled the parka hood from the face.

He was alive! But, though Pat did not recognize it, the eyes were already glazed with the promise of death. The marine couldn't speak. His lips moved, his hands groped toward his legs, his features twisted with horror and with pain and with realization. Pat put his glove to the wrinkled forehead, as if to wipe away the terrible visage. He thought of Pappy whose face had been frozen in his death agony. "Get you to doctor, hospital. We'll get helicopter," he promised, believing it.

Rackarackaracka. The machine gun coughed again, spattering the earth behind them. Pat gathered the limp body in his arms. He walked, straining under the load, lurching drunkenly toward the creek bed. He did not hear the frenzied chatter of the enemy guns. He heard the gurgling voice of death; he heard his own command that had smashed the man down.

Lock took the body from him. Pat bent over the radioman. "Get a corpsman," he said. "Pain must be bad. Got to give him morphine." Lock didn't move. "Go on! When I tell you to do something, do it!"

"He's dead, Cap'n."

"No, he's not ... he's ... we'll get him back to a doctor ... not dead. Look. Not dead!" The face was relaxed. Pain and horror did not show. But it was a dead man's face. Pat was trembling. "Shouldn't have made him come in," he said dully. "Ordered him to. He was resting a minute. Safe. I ordered him ..."

"Better get that radio," Sanchez said.

"No!"

But Sanchez was already gone; and Pat watched breathlessly while the marine retrieved the set without being fired on, and returned. "Demette wasn't a big guy, and this damn things heavy."

"I didn't even know his name," Pat said.

"Wasn't a bad feller," Lock said. "Sorta stuck on hisself ... but I never knowed him real good. Fergit his first name ..."

Sanchez moved the body and laid it in the snow. "When he checked in the C.P. this mornin', he was feelin' bad. The crud. With this cold, it bothered him awful... He was bitchin'."

Pat lay back. The magnitude of Fate's workings confronted him. If he had run last ... if he had not ordered the man to bring in the radio ... if he had not left his .45 on the ground for someone to give the Chinese prisoner, Monk would have carried that radio. The marine would still be alive; and Monk would have lived a week longer. Could that be true? Was death only an accident?

Allison was back on the air: "We're ready, Captain."

Pat wavered on the brink of decision. He wondered what Andy would think, would do. Artillery or air might silence the enemy mortars. Without such help, the company might suffer more casualties. One man's blood already covered him.

The front of his parka looked like a butcher's apron. And yet, to delay might invite still more.

From out of the sunlight before him, above him, came a gentle rustle, a sigh. And then the earth was convulsed. As if ... as if a runaway freight train with a thousand cars had ripped a railing and fallen, fallen, fallen, crashing against a steel roof five hundred feet below.

"Artillery!" Pat, wedged into the bank of the creek bed with Lock and Sanchez, had shrieked the word, giving hysterical voice to the terror in his mind. "They're throwing artillery at us now!" In the instant of silence before the next convulsion of the earth, he held his eyes closed, afraid to open them, afraid to face the two marines now that he was exposed, now that they had heard the anguish in his voice.

Then Chuck Cagle checked in, his voice as casual as if he were calling from the Christopher Street apartment he was always talking about. "We're chomping to go. Too close here to stick around. My people been eating Tootsie Rolls ... and they're gassy!"

They all heard the beginnings of a nervous chorus of laughter as the transmission ended. Lock winked at Sanchez. "That there's one sharp sonovabitch," he whispered admiringly.

Cagle's message, despite its hint of bravado, its earthiness, offered Pat release, snapped him back to reality, forced him to action. He ordered the concentration of white phosphorus. It struck in spreading clouds across the crest. It was a startling, even beautiful sight as the milk-white smoke foamed up, casting fire-bright embers. The marines started out of the creek bed that had imprisoned them.

Answering Pat's call, Skinhead promised artillery support as soon as an aerial observer could reach the position. Stretcher bearers passed by, carrying wounded to the rear. The advance continued up the ridge. Allison moved at the head of his outfit, guiding on the high knuckle on the left. Cagle was walking before his men, climbing toward the saddle between the two knuckles of the fist. They were meeting only light enemy fire.

Pat held his breath, hoping desperately the attack would succeed. Then the smoke began to break, providing clearer vision for the Chinese. An ever increasing choir of their weapons was heard. One hidden machine gun put up an impenetrable shield before them. Marines fell and hugged the earth. Allison on the left and Cagle on the right were both stopped midway up the ridge. Their light guns began a stuttered reply to the enemy, but they could not regain the fire superiority that would allow them to advance.

Now is the time. Now. I've got to lead them ... "I'm going up," Pat told Sanchez and Lock. They started to follow him. "You stay here!" He took the 536 radio from Lock, and pulled over the ledge. "Watch me. I'll signal for you when ..."

And then his own voice was stilled by the whisper, the deadly murmur again. He shuddered as another shell dropped behind them, hurling rock and earth like a giant steamshovel run amuck. Pat wanted to stand. But something stronger than he opposed his will. He wanted to show courage, to prove himself, to rush forward, to yell and charge, to awaken his men. But he could not. He crawled on toward the blasted crater where he could see the whole front. Too few marines were firing. Many lay as if mesmerized. "Return fire!" he shouted. No one seemed to hear him. He called his platoon leaders. "Less than half your people are firing ..."

"Always some that get clutched up." It was Andy. He had slipped into the crater.

Pride had prevented Pat from calling for his help. Now, seeing him there, feeling his strong, calm presence, he knew a surge of relief, of something akin to affection. But he said, "What are you doing here? I told you ..."

Andy ignored him. "We're going to have to gung-ho up there."

"Can't. I can't order them to walk into that fire."

"Maybe you can't." Andy started to hoist himself over the lip of the shell hole.

Pat held his arm. "Wait. We ought to get counter-battery soon."

"Wait? Fritter away more time and more lives?"

"What do you think's going to happen when they stand up?"

"Got to take a chance. Can't stay here and get picked off."

"I'm not going to gamble with lives!" Pat heard himself shouting above the clatter of weapons. Then a shell blasted a geyser forty yards away; and he flattened himself, lay there clasping his body to the earth as the sky tilted and debris fell.

"Gamble?" Andy was sitting beside him, staring at him. "At times you've got to gamble and sometimes make mistakes. If you don't, you just give in to being licked. It's the nature of things. People get killed. And if you're not prepared to give the order that may murder them, you've got no business in command of troops!"

"But the odds against—"

"You can shorten the odds but you can't eliminate them!"

Pat didn't answer. He saw Andy vault from the crater and race across the ridge to Allison's position. He heard him rallying the stalled attack, listened to his radio while messages were exchanged between the two platoons. Brought them this far ... Got to go ... rest of way. Andy said ... can't give order ... no business in command ... He crawled forward, his heart thumping in painful spasms.

An enemy machine gun still placed murderous fire on his troops. But where ... where? Can't see. If you could see. Again. In an arc above, from left to right. Not fixed. Swinging free. The puffs of earth moved like a writhing snake through its pattern again. The vortex ... apex ... cone ... triangle. If you could see ... Then, searching for the telltale muzzle blast, searching the area where it must be, he saw a flicker of light, a puff of snow fifty yards before his forward platoons. It came from scrub growth a bit too isolated, a bit too free of snow. Flicker ... puff ... flicker ... puff ...

Andy was calling on the radio: "Stand by now; we're ready to move, Chuck."

Pat cut in. "Belay that order." He identified himself, and ordered the platoons to take available cover while mortar fire came in.

Andy raged back. "Able Six! This is Able Five!"

"Get off the net," Pat said. "Get off the net while I use this radio." Then he called The Horse, and ordered fire on the machine-gun position.

"Nothin' left but W.P., sir."

"Fire it. Will observe."

The platoons held fast. The white phosphorus burst well over the target. Pat moved it in, adjusted it. There was a direct hit on the emplacement. He watched, horrified, as the weapon tumbled over and the enemy crew scrambled. There was a shriek as one of the Chinese, screaming with pain and fright, plucked at the burning chemical that ate into his flesh. He ran straight toward the marines, then fell and rolled over in the snow.

Andy charged across to a position between the two platoons. "Let's go," he yelled. "Let's get the bastards!" His husky roar sounded across the ridge. "C'mon, you gyrenes, Semper Fi!"

Suicidal, Pat thought. Stupid to stand up like that. Not necessary. And yet, he would have mortgaged his soul to do what Anderson was doing. He wanted to do it. But he could not bring himself to move. Legs and arms refused to work. He looked toward the crest. Andy was standing there, above his men, his voice trembling with passion, blind fury in his eyes. "Semper Fi!" he yelled. "Semper Fi!"

The marines stormed forward to take the ridge.

12

The moon lay cold and yellow in the cradle of the distant hills. A moaning wind drove fresh white flurries before it; and the spent and weary men of Able Company rested uneasily, knowing that this was but a respite from battle, that before first light they would be ordered from their meager comforts, across yet another valley. Crouching in the holes they had carved from the frozen earth, they waited their turns in the warming-tents, tightened the hoods about their faces, peered anxiously toward the front.

The command post was set up in the blasted creek bed. There the order for the next day's attack had been issued. There Pat and Andy stood watching the platoon commanders trudge up the slope to their positions.

"Not a bitch. Not a gripe from them," Pat said, leaning against the bank. "They just looked at me as if they hadn't heard right." He beat his arms against his sides. "Usually the condemned have a last meal and a chance to protest to the padre."

"Nobody argues with orders," Andy said.

"I'd like to argue with these." Pat took off his gloves and blew in his hands. "What are our chances?"

Andy was rubbing the circulation back into his face. "If it's done right, if nobody fouls up, we'll make it." He stretched, reaching his short arms high over his head. "But nobody's a good insurance risk out here."

"Can't understand it. We're going forward alone, in a full moon, across nearly a mile of table-flat terrain." Pat flexed his hands and cracked his knuckles. "No concealment. No cover. An entrenched enemy looking down our throats."

Andy called to Justus, Sanchez, and the other command post personnel who were talking noisily twenty yards away. "Knock off the grabass down there!"

Silence answered him. He looked up at Pat. "Relax. You're fighting the problem."

"It's a job for a whole battalion, not for one under-strength company—and after what we went through today."

"Wish I had a cigar," Andy said. Seeing Pat's perplexed expression, he laughed. "Stay loose. Once we get there, we'll have a lead-pipe cinch compared to the other outfits. All we have to do is outpost the high ground. Just sit out there and watch frozen Choisin, keep the Chinks from cutting the road to Yudam-ni."

"The plan's logical enough. But two hundred men attacking in twenty-below weather against no one knows how many ..." Pat hunched his shoulders, and slumped to the ground. "Even to defend it! On the map it looks like three hills, not one. It just doesn't make sense."

"Everything has to make sense for you, doesn't it?" Andy slipped down beside him. "Don't think too much, Pat. Don't line up your figures, add them, and try to prove totals. Some things never add up, even if you juggle the figures. The only thing that needs to make sense for us is killing goonies." He spread a poncho and raised it overhead. "Let's smoke your cigarettes."

Pat pulled the shelter over him. They crouched there, huddled together, curtained from the night by the improvised tent. They smoked, the glow alternating, lighting one face and then the other: one flat, ghostly-white with a bushy beard and green eyes heavily overlined with prominent brows; the other with dark brown eyes, strong features taking on a new look of leanness, and a black bristle on his cheeks.

Luxuriating in the warmth and the silence and the pungent smell of tobacco, Pat relaxed. Long, long day. Never forget. Never.

He relived the terror he had known when the Chinese counterattacked: His men giving ground, slowed, halted, then clawing their way back up the ridge. The enemy holding stubbornly. Chinese guns, secure in distant redoubts, smashing at the ranks of Able Company. Marine guns, in deep defilade five miles back, pounding at the defenders. Artillerymen of both sides trapping, murdering the helpless infantrymen.

(But what *if?*: What if he had foreseen the danger of counterattack, had consolidated the position more rapidly, had gotten a protective barrage down before his lines, had been ready when the enemy struck back? What *if?*)

And more: The two marine artillery shells that exploded in the midst of his troops. His feverish calculations to absolve himself of the error. The artillery officer's sober regrets: "One of those things. Short round. Nobody's fault." But there were the bodies of the dead. He had rushed to the spot, had carried a man with one arm gone to the aid station. The marine had been conscious, in agony. But the morphine was frozen. "Can I help you?" Pat had asked. And the pinched, grimacing mask had relaxed briefly. "My ID bracelet ... find it, will ya, Captain?"

(But what *if?*: What if he had not, frantic with urgency, called for fire on target? What if he had started at longer range, walking it slowly back toward the crest? If ... If ...)

He had lain in a shell hole later, relaying requests to the Corsairs as they pursued the enemy by fire. He had seen Andy above him, heard him shouting orders. He had felt the sluggish response of his body, the strain to master it, to force it to his will. It had been like ... like the split second of awakening from a nightmare ... when the sleeper fights free and returns to consciousness.

(No end to *if*: Through that long, bitter afternoon he had thought how it might have been, what he might have done. If there had been more time. If he could have known. If anything could be predicted ...)

There had been earth-quaking tremors. Screams. Huckabee and Choy, covered with the blood of the wounded. The Horse, his homely face contorted as he lifted an ammunition carrier's body. Goober drop ping beside him. "Is he all right? Is the lieutenant all right?" And all around them, the sleepwalking figures of the men, pressing forward.

More sustained horror in one day than a man would normally meet in a lifetime, Pat thought. His differences with Andy, his own battle with himself, seemed unimportant compared with all that he had seen and felt that day.

Andy broke the long silence. "You've never been on a night attack before."

"No."

"Control's a problem."

"Imagine so."

"Awful easy to make a mistake."

"If we can just get across the open area before it's light, Andy ..."

"One mistake. That's all it takes. It can cost you."

"I know."

"It'll be rough if we're caught out in the open. Might have to change plans in a hurry."

"I've thought of that."

"Tricky business. Awfully tricky."

Pat cupped his palms around the fiery tip of his cigarette. The heat entered his hands, rushed up his arms, and suffused his body. He did not want to think of later that night or of tomorrow or of what might lie ahead of that. There was danger in thinking ahead. He thought instead about the moment, about the glow on his face.

In the dim light, Andy watched him. Afraid. Not sure of himself, he thought. Leaning toward Pat, he said, "Maybe I'd better go up with the platoons tonight."

"I thought you'd be with me."

"Somebody's got to be at a central position where he can be reached, where he can call in support. That's your job. I'll be more help to you if I'm on top of the situation."

"I don't know ..." Pat held the stub of his cigarette, feeling the burn of it on his fingers. To relinquish even a measure of command ... He hesitated, seeking some way to justify his action.

"Well, what do you say?" Andy nudged his shoulder. "You hold things together. I'll keep them moving up front."

"I suppose ... that'll be all right, Andy."

"Good."

"Probably the best way." The air was stale and smoky beneath the poncho. But it seemed warm. Pat was reluctant to leave it. Despite his concession, he felt a sense of relief, like a relay runner who, having exhausted himself without advancing his team, hands the baton to a better man.

"For a first go, you really did okay today."

Pat nodded, grateful for what he considered a noble lie. He lifted the poncho and slipped out into the frigid, snow-swept night. Warmth fled his body.

Won Kook Choy, watching the command post from a crater only thirty yards away, saw Pat and Andy start up the slope to check the forward positions, saw them pick their way, pulling themselves forward through the heavy flurries of snow. It will be soon now, Choy thought. With a last look at the creek bed, he moved silently and carefully toward the lightly defended flank.

From there his view was unobstructed. He stretched his slim, short body, and lifted his carbine before him. He did not expect to wait long, but the hate and anger that drove him added length to each minute. He had made up his mind to kill; but the fact neither thrilled nor sickened him. He had no thought of consequences, no thought of the act as murder. It was justice, he had decided, and retribution.

Footsteps approached. He huddled into the snowbank and held his breath, fearful of discovery, already plotting an excuse for his presence. "... but I can predict the next step before it happens. Been with Andy a long time." It was Lieutenant Cagle, his voice low, muffled. "Can see it now, with Patrick. Same old routine."

They came closer. Lieutenant Allison's boyish voice: "How do you mean?"

"Same thing with the last guy. What was his name? Stepped on a mine outside of Kimpo ... McGaughey, I think ... Andy had him so shook up he didn't know whether to poop or go blind." Cagle fumbled with the buttons of his trousers and finally had to take off his gloves. "Far as Andy's concerned, if Cates, Shepherd, and O. P. Smith rotated as skippers, they wouldn't suit him."

Allison motioned to him to lower his voice. "Been with the outfit so long, before the Brigade was formed, I think, that the men are like his own ..."

"Properly loyal, my good and faithful Annapolis grad. But you're talking like a man with a paper rectum." He shivered and turned his back to the wind. "The men! Hell, the men don't mean a damn to Andy. And you don't. And I don't. He's not capable of that kind of feeling. Joe Anderson loves the legend of Andy. And Andy loves Able Company. Andy's Able. Hard-hitting Able. Volunteering Able." Coughing, he drew on wool inserts, and pulled his gloves over them.

"It gets any colder, I'm going to give this up. My bladder be damned."

Allison laughed. "About Andy—he's got what it takes just the same, Chuck. Not a man in the outfit who wouldn't follow him to—"

"Come off it." Cagle was hugging himself, kicking one snow-caked boot against the other. "Not a marine anywhere who wouldn't follow you or me or anybody else with the hashmarks or bars."

"So you're coming around to believing the pitch about The Corps," Allison said, smiling.

"C'mon, c'mon, I'm freezing ... too damn' cold for a Semper Fi lecture ... but sure I believe it." He took a few steps, then turned to wait for Allison. "Believing—that's the ticket. That's what makes it so. Put on the blue uniform and you're eight feet tall. Offer a good product. Boost it with the power of advertising, the saturation message. LSMFT—ad infinitum, ad nauseam. Always works."

Choy could see them. Cagle, as always, was clean shaven, neatly uniformed. Allison's lean shadow was pointed across the snow in the moonlight. They were only ten feet away.

Allison started up the ridge. "Always over-simplifying. Guess it's a habit in your business."

Cagle laughed. "And your business? The old class ring entitles you to membership in the Stupid Brass Protective League. Get that trinket and automatically become candidate for general in World War III!"

They walked away. Choy relaxed again. He searched the flank, looked down at the mortar section and the ammunition dump, estimated the distances. He stifled an urge to cough. I am going to kill, he told himself. He whispered it, so he might hear the sound of his own voice admitting it. "I am going to kill."

A few years before, he would have probed the subject. He and his fellow instructors, sitting in the disordered rooms of their idol and teacher, would have talked the night away, arguing the philosophic and legal and psychological aspects of murder. Or Hate. Or Fear. Or Unity for Korea. Or Love. Or Rhee's distrust of democracy. Anything, so long as they might talk. Talk, but never act. Talk the life and the juice out of any subject. Insulated from reality, they were too ready to hear every side and to ally themselves with none. They had been great talkers in those days. Days when Korea needed doers.

He could see his teacher now, as the last of his seven children filed by to be solemnly bidden good night. He could imagine the warmth in his face as he turned back to his disciples; he could see the serious brown eyes, and the index finger stroking delicately on the stringy goatee. "Murder? Does a man ever have license to kill? And what of killing in war?" Then the sly smile as he leaned back in his chair and lit his pipe. And the chorus of argument, each man eager to impress, to quote the obscure from the works of the great, to twist from context the words of Confucius or Plato, the French encyclopedists or Kant, Gandhi, or Marx.

Choy could remember those scenes so vividly, could recall the intensity of their reactions and the pathetic inability of any of them to face the need for action when talk had been exhausted. And he had been as lost as the others, as vain, as blind. What would he have said in such a conversation on murder? He would, he admitted, have quoted from the United States Constitution, that no person shall be deprived "of life, liberty, or property, without due process of law." And he would have done so not because it was particularly relevant, but because it would have pleased his teacher. He would have quoted Voltaire, in French, though none of the others understood the language. And then he would have translated, patronizingly, proving nothing except his gift of memory:

" 'Twenty years are required to bring man from the state of a plant, in which he exists in the womb of his mother, and from the state of an animal, which is his condition in infancy, to a state in which the maturity of reason begins to make itself felt. Thirty centuries are necessary in which to discover even a little of his structure. An eternity would be required to know anything of his soul. But one moment suffices in which to kill him.' "

What would his old teacher, his old friend, think of him now? What would he say of his Christian brother, the product of the mission school? What would he say of his intention to do murder? "The world takes its own revenge on evil," he would tell him. "Trust God and trust the Americans."

The old man was gone now, like everything else Choy had believed in. And he had died a victim of his own belief. "You will do more for our country by teaching its sons in the University than you will by fighting the Communists," he had said. "In time, Korea will be united. Trust God and trust the Americans."

But the Communists did not trust God. And the Communists had known the Americans far better than either of them, Choy reflected. He had known the Americans of the textbooks. The white-wigged Washington who led rabble to victory. The wise, worldly Franklin. The great, versatile intellect, Jefferson. Madison, who fashioned the magnificent instrument of the Constitution.

Lincoln, preserving his nation "conceived in liberty," freeing the slaves. Wilson, the visionary, the naive dreamer. Roosevelt, a cripple who somehow embodied the strength, the vitality, the imagination, the ingenuity, the courage of his people, a people who had explored a continent, built a new world... Those were the Americans both of them had known.

But the Communists knew the real Americans. And now that he could see them, he knew the real Americans, too. Foolish, given to bragging. Children, eager to be liked. Involved, yet rejecting involvement. Impotent in all their power. Substituting technology for courage. Running. He had seen them. Outgunned. Outfought. Then Inchon. And he had joined the marines, and entered the rubble of Seoul with them.

His family was gone. Mother. Father. Two brothers. They, too, had trusted the Americans—although the Americans had not trusted them. While Korea had cried for arms to defend itself, America feared those arms would be used for offense. She trusted the Communists, instead. And then, defenseless, Seoul fell to the first onslaught from the North...

He had left the skeleton of masonry that had been his home, and gone to the mission. The Red Cross was in charge. Only his youngest brother had survived. Six years old. He watched the child at play. Demented. Crazed by the horrors of his experience. Unable to control his body. And other children of his age danced around him, pointing at his grotesque movements, laughing at him. Laughing.

Yes, "trust God and trust the Americans!" Not the Americans you read about, but the Americans you are with every day. Trust Cagle—brash, unschooled, intolerant. Trust Allison—dull, colorless, dependent. Trust Pappas—a follower, a simpleton who believes God is always in His Heaven and all is always right with the world. Trust Anderson—a man of courage, but without sensitivity, culture, vision, or purpose. Trust Patrick—weak. What else could be said for him? Even his officers realized that. Weak.

It was a measure of them all that they did not comprehend what had been wrought despite their apathy, their ignorance of the world, their inability to understand the enemy. Here, in Korea, the decisive battle could be won. All Asia, even now rubbing the seeds of sleep from its eyes, awakening with a bitter taste in its mouth, would see that there is an alternative to subjugation, that it need not choose between colonial domination or Communist enslavement. Yet none of these Americans had a sense of mission, none of them wanted anything so much as to go home. Not one saw the ideal within grasp. Not one valued anything—peace, freedom, dignity, principle—more than he valued life itself.

Choy thought he saw movement out front. He snapped the safety off his carbine, and hunched deeper in the snow. But no one appeared. He made himself relax, and settled down to wait.

13

First Sergeant Wallace Goober tugged his trousers over the heaving immensity of his belly, left the command post, walked the length of the creek bed, and sat down. Before him, their faces shielded from the bleak night, eight marines lay stretched side by side. They did not speak.

Goober checked the dogtags on the frozen chests, compared the names and serial numbers with those on his report, and finally covered the faces. He knew only two of them. Demette was the kid with the crud. The other one was called "Pappy," and had bad breath. Goober was kneeling behind them; and without realizing what he was doing he pushed back the hood of his parka and took off his helmet. The bitter wind attacked his damp scalp, but he did not notice.

He wanted to talk to someone. But the skipper was busy. And the others ... What drove people away? What did he say or do? Somehow, he could not get through to them. No one knows me, he thought. No one ever has. No one has ever tried.

He thought of Grace. The past surged through the conduits of his mind, obliterating the present, the bodies, the Korean night. Pressing his thumbs to his temples, he suffered through all the sordid detail again. He hated her with undiminished fury. "I don't want any part of you, Wally. Think I can stand you touching me? Oh, God, leave me alone, alone..."

The familiar ache of frustration and loneliness and self-pity tore at his chest, became unbearable. He replaced his helmet. "Maybe you're better off," he said aloud to the eight draped forms. "Better off ..." He clambered up the creek toward the command post.

A foot slipped behind him. The sound, coming out of the silence, invading his thoughts, jolted him. He threw himself to the ground and raised his carbine. The exertion made him gasp. "Halt!" he called, his voice cracking with tension. "Give the password."

"Grable," Lock Justus replied amiably.

"Betty," Goober whispered, after a moment when he had been unable to remember the countersign. I'm shook, he told himself. "What the hell you doing here, Justus?"

"Been crankin' up the jeep. Cap'n's orders." Lock followed the first sergeant. "Want a drink, Top?" He offered a smoking ration can.

Goober took it and sipped. The liquid was bitter, but deliciously hot. "What's in this stuff?"

"Drained a mite of vodka from the radiator, mixed in some coffee and snow. Prime, ain't it?" They came to a barrier where the creek bed narrowed. "Open up," Lock said.

A poncho was raised. Sanchez poked his head out. "C'mon in before it gets cold in here."

Goober bent over, and managed to slide his hefty body inside. Lock followed. A container of heat pills was ignited in the center of the smooth, snow-packed floor of the shelter. The roof was made of stretchers lashed together and covered with earth. The sides were supported by empty wooden ammunition boxes. The earthen walls at front and back had niches carved into them to hold toilet paper, ration cans, a cracked mirror, two combat packs, Sanchez's souvenirs, and two rifles. Sanchez, Huckabee, and The Horse leaned against one bank, Goober and Lock against the other. The five men sipped their vodka toddies, and took turns extending their hands over the flickering fire.

Taking a bill from a wad of captured currency, Sanchez held it over the flame, and lit his cigarette with it. "This beats workin' for a livin'."

Goober checked his watch. "It's 0100. You'll be workin' before long."

Lock was taking off his shoes and socks. "That's what burns a hole in my hiney. We're nearly clean and pretty dry. Rifles are fit fer a boot-camp inspection. Me and my bunky got us a good place fer some sack drill. We got somethin' to drink, got ever'thin' a man needs 'cept maybe some poontang, an' we gotta go gung-hoin' again."

"That's all worries you?" Goober held his cup over the fire. "You realize we're going out in the middle of nowhere with nobody on our flanks, and Battalion miles away, and the goonies on the move?"

Massaging a foot, Lock eased it toward the fire. "All that ain't my never-mind. All I know is I gotta be here. What frosts me is I'm already loaded like a swayback mule." He tugged at each piece of clothing. "Long johns, shirt, sweater, vest, trousers, shoe pacs, gloves, parka, helmet. Then I got my M-1, bayonet, cartridge belt, two bandoleers of ammo, two grenades, chow, extry socks, an' my poncho. Top of that, I gotta pack that heavy 300. Me, a little feller. Goat's built like a breedin' bull and all he's got's that toy 536."

"You're breakin' my heart," Sanchez said. "I got mucho troubles of my own."

Goober drained his cup; and Huckabee offered his. "I had plenty," the corpsman said.

"Thanks." Goober took a long drink, and belched. "You know, Justus, the last two radiomen who carried that 300 are laid out."

"How come you're so cheerful all the time?" Huckabee said.

"Well, I ain't no communicator; and I ain't superstitious," Lock said.

"Those feet look bad," Huckabee said. "Got that bluish look. Better take care, Lock, or you'll get shipped back with frostbite."

"If'n I could be sure of that, I'd walk around barefoot and in my skivvie drawers."

"They'd send you back to Japan," The Horse said.

"Not me. I'd never get a clapshack in Tokyo. I'd wind up in Koto or Wonsan. My luck stinks."

"My mouth's sore," Sanchez said. "Got it chapped or somethin'. Can't hardly open it."

"I'll fix it fer you tomorrow," Lock said.

"How?" The Horse asked. "Huck couldn't do nothin' but give him some grease."

"Thing to do," Lock said, "is use an old hill-country recipe. Gotta find a man who never has seen his pa, and get him to blow in it."

"You're nuts!" Sanchez said.

"It works."

"Goat, you gonna let some bastard blow in your mouth?" Huckabee was giggling.

"All you got to do is find a bastard," Goober said. "And that won't take much doing around here."

"Okay. Laugh. Suffer!"

"Any scuttlebutt?" Sanchez asked Goober. "I don't like this night business."

"You and me both," Huckabee said. Raising his hands in an attitude of supplication, he drawled, "Lawd, take care ob this hyar nigger..."

The others laughed. "I think you're real funny," The Horse said, his pocked face drawn in a frown.

"Skipper's going to honcho when we jump off," Goober said. "We'll be okay. You see him this afternoon? You see what happened when he got up?"

"Thought he'd gone ape, the way he hollered up there," Lock said. "Looked fer a while like the cap'n was gonna bawl before he come. Right, Goat?"

"Captain was all right."

"He was skeered. Got limp as an old man's pecker when them mortars opened up."

Huckabee had taken the mouthpiece from his bugle, and was cleaning it. "He did pretty good. Doesn't raise the devil like Lieutenant Anderson, but he got things to workin' 'fore long."

"The skipper's got guts," Goober said. "He gets right up there like the squad leaders, right in the middle of it, wearing that red thing around his neck, like saying 'screw-you' to the goonies."

"Nobody like him," Lock said.

"No need throwin' off on the captain," Huckabee said.

"Tell you one thing," The Horse said. "He damn' well knows how to observe fire. Had my second round right on that Chink gun."

"He was shook," Lock said. "Me and Goat oughta know. With him nearly ever' minute."

"Sure he was shook, just like the rest of us," Sanchez said. "But you seen him go out after Demette. And he hauled up that ridge before the skipper got there. Nobody says a company commander's gotta be up with the squads..."

"What you know about it, Sanchez?" Goober lit a cigarette. "Company commanders is supposed to lead, right? The Book says—"

"Aw, shove The Book! My mouth's sore. I don't wanna argue. Think what you want."

"Who'd you rather be with in a fight?" Lock said.

"Can it! Stow it! Blow it!"

"You got doggie brains, Sanchez," Goober said.

"What's wrong? You got a wild hair or somethin'?" Sanchez had not intended to defend the captain, but it had come to that. He resented it. "You see the Old Man out in front of the regiment?"

"No, but-"

"You see Skinhead down here honchoin' the company? Hell, no!" "That's got nothin' to do with it," Lock said.

"The hell you say!"

"That's right," The Horse said. "Either of 'em could if they wanted. But they don't. No sense downgradin' the captain 'cause he don't run somebody's platoon or squad."

"You wasn't there," Lock said. "I say he was skeered, skeered as at nigger at a Klan meetin'!"

"Why don'tcha dry up?" The Horse said.

Huckabee laughed. "You show me somebody who's not scared, and I'll show you an idiot. I'm scared so bad sometimes, I turn white enough to run for governor in Alabama." He struck a pose, one hand raised. "A vote for Huckabee is a vote for the peepul!"

Goober laughed at him. "You're a jackass, Huckabee. But you're all right."

The conversation dwindled. They sat there quietly, as if by mutual consent. Sanchez used a toothbrush on the sights of his rifle. Goober polished the stock of his carbine. The Horse changed his socks. Lock shortened the straps on the 300 radio. Finally, Huckabee, who had been tying his bugle to his pack, spoke. His voice was so charged with conviction that everyone stared at him.

"You know, fellas, somebody that's built like Lieutenant Anderson, somebody who just don't fear anythin', well, you don't see people like that much. But when a man can have that fear, when he's so panicky his sphincter is suckin' air, when a man can stand up and go anyway, why, that's really guts. That's God's courage ..." Goober rubbed out his cigarette, smothered the fire, and crawled to the entrance. "Huckabee, you're the gawdamn'dest coon I ever knew!"

In a few minutes Huckabee left. "Be sure your feet are dry, Lock. Don't like how they look," he said as he slipped outside.

The Horse leaned close to Lock. "Why don't you watch your mouth in front of Huck?" he asked angrily. "You got to say 'nigger' and 'cocabola' and 'coon'..."

"Hellfire, Horse, I don't have nothin' against him. Jezuz, I've known niggers all my life. They leave me be, I leave them be ... but I don't run with 'em."

The Horse grunted, and followed his friend outside. Huckabee was a few yards away, walking toward the command post. "Huck?"

"Yeah?"

"Aw ... nothin'."

"What is it?"

The Horse stopped beside him. "It's like you're two people ... I mean, you make yourself out a idiot one minute ... and then you say somethin' makes me know it's you after all." He rubbed his forehead as if to clear the musty passages of his mind. "Wish I could ... not much at explainin' stuff. I mean, I think somethin' real clear. See? And when I try to say it out ..." He shrugged.

"What's botherin' you, Horse?"

"Tried to tell you lotsa times. You get mad ... Huck, it's like when you call yourself names and make cracks about yourself and talk about turnin' white. That kinda thing ..."

"Everybody else was jokin'. Wasn't just me."

The Horse sat down in the trench before the mortar section. "Naw, you don't get me." He spoke softly, slowly, as if he were in pain. "Y'know why Goober said you're okay? 'Cause you act like what he thinks a Negro's supposed to be. Always happy. And silly. And humble. He called you a coon—and no wonder. Y'call yourself worse. And you drawl ... Yeah, you drawl. Sometimes you look and sound like-like—in a movie or somethin', the whistler with big eyes goin' through the cemetery ..."

"You're just lookin' for somethin.'"

"I'm not. I see it. Why you got to try to act like—like what you're not? They'd like you better if you was ... just like ... usual. Like you are with me. Like you slip up and let yourself be with them sometimes."

"You don't have to stay around me, you know. You don't like the way I act, don't do me favors." Huckabee began to build a mound of snow, patting it with his glove.

"Now don't go gettin' the red ass."

"I'm tired of you nitpickin' at me."

"I don't mean to. Huck, you been to school and know about lotsa things, and feel ... feel things ... and know your job. In lotsa ways, you're better than lotsa guys."

"I don't want to be better. I just wanna be like everybody else." He swallowed and cleared his throat. "That's all I want. You expect me to be solemn and correct their grammar and talk like a schoolteacher?"

"No ..." The Horse wanted to explain, but he could not phrase his thoughts. Finally, he said, "All you gotta do is be your own self and pull your weight." He knew that he was hurting Huckabee, but he couldn't stop. He had thought about it many times; and he believed every word. In his mind he saw the white circle of light, heard the clang of the bell, the crowd's merciless voice, felt the hand on his bare back, pushing him forward. "A clown's okay t' laugh at," he said. "But nobody figures he can count on a clown. Nobody wants t' trust a clown with his life ... I just can't make you see ..." The Horse put his beefy hand on the other man's shoulder. "Huck, I'm tryin' to be your friend."

"Friend?" The keen, handsome face, illumined by the moon, turned up to him, then quickly turned away. "You're not my friend. You're ashamed ..."

"No"

Huckabee shook his hand away, and walked off toward the command post.

Choy was cold. The half-hour of lying prone in the snow had chilled him to the edge of numbness. His body ached. His muscles protested. He rolled over and tried to flex his arms and legs. A glimmer of doubt arose. Perhaps he had been wrong.

The platoons were beginning to move. He could see dark forms coming down the slope, slogging toward the opposite flank and the line of departure. He could hear the hoarse whispers of NCOs directing them. He turned again. His patience had been rewarded. His quarry appeared. Choy pressed his cheek to the stock of his carbine and centered the blade in the sight. He had seen the Americans, weak and vacillating, confusing mercy with justice. His victim moved closer. When he reached the centerblade, Choy let the carbine swing easily, lined up the target, fired.

14

The sharp snap of the carbine pierced the stillness of the night. Orders, movement, conversation froze in mid-passage. The men had been warned to speak in whispers, to move softly, to strip any object that might make a noise. They had been told that stealth was their best hope for safety. Now silence hung like an unresolved chord. Another shot. This time the muzzle blast, like the spurt of a match in darkness, revealed the direction of danger.

When George Pappas reached Choy, the interpreter was already surrounded by men who had crawled to his side and were gazing anxiously through the falling curtain of snow, seeking movement, a silhouette, a figure at which to fire. Choy stood there, calmly replacing the two bullets in his magazine.

"What did you shoot at?" Pappas whispered.

"He is out there."

"How many?"

"Only one"

"Where?"

Choy strode into the cutting wind that whined over the shoulder of the ridge. Pappas, wary, followed. They found him. You-all lay face down in the snow, one side of his uniform bloody, fingers working convulsively. The lieutenant looked at Choy, accusation in his eyes. "You should have recognized him."

"I did. I was waiting for him."

You-all made no sound. Pappas worked quickly over the flesh wounds, one in the shoulder, the other in the leg. He passed the word for a corpsman, ordered the curious men surrounding them back to their units, sent the interpreter with a sergeant to the command post, and helped carry You-all to its shelter.

The men in the creek bed, their faces smeared with mud to dull reflection in the moonlight, looked like angry, dirty-faced ruffians as they listened to Choy's impassive explanation.

Andy broke through the ring around You-all. Bending over him, he grasped the collar of his uniform. "You piss-ant!" he said, his voice taut with suppressed fury. "You sonovabitch!" The boy choked and put his hand up to fend off a blow. Andy raised him to his feet, still holding his collar. He slapped him full in the face; then, with his free hand, twisted the wrist slowly, with cold hatred, until the fabric in the armhole tore, and You-all was bent double. The boy grunted, but made no outcry.

"Let him go," Pat said wearily. "The bastard's too filthy to touch."

Andy spoke in even measures, slapping the sullen face, bending the arm, as if he could smash the defiance from the stony gaze and wring a protest, a plea from the contorted body. "We took you in ... and fed you ... and put clothes on your back ..." Sweat beaded on the boy's face. His features twisted in pain. Andy's voice was muted, as if he were confiding a desperate plan. "People were shot at today with our own weapons ... with the M-1 you took ... and the carbine ... And the goonies knew exactly where we'd be today ... 'cause they had my map ..." He shoved the arm back savagely, and yanked the boy to him. At last, You-all screamed, a high-pitched, agonized child's wail.

As if that were what he was waiting for, Andy released him. You-all fell, then dragged himself away, cowering against the rocky wall of the creek bed. Andy took his pistol from his holster. Glancing over his shoulder at the others gathered around them, he said, "You people clear out of here." All but Pat started to move back. "I'm going to kill him," Andy said, huskily.

Pat walked up beside him. "God knows he ought to be killed. I wish we could ..." Who would find out? he thought. Who would criticize him if they did? What more provocation did you need to kill? He could just turn his back on it all, walk away, let Andy do what, by any sane standards, he had a right—at least a reason— to do. And yet, to allow it ... in cold blood ... He said, "Put your pistol back." Then, in answer to the startled disbelief in Andy's eyes: "I know. I know. Don't you think I care that he's been stealing, killing? But to—to murder him like this—it's just not ... it's not the way." "You got a better one?" Andy snapped at him. He sighed, began again, quietly, reasonably. "Have enough sense to listen to me this time. You know how that Chink got your .45?" He seated the magazine in the butt of his pistol.

All the anxieties and pressures, all the fear and guilt of the week before, all the uncertainty and terror and torment of the day, the moment, the night ahead, buffeted Pat. His mind groped for a way out of the situation. But the decision was too clear-cut. Allow the boy to be murdered. Or prevent it. "I don't like it any better than you do, Andy," he said. "But we've got to send him to the rear."

"The way you sent that Chink prisoner to the rear?" Andy pulled back the receiver of his pistol, seating a round in the chamber. "Maybe you don't know any better, but I do. Once he gets away from us, he'll get his knuckles rapped, and that's about all."

Pat felt the sweat running down his sides, felt the involuntary quiver of the muscles in his neck. He wished that Choy had succeeded, that it was all over with, done, a fact that he would have been forced to accept. He started to speak, but his mouth was dry. He cleared his throat. "He'll be taken care of, Andy."

"You're goddamn' right about that!" Andy turned away, and walked toward You-all.

Pat's patience was exhausted. Anger took over, and mounted: At the boy, who surely deserved death. At Choy, who had discussed his plan with no one. At Andy, who was treating him with the patronizing disdain of an adult toward a confused child. The all-knowing lieutenant and the green captain. The capable exec and the bumbling CO. "I gave you an order," Pat said evenly, fighting to still the tremor in his voice. It was no longer just a question of You-all. It was a question of his authority, of his right to make the decision.

"Christamighty!" The pistol dangled at his side as Andy faced him. "You listen to me," he said, his voice grim. "I'm not asking you to watch. I'm not asking you to take responsibility. I'm not asking for your permission. I'm not even asking you to act like a marine!" He moved forward; but Pat stood firm. With a quick, catlike stride, Andy shoved him out of his path.

Pat grasped his arm, jerked him off balance and, gripping the front of his parka, flung him back. "Don't try that again! I've had enough out of you!" He shoved his hands in his pockets, holding the lining to keep from reaching for Andy again. He could see Huckabee, Justus, Sanchez, Goober, and Choy, all staring at them. "Put that weapon away," he said deliberately. Andy did not move. "Now!" Pat said. "Or, by God, I'll take it away from you!"

The two men faced each other, rigid, unblinking, panting, puffs of their frosty breaths hanging between them.

"I said to put it away," Pat told him, warning in his voice.

Andy chewed at his lower lip. He pounded one fist against his leg. Words formed. Rage surged within him. He wanted to fight. He wanted to feel his fist in that too handsome face, wanted to see it bleed, wanted to pound the bigger man to the ground, and look down at him. But his training and discipline rebelled against his instinct and his nature. And, when he glanced at the men, waiting for him to speak, to act, there was nothing he could say or do. He removed the magazine from his pistol, cleared the weapon, and shoved it into his holster.

Pat caught his breath. "I know how you feel," he said, trying to relieve the tension. "You're right in a way; but you can't kill someone ... just like that ..."

"What a bunch of crap!" His exec stalked past him, and picked up his pack and poncho.

"Just a minute!" Pat checked the rising timbre of his voice. He had to maintain some semblance of authority, of control. "I've got something else to say to you."

"Save it. I've got a job to do." Andy vaulted over the bank.

Pat confronted Choy. The interpreter had surprised him. He hadn't believed there was any violence in the man. "Choy, I've disagreed with you, but I had the idea that you knew the difference between ... that you at least ..."

"That I had principles?" Choy met his gaze. "Principles mean nothing if they are not put into action."

Pat walked past him. "Top, I want him moved to the hut by the road," he said, nodding at You-all. "You stick with him and Choy.

Keep them with the rear echelon. Bring them up when we take the objective. I'll send both of them to Battalion in the morning. You understand?" Goober nodded. "Answer me, dammit!"

"Aye, aye, sir." The first sergeant gave orders, collected his men, and had You-all earned out of the ditch.

"George, you better get back to your platoon," Pat said to Pappas. "I'll go with you. The rest of you get your gear." Huckabee, Sanchez, and Lock slung their packs. Pat checked his watch. "We jump off in twenty-six minutes."

The two officers started toward the road that ran at right angles to the position and parallel to the objective. "Don't know which will hurt us more, this weather or the Chinks," Pappas said.

"Guess I handled that badly," Pat said, hoping to hear a denial. "War stinks," Pappas mumbled. "Guess somebody said that before"

"We were good to that kid."

"I think Choy suspected him for a long time."

"He was ashamed of him," Pat said. "And I don't think he trusted us to do anything about it."

"Maybe he's right in a way. What can you do to a kid?"

"If I were in Choy's place ..." Pat's voice dropped. From far off he thought he heard a truck, the protest of gnashed gears, the hum of a motor straining on a hill. "You hear that?" Pappas shook his head. Pat waited for Sanchez, Lock, and Huckabee to catch up. "You hear something, sounded like a truck, coming from out front?"

"Seemed more like out on the left flank," Sanchez said.

"Couldn't have any transport around here. Battalion's already pulling back." Pat listened again. "There! Hear it that time?"

"Probably a long way off," Pappas said. "Sound carries for miles out here."

They reached the road. "I'll be up to check with you in a few minutes, George," Pat said.

Pappas stood on his toes and breathed in Pat's ear. "I know what you were getting at ... he began. But he thought better of it. "See you."

The growl of motors sounded again. Pat hesitated, all his senses alerted, listening until it was silent again. "Get some mud on that buckle, Justus. Stands out like a flashlight."

"Aye, aye, sir."

"You men can wait in the hut out of this wind. I'll send for you when I'm ready to move out." He trudged off down the road to check his platoons.

The men crossed the road and slipped under the makeshift blackout curtain that covered the doorway. The small room was crowded. Goober sat by the Coleman lantern, helping Firesteen clear a stoppage in a BAR. Two men were already sleeping on the mud floor. Lock and Sanchez flopped against a wall. Huckabee examined the four frostbite cases who were awaiting evacuation. They lay on stretchers, cheerfully exchanging diagnoses, commenting on one another's green-black legs and fingers. You-all was crouched in one corner. Choy stood beside him, cursing.

"Knock it off," Goober said. "If I could get away with it, I'd let you brain him once an' for all."

"He says his comrades will know how to deal with traitors like me. They will cut my hands off." Choy spat on the boy. You-all's face was distorted with hatred. He wiped the bandage on his shoulder, slipped over the ground, and leaned against the wall close to Lock.

"Get away from me, you bastard." Lock moved back. "I'd like to wrap a block of C-2 'tween yer legs!"

Goober disassembled the BAR bolt and handed Firesteen the firing pin. "I was hopin' the skipper would finish him."

"He woulda," Sanchez said. "Captain stopped it."

Lock worked his toes painfully in his boots. "I thought maybe those two fellers would fight. I'da liked to seen that."

"Skipper would have coldcocked him," Goober said.

"I don't know," Sanchez said. "Patrick sure had his Irish up."

"Snowed hell outta me when he grabbed the skipper by the stackin' swivel," Lock said. "Gotta give him credit. Where I come from, you don't mess with a feller you ain't willin' t' fight him."

Goober worked the action in the automatic rifle. "Musta been froze-up, Firesteen." He handed it to him. "And what the hell you doing carrying a BAR, anyway?"

"I got the hottest fire team in the division," Firesteen said. "Two BARS, two M-1s, and an extra Tommy gun."

"I gave you that BAR and Tommy gun," Lock said. "Goat and me borreyed those pieces from the First Marines."

"Gave?" Firesteen scowled. "Cost us a slopehead flag and two months' coke rations."

"I don't want to know about it," Goober said. "You knuckleheads got to steal, don't take stuff off other marines."

"All I know," Firesteen said, "is my outfit can put out damn' near as much fire as a squad. Like my dad, he should rest in peace, used to say, 'Melvin, it's always best to be in business for yourself.' "

"Them's my sentiments," Lock said, laughing.

The Horse came in. "Captain's waiting for you," he told Huckabee. "Lock and Goat, too. Top, he decided to keep my section back till it gets light. Can't shoot now anyway."

Justus, Sanchez, and Huckabee got their things together. "I'm leavin' all my souvenirs in here," Sanchez announced to the rear-echelon men. "And they damn' well better come up with the rest of the gear."

The Horse stopped Huckabee at the door. "Want me to watch out for your sleepin' bag and pack like usual, Huck?"

"My stuff'll be all right," Huckabee said, not looking at him. "You still pissed off?"

"Never mind."

"Okay. You wanna be one way ..."

"No call for you to worry 'bout how I act." Huckabee pushed by him, and joined Lock, Sanchez, and Firesteen on the road.

"Feet are killin' me," Lock said.

"Got a rotten feelin' in the pit of my stomach," Firesteen said. "Be glad when this one's over."

"Don't fret, Mel," said Lock. "You get kilt leadin' Firesteen's Fireball Fire Team, I'll write a letter to yer wife, tell her you bayoneted fifty goonies, and died a hero with a bullet up yer hiney!"

"Who's gonna teach you to write?"

"Same guy taught you t' screw," Lock said. "And I hope he does a better job on me!"

"Go to hell, Justus."

"Be nice down there tonight. Cold 'nuff up here to do a job on that ole brass monkey," said Lock.

"Good luck, Mel," Sanchez said as they came to Pappas' platoon. "Thanks."

"It's not gonna be bad, Mel," Huckabee said. "Don't you think about it. Think about gettin' mail about your baby soon."

"Yeah," Lock said. "That's a good dumb way t' die."

Pat appeared across the road, and motioned to Lock, Sanchez, and Huckabee. They trailed behind as he threaded his way through clusters of men. Andy was standing alone. Like the others, he was in blackface, swaddled in hood and parka. But the red swath about his neck, the bushy beard, identified him. The platoons were in column, the company in wedge formation. As Pat approached, Andy raised his hand, signaled forward, and started across the paddy.

The men followed. Bent over by instinct and the weight of their gear, they looked like an army of hunchbacks as they filed past on either side of Pat. They plodded along—shadows in slow motion-testing their footing, conscious of every sound, thankful for the fitful moaning of the wind that might drown out a boot that creaked, a sneeze, a cough, a cleared throat, the crunch of snow and ice, the cinching of a pack strap. Any of the things that might expose them, might call forth death from the sleeping ridge. The last of them stepped off into the frozen paddy beyond the road. The point of the wedge had already slipped into darkness.

Pat whispered to his group, "All right. Let's go." Lock, Sanchez, and Huckabee followed him.

The advancing marines had churned the paddy into lanes of ice, slush, and water. It seeped into Pat's boots. As one foot pulled out, and he stepped again, he could hear two hundred other boots being put down, withdrawn. Enemy sentries would be alert. He tried to measure how far the sound could travel. He wondered if the Chinese, even now, might be watching, listening, awaiting them. He tried to think of something, anything that would displace his consciousness of freezing feet and face, aching back, watering eyes and the formidable ridge ahead.

His anger returned as he recalled the scene in the creek bed. Have to deal with him. Must. But how? Even now he was depending on Andy, allowing him to assume at least part of his burden. Even now, despite the man's perversity, he had to admire his strength and courage. But there could be no excuse for the unrestrained behavior; and, he thought, no excuse for his own failure to silence him. If Skinhead had witnessed the scene, he would have relieved them both. The simplest thing would be to put Andy on report. For insubordination. But that would be an admission of his own weakness, his own inability to handle his company ...

He stepped up on a rocky outcropping that ran along one side of the paddy. The footing was precarious, but it was drier. Lock was at Pat's elbow, breathing hard, balancing himself on the rocks like a tightrope walker. Suddenly he stepped off into a jagged crevice and fell to his knees in icy water and snow. Pat frowned at the noise, and offered his hand. Sanchez and Huckabee helped him pull Lock free and hoist the bulky radio. Pat was aware of the steady beat of his heart, of the sweat that beaded and froze on his upper lip, of the seep-squish as one foot was placed before the other.

The truck sound again. Closer this time. The four men halted, listening. "Probably miles away," Pat whispered. "Let's move."

15

At the hut, three hundred yards to the rear, Goober heard the noise, too. He strained to identify the sound of the approaching vehicle. Closer. Still closer. "Could be a goonie tank," he said to Choy. "Back here prowling."

The Korean walked across the dimly lit room to where You-all slept on the floor. He kicked him awake. The boy cried out, and sat up groggily, blinking. Choy questioned him. There was a hesitant, sullen reply. The interpreter cursed, and slapped the bruised face. "He says the Americans will all be dead by morning."

"You ain't gonna die of old age yourself, Buster," one of the demolition men said.

Another marine picked up his rifle. "I'd love to have an accidental discharge."

"I was 'bout to have one myself!" A frostbitten rifleman propped himself up on his stretcher. "Workin' up a dream. Had the back seat in the bushes, had me a chick—smelled like shiny lipstick and Sen Sen—and I was ready to make out." Laughter.

"Knock it off, dammit!" Goober was in the doorway again, listening. But he could hear only the wind. He lumbered over to You-all and grasped his jacket. "What about it, you yella sonovabitch, that a tank out there?" The boy glared at him with unconcealed contempt.

Choy repeated the words, the intonation, detesting Goober and the boy. "Well, you yellow son of a bitch ..." Then he launched into an angry flood of Korean. You-all backed away. Choy grabbed his wounded leg, dragged him back to the center of the room, and repeated the question. The boy, grimacing with pain, rubbed his leg, and would not answer. The interpreter followed Goober outside.

The first sergeant tried to shut out the sound of conversation behind them, the sound of Choy's breathing and his own. The wind flailed him, and his heavy body shook in a spasm of chills. The grind of gears again! They left the hut and walked through the snow to the creek bed where the old C.P. had been. Less than a hundred yards away, its turret shining in the moonlight, they saw a Russian tank. A Chinese soldier was behind a machine gun, scanning the area. Goober ducked, his body quivering with cold and anxiety. Not fear. He assured himself he was not afraid. "They're snowed," he whispered. "They expected to find us crapped out up there."

"The boy," Choy said. "He led them in."

They hurried back to the hut. No time, no weapons to fight a tank, Goober thought. The Book said ... Had to get word to Battalion and the skipper. Had to get his wounded out. The Chinese could not miss the hut when the tank reached the road. He cursed the captain for not leaving him a radio. "Those of you can walk, get out on the double. We'll carry you other people. Take up positions on that ledge about fifty yards behind here. Nobody fire unless I give the word. We'll try to play doggo."

"I will go to the company," Choy said.

"No. I got orders to stay with you and that punk. Wait here with him. I'll be right back, help you load the bastard." He called the corporal who was acting as supply sergeant. "Get down to the mortars. Tell The Horse to move his people in with ours. And tell him I want a volunteer to send to the skipper."

The two Koreans were left alone, two shadows in the dark, bare hut, aware of each other.

Deliberately, knowing what he was going to do, Choy picked up Sanchez's saber from the stack of souvenirs. Man of principle, he thought, recalling the captain's accusation. Educated man. Modem man. Christian man.

You-all slouched in a corner, watching him, watching the saber that swung in his hand. "You are right," Choy said, and was surprised at the weakness of his voice. The boy began to edge along the wall. Choy blocked his path. "A traitor should lose the hand he raises against his country."

You-all retreated, limping, feeling the shocks of pain in his leg and his side, holding the thatch behind him. His eyes narrowed; his gasps were audible.

"It is an enigma, is it not?" Choy spoke softly, in Korean, and moved closer. "These Americans you hate, they are your only hope." He cleared his throat, trying to wait out the shortness of breath that made his voice quiver. "Do you know what is an enigma? At sixteen years, it is time you knew."

You-all tensed, braced himself, and lunged toward the doorway. Choy held out the saber, tripped the limping boy, and stood over him while he tried to replace the bandage on his leg. "Your masters have neglected your education," Choy said.

"But of course the Communists have no enigmas. They are positive about everything."

Sitting up again, You-all began to inch back, supporting his weight on his hands. He finally managed to stand. Choy swung the blade, and ripped the pocket of the marine jacket the boy was wearing. You-all staggered away, clinging to the wall for support. His tormentor prodded him with the saber. For the first time, You-all spoke. "Soon the Americans ... will be gone ... and we will be masters in Korea, in Asia, in all the world ..."

"The Peiping radio," Choy said bitterly. "They do not even give you a resounding phrase with which to die. No martyr's defiance. No patriot's appeal." He looked at the boy as if for the first time. "Say, 'Long live the revolution!' Say, 'Forgive them ... for they know not what they do.' " Choy's voice rose. "Do you recognize either of them?" he asked, as if he expected an answer. "No. You are Zarathustra's man." He rested the gleaming point on the horrified boy's throat. "But, then, you do not even know that, do you?" Transported beyond the moment, he reached back in his memory. " 'Without demanding reason ... you would sacrifice yourself ... to earth in order that earth may some day become superman's ...' " He pressed the saber against the yielding flesh. "But they have not taught you Marx," he said. "Surely not Nietzsche."

"I am not afraid," You-all said, shivering.

"No," Choy said. "You would not be. You are like the rest of your kind. Better at dying than you are at living." He saw the boy's bleeding face, his tom clothing, his wounds, his wild eyes. Broken. Beaten. Dirty. Ignorant. Weak. Defenseless. And his hatred was mellowed by pity, by the knowledge that he was looking, in reality, at the plundered mass of his people. He had only to press home the saber to still the frantically beating pulse beneath its point. He felt his hands damp in his gloves, wet with perspiration; he felt the trickle on his back, on his sides. It was not like sighting his carbine across the cool expanse at a target. He could feel the life beneath his hand. He took the saber away, shaken, knowing that he did not have the strength to kill.

"We shall win," You-all said, rubbing his throat. "We are strong; and you are weak!"

Blindly, without ordering the motion of his hand, Choy struck at him, and smashed him to the ground. You-all screamed. Choy plunged the weapon. In the hysteria of his rage, he chopped at the offending hand that groped toward him. He picked up the grisly object, looked at it, unseeing. At his feet was the sound of death, like the gurgling of pipes in a deserted cellar.

Goober found him there. "Heard a scream," he said breathlessly. "What happened?"

"He tried ... to escape."

Goober stared at the horror on the ground, saw what Choy held in his hand. "My God! You're crazy!"

Choy dropped it, fought off dizziness. Then, wiping his hands on his trousers, he ran out of the hut, toward the distant company.

It was Lock who heard the slushing of footsteps behind them. He told Pat. They watched the embankment where any pursuer would have to climb out of the paddy. The wind swirled snowflakes across the valley, blowing the mist before it, sweeping aside the comforting illusion of concealment. Low-scudding clouds still filtered the moonlight. Pat looked up and searched the bowl of the sky, but saw no break there. "Lucky those clouds are so thick," he whispered.

"Moon gets through again, it'll light this place up like a ballpark," Sanchez said.

While they waited, Able Company moved on to within a thousand yards of the objective. Slowly, nearly silently, racing dawn, racing against the moment of discovery. A figure, stooped, running, came toward them. "It's Choy," Pat said. The interpreter, soaked and shivering, fell beside them. He reported the tank. Even as he spoke, Pat was visualizing the panic that might result if his company was struck from the rear.

"Sanchez, you go up to Lieutenant Pappas. Get me his bazooka team. Get a move on!" His mind worked in a frenzy. "Huckabee, do what you can for Choy. He's damn' near frozen." Foremost in his thoughts was the image of a great steel juggernaut charging through the darkness, not knowing what inviting targets it would blunder on.

Sanchez returned with Firesteen and another marine. "Bazooka-man got shot up yesterday," Firesteen said. "Loader's got frostbite. But I've loaded the thing plenty. And this guy says he's a expert gunner."

"Yes, sir." The other volunteer was a ferret-faced man who had been a battalion cook a week before, and had been sent forward as a replacement. "Learned with a 2.36, Captain. But this 3.5's the same thing practically."

"All right," Pat said, pondering his next move. "Justus, you go with them. Take the 536 so you can call me in an emergency. But don't use it unless you have to. I'll be up with one of the platoon radios." Lock walked over to where Huckabee and Sanchez were massaging Choy's arms and legs. He took the small radio. "See you, fellers."

"You got bad feet, Lock. Been gettin' worse right along. You got no business goin'." Huckabee stood. "I'm gonna tell the captain." Lock could feel the flakes of ice inside his boots, the numbness at the tips of his toes. "You fret 'bout yer own feet, swabbie. I'll handle mine!"

Pat was giving instructions to Firesteen. "You're in charge, Corporal. Don't take unnecessary chances. And don't let it get past you."

"We ain't gonna try to win no medals," Lock said.

"Remember, we're on radio silence. Don't use it unless you're in real trouble." Pat watched them start across the field, and knew a restless stirring of uncertainty. Andy had the experience. It might be wiser to talk to him first. But there was no time. Perhaps he should have gone himself. And yet, his place was ... where? Could you send men out to face what you would not face yourself? He considered that, and then made his decision, measuring it by only one ruler: What would Andy do? "Sanchez, you keep moving with the advance. Pass the word to Lieutenant Pappas. Have him inform Lieutenant Anderson. Tell him to press forward. Battalion's too far back to send us an anti-tank team. But give them an alert signal." Before Sanchez could ask a question, before Pat could deliberate any longer, he darted after Firesteen, Lock, and the bazookaman.

He caught them as they were descending into the paddy, and led them toward the company rear, pushing them, refusing to let them rest. Driven by the urgency of intercepting the enemy, they were panting with effort. Sweat drenched them, enveloping their bodies in a frozen sheen. They stumbled on, alert for the sound of motors. One hundred yards. Two hundred. Four hundred.

"Sir?" The bazookaman was plucking at Pat's sleeve. "Sir, I got a gut ache." He bent over, cradling the tube in his arms. "Something awful."

"What?"

"My gut hurts, sir. I got to do something about it."

Pat took the weapon. "I'll carry this for you. Just try to get your mind off of it. We've got to keep moving."

They crossed another fifty yards without hearing the tank. Pat, balancing on the paddy dikes, waited for the others to catch up. The wind was stronger now; and he reasoned that it might hide the tank's motors ... or might sweep the clouds away, revealing them all. He was worried, too, about the fate of the company rear echelon—Goober and his wounded, The Horse and his mortar section. But he convinced himself that the silence meant they had not been discovered.

"Can't help it, sir." It was the bazookaman again. "I got to stop."

"We can't. Not now," Pat said. "Put it out of your mind."

"I gotta go, sir."

"Hold it. You've got to hold it ..."

"Can't. Sir, I been trying, but I can't."

"Don't you understand? There's a tank somewhere out there. If it gets past us—"

"Captain, I know. And I'm sorry. It just hit me all at once."

"I can handle that bazooka, Cap'n," Lock said. "He can stay here with the radio."

The radio! He had told Sanchez to call Battalion on the other set. But surely it was an emergency. It had to be done. And yet, if the enemy intercepted that call, they would be alerted. The attack might be doomed. "Can't leave him alone," Pat said, thrusting the other thoughts aside.

Firesteen sat on the rocks running along the paddy's edge. He eased the canvas carrier that held the four rockets on his shoulders, and unslung his automatic rifle. "Might as well take a break, sir. We won't be fit to do any shootin', we don't crap out a few minutes."

Pat motioned to the bazookaman. "Hurry up!"

The marine sighed with relief. "Thank you, sir. Oh, man ..."

Lock sat beside Firesteen. Pat slogged a bit farther through the paddy, and then got to his knees, listening. Above the wind, he thought he could make out the truck-sound he had first heard nearly two hours before. But now he knew it to be the tank. He turned. "Tell him to hurry it up!"

Firesteen spoke to the bazookaman. "Get a move on."

"Yeah," Lock whispered. "Or he'll have y'doin' it by the numbers."

"Can't get these back buttons, dammit!"

"Give him a hand, Lock."

"Aye, aye, Corporal, sir." Lock walked over to the distressed marine. "Make it speedy, buddy-roe. That's a hell of a place to get frostbite." He joined Firesteen again. "Mission accomplished, General, sir."

"I'll give you the Order of The Tuchas for that."

"Took-us. Means hiney, huh?" Lock smiled, and began counting off his vocabulary on his fingers. "*Smuck ...*"

"SH-muck," Firesteen said.

"That's what I said. Smuck, puhtz, momser, shtup ... I keep learnin', Mel, I'll be talkin' Jewish right good."

Firesteen grinned. "You don't know nothin' but dirty words."

"Them's the only ones you use."

"Hey, one of you fellas!" The bazookaman was whispering urgently. "Need my helmet."

Lock took it to him. "You sure I can't get you somethin' t' read?" he asked with exaggerated politeness.

Listening to the conversation behind him, Pat wondered at their calm, at their ability to forget present danger, to laugh, as if the cold, perilous present did not exist. He heard the tank again, and was certain that there had been a flicker of exhaust no more than two hundred yards away. He thought of the radio call to Battalion, and hoped desperately it had not revealed their presence to the enemy. "Hurry!" he whispered. "We've got to move."

The three men joined him. Pat slogged ahead; and they followed, pushed by the wind at their backs. They worked their way across the area until they reached the midpoint between objective and line of departure. The company was five hundred yards behind, the rear echelon more than four hundred yards in front of them. Firesteen stopped, and pointed. "There's the caviar can, Captain."

Pat could make out the snow-shrouded silhouette of a T-34 tank. It edged forward and nosed through a ditch, heading for them. "Gotta try to catch her broadside," the bazookaman said. "Can't get a good shot at her from here." They moved on, snow and wind whipping their faces, their aching limbs demanding rest. "Far enough," the bazookaman said. He spoke hoarsely, his breathing uneven.

Pat gave him the launcher. "Better let me take that BAR, Corporal. You've got enough to carry."

"Beg your pardon, sir. But I'd just as soon keep it myself if it's all right with the captain," Firesteen said. "We'd better go on alone from here."

Pat nodded. "Get as close as you can, but be careful," he whispered. He waited with Lock while they tried to flank their target.

Firesteen fitted a 3.5 rocket into the end of the launcher, connected the wires, and tapped the man's shoulder. "Don't miss, cobber."

The marine shrugged. "Never fired a shot at a real target before." He crawled toward the tank that rolled on across the frozen paddy, narrowing the distance between them. He knelt, aimed, fired. The back blast threw a sheet of flame behind him, lighting the area. The rocket smashed against the hull, and skidded off a corner of the armor. Firesteen lifted his rockets and his BAR, and lunged forward to reload. But the gunner in the tank turret was alerted. He fired a stream of tracers. The bazookaman crumpled. Firesteen charged ahead, fell beside him, wrested the tube away, and was tugging at another rocket when the gunner fired again. "I'm hit!" Firesteen shouted.

Pat rushed toward them. Lock, limping, followed. The bazookaman lay on his back. "Dead," Lock said. Firesteen was on his knees, trying to lift the bazooka. "You okay, Mel?"

Rackarackaracka! The familiar rhythm of the enemy weapon began again. Pat pushed the other two down. They pressed themselves into the snow as the bullets whipped overhead. "Get Firesteen back to those rocks," Pat said. "Stop the bleeding."

"Never make it," Lock said.

"Just my leg, I think," Firesteen told them. "Bums sorta. Gotta stay calm. Mustn't get excited. Shock. That what you've gotta worry about. I'm all right." He was speaking to himself as if he were comforting another man.

Rackarackaracka!

"Hellfire, man, get a shot off at them!" Firesteen said, gasping. "I'm okay. Can move fine."

Pat stripped the BAR magazines from the corporal's belt. "Get out!" he yelled. "Lock, get him back to the rocks."

He tapped the magazine in place, rested the bipod legs before him, and fired at the tank, which had stopped now, seventy-five yards away. Following the path of his tracers, he adjusted the fire and swept it across the turret. Lock was wrestling Firesteen to his feet, taking the canvas carrier and the rockets from him. "Go on, dammit!" Pat shouted. He pulled out the expended magazine and tapped in another. The turret gunner, who was pinned behind his machine gun, fired another burst, blindly; and the earth ten feet in front of Pat bubbled with snow.

While the two marines moved back, Pat timed short bursts from the BAR, covering their withdrawal. The enemy fired twice more, both times overhead. "Made it, Cap'n!" Pat heard Lock's voice well behind him. His ammunition expended, he slung the BAR and reached for the rocket launcher. The bazookaman lay beside it. Pat had the feeling that he must do something with the body. The dead man appeared to be thinking, eyes closed tight, sharp, fine teeth biting his upper lip. His pinched face was ghoulishly white as the earth.

Rackarackaracka! Pat was startled by the thud of bullets striking beside him. He heard Lock calling him again. The growl of the tank. The sharp intake of his breath. Lock yelling once more. He had to get back. The rocks were only thirty yards from him—the distance from third to home, he thought—but they seemed incredibly far away. Grasping the two weapons, he began to push himself back, foot by foot.

"Cap'n! Get outta there!"

The tank had stopped. The machine gun traversed the area, raised its sights, and traversed again, this time sewing a line across the body of the bazookaman. Pat saw it heave like a headless chicken, felt the jolting of his heart when bullets laced the spot where he had lain only minutes before. In desperation, he held the BAR and the launcher under his arms, stood, and raced toward the rocks, keeping low and weaving across the rutted paddy. The bullets were striking closer, and though his body felt unbearably weighted, fear drove him on. He dropped beside Lock and Firesteen.

"Mel's okay. Lucky character caught three slugs in his took-us!" Lock fired his rifle once more, let the clip eject. He took the bazooka from Pat, who was trying to catch his breath. "Load me, Cap'n. They's comin' on."

"Where ... are the rockets?" Pat asked, still gasping.

"Oh, Lordie, I dumped 'em on the way in! Couldn't make it with Mel ..." He pointed to the canvas carrier, plainly visible ten yards away, and started to get up.

Pat didn't have time to examine his fear. The one overpowering fact was that his company could be decimated by an unexpected assault coming out of darkness. He pulled Justus away and crawled out of the crevice. It was as if he were impelled by some force outside himself. Though he heard the stutter of the enemy gun, heard the crunch and spin of tracks on the ice, heard Lock's M-1 firing, the sounds occupied only one compartment of his mind. The rest was devoted to a single purpose: to get the rockets and return with them. He had the carrier strap, jerked at it, lifted it, turned, all in the same instant. Then the rock formation was before him. He tumbled, and fell into the trough of granite.

Firesteen pried Pat's fingers from the strap. Only then did he realize that he had made it. He had no recollection of the dash back. "Let me," he said. The rocket was inserted, connected. He heard the motors roar again, and looked over the protecting shelf at the approaching tank. Range shortened. Seventy yards. Sixty. Fifty. "Fire!" he yelled. The rocket smashed into the sand-bagged front of the monster, and blew dirt high in the air, but failed to penetrate.

"I'm a *shlemiel*," Firesteen said. "Shoulda got off a broadside round out there ..." He winced, and held his glove tight over his ripped buttocks.

"Quick! Another round," Pat said. They saw the gunner drop out of sight, heard the hatch clang shut. Then the muzzle of the big gun inched around, searching for them. The barrel swung, pointing like a steel finger. It rested on them. "Down!" Pat yelled, throwing himself at the others. There was a ring of fire and smoke, a shattering impact. He felt his head jerked back, felt the shuddering of the earth. He was dazed. His mind seemed suspended, independent of his body. His helmet had been blown off. He started to tell the others about it. Then he saw the tank again, imagined it smashing him to powder. The thought transfixed him. It was less than forty yards away.

"Cap'n!"

"Load! Load!" Firesteen shouted.

Each simple manipulation became intolerably taxing. The brain ordered the muscles. They responded sluggishly. Pat concentrated on lifting the rocket, raising it, inserting it, pushing it, seating it, connecting the wires. And all the while, he knew it was too late. He tapped Lock's shoulder. He saw him pull the trigger. But the launcher did not fire. Then he saw that one of the wires had pulled free. Lock ducked beside him. Cursing his own error, Pat took the weapon from him, and stood to fire it himself. "Connect the wire," he said breathlessly, staring at the oncoming tank.

"No!" Lock shouted. "Can't!"

Firesteen reached for Pat, and pulled him down. "Too late, Captain!" They were wedged against one another, faces pressed together, arms and legs intertwined. The weapon was jammed down on their shoulders. "My ass! Oh, my ass!" Firesteen said, groaning.

Pat closed his eyes, knowing he would never open them again. A great weariness came over him. The last thing he had seen was the strip of beaded rivets on the tank's hull as it bore down.

16

Pat crouched, body and mind paralyzed by the approach of death. For a terrible instant, the tank's belly loomed above. Then, like an enormous piledriver, it smashed down, tracks grinding at rock, exhausts spewing. All the pulses of Pat's body thumped as one. He was bathed in sweat. His teeth were clenched as if driven together. His eyelids, closed tight, were weighted, gritty. Fumes choked him, seared his nostrils; and he gasped, sucking for breath, and tasted powdered granite on his tongue. He felt the weight of the launcher cutting into his shoulders, the throbbing of Lock's heart pressed to his, the tensing of Firesteen's muscles behind him. Screeching in his ears, deafening him, was the piercing scrape of metal against rock, like chalk screaming on a blackboard. The great tracks rose, poised, then dropped, spun, caught, pulverized the earth—and rumbled on!

He opened his eyes unbelievingly; it was like coming out of a tunnel into the open again. He saw the valley, the screen of clouds over the moon, the faces of his men. He filled his lungs with cold, pure air.

"You ... all ... right?" he asked, choking on the words.

"Now we got 'em," Lock said, his voice rasping. He set the launcher in position, resting it on the granite ledge of the trough that had saved them. "Got 'em where ... hair is short!" The broad, lightly armored rear deck of the tank was only ten yards away. It took both Lock and Pat, working in a fury of concentration, to load the bazooka.

"Steady," Firesteen said weakly. "Don't shoot ... too high."

The trigger sent the electric current to the rocket fins. There was a whoosh that blasted a trail through the snow behind them. The projectile burrowed its nose in steel, exploded, ricocheted flaming metal through the tank's interior.

Lock's mouth worked. He screamed. It was a barbaric yawp of triumph. Firesteen was grinning hideously, tears of pain on his face. Pat laughed uncontrollably, conscious of his laughter, yet surprised by it.

The second projectile was prepared, fired. It sizzled through, found its target. Black smoke poured from the ports. The hatch opened. A soldier scrambled up. He stood posed there, a thick-set man with a fur cap too big for him, waiting, as if he had forgotten something. Blue light, like the flame from a welder's torch, leaped after him. It turned to orange, and he was silhouetted against its glow. Then a cloak of fire enveloped him. He curled up like a dying ember, and fell back into the pyre.

"Got to get out ... before ammo goes." Pat pulled himself from the niche in the rocks. His cramped, bruised body ached; his head reeled with fatigue and cold as he helped the others. Firesteen moved in a crouch, dragging one leg, pressing a bloody rag to his wound. Lock limped painfully on swollen feet. Pat found his helmet, slung the radio, the BAR, the M-1, and the launcher. Together they slogged past the inferno. An unreasoning desire to wait there, to soak in the warmth, to thaw, overcame them. Leaning on one another, they reveled in the fierce heat whipped toward them by the wind. Pat smelled the charred, singed-fowl odor of burning flesh. He held his breath, closing his nostrils to it. Despite himself, he sniffed again, in curiosity, in clinical appraisal. The snap of exploding cartridges aroused them. They pushed on. Wayward bullets hummed around them. They dropped to their knees and crawled.

A shell detonated, hurling shrapnel and fire. Firesteen jogged a few steps and fell. Pat gave the radio to Lock. "Run!" he shouted. Grasping the corporal's waist, he tugged him, protesting, over a shoulder. Then he cradled the weapons in his arms, stood shakily, and doggedly strode ahead. Twice he stumbled and almost fell, but he plodded on, fighting exhaustion, suddenly aware of his drunken shadow, projected on the snow by the fire behind them. A hundred yards away, all three dropped to the earth, spent, eyes shut against the wind, their breath coming in deep, wrenching sighs.

Pat tried to remember whether he had tended Firesteen's wound. He slid across the ice, looked at it, at the blood still seeping from the frozen clot. The corporal lay on his stomach, weak from loss of blood and from exertion and shock. Taking the towel from his neck, Pat tore it between his teeth, and bound the ripped flesh as well as he could. He found a morphine syrette in his parka, but it was frozen. "Put in it your ... Put your mouth it ..." His tongue stumbled over the simple phrase again; and all three of them laughed. Shrill laughter, verging on hysteria.

"Put... it... in ... your ... mouth," he managed finally. "We'll use it ... when it thaws." There was more feeble laughter; and they lay back in the snow.

Hours had moved so swiftly that Pat could recall little of the detail. He could not logically explain his exhaustion in terms of freezing wind, the night without sleep, the argument with Andy, the intermittent dashes across the paddy, the immediacy of danger, the frenzy of battle. He could not understand the rebellion of his body, his lightheadedness, his sluggish mind, his apparent inability to command his own reflexes. Taking Lock's boots in his hand, he began to unlace them.

"Better rest ... while y'can, sir."

Pat rubbed his eyes, and focused on his task. "I'm all right."

"Yes, sir," Lock said. "And I'm okay. Mel's okay, huh, Mel? Okay. Okay ..."

Twenty-below cold and wind and water had worked on Lock's feet. Before the boot was off, Pat could see the telltale green-black color, the turgid flesh of frostbite. He laced the boot again. A violent bellow came from the vitals of the blazing tank, a hundred yards behind them. Pat was shaken as it rumbled and shuddered like a great beast in its death throes. He checked the luminous dial on his watch. The company, hidden somewhere in the snow before them, should be nearing the objective by now. The first pearly flush of morning was fingering the fringes of the night. The enemy could not be deceived much longer. "Let's go," he said.

He tried to carry Firesteen. "No, Captain. Not ... that pooped. Can walk."

Though Lock protested, Pat took weapons and radio. They slogged toward the company, helping one another, resting briefly, then pushing on. "Cold," Lock mumbled. "Cold ... as—as—"

Firesteen took the syrette from his mouth. "Can we stop? A minute?" He asked wearily.

"Not yet. Little farther," Pat said.

"How far you think?" Lock said.

"Hundred and fifty, maybe two hundred yards. Can't see yet." Pressing against the wind, ducking his head to breathe, Pat tried to plot his actions should the company fail in its attempt at surprise. Must have artillery, maybe air. But such help would have its danger, a short round, a misplaced bomb. He tried to recall the bursting radius of a 500-pound bomb, of a 105 shell, of a 155, of a napalm tank. The figures were fogged, illusive. He stopped and closed his eyes, concentrating. It was important that he remember. He had to know. The weight of the radio and weapons pulled on his shoulders, stretching the muscles in his back. Must know ... can't ask Andy. Won't ask Andy anything. Must know. Lock and Firesteen fell at his feet. Pat was near collapse himself. He wanted to stretch out beside them, sleep, regain his strength. But first, he had to know ... now. What was it he was trying to remember? "Get up!" he ordered them.

"Minute ... in a minute," Firesteen said.

"Can't we rest ... just a spell, Cap'n?"

Pat dropped beside them on the ice, his eyes searching the fading night. He gave Firesteen the morphine and retied the soaked bandage. No one spoke. They lay there, half dozing, until a new and frightening sound invaded the silence. It was like a deadly orchestra tuning up. Even as they listened, it swelled in a dissonant crescendo. They could see staccato bursts, muzzle blasts, and tracer fire. From holes along the crest and from clefts across the forward slope of the objective, hidden guns joined the cacophony. The enemy, Pat reasoned, had been alerted by the explosions in the paddy. They were still unable to see the marines scattered below them, but knew they were there.

Pulling Firesteen to his feet, Pat braced him, and gave Lock the launcher tube to use as a crutch. "Got to hurry." They hobbled on. "Was trying to remember ..." But his mind failed him. It was important that he remember something, but he could not recall what it was.

From somewhere up ahead, they heard the urgent call of "Corps-man! Corpsman!" The awakening sky was giving definition to the contour of the ground, to the paddy dikes, to the distant rocks that had been their refuge, to the swaddled shapes moving in the gray light of dawn.

Lock pulled up on his crutch and stopped, staring at the objective, now only two hundred yards away. "Looks like ... a girl ... who got knocked up."

Pat saw the massive caricature before them. The objective was shaped like a huge reclining figure of a pregnant woman. On the left, the craggy head, and then the gentle rise of a breast. On the right, the higher, swollen belly, and then the leveled thigh. "Does look ... like that."

"Like in ... her sixth month, huh?" Firesteen said.

"Bad girl. Call her Bad Girl," Lock said.

"Yo!" It was Sanchez. He was waving to them. They stumbled toward him as he rushed across the snow. "You guys been a long time," he said. "You all right, Lock?"

"Lost my toenails," He gulped, leaned on his friend. "Hope to die, Goat, yer ole buddy's 'bout shot his load."

Firesteen had dropped behind. Pat saw him falter. He and Sanchez started for him; and Sanchez got there in time to catch him. "What's wrong?" he lifted Firesteen easily, and carried him in his arms. "Hey, Mel!"

"Wounded," Pat said. "He's out."

Lock pulled back the hood from Firesteen's face. "Poor guy. Have a hell of a time explainin' gettin' shot ... in the hiney ... in the took-us." He grinned and began to shiver, his teeth chattering wildly. Pat took his arm, and helped him to the command post.

Huckabee left another casualty, and went to work on Firesteen. While Pat watched, he took a bottle of plasma from its nest of warmth between his legs, and prepared his patient to receive it. Choy had stripped Lock's boots, and already had him on a stretcher, covered with blankets.

Sanchez was at Pat's elbow with the 300 radio. "Captain, I got the poop to Lieutenant Anderson. Chancellor Six been callin'. Skinhead wants you to check in pronto." He waited for acknowledgment while Pat tried to order his thoughts. "I said Chancellor Six wants ..."

"Yes." First he had to see Andy, find out what the situation was. Superior firepower would be needed. Artillery for sure. But that could not be requested until he knew the actual situation. "Come on," he said to Sanchez. "Take radio. Going up."

"Can you make it, sir? Want me to get the lieutenant?"

Pat ignored him. Must do something, he was thinking, before enemy observers could blast at will in the open valley. Fighting back overpowering fatigue, he shambled forward. All around him, hidden in the swirling snow, were marines of Pappas' platoon. Enemy fire was reaching into the area, and the men cowered behind rough parapets of ice. A hidden rifleman began shooting at him. He was aware of it but felt strangely unconcerned, driven on by the knowledge that at any moment the enemy might destroy his company by a resolute charge into its midst. "Take cover," he told Sanchez. "Set up radio. Wait here."

He searched for Andy, his burning eyes peering ahead. Depend on Andy, he thought groggily. Andy again. Don't know what's going on. Suppose they hit us now? Who would control fire? Who would maneuver? Who would rally the men, force them to fight? He didn't even know where they all were, or how many casualties they had suffered. But Andy would know, he assured himself. And then he saw the familiar red muffler. Anderson was standing in a circle of boulders, looking as impregnable as the ridge they had to take. He was pointing to the swollen belly of the objective, talking to the ape-like form that was George Pappas. Relief surged over Pat. He started to jog ahead, despite the erratic sniper fire. And then he stopped as suddenly, regaining his breath and trying to clear his mind, to be calm and in control of himself.

Andy greeted him as if there had been no argument. "God damn', man, where you been?" Pat started to answer when another sniper, lodged somewhere on the breast of the ridge, began firing at the trio. Pappas dropped to the ground and rolled to a shallow dip in the snow.

Pat plunged after him. "We got the tank," he said. Andy still stood there, looking down at him. Pat steeled himself and got up again. As long as Andy stood, he would stand. "I said ... we got the tank." His throat was raw. It hurt him to yell over the wind. And the bullets were whipping too close. His mind wavered.

"Saw it blow out there. Who got it?"

"Justus, Firesteen, and me." He gulped. "Lost the bazookaman."

"Justus, Firesteen, and you, huh?"

Pat nodded. A knot of pity tightened unaccountably in his throat. He thought he was going to cry, without knowing the reason for the emotion. He realized only that he had come through an ordeal, and it was important that Andy understand it. A bullet chipped a rock only five feet away.

"Who handled the bazooka?"

"Justus." The next shot whined closer, ricocheted. It was a madman's game to stand that way, in full view of the enemy, protected only by luck and the dim light. But he would not be the first to drop.

"So Lock has a tank to his credit." The innuendo was there, jutting through his words as the surrounding boulders jutted through the snow.

"Yes."

"Bring the dead man in?"

"No. I—I thought—the rear echelon ... they could pick up the body ... when they come up." He hadn't thought of the man since he had left him; and in that moment he saw the pathetic face once more, teeth gripping the upper lip.

"We never leave our dead," Andy said.

"Didn't leave—" Another shot from the sniper, this one striking behind Andy. He didn't flinch.

Pappas had crawled closer. "Get down!" He pulled at Pat's leg. "Captain!"

The single shots from the ridge grew into a volley. Pat started down, was bent over when he saw Andy's smile. He forced himself erect, blinking his eyes to clear his vision. Andy was talking to him. "What ... What you say?" Pat asked.

"Where's Firesteen and Justus?"

"Back at C.P. Firesteen got nasty flesh wound, lost... lot of blood. But he'll be okay. Justus ... frostbite. Pretty bad. We were in a crevice ... and tank rolling right down on us ..." A machine gun took up the task against them. *Rackarackaracka.* It chipped away, its beaten zone ten feet before them. All the gunner need do was raise the sight. Pappas tugged at Pat's legs, and dragged him down behind the rocks.

Andy walked over slowly, and sat down beside them. The machine gun sprayed overhead. He pinched his bearded cheeks, and leaned back lazily. "Enough sea stories. Better get things moving. Chuck and Stringbean are going into position. Ought to be set by now."

Sanchez tumbled over the rock shelter with the 300 radio. "Told you ... stay back," Pat said.

"It's Skinhead," Sanchez said. "Called again. He's hotter than a two-dollar pistol."

Pat righted the set, then called Chancellor Six, his voice trembling, his whole body racked by shivering he could not control. Skinhead answered. Hesitantly, trying to steady his voice, Pat reported his position. "Checking now, sir. Will request ... fires soon as I'm ... as soon as ..." He tried to think of the right word, the word ... "When I'm briefed," he gasped at last.

Making no attempt to disguise his anger, Skinhead lashed at him. "For the past two hours my only contact with Able Company has been with your runner. You ought to be abreast of the situation. You're up there to fight your company, not to play marine!"

Andy was scratching his beard. Pappas had crawled away, as if he were not listening. Sanchez was watching him. "Yes, sir," Pat said dismally. "Will call you. Out." He was confused. What, after all, was expected of him? His drowsy mind dealt feebly with the question. He had been trying to ... to do what? Now, because he had not planned, because he knew nothing of the disposition of his men, he was powerless. He had gone off on a diversion, abdicated his post, turned over his command. And yet ... out there in the paddy he had known a pride, an exultation, he had never known before. Because ... Because ... He took off his gloves, rubbed furiously at his face and eyes, and breathed deeply. Though he was vaguely aware of his failure, he did not regret it. He knew only that he would not erase his error if he could. "Andy ... got to move people on line. Get base of fire ... going."

"What you going to have them shoot at?" Andy grunted. "You see anything up there? We get them all bunched up, it'll be just in time for their artillery to clobber us."

Andy was right. Should have thought of that, Pat's muddled brain told him. "Get Stringbean, Chuck. Want a report. Got to put out order ..." The important thing was to do something, to act, at once. As he had earlier. As he had when the tank charged toward them. It was getting lighter, and their vulnerability grew with the onsweep of day.

"I've already put out the order. Been waiting for them to get set, and call in some artillery. Sent a runner for that radio ten minutes ago ."

"Thought we'd send Stringbean's people around right flank," Pat said. "Move Chuck on other ..."

"Here's the dope on the artillery preparation."

"Wait a minute. Want to know where my people are ..."

"Haven't time for a briefing session, Pat," Andy said pleasantly. "Now you call me in some artillery. Some air, if you can. I'll get the troops up there."

Pat listened, noting the requests for fire support. "Got it. But want to be sure we ... coordinate between assault echelons so ... won't be firing ... into one another."

Andy ran his finger under the red muffler. He stood up again and surveyed the head, the breast, the belly, the thigh of the objective. "Yeah, I know all about it."

"And, George. Passed your platoon on way up. Too many people flat on their backs. Want them moved. Right now."

"Will you get hot on that radio? We haven't got all day," Andy said. "George, be ready to move. They catch it too bad, I want to throw you in. Take off." Pappas left them. Pat was still sitting. "You've got your map, haven't you?" Andy asked. "Better get to it. Probably let us have 155s. They're five or six miles back; and I want you to be sure they know exactly what they're supposed to be shooting at." He nudged Sanchez with his foot. "Get down to Lieutenant Cagle and tell him to get all the extra grenades he can from third platoon." Sanchez scampered off.

"Maybe it would be better to send Allison up on opposite side of Cagle. Good cover," Pat said. "Would divert the Chinks. Frontal assault is too—"

"A double envelopment ... Well, that's probably the school solution." Andy dismissed it. "I told you, Pat. I've put out the order and I know what I'm doing. Now, fergodsakes, call in some fire for me." He climbed up on a boulder, and looked over the front.

Pat stood below him. "Andy, I've got to know what's going on. I'm responsible..."

"What did you want me to do? Sit here with my thumb up my ass, waiting for you?" He lowered his voice. "I've started the show, Pat. Now let me get it on the road."

The machine gun fired again. Close. Pat involuntarily dived for cover. When he looked up, Andy was gazing down at him. Then he jumped the four feet into the snow and moved off toward the left flank. Feeling the sting of tears in his eyes, Pat watched him go.

17

The marines of Able Company took the rocky island in the shoreless sea of snow. They took it though half their weapons would not fire, and a short round had killed six men, and their feet and hands and faces were numb. And when they reached the crest at dusk, they left the slopes littered with torn bodies and the broken tools of butchery.

They tried to carve shelters from the unyielding earth, but broke their entrenching tools. They huddled instead behind flimsy walls of ice. They tried to eat, but could not thaw their rations. They melted snow, drank the warm liquid, and chewed on Tootsie Rolls. They tried to repair their weapons, but oil froze on the working parts. So they boiled them in water, dried them quickly, and applied hair tonic.

The enemy punished them unceasingly. Chinese guns pounded the head, the breast, the belly, the thigh of the ridge, blasted great craters, churned snow and ice and rock. Mortars ripped their puny shelters, destroyed a machine-gun emplacement, maimed five men in one squad of thirteen, killed a corpsman, a demolition man, three riflemen. The enemy fired with impunity. Marine artillery was silent. Able Company's frozen radio had lost contact with the rear. Relentlessly, explosives tore into the disputed ground until the whole earth seemed to shudder in violent convulsions. And then, suddenly, unpredictably, it stopped.

Pat and Andy crawled out of the command post. "Right up there," Pat said, pointing to a column of granite that stood like a nipple on the breast of the ridge. "We'll use it for the OP. When it's dark, we'll be able to spot their flashes, get counter-battery on them." He rubbed warmth back into his nose. "If we can just get our radio working."

"Yeah, 'if'!" Andy caught his breath as the wind rushed at his face. "If the radio worked ... if we knew what was going on behind us ... if the weather wasn't lousy and planes could get in ... if the artillery hasn't displaced ... if the Chinks don't decide we're softened up enough for a counterattack." He laughed. "If they'd just pack up and go home!"

A wireman joined them. "Sanchez said you want some sound powers strung, Captain."

"Right up there at the observation post," Pat said.

The wireman stepped between them to get a better view. "You want platoon lines run up, and a line from here, then?"

"Yeah," Andy said. "And two lines to the mortars. One alternate." A sniper fired from somewhere in the limitless expanse of snow. The wireman dropped, clutching his chest. Pat tore open the parka, and bared the wound. There were crimson bubbles there; and as the marine panted, the bubbles moved. His lips trembled, but no sound came. Before they could get him to the aid station, he was dead.

"You just can't figure it," Pat said later when they returned to the C.P. "All three of us standing there. Could have hit any one of us; and he picked him. Why not me? Or you?"

Andy smoothed out his sleeping bag, and lay on top of it. "No reason. Might have been aiming at you, and hit him. Might have figured he was the officer. An accident. Who knows?"

Pat lit a cigarette, holding his bare hands over the match until it was snuffed by the wind. "Thought about that this morning when everything seemed to be caving in on us. Funny how the damnedest things strike you at times like that ..." He was speaking softly, mulling over his thoughts. "You feel ... well, when you're that close to death, and everything says you're going to be killed, and then you aren't ..."

"I'd give my chair in Heaven for a cigar," Andy said, stretching. Pat wasn't listening. He was still groping for words. "I mean—" He hesitated. "We were right under that tank's gun. I could damn' near see the rifling. They had us dead center. Couldn't miss. And, somehow, they fired overhead. We were safe ..."

"Proves my point. It's all an accident." Andy reached for Pat's cigarette, puffed on it, and handed it back. "Take that gunner that fired at you—and missed. Why? Not because some just, merciful God blinded him for a second ..."

"Who knows why?"

Andy took the cigarette again, inhaled, and let the smoke out his nose. "You know why that gunner missed? Because his eyes were bleary. Because he didn't sleep last night. Because he'd lost his only bag of rice at goonie stud poker. Because the guy that won his chow cheated. Because the cheat met a rummy in Shanghai five years ago who showed him how to palm a card." He returned the stub of the cigarette. "And why did he show him how? Because the rummy happened to have a singsong girl with hot pants earlier in the evening, and sex made him talkative. Because the broad had been booted out of her house for holding out on the madame. Because her old man sold her to buy himself a funeral. Because ... Because ... Hell, there are ten thousand becauses." He slouched back, arms folded clumsily. "But if you're looking for a reason that makes more sense than bleating about God, just figure that goonie missed you this morning, the twenty-sixth of November in the year of Your Lord, nineteen hundred and fifty, because two old Chinks fornicated twenty years ago." Taking off his helmet, he propped his head on it. "You follow me? Life ... death, it's all an accident."

Pat doused the cigarette, stripped it, and let the tobacco fly in the wind. "But you plan. You pick out where you're going. You work..."

"People sweat and dig and cheat and whore and steal, and they can still end up with nothing." Andy sat up again, twisting his head, working the stiffness out of his neck. "All you can do is blunder along, doing the best you can. Nothing ever turns out the way you hope, does it?"

Flexing his hands, Pat pulled on his gloves. "Still, don't you have to try?"

"So try." Andy yawned. "Fifty men died today—at least that many. We've got nineteen dead. The Chinks probably twice that. But the old world repopulated itself a hundred times in the same few hours. It won't miss them at all." He paused, twisting a curl of beard. "If something's going to happen, it's going to happen. You're nuts if you think you can do anything to stop it."

Pat massaged his arms, trying to relieve the numbness. "So it's inevitable to live. Inevitable to die. Inevitable to suffer. Inevitable to get nowhere." He shrugged. "You really believe that, don't you?" Of course he did, Pat thought. That's why he was not afraid.

"Life stinks," Andy said. "But what the hell."

"It's the only life we've got."

Andy nodded. "That's the idea. Just can the pretty notions, and remember it's all an accident. Any breaks you get along the way, any fun, any love ... they're all to the good, all because you happen to be in the right place at the right time." Deliberately, he pounded his fist into the snow at his side. "It's like rape. If you can't prevent it— and you can't—relax and enjoy it."

Pat sought some rebuttal. He believed Andy was wrong, wrong for himself and wrong for most people. He saw him at one pole, in a universe ruled by chance and coincidence where there was no law, where life, death, the growth of a seed, the rising of the sun were all fortuitous.

He saw his mother at the opposite pole, in a universe ruled by a stem yet benevolent personal God who, enthroned among the stars, dispensed justice, rewards and punishment in direct ratio to the homage, prayer, and piety offered Him. No matter what realities confronted her, she had her answer.

When his father lay trussed and bandaged, fighting to draw breath from his crushed chest, she had told Pat that prayer could save him. And Pat, burdened with guilt, had left the hospital, and knelt beside his bed in that stifling apartment in Knoxville, repeating every prayer she had taught him, reading his Bible, forcing himself to see the blurred words. And he had awakened in the early morning, his head against his bedpost, the Bible on the floor beside him, opened to Ecclesiastes. And he had known, with the terrible certainty of youth, that his father was dead.

When he had finished his first semester in college, and there was no money to return, his mother, with simple insistence, had told him he must pray for it. She prayed. He worked for six months, mixing concrete during the day and sanding floors at night. She prayed. He found a part-time job at school, stoking furnaces. When he started classes again, it was with his mother's assurance that God had given him guidance, that prayer was responsible for tuition and books and lab fees and rent and food and clothing.

And later, when his summer's savings had been expended to pay for his two weeks in a hospital with a ruptured appendix, prayer was still the answer. She prayed. He joined the Marine Corps' V-12 training program. For the first time, he studied with a full stomach and in warm clothes and with a little cash in his pocket. The work of Providence, his mother told him at his graduation. Faith and Prayer and Piety worked miracles.

Somewhere in between, Pat believed, between Andy's bitter negation and his mother's unquestioning faith, were many others like himself. But, like most of the people he knew, like Ann, like the men he worked with, like the marines around him, he had not formulated his ideas into a cohesive whole. He had hot consciously pruned and selected and rejected. How many people had? How many could say: This I believe. This is my philosophy.

Andy was curled up under his poncho, his eyes closed. Pat whispered, "Andy?"

"Yeah?"

"About this morning ..."

"Forget it. The little bastard got his." He unbuckled the strap on his helmet. "I was pissed off. So were you. We yacked at each other. I'm sorry. You're sorry."

"We can't go off in different directions. I've got to fight this company. You can help me."

"Sure." Andy opened his eyes. "Better get some sleep. It'll be noisy around here tonight."

No use discussing it, Pat thought. Better let it go, start off clean. Though his body was sore and bruised, though his eyes ached, he could not relax. For a long time he lay rigid, listening to the tireless wail of the wind, watching the fresh snow cover the scars of the ridge, coating it in sterile whiteness.

Sanchez dropped into the bomb-scooped crater, lost his footing, and sprawled alongside Pat. "Sir ... got the radio goin'!" He was out of breath, gulping for air. "Musta been froze, 'cause soon's it sat in front of the fire ..."

Pat got up quickly. "Did you get Battalion?" He helped Sanchez to his feet.

"Yes, sir. Took some time, but I raised 'em. Signal kinda weak. Don't know how long them batteries is gonna last."

"Any word?" Pat asked anxiously. "Did they tell you anything?"

"Said to get you on the double. That's all."

Pat followed Sanchez along thirty yards of slippery, icy path. Bodies were ranged on either side; and he counted as he passed. Nineteen. The draped ponchos were already weighted with snow, molding them in white conformity. The dead differed from each other only in the size of their protruding shoes.

Entering the aid station, Pat saw The Horse checking the mortar shells, medical supplies, and grenades Korean laborers had brought from the rear. Others were carrying laden stretchers from the one warming-tent that had survived the shelling. A line of marines stood outside the entry flap, awaiting their allotted ten minutes of warmth before returning to the freezing wind and their burrows in the earth. Goober and Huckabee were kneeling beside an overturned ox cart, checking the casualty list with the sergeant in charge of the working party.

"Hold the litter bearers up for a few minutes, Top," Pat said. "May want to send a message back."

Goober stood. "The skipper said to move them out fast as I could. It's getting dark."

"Just be a few minutes."

Goober muttered something unintelligible.

"What was that?" Pat asked sharply.

"Captain, don't you think ..." He changed his mind. "Aye, aye, sir."

Inside the tent, Sanchez was working at the radio. "Chancellor Six. This is Able Six. Over. Chancellor Six ..."

Men encircled the small red belly of the stove. Bottles of plasma were suspended from the canvas roof, thawing. The wounded still awaiting evacuation lay on stretchers on the ground. As Pat moved among them, Lock Justus caught his trouser leg. "How's it goin', Cap'n?"

Pat smiled. "What are you still doing here?"

"Waitin' my turn. Don't let it out, but I'm okay. Just one foot. If that chancre mechanic Huckabee wasn't skeered of me, he wouldn't'ta tagged me at all."

Pat gave him a cigarette and lit it for him. "When we get back,
I'm putting you in for a Silver Star for that tank we got this morning. Firesteen, too."

Lock grinned. "Man, the sea stories I can spin on liberty!" ' "Hi, Captain." Firesteen lay face down on the next stretcher. Choy was changing the dressing on his wound. "For a while there, I was thinkin' I'd get a star all right—a Star of David, three feet high and six feet above!"

"How's it going?" Pat asked.

"Great, now," Firesteen said. "But Huck musta put thirty stitches in my ass."

"Took-us!" Lock said. "Them goonies damn' near reamed him a extry one."

"Think I got a chance of gettin' stateside with this, Captain?" Firesteen said. "Ow! Dammit, Choy, take it easy."

"If'n you wanna get back," Lock said, "make out yer sufferin', hurtin' like a cat with his tail in a threshin' machine."

Sanchez was still calling Battalion. "... this is Able Six. Come in Chancellor Six. Chancellor Six ..."

Huckabee held open the tent flap and pointed to Lock. Two Korean bearers came in and moved the stretcher. "Wait a minute, you yobos!" Lock yelled. Turning to Firesteen, he said, "You owe me two cans of franks and beans and four coffees, Mel. I tole you I'd get outta here 'fore you."

"Check with me at my apartment in Pittsburgh," Firesteen said, laughing. "Me and the wife and kid'll be glad to feed you."

Lock took the canteen that lay beside him, and handed it to Pat. "Cap'n, there's 'bout three swigs of vodka left. You take it."

"You'd better keep it for the trip out."

"Go on. Hellfire, it's a fair trade, ain't it? Hope to die yer gettin' the best of it. Yer gettin' the vodka and all I'm gettin's a Silver Star." Pat took the canteen and shook hands with Lock. "Take care of yourself."

"Sure." The Koreans lifted him and started for the tent flap. "Mel, you write me if'n that baby comes through. I got money on it. And take care of my bunky, Cap'n. Goat'll be lost without me t' do his thinkin' fer him."

"So long, Lock," Sanchez said, pausing at the radio.

"You done tole me that five times already. So long, you ole sonova-bitch." Lock waved as he was carried outside.

"Gonna miss that damn' hillbilly," Firesteen said. "Coulda had him talkin' Yiddish in another coupla months."

One of the other casualties, a machine gunner with shrapnel wounds in his face and chest, was moaning. Choy went to him. "I think you need morphine," he said.

The marine smiled wanly. "Gimme a shot, bartender."

The radio started buzzing with static. Pat knelt beside Sanchez. "Chancellor Six. This is Able Six. Come in, please …"

There was a disturbance outside the tent. They heard Huckabee's voice: "Go on back to your outfit, and let me be. I'm one tired nigger."

The other voice was charged with anger. "Don't give me any of your crap, dammit! You hear me?"

"I hear you," Huckabee said. "But that's all I got to give."

"What the hell's the idea? I got people still here was hurt this mornin'; and it's damn' near dark already."

"I'm gettin' them out fast as I can. Have to wait for carriers."

"When I tag somebody, I'm not playin' jokes. I mean for 'em to get out."

Pat looked outside. One of the platoon corpsmen was facing Huckabee. The others in the aid station had stopped work and were watching them. "Take it easy," Huckabee said. "Those in worst shape I send out first. Doesn't matter when they get hit. It's the ones who need surgery—"

The other corpsman pushed him. "What makes you think you know better than me who needs what?" he asked, raging. "Next time I send somebody back, you better damn' well move him!"

Pat had an impulse to stop the exchange, but he held back. Andy had predicted trouble. Now he wanted the prediction refuted. Huckabee had to assert his authority if he was going to do his job. Pat waited, hoping he would order the corpsman out of the area, curse him, even hit him. "I do the best I can," Huckabee said.

"You damn' coon," the corpsman said. "That's not good enough for me!"

Huckabee turned his back. The other sailor grabbed him, spun him around, and shook him. "I oughta clobber you, you black bastard!"

There was a sound at Pat's elbow. Choy was standing beside him, listening. "It always comes to that, doesn't it, Captain?"

Pat disregarded him, and walked outside. The Horse had reached the two men. He jerked the platoon corpsman from behind, pulling him off his feet, snapping his head back. "Get outta here, swabbie," he said, his voice charged with anger.

Huckabee stepped between them. "I don't need your help," he said, mumbling, averting his eyes. "I can take care of myself."

"Then do it!"

Goober parted them before Pat could interfere. "Let's get this squared away," he said to the platoon corpsman. "When Huckabee tells you something, that's me talkin'. That's the skipper talkin'! General Cates! Harry Truman!" He pushed him away, and faced The Horse. "Get your ass in gear—back to your mortars!" He glared at Huckabee. "You don't know how to boss your people, by God, I'll see the skipper gets somebody down here who can. A guy talks like that, roughs you up, knock him on his duff!"

"Captain!" It was Sanchez, calling from the tent. "Got 'em!" Skinhead was on the radio. "Can't talk in the clear. I'm sending a message to you. How are things? Over."

"Supplies you sent are a help. Need more illuminating shells, extra batteries." There were so many questions Pat wanted to ask, but knowing that the enemy might be monitoring the transmission, there was little he could say.

"Have some news," Skinhead said. "Get this: Pluto's friends ... across the ice rink ... are toothless now. Over."

Pat was frowning, unable to puzzle out the battalion commander's meaning. "Say again your last transmission. Over."

Skinhead spoke more slowly this time: "I say again: Peter-Love-Uncle-Tear-Oboe ... P-L-U-T-O ... Pluto's friend's ... Disney's Pluto ... across the ice rink ... are toothless now. You read me? Over."

The doggies, the Army unit across from Able Company on the east coast of the reservoir, had been hit and were defenseless.

"Chancellor Six. This is Able Six," Pat said. "I read you five-by-five. Over."

Laughter answered. Then: "Pluto's friends had two bats of sloggers, some cannon cockers ..."

Army had two battalions of infantry and some artillery ...

"... We hear no barking," Skinhead said. "You with me? Over."

The marines had lost contact with the besieged Army troops.

As they talked, the stern tone, the evasiveness of the battalion commander's answers to other questions alarmed Pat. He wanted to know how they stood, whether they would be withdrawn, where the division would set up. And he could ask none of those questions and expect an answer. "We're in good shape," he said, as if he were addressing the enemy. "In damn' good shape. Mighty cold, though."

"I know," Skinhead said. "Under twenty-below here." Then, the pained sound of his voice again, as if he were trying to communicate something. "Keep contact, Pat. Of course you know where the Chinks are. But keep contact." Pat knew only vaguely where the enemy was. And Skinhead was undoubtedly aware of it. What was he trying to say? "And watch for any strays of the canine variety..."

Be on the lookout for any Army stragglers.

Pat read ominous hints into every word. Finally, he asked to speak to the artillery officer. "Want to plan for tonight."

"You know what they say in the cannon cockers' song?" Skinhead asked. "About the caissons—in reverse."

Pat nearly blurted the lyric, but caught himself. The inference was clear enough. The caissons were rolling along—in reverse. Rolling away. Rolling out of range, leaving them to be pounded. The guns closest to them, at Hagaru, could not help either. Their fire was masked by the intervening hills.

When Skinhead signed off, Pat knew his worst fears had materialized. The company was sitting alone, six miles from the nearest friendly lines, the final bastion between the enemy and Division. And the Chinese were attacking.

He climbed back to the command post, and found Andy still asleep. He shook him. "Andy!"

He lay there, like a stunted red bear in hibernation. His head, cushioned by his beard, lolled on his chest. He roused slowly. He had been dreaming.

Don't. Don't say anything, darling.

Who loves you?

You do.

Who's good in bed?

You are.

You'll many some big-bosomed blonde now.

Don't. Please don't.

I'll haunt you if you do ...

Andy blinked at the white world of snow and ice, felt it, cold and numbing; smelled it, damp and penetrating. Reality dissolved the dream of the all-white hospital, the loathsome odors, the whispered hallway conferences, the secrecy and humiliation and false cheer—and then death, and overwhelming guilt.

He stretched. "Well, what is it?"

Pat reported his call from Skinhead, the loss of artillery support, the promise of a detailed message, the implied warning in the Army's entrapment across the reservoir. Together they climbed to the observation post. "The men have already given the ridge a name: Bad Girl," Pat said. "Justus came up with it."

"Getting soft," Andy said. "Usually it's Slaughterhouse or Cemetery or Massacre or some other pretty handle."

"I think we ought to tell our people exactly where we stand," Pat said. "They ought to know we're up against it."

"Tell them nothing," Andy said. "You'll just get their imaginations going. They'll be making up scuttlebutt, panicking each other."

"You don't trust them, do you?"

"I don't trust anybody."

They stood at the crest. Off in the distance, they saw furling light against the darkening sky. "Could be the Army people, burning their trucks."

"They had some help," Andy said. "That's for sure."

Pat nodded. But he had not heard him. His eyes were fixed on the orange glow that spread on the horizon like a sunset.

18

Five miles away, across the glassy face of the frozen reservoir, fingers of flame clawed the sky. Dead lay crumpled along the road. Wheels spun on an overturned truck. Enemy burp guns coughed. An automatic rifle stuttered a reply. Only the whimpering chorus of the wounded interrupted the deadly conversation.

A soldier lay cowering in a ditch. Above him he heard the enemy jabbering, heard a dull explosion, screams, footsteps. Beneath him, surrounding him, were dead men. A lifeless, frozen thumb pushed against his glasses. The truck above him was afire. The dying men inside began to scream in disbelief, in terror, in agony. An American voice shrieked hysterically. The soldier buried his face in a dead man's shoulder, trying to shut out the sound, trying to stifle his own sobs.

His mind was in chaos. There was no chronology to the past hours. Incidents, faces, conversation—these were amazingly clear, sharply defined. But time was jumbled and confused.

He remembered the ambush of the convoy. Naked bodies in the road. His radio smashed. Men trapped in vehicles. Men milling about in wild disorder.

He remembered the communications officer, lying in the snow beside his wrecked jeep, his hand to his stomach, blood oozing between his fingers. "Knew we shouldn't have tried to barrel through ... can't fight from trucks ..."

He remembered crossing a stream. Marine planes had come over to help. The men had cheered. The roar of the motors alone had silenced the enemy. Then, inexplicably, the pilots had bombed and rocketed their own troops.

He remembered the only order he had been given. A sergeant with gaping spaces between his teeth had said, "Keep going west. Marine lines across reservoir. Get back best you can. Every man for himself."

He remembered the three men with him. They were wounded by machine-gun fire. He had dragged them to the ditch where they died. Then he was alone.

When he dared listen again, it was nearly quiet. He heard the sigh of the wind, the snap of burning wood and canvas, the jabbering of the Chinese as they searched the wreckage. His hands were freezing. He held them against his mouth, blew on them, rubbed them together. His gloves were gone. He had given them to one of the wounded aboard the trucks.

He considered surrender. He could just give himself up. Give his name, rank, and serial number. And he would be out of the war. But that would be cowardly. And he had sworn only that morning that he would die before being guilty of cowardice again.

There had been the lieutenant—a solemn young West Pointer with red hair—whose name he knew so well, but could not recall now. "Fight! Don't run," he had shouted as the platoon melted away. "Damn your lousy souls to hell! *Don't run!"*... It seemed so long ago. The soldier wished that he had stayed with the officer. He had wanted to, though he had known it was hopeless. There was something so pathetic in the fury of the slight, pale young man shouting to men who would not listen. All the others ran. So he had run, too. When he looked back, he saw the officer cursing them, then turning to face the enemy alone. And he had wanted to go back, but had been too stupefied by fear to do more than watch as the Chinese swarmed over the position.

Now, cautiously, the soldier pushed up on his elbows. West. Go west. The reservoir. He crawled down the ditch, sliding over the snow, alert to each sound, each shadow. It took him half an hour to cover forty yards. As he started to pull himself out, he heard the crunch of footsteps ahead. He burrowed frantically into a clog of bodies. An enemy scavenger worked over him. He could smell the urine-garlic odor. He could feel hands on his boots. He held his breath, kept his limbs rigid, imagined the man debating on the size of his feet. His leg was dropped. The Chinese began to strip the body on his right, grunted as he pulled a dead man's boots, cursed as he bent frozen arms to remove the parka. Then he returned to the soldier and picked up his hand, discovering the wrist watch, the diamond ring. He slipped off the watch, pulled at the ring. It was tight. He twisted it, bending the finger until the soldier thought he must scream. Another tug at his finger. A harsh voice called out of the darkness. The enemy yelled a reply. The soldier felt the damp breath of the Chinese on his hand, felt the slimy tongue on his finger, the teeth below the ring, pulling at it. At last it came off. The enemy climbed back to the road. The soldier dared breathe again. The saliva had frozen on his finger. He plunged it into the cleanliness of the snow, and lay there trembling, too weak to move.

Come on, boy. Why not take something for a change without making a big deal over it? Picked the ring up in Chicago. There on business, figured I'd fly out here, spend a day, see how you were getting along. Wasn't any call for you to run off. I didn't mean to push you into the plant ... But now you've done it, I told your mother I'm glad you joined the Army. Shows spunk. Independence. That's the kind of man makes good in business these days. Besides, it'll give you time to make up your mind. Two years, you'll be tickled to death to forget the farm idea ... Okay! Okay! You don't, we'll work something out. But, Hell's molasses, I pack more meat in a month than you could raise in twenty years! ... Sure your father was a fine man. Didn't know him too good, but the little I saw him—when I used to drive you out and pick you up every six months—I liked him. Hard worker. Honest. And he didn't hold no hard feelings over your mother. But, face it, he never had a pot to pee in or a window to throw it out of, did he? When I married your mother, he had most everything she owned in hock, sent her stuff back for years after ... Two hundred and more acres and up to his armpits in debt half the time ... Now, put on your hat and let's go into town for a steak. And we'll call your mother. Make her feel better. Just act like nothing happened. And take the damn' ring, will you? Three carats. Diamond is something a man can always get his money out of ...

Lying there, shivering and alone in the wilderness of snow and ice and mountains and death, the soldier examined the ground before him, saw how it sloped gracefully toward the reservoir, fifty yards away. Moonlight coated it, giving the ice a glittering sheen. Like the east pasture, he thought. In clover. And the barn would be over there, by the road. And the fence would run a broken line around the edges of the ice. But there'd be no ice. It would be summer. There'd be cattle drowsing in the heat, grazing in the bending field of wildflowers. There'd be the smell of freshly turned earth, and the corn standing in soldierly rows ... His mind dallied with the past for only a second, then turned to reality again, to the churning wind and the whirlpools of snow.

Dragging himself out of the ditch, he worked his way painfully toward a clump of scrub pine. The path was unmarked. The enemy surrounded him. Yet he found his alertness had increased. Everything seemed in sharper focus. Off on the right he saw two cigarettes glowing. On the left, the light from the burning trucks still flickered dully across the hillside. There was only one choice. Straight ahead. He pushed forward, careful to slide his body with the moan of the wind, picking his way in shadow, out of the moonlight. Suddenly he was aware of someone clearing his throat, coughing, spitting. Up ahead. He got behind a tree, hugged the trunk, waited, his heart thumping. It had taken him more than an hour to come that far. He had brushed capture or death. And now, within ten yards of a chance, he was blocked.

He watched the Chinese sentry—a frail little man—a shadow's length away. He was putting on GI boots, tossing his sneakers aside. He jabbed a finger in his nose, probed, examined the results, flicked it away. The soldier watched as the enemy took a can of American rations from his pack and began to pry it open with his bayonet, his face furrowed in concentration.

The soldier was hungry, too. He wondered, in a moment of fantasy, what would happen if he stepped up to him and said, "How about some chow, buddy?" But fear would undo them both, he thought. One would have to kill the other. He heard voices coming from behind, the sound of slogging through snow. He edged back, seeking concealment in the scrub pines. Three Chinese passed so close to him that one kicked snow in his face. He lay there trying to still the spasms that shook his body.

The three Chinese surrounded the sentry. One raised his voice. Another laughed. The little man got up and held out his can of rations, offering it. Each refused. Then all three fell on him, one sitting astride him, one holding his arms, the other ripping his coat open, searching him. The soldier watched, hypnotized, as the sentry cried out, gesticulating. The tallest Chinese rubbed snow in his face. The others went through his clothing, laughing when they found several more cans of rations. They let their victim up and turned away. He followed, protesting. The big man smashed a can into his cheek, knocking him down. And as he fell, he ripped the palm of his hand on his opened ration. The others stood over him for a moment, then left him there.

The soldier listened until he could no longer hear them, until the only sounds were the wind and the whipping of the tree branches and the sobbing of the Chinese sentry. The man had moved to the tree trunk where the soldier had hidden earlier. He still clung to his can of food in one hand, and licked the bloody wound in the other, his body heaving with deep sobs, tears streaking his face.

I have to kill him, the soldier thought. No other way. Phlegm rose in his throat, and he rubbed his stiff fingers across the knot there. But it had to be done. And he had no weapon. He felt his belt. His radio repair tools—pliers, a screwdriver. Carefully, he slipped the screwdriver out. It scraped the leather holder, and he froze in dread. No reaction from the enemy. The Chinese was leaning back against the tree, still holding his wounded hand to his mouth.

The soldier palmed the tool so it would not gleam in the moonlight. It was a poor weapon, he thought. Blunt. The enemy was wearing a parka and a padded uniform. He would have to stab him in the neck ... or the eyes. He swallowed a lump of revulsion. He had never killed before. Although he was among the first troops to reach Korea when war began, he had never fired a round from his rifle. He didn't really know how to kill a man. Once, in basic training he had seen a movie called "Kill or Be Killed." It showed how. And he had been sick. Now he had forgotten the details.

The idea teased him again: Why not walk up to him, with hands raised, and surrender? Just give name, rank, serial number. Protected by law. Nothing cowardly about it. Not when you can no longer fight. But he could not convince himself. With new resolution, he tightened his fist about the handle of the screwdriver, and slipped across the snow, closer. He would have the advantage of surprise.

His heart seemed to stop beating. All time was suspended. He could already reach out to touch the man. He could hear his adenoidal breathing. He promised himself he would jump on ten. One ... two ... three ... The acid of fear ate into his resolve. He took off his glasses, put them in his pocket. Eight ... nine ... Not the eyes. The throat. One ... two ... He eased himself erect. Seven ... eight ... nine ... He took a step. The sound made the Chinese turn.

The soldier hurtled forward, and fell headlong, sprawled on the lip of the frozen reservoir. He felt hands on him, pulling him back, sliding him across the snow. He lay there, his body shuddering with cold and terror, waiting for the shot that would finish him.

The enemy lowered his rifle, and looked down at a homely boy, about twenty-three, prematurely bald, with jutting chin and high forehead. He saw the heavily lashed, wide brown eyes protruding from a sad, wizened, meager face. He heard a quaking, hoarse voice repeat, chanting, "Pfc. Woodrow Dorn, 868432151, U.S. Army ... Pfc. Woodrow Dorn, 868432 ..."

Pat checked his watch for the fourth time in as many minutes. Andy's patrol had been out for three hours. It was 0350. He was twenty minutes overdue. "Maybe I shouldn't have let him go. Suppose we get hit before he gets back?0

"This moon," Pappas said. He forced down Chuck Cagle's head, and ran the clippers up his neck. "Slow going in light like this."

"Pay attention to the customer, George," Cagle said. "I'm a big tipper."

"Crazy time for a haircut," Pappas said.

Cagle yawned. "I'm a busy man."

"Think I'll go up and see if they've been spotted," Pat said.

"No need," Pappas said. "Asked Stringbean to call on the sound phone when they come through his lines."

"Stick around, Captain. Ought to let George trim that goatee of yours. You're beginning to look like Mephistopheles."

Pat glanced at his runner, who lay under a poncho across the crater. He had the phone. "Sanchez?"

"Just catchin' a smoke, sir. No word."

"Little more off on top," Cagle said. "You know, George, I've got a notion to stake you to a shop in New York. You've got the touch of a first-class barber."

"Not me," Pappas said, laughing. "You couldn't give me the franchise in the Waldorf. I get home, I don't figure to do any haircutting. We sold the shops. Got a barber and beauty parlor supply house. The old man's going to retire; and I'm going to take over." He ran the point of his scissors around Cagle's ears. "The way Texas is growing, it's time to branch out. Get men on the road, open another warehouse. Advertise."

"You get big enough, I'll handle your account. I'll be BBD & O's youngest VP by then. Favor to an old buddy I knew in The Corps— once a marine, always a marine."

Pat was retracing his actions over the past few hours. He had reconnoitered the terrain again, and made minor changes in the organization of the ground. Allison was defending the head, Cagle's battered unit the breast, and Pappas the belly and thigh of the ridge. He had walked the main line of resistance, assigned alternate positions on the final protective line, designated new boundaries and limiting points, planned the mortar barrages for the dead space, and set up another listening post. What Andy had neglected to do, he had handled himself. And that had involved some changes. He was uneasy about Andy's reaction when he returned. He looked at his watch again. 0356. "Houston's a big town, isn't it?" Cagle said.

"Sure. Been growing like crazy. Doubles in population all the time," Pappas said. "Going to be one of the biggest cities in the country some day."

"I was thinking," Cagle said. "Might be a good place for an agency. Hate to give up the fifteen grand I'm making now ... but I'd be willing to struggle for a few years."

Struggle for a few years ... The words were caught up in Pat's mind. The last night before he left Washington. Aboard her parents' sloop with Ann. The two of them stretched on the deck beside the forward hatch, watching the mast above them as it rocked like a metronome against a blue-black sky.

And he had damned the war, damned Truman for involving the country, damned the Marine Corps for involving him. "I've had my war. There's so much I want to do that I may never do now."

And she had said: "You're using the war as an excuse. Suppose it was over tomorrow. Would you be willing to *struggle for a few years?* Would you give up your job with Walt? Start fresh? Design according to your own standards? Suddenly shun compromise? Would you do all the things you've told me you want to do?" He had watched her face in the amber glow of the anchor light as she leaned over him. "Would you, darling? Would you chuck everything and do it? Give up that car with all the gadgets and the flossy apartment your mother hates and the golf lessons and all the rest? Really?"

He had had no answer. He had got up without speaking, and stepped out on the bowsprit. Holding to the forestay cable, he had watched the shafts of light across the Potomac as planes slipped down to the airport. And he had known she was right. He would do none of those things. War or no war. Leave Walt? Because it was the firm name, not his on the blueprints? Because corners were cut? Because his plans were consistently modified? Because taste and integrity were always secondary to the client's whims? What beginning architect didn't have the same complaints?

She had come up behind him on the slim footing; and he had steadied her. They had stood there, suspended over the pale green river. "Well?" she had said, waiting for his answer.

And he had lied. "It's the damn' war ..."

Now, sitting in his command post, Pat could admit the truth. He wanted only what he had left behind. He had struggled long enough to attain it. He was not willing to *struggle for a few years ...*

Sanchez called for silence. He held the receiver to his ear. "Patrol's comin' in."

Pat bolted, with Pappas and Cagle behind him. They hurried to Allison's position where the patrol had cleared the lines. Andy was sitting in the snow, one boot off, rubbing his foot. "Chinks are moving heavy stuff behind that ridge four hundred yards to our left front. Looked like a battalion of them. You could hear them yacking like they owned the place. Fires going, everything."

"Just a battalion," Cagle said, frowning. "Well, that only makes it about four to one."

"Let him finish!" Pat said. "Go on, Andy."

"Counted three big guns. Looked like 76s. Not dug in, seemed to be waiting for something."

Pat cursed. "If we could just get some artillery on them!"

"Your 'ifs' again!" Andy pulled on his sock. "Coming back, we skirted the reservoir. Picked up a dogface that made it across. Died by the time we got him in. Back wound. But he said there are men out on the ice somewhere, a hundred or more. Some hurt. Most headed south, and oughta hit our lines closer to Hagaru. It's the remnants of the Army lash-up that got clobbered today."

"We'll have to go out and look for them," Pat said.

"You think the Chinks can still move up on us tonight?" Allison asked.

Andy shrugged. "I don't know what they'll do, Stringbean. But that's not a Boy Scout meeting they got going over there."

PFC Woodrow Dora, bare hands raised, knelt at his captor's feet. The Chinese was circling him, his rifle held in his armpit, blood seeping from the ripped palm that rested on the trigger guard. The soldier, terrified, fearing a shot from behind, revolved on his knees, keeping the enemy before him.

The Chinese spoke in a curious, gravel-throated voice, and gestured to his prisoner to stand. Dorn got up, still holding his hands above his head. The bitter wind had made them numb. He tried to work his fingers. Stabs of pain ran down his arms into his shoulders and back. The enemy stood looking at him, his thin, dirt-streaked face puckered in a frown. Then, prodding him, he drove him back toward the road again.

As they started through the pines, they heard laughter, loud voices, footsteps coming toward them. Dorn stumbled, and regained his balance. Fear choked him. The wind beat at his face. His arms felt weighted. He shivered violently. The Chinese spoke again, forcing him to the snow, and then pulled his hands down. They were bent over, hidden by the underbrush and the pines, side by side, like small boys playing hide-and-seek. The Chinese was breathing with effort, blood from his torn hand dripping in the snow, the other supporting the rifle, holding his prisoner at bay.

The same three men who had robbed and beaten the sentry twenty minutes earlier had returned. They called out, searching the shore line. The Chinese was chewing his lips anxiously. He and his prisoner could see the others clearly as they went through the deserted pack, found a blanket, the screwdriver Dorn had dropped, another can of rations, and a bag of meal. Then they walked off, talking, examining their spoils. Dorn glanced at his captor. There was a splotch of red on the snow beneath his hand. The Chinese, sighing with relief, was licking his wound again. The soldier reached under his parka for his first-aid packet, unsnapped it, and brought it out.

The Chinese, seeing the motion, jumped to his feet, and painfully swung his rifle. Dorn dropped the packet. The enemy backed off, as if expecting it to explode. When it didn't, he came closer, and probed it with the muzzle of his rifle. He bent over and picked it up. As he did so, he broke wind. Shyly, he looked at Dorn, and giggled. Dorn smiled, heard himself chuckling, then laughing softly. They both put their hands to their mouths to still the sound, and, looking at each other, laughed again.

Sitting beside him in the snow, the enemy wiped his face on his sleeve. Dorn ripped open the first-aid packet, took out the bandage, and offered it. The Chinese put it in his palm, but could not hold the rifle and tie the gauze. Dorn, moving slowly toward him, took his hand, tightened the compress and tied it.

The enemy nodded, inclining his body in a slight bow. Dorn did the same. The Chinese stood, his rifle at his side, listening. He motioned Dorn to move on. The soldier plodded toward the road. They had walked only a few yards when the Chinese whispered something, came up to the soldier and turned him back toward the reservoir. They stood for a moment, looking at each other. Then the Chinese nudged him, pushing him ahead.

Dorn dared not hope for the impossible, but he was confronted by it. He had seen the enemy bum wounded, loot and scavenge. He expected no mercy. He had heard of prisoners being released—for propaganda purposes, to carry messages. But this was different. This man held the power of life or death over him, and chose to give life. He's letting me go, Dorn kept repeating to himself. Letting me go. When he reached the edge of the frozen reservoir, the enemy halted him, and signaled to him to wait. Retrieving his half-eaten can of rations from the snow, he brought it to the soldier. Dorn took it. He wanted to say something. But the few Chinese words he had learned were all curses. He could not say "Thank you." Putting the corned-beef hash in his pocket, he kept his hands there to warm them. He was trying to think of some word, something. "Very good," he said, *"Ding Hao."*

A smile quivered on the comers of the enemy's mouth. *"Ding Hao,"* he repeated.

Dorn offered his hand. The Chinese looked at it and, without taking it, backed off. The soldier started walking, then running across the ice. When he looked back again, the Chinese was still standing there, watching. Then he raised his wounded hand, palm up, in a gesture of farewell.

The reservoir seemed one vast plain, slick in the moonlight, with the cutting wind boiling over the rim of the earth, and sweeping across it. West ... West ... Sun rises in east and goes down in west, Dorn thought. And the moon?

As he trudged on, losing sight of all but the circle of ice around him, he tried to account for the phenomenon of his release. The wind battered him, drove him to his knees, making him slip and fall comically. But each time he stood again, mechanically, and pushed forward. As time passed, he could no longer concentrate. He remembered only that he must not stop, must not lie down. Men died in blizzards because they slept.

What was the story about a little dog and the man who froze to death so close to camp? Jack London ... Shep had been his dog. Dead. With his father, dead. Man and boy had walked the fields together, stopping to pull a radish, eating it with the grit of earth still on it, drinking lemonade from a Mason jar. Rarely speaking. And once Shep had found a lost cow, bellowing, in labor. For an instant Dorn could see his father, see his feet planted in the animal's belly, see the horny, sinewy hands grasping the calf's emerging forelegs, tugging it into life. And later, they had come home, tired and sweating. And they sat on the floor of the sitting room, and picked the burrs from Shep's fur ...

He was in a stupor of exhaustion now. His eyes, nearly shut, were dull, pallid, as listless as his gait. Only when he stood again to move on, only when fear pushed him to his feet in a moment of logic and sanity, did those eyes flicker, and then with the brief flash of desperation.

He rested again, on his knees, his head bent above the ice, his arms shielding it from the incessant wind. Mustn't lie down. Must keep going. Count. To fifty. Then get up. West ... must go west ... How many miles had he come? Easier to die. Now he would freeze to death, would stay there, preserved, like a chicken. And with spring, there'd come the thaw. And his body would float away, be fished out, bloated and stinking.

Like the men on the retreat from the Naktong. Only last summer. The blistering sun, the sweet stink of death, the unburied bodies, swollen, puffed, skin popping from featureless faces. Everywhere men were moving back, and people were calling, "What outfit you from, Mac?" And no one seemed able to stop it. Until they were miles from battle. And a colonel had stood in the middle of the road, pointing a pistol at them, ordering them to regroup ...

Now Dorn counted to fifty twice. Had to move on. Had to. He could not reckon time. He could not determine distance. He could not gauge direction. The wind hammered at him until he couldn't breathe. He turned his back to it. He kept his hands in his coat. When he tried to eat the food he had been given, he could not hold the can long enough. He put the frozen chunks in his pocket, warmed them in his hands, then put them to his mouth. Shuffling on through the interminable night, he groped his way toward dawn. Each step became more difficult. Gradually, he gave in. He rested longer, still longer, forgetting the groaning ice, the restless noises of the wind.

Ray will be a Gold Star mother ... sniffling in one of those postage-stamp handkerchiefs, all lace. Her sharp little voice quavering, looking out her window, one hand on the beige lace curtains, the room smelling of furniture polish and face powder and cologne. And Harry standing beside her in his gray or blue or brown homespun suit trying to comfort her. Poor Harry. Good, decent, fumbling Harry. Stepfather Harry ... Once, when he was only twelve, and Harry and his mother were just back from Europe on their honeymoon, he had taken him to the slaughterhouse to show him around. He had stood in the killing room, seen the great dumb beast struck, fall to the concrete floor, its muscles jerking. And he had turned away, only ten face the great tubs of lungs and livers, kidneys and tongues and testicles. He had looked for the door, had seen men working over the carcass with sharp knives, tearing at the hide ... and he had fallen forward, and vomited into a tub. It was a joke Harry told to company that night... He had hidden in his room. Harry had found him there, had taken him to town, on the streetcar ... And they had their picture taken in a booth where you put in a quarter. And they went to the movies ...

Dorn found himself shaking with silent laughter. He was going to die. He couldn't keep going. His legs buckled when he tried to stand. His eyes seemed to scratch against the lids. For the first time, he remembered his glasses. One lens was broken, but he put them on. Now the mountains seemed closer. But he could not be sure. Only the wind was the same. And the cold. He felt drunk.

The brandy was found in the loft, among the rotting cornstalks. And he had finished the bottle with one of the neighbor boys. His father had found them, giggling and reeling in the hay. He had carried them both in, put them in the bath ... hot water. Steaming hot water and piny soap. And he had laughed and laughed. "Little likker head, you! Stay outta my barn when you go on a binge." Laughing. Hot. But the barn was a sweet place, a warm, secret place. And in the night, when a boy's sixteen and has a girl ... The pinch of boards on his back, the marrow-chilling delight of yielding lips, and the fumbling, the whispered directions ... firm, pointed breasts against his chest, the squeals and turnings and half-uttered protests. No face to remember. But the white, shining mound of her belly, the dimple of navel ... And the pigeons scolding from the rafters high above ...

He could not stand. He shook his head, blinking. Suppose, he thought, suppose I've been going in circles? Suppose I step on shore, and I'm back where I started? He fell again, lost his glasses, felt for them. "What's the trouble, Woody, you outta gas?" his father would say. Yes. Out of gas. And on my ass. Out of gas. On my ass. A pretty pass ... Just a minute now, gonna lie down, but just a minute ...

He closed his eyes; and at once he heard a sound. It was the click of a safety going off. His heart stood balanced on the brink of terror.

"Halt and give the password!"

The voice was only a few yards away. An American voice! He tried to speak, but the wind froze the words in his throat. At last, "GI," he croaked weakly. "GI." George Pappas was standing over the soldier. Woodrow Dorn saw the blurred visage staring at him. "Out of gas," he murmured, collapsing. "Pretty pass ..."

19

Able Company, gripped by cold and tension, began its third night on the isolated ridge, awaiting the onslaught of the enemy.

In the command post crater, Pat tried to sleep. He lay there in the darkness, watching the flare shadows ride over the jagged rocks above, hearing the constant drone of the wind, a sentry's challenge, Andy's uneven breathing. The day had seemed endless, pervaded by a sense of impending disaster that grew with each patrol's return, with each garbled report from an Army survivor, with each agonizing minute of unnatural quiet between devastating Chinese bombardments.

Burying his face in the lining of his sleeping bag, he closed his eyes and inventoried the situation yet once more. Two days had passed since Andy's patrol had spotted the Chinese, since Army stragglers had first wandered into the lines. Frostbite and wounds had cut the company's strength from 250 to 195. Those men were cold, hungry, with hands bleeding from futile digging, their bodies racked by exposure and sleeplessness. And they were spread thinly, without a reserve, over a 400-yard perimeter. Morphine was in short supply. The plasma was gone. The illuminating shells, which could help spot a night assault, were all but expended. Artillery, which could plague the enemy in his assembly area and disperse him in the open, was still out of range. Planes had been unable to fly in the snowstorms of the past few days.

There had been a series of terse messages from battalion. Two supply parties had come in. Another was on its way with replacements. Then the 300 radio had gone out again.

Pat's limbs ached. His weary body demanded sleep, but his taut nerves would not release him. The scrape of an entrenching tool, the muffled steps of men plodding by for brief haven in the warming-tent, the echo of distant gunfire, shook him, brought him back instantly from the edge of consciousness.

Choy appeared, nodded to him, then dropped to the snow. "Sanchez, you will wake me, please. In one half-hour. Then I will let Huckabee rest." He closed his eyes.

Pat got up. Sanchez was at his side at once. "Want to check the patrols coming in," Pat said. He covered Choy with his own sleeping bag. The interpreter looked up at him, and tugging the fabric around his neck, smiled wanly. Even so fleeting an acknowledgment surprised Pat. If for only an instant, the Korean seemed disarmed.

They passed Andy, who lay in untroubled sleep a few yards away, and climbed to the observation post. Huddling together out of the wind, they leaned against a canted pillar of rock, and searched the moonlit night. Somewhere out there was the enemy, an enemy who had waited two long nights, two longer days, and still withheld his assault.

The two men, hoods pulled tight around their faces, roamed the ridge together. They routed out an exhausted marine who had zipped himself into the straitjacket of his sleeping bag. They field-stripped another man's carbine, rubbing the parts until friction melted the film of ice and cleared the stoppage. They shared chunks of frozen fruit salad with a machine-gun crew. They listened to a corporal's suggestion that a two-man team move from hole to hole through the night, keeping at least one man awake at every position. Within an hour, Pat had the first team operating.

When George Pappas returned from patrol, they were waiting in his platoon C.P. "Nothing," the lieutenant said. "Not a damn' thing. Plenty of tracks, some of them within fifty yards of us. One place, near a narrow road, they'd used for a head. Two or three people, probably. Maybe observers for when they were clobbering us with those big guns." With both hands, he rubbed the frozen tip of his nose. "But not a sound. Not a light. Like they'd just taken off."

"Any ideas, George? Anything else you think we ought to do?"

"We're doing everything we can. You did a damn' fine job organizing the ground. You think maybe they pulled out, bypassed us?" Pat clung to the moment of praise. Andy had only grudgingly agreed to his changes in the defense. This was the first statement of outright approval he could recall since he took over the company. It buoyed his confidence. "No. I don't think they pulled out. We're too big an outfit on too big a piece of terrain, planted right in their path. We've got observation from here that commands the whole area. They know that. Once we get air and artillery support, we can bottle up any big movement. They know that, too."

"Then where are they?"

Ten minutes later, when Pat and Sanchez sat with Stringbean Allison in his platoon command post, the same question was repeated. "What goes with the goonies? Where are they?"

Pat hunched his shoulders. "The longer they hold off, the better chance we have of beefing up."

"I don't know," Allison said, frowning. "We're hurting with the cold, Captain. Frostbite. Malfunction of weapons. And our people can't go on eating and drinking as they have been. There'll be so many cases of fluid drive around here ..."

Huckabee had told Pat the same thing. "But the Chinks are cold, too," Pat said. "Probably colder."

"Captain, they any colder than me, they're peein' ice cubes," Sanchez said.

Pat got to his feet. It was time to catch Cagle's patrol. Sanchez went with him. As they walked across the ridge, Pat thought about Allison. A kid himself, no more than twenty-two. And a regular officer. He would spend his life killing, or preparing to kill, or teaching others to kill. But then, he mused, which of us won't? The drafting board, the T-square, the specifications, the blueprints, the petty arguments and frustrations of his work seemed part of another existence. I've spent two years at my profession, he thought. And twice that being a marine. They stopped to rest after a long climb. "What do you do on the outside?" he asked Sanchez.

"This is the only full-time job I ever had," Sanchez said.

"What are you going to do?"

"I don't know, sir. Thought about it, but I just don't know." Chuck Cagle had constructed a shelter by hanging a poncho over two boulders, and packing the top with snow. Pat and Sanchez crawled in after the lieutenant. "Not as cozy as my nest in the Village," Cagle said. "But it'll do." He lit Pat's cigarette. "Man, I'd like to get in a tub of hot water, soak in it for an hour, get myself doused with shaving lotion, put on a shirt so starched I'd have to fight my way into the sleeves, mix up a vodka martini ..."

"What did you see out there, Chuck?"

"Absolutely nothing." He held his cigarette close to his face. "There are signs of them, all right. Footprints. Comm wire. Scraps of chow. But no goonies."

"Hear anything?"

"I'll tell you, Captain. I had eight men out with me. And every one, at one time or another, swore he heard something. I didn't. It's even colder out there. Everything's in boldface. It's like the wind's in italics. And there's a smell to the snow. You think you hear something, but it's only your own heart beating. A guy swallows, you can hear it."

Pat ducked his cigarette. "I don't know what else to do. Don't want to send anyone any farther out."

"Nothing to do but wait."

At that moment Goober thrust his head into the opening. "Supply party just got in. Message for you."

While the first sergeant held matches for him, Pat read the form. Not even in his imagination had he envisioned such news. The battalion, now with the two regiments at Yudam-ni, was withdrawing. As they had feared, the enemy threatened to cut off the scattered marine units; and the division was forced to regroup, to pull back to Hagaru. Able Company would remain in position while the others moved down behind them. No word on eventual withdrawal.

"Think I oughta wake Lieutenant Anderson, sir? He might want to talk to ..."

Pat hesitated. Before he could reply, Cagle said, "Anybody who can sleep now deserves it. No need to wake him."

"Of course not," Pat said. "I want to see the man that brought this."

They hurried to the aid station. There Goober took charge of the mortar shells, medical supplies, warming-tent, stove and machine-gun belts that had just arrived. Sitting in the shelter of the wrecked cart,

Pat questioned the sergeant who led the supply party. "Where are my replacements? They told me you'd bring in some men."

The sergeant spat tobacco juice, then covered the stain. "Don't know about that, sir. Called me from chow, told me to take these here yobos, and load some gear. Seems they got word from Yudam-ni."

"Didn't you come from First Battalion?"

"No, sir. First Marines. Hagaru. Chinks got roadblocks between here and Yudam-ni. Scuttlebutt is the Fifth and Seventh are gonna have to fight their way down." He pointed to the Korean laborers who were bunched before the entrance of the warming-tent. "Damn' near ran into a Chink patrol gettin' here. Had to sit on the gooks. They was hot to trot."

"The Chinese are operating in the rear?"

"Just small outfits mostly, I guess. But they say the hills stink with 'em."

Pat realized that the situation was even worse than he had understood from the message. Two regiments were cut off above him. It would take time for them to fight their way back down the road to Hagaru. He was expected to hold, probably with little help. "They promised us those men. They promised us!" he said. Then, noticing the sergeant staring at him, he said, "Thanks. You did damn' well to get to us. Better saddle up and get moving."

"Yes, sir. It's two miles to where we meet the trucks, four more to Hagaru."

The wounded were being led or carried from the tent. Huckabee had unpacked some of his supplies, and was giving morphine. "Don't look good, does it?" It was- Goober, standing beside Pat. "I got the pitch from the sergeant."

"If only we were up to strength ..."

"Got a hell of a lot of ground to cover. We cave in anyplace, there's nothing to counterattack with." Goober pulled at his ear, thinking. "Might take most of the mortar section, use them in the line ..."

"Could make a reserve out of them," Pat said. "That's a damn' good idea, Top." The possibility excited him. It offered some hope of resolving at least one problem. "Now, if we had even a few more to send to the platoons ..."

"How about putting some of the walking wounded back in? Hell, as long as they can shoot ..."

"Top, you should have come up with this before! How many walking wounded, including the Army people, do we have going out?"

"Ill check with Choy," Goober said, pleased. "He's got the list."

"I forgot to wake him," Sanchez said.

"Well, go get him, knucklehead!"

By the time Goober and Pat had worked out their plan and called The Horse to a meeting at the C.P., Sanchez was back. "Fifteen doggies going out. Nine of ours," he said, breathlessly. "And Choy and Lieutenant Anderson are on the way."

Pat walked among the men, ignoring those who lay unconscious or groaning or sedated on the stretchers. A marine was talking to a soldier who stared as if he could not see. Another man was catching snowflakes on his tongue, grinning stupidly. Marines and soldiers supported one another. "Some of 'em are bad shook," Goober said. "Doggies had a real rough go."

"I'm asking for volunteers," Pat said to the men. "We need everyone we can get to help us hold on here for a few days. Then we'll all go back together." There was no response. Of the twelve standing, not one looked at him.

Then a marine, a rifleman who had lost a finger, walked to the pile of weapons and selected a rifle. "What the hell, I'll stay," he grumbled. "Can you use that hand?"

"Sure he can," Goober said. "He's in swell shape. Still got his trigger finger."

The marine made the traditional "Semper Fi" gesture. "And my social finger," he said. Laughter.

Mel Firesteen hobbled up. "I don't volunteer, dammit. But there's nothin' wrong with me but a sore ass."

Pat was about to refuse when Andy stepped up. "Okay, Firesteen. You going to be gung-ho, get back to your outfit."

The two men started off, Firesteen leaning on the other marine, limping. He stopped and spoke to the supply sergeant. "How about gettin' some mail up here, Sarge?" Without awaiting a reply, he clambered up the ridge.

Pat walked among the soldiers. "Well, how about it?"

Andy called him aside. "A bunch of doggies aren't gonna be worth a damn. But if you want them that bad, stick them in a hole. Don't ask questions."

Pat approached the men again. "Any of you willing to pitch in?"

A tall, stoop-shouldered Negro sergeant stepped forward. "I'd stay, sir. But wouldn't be much use. I'm in motor transport."

"Thanks," Pat said. "Give your name to the first sergeant. Top, send him to the machine-gun section with the first platoon."

"You're asking for trouble," Andy muttered. "One of these pogues starts running, some of our people are liable to get up and follow."

"How about you?" Pat asked the next man in line. "What do you do?" .

The man stammered something unintelligible. He seemed nervous, ill at ease, like a new boy at school. "I lost my glasses, Captain. I don't see too good with my left eye." He looked at his feet.

Pat thought he might cry. To give him time to recover, he said, "What's your name?"

"Pfc. Woodrow Dorn, sir. If you ... want me, I'm a radio operator."

"Good. We need one badly. Sanchez, take care of Dorn. He'll stand listening-post watch with you. Right now see what he can do with the 300."

Pat worked down the line. Of the eight still standing, five offered to stay. He accepted three of them. As they walked off to the depleted units above, Andy watched them. "We're sure as hell going to have trouble from them," he told Goober.

"I don't think so," Pat said, overhearing him.

The supply sergeant yelled at the Koreans. They picked up the litters and stood waiting. Pat sent back a message on his strength and situation, requested an air drop of new radios, stretchers, blankets, warming-tents, stoves, and additional ammunition. The group moved off into the night.

Pat, Andy, and Goober started for the command post. "Wally gave me the scoop on what gives at Yudam-ni," Andy said. "Didn't I tell you something like this was going to happen?"

"Sure did," Goober said. "Weeks ago."

They stopped on the path, let Huckabee and Choy pass them, and watched as they laid the twenty-fourth body among the dead. The corpsman let his burden slip down, and left it. "Mr. Allison's runner," he said as he returned to the aid station. Choy forced the stiff arms to bend, crossed them over the torn chest, and packed snow on the edges of the covering poncho. When the others walked by, he looked up at them, but did not speak.

Pat stretched out on his sleeping bag. He looked at his watch. "It's 0210. That's four hours and fifteen minutes since they last worked us over with artillery. You'd think, if they were coming, they'd move up under a concentration..."

Andy said, "They'll come."

20

Jesus Sanchez came awake like any creature of the night, instantly aware, tensed for action. Woodrow Dorn, speechless with fear, was pointing to a clump of poplars that stood a hundred yards beyond the listening post. Sanchez stared, blinked, stared again. An illuminating flare rode overhead, briefly turning night to day. He watched for movement, the glint of metal, regular shapes on the irregular terrain. Nothing. "Where?" he asked. The wind was silent for a moment, and the whisper sounded like a growl in the stillness.

The skinny arm was extended again. Sanchez looked down it at the field of snow, the swaying trees tipped in moonlight. He spoke in the soldier's ear. "That's the second time you woke me in ten minutes. There's nothin' there, dammit. Nothin' but snow and trees and a few rocks and bushes." Dorn's teeth were chattering. "Now stay loose. Don't get so clutched up!" Cuddling his rifle, Sanchez held the sound phone to his ear. "I'm gonna crap out, doggie," he whispered. "You hear somethin' or see somethin'—really somethin'—you shake me." There was no answer. Sanchez sat up again. "You all right?" Dorn swallowed visibly. Sanchez shook his head. "Fer cryin' out loud, doggie, why don'tcha say somethin'? With this wind, nobody's gonna hear a whisper."

"How far are we ... from the others?"

"Fifty, maybe sixty yards." He stifled a yawn. "We got it made. If we spot the goonies, we call company, pull the phone, and haul ass back to Bad Girl." He leaned against the bank again and closed his eyes...

Dorn touched his sleeve immediately. "I don't see too well out of one eye."

"Look sharp with the good one."

The soldier slipped into the shadow of a rock, and fixed his gaze on the front. In a moment he was over Sanchez again. "The bug-out route. Nobody told me where it is."

Sanchez groaned, and propped himself on his elbow. "What the hell's that?"

"Where ... you bug out, pull back. We always had a bug-out route in advance ..."

"You mean run? Turn tail?"

"If we're outnumbered," Dorn said, hesitantly, afraid that he had blundered. "If things get too tough ... and we have to take off."

"We're never outnumbered. And things don't get that tough. You get that crap outta your head, doggie. Get any ideas like that around here, and somebody's liable to put a bullet up your butt! Here we are and here we stay, 'til told different. Now, stop actin' like a gutless wonder and let me sleep. You had yours."

The soldier was trembling, his face within inches of Sanchez's. "I'm no coward," he said. He fought back the quaver in his throat. "Don't you say I'm a coward!"

Sanchez was instantly contrite. "I didn't mean you was yella," he whispered, reaching out to touch Dorn's arm. Dorn recoiled. "Hell, doggie, you ... aw, will you stop the blubberin'?" The soldier moved away, and Sanchez finally slid over to him. "A guy that had enough guts to come out over that reservoir on his own ... why, hellfire, you got plenty of guts, doggie." No answer. "What's your name?"

"Woodrow Dorn."

"That what they call you?"

He took a deep breath. Everyone had always called him Woodrow, except his father. "Woody, if you want."

"Okay, Woody. Mine's Sanchez, Jesus Sanchez. The guys call me Goat." He smiled, and his teeth gleamed in the moonlight. "You want me to shoot the breeze with you?"

The soldier shook his head. "I'll do my turn."

"I don't mind. Hell, I ain't tired."

"No."

"Okay."

Another illuminating shell burst overhead. Sanchez unhooked his chin strap and lay down again, pillowing his tangled, curly hair on his helmet liner. He's shook real bad, he thought. Had a rugged time. Looking at the soldier, he saw that he was leaning forward, his eyes straining into the darkness. "Nobody's gonna leave you, Woody. I don't leave you. And you don't leave me. Okay?"

Dorn looked at Sanchez's face, dark and full of power, and somehow it reassured him. "Okay."

"We get relieved in forty-five minutes," Sanchez said. "You call me for sure in twenty-five."

"No watch," Dorn whispered. "They took it."

Sanchez removed his wrist watch and handed it to the soldier. Two weeks before, he remembered, he had taken it back from the Chinese he had killed. That damned watch. It seemed that everything, even his being here, in Korea, had started with that watch. He stretched, then huddled in the lee of the bank. He did not sleep.

The street light on the comer, lighting his barren world and the world of Central Park West. Filth on the edge of luxury, rotting tenements where boys played stickball on the steaming asphalt streets, cursed the cab drivers, snatched pocketbooks in the park at night, stole tires from parked cars, seduced their cousins, and had gang shags on the roof, screening themselves with clothes borrowed from the sagging lines. ("Not you, Jesus. You and me, we're not animals. We'll go to church and look in the windows on Broadway, and have ten-cent orangeade at Nedicks, and stay out of trouble.")

And all about them, the mangy, scabby dogs, children eaten by flies, and beaten by the older children. The faces of the women, grown old too soon, with sunken eyes, twisted mouths, hair hanked in greasy strands, hand-wiped, brat-wiped aprons. The smells of boiling laundry and dirty diapers and cheap liquor and rancid meat and broken plumbing. ("Listen to your sister, Jesus. While I work, you go to school and learn your lessons.")

The policeman is your friend. All men are equal. God is good. New York is the biggest city in the world. Swallow chewing gum and seeds, you get appendicitis. America is a melting pot. Abraham Lincoln was born in a log cabin. Honesty is the best policy. The battle of Hastings was in 1066. Benjamin Franklin tied a key on a kite tail and invented electricity. You are your brother's keeper ...

There was always the refuge of the church, the cleanliness, the quiet, the regal splendor and richness. He would wait in line before the confessional, drop back, give away his place, only to remain a little longer. But in time you had to go back to the squalor, the filth, the ugliness, the misery, the inhumanity of men feeding upon one another. His people, against their nature and their will, were molded by cunning and cruelty and vice. They had come from a simple land, were simple people. And they had been infected with the city-bred disease. The floors, ceilings, sills, walls, steps, roofs, streets, were impregnated with the bitterness of their lives.

He remembered little about his father. Only that he was dark and wore his hair long around his ears, and had a way of pinching you on the cheek, and could sing bass, and smoked long, thin black cigars. He thought of him, always, upside down. He would come home from school. And his father would still be sleeping before going on the night shift. Jesus would look in on him, see his face, upside down, the mouth where the eyes should be... In his coffin, he had been that way, too.

Upside down ... The priest was young and had a scar on one cheek, and could tell you DiMaggio's batting average.

Sanchez's mother, in her last years, used to hold his head between her thighs, and beat him with a wet towel, cursing in Spanish, sweating, eyes wild, and the thin stain of snuff dripping from the comers of her mouth. Then, weeping, kissing him, making him promise to stay away from those bad boys, to go to communion, to learn his lessons. ("She's dead and better off, Jesus. I'll take care of you. The two of us. We'll amount to something.") His sister's love had been another sanctuary; and he repaid her with fanatic devotion.

And life was better. His sister worked. He went to school. On Saturday nights, they would eat roast beef on Times Square, and then walk across to Fifth Avenue, to St. Patrick's. Then she had to work at night; and he saw too little of her.

But there was more money. Trips to Coney Island in August. The girls with dirty underwear you bribed to go under the boardwalk. The clop-clop of feet above, the heavy breathing and the smell of the ocean and the musky smell of sex, and the feel of sweaty flesh and sand grit, and afterward you couldn't stand the sight of the thin little mouth and the hollow cheeks. So you lost her. And you bought a hot dog at Nathan's and listened to the man who sold soap and proved the brands were no good, and leaned against the facade of the Half Moon Hotel, watching the rich get pushed in wicker chairs, and found you still had enough left for the subway and a combination ticket to Steeplechase.

And once, when he wanted to buy a birthday gift for his sister, he listened to the other boys, followed their directions. For two hours he hung around the park, waiting for a queer to make a pass at him, so he could mug him. But no one came by. Only a woman in a car with a right-hand steering wheel, and she gave him five dollars for changing her tire. And he knew it was God's will he should not sin. And he gave himself his own penance. (Fifty Hail Marys and fifty Our Fathers, said before he slept that night.) The next day he lit candles for his mother and father, and bought his sister a red cloth pocketbook and a red scarf and red gloves. And when she wore them, she was very beautiful and made him take ten dollars and kissed him and cried.

And later ... Later, there was the watch ...

Between sleep and waking, Sanchez groaned. Dorn glanced at him, restrained an impulse to muffle the sound, and began to search the night once more. There was over a hundred yards of flat terrain. Then a clump of poplars. Forty yards away, on the right, was a road that lead to the reservoir, the road he had come over two nights before. Far off, another mountain rose out of the snow. And the moon sat atop it.

He saw a mound out in the darkness, beside the road. Or it could be a man, bent over. Cautiously, fearing what he might discover, he looked away, then quickly looked back again, as if to trap it. But it had not moved. And yet, there were two mounds now. Where had the other come from? Surely it had not been there before! He leaned forward, peering across the glistening snow. He would keep his eyes on those mounds. The enemy could be coming up the road, infiltrating, standing right there, watching ...

Fifteen minutes passed. His eyes were watering. He held his hand over the broken lens. He was lucky to be there, he told himself, lucky to have survived at all, to have had food and hours of sleep and warmth. All he had to do was to stay for a little longer. Then they would be relieved, and he could go back with the others. Maybe he could get the radio to work. He wanted to do that, to prove his worth. To himself. He had wanted to be evacuated with the others, but the captain had reminded him of his own lieutenant, and he could not refuse. He felt, vaguely, that he owed the captain something. He closed his eyes to rest them for a moment.

Near the road two mounds rose, stepped forward. Bushes before the poplars came alive, moved. From behind a line of pine trees, shadows emerged, melted into the snow.

The casing on an illuminating shell burst above. The snap awakened the soldier. At once he realized he had dozed off. How long? He looked at Sanchez, and sighed with relief when he saw that he was apparently asleep. Then, frantically, he stared out at the snow. His eyes riveted on a rock. Or was it a bush? He had not seen it before. Arms? Or branches? A man, crouching, with rifle extended? It moved! Or was the wind bending it? He looked away for a second, then back to the road. The mounds had disappeared! His mind reeled. My God! They were there, two of them. And now they're not there! He searched, desperately. Of course. They were on this side of the road. Or were they? Had they been on the other side at first? Or was it a trick of moonlight?

He wanted to wake Sanchez. But he had to be sure. It could be his imagination, he thought. He tried to recall all the detail he had memorized at the beginning of his watch. Hie distances. The spaces between tree and bush and rock and road. How many mounds were there? And on what side of the road? And that scrub growth before the clump of pines, why hadn't he noticed that before? He thought he heard the sound of footsteps sloshing in snow. But the whine of the wind deceived him. Wake Sanchez, he told himself. The company is dependent on a warning, your warning.

He counted five mounds along the road. Now he was sure there had only been two. But they were stationary. Three were up the road. Perhaps he hadn't remembered them. He waited for the next illuminating shell, heard the thump of the mortar, saw the projectile arch like a streaming meteor, heard the casing blow. The flare rode high above, floating gently, lighting the night with dazzling brilliance. Just before it died, he thought he saw movement from the corner of his eye, and turned to face it. On the road. He caught his breath. His stomach churned with nervousness. Another mound had moved. Surely it had moved. But everything was still. He waited for another flare. Still another. One more, and then I'll count to fifty, he promised himself. And then I'll wake him. One more flare ...

Pat shook the bottle of plasma, but flakes of ice choked the neck, and only a trickle ran through the tube. He edged closer to the stove in the center of the tent, and pinched the rubber. "Should we try another?"

Choy and Allison were squatting beside an unconscious marine on a stretcher. The interpreter looked up. "They are all the same. Frozen." Andy came in, and Pat made room for him by the stove. "I told Huckabee to pitch this tent beside the other one," Andy said. "What was the idea of moving it into the C.P., and having two aid stations nearly a hundred yards apart?"

"Thought it best to disperse them," Pat said. "Goober's helping Huck at the other tent. Choy's going to take charge here."

Andy broke a board off an ammunition box and fed the fire. "Too damn' many people trooping through the C.P."

Pat wasn't listening. He was turning the bottle of plasma in his hands, trying to force the liquid. "Doesn't seem to do any good."

"It does not matter," Choy said. "This one will die anyway."

"But it's only a leg wound," Allison said.

"Shock," Andy said. "Some of them are torn apart and sheer guts keep them alive. Some, like this one, go—" He snapped his fingers. "Like that!"

Choy withdrew the needle. "The great pity is that they die without even knowing for what they are dying." He took the bottle from Pat. "That is the great advantage the enemy has over you."

Without answering, Pat took water to the only other wounded man in the tent. He raised the marine's head and let him suck thirstily at the canteen.

"No time for thinking about causes and issues," Allison said. "You're too damn' busy just trying to stay alive."

"Hell, if you start thinking, really thinking ..." Pat shrugged impatiently and came back to the stove. "This is the whole world. Right here. Nothing else. Punch-drunk fighters on either side, slugging it out."

"And the rest of the world sits in the stands, cheering for their side between gulps of pop, bags of peanuts, and time out for the comfort station." Andy rubbed burn ointment over the thin line of his lips. "Nobody much gives a damn as long as it's somebody else in the ring."

"I think you're wrong there," Allison said. "We're here for a reason, and even the people who don't have to do anything but watch know it."

"All right, Stringbean," Andy said, holding his hands over the stove. "A Regular always finds good reason for a war. There are always some eggheads like you who need slogans on their battle flags. I'm talking about the public."

"So am I," Allison said. "My dad's no Regular. And he's no egghead. He's a mechanic for Buick at Flint. And he wrote me, right after I got over ..." He squinted as he tried to remember the words. "The idea was, this is maybe the most important war ever. 'There's got to be some law and order in the world'—that's the way he put it."

"Then your old man's an exception," Andy said. "Let's face it. The people at home don't give a damn about the issues. How many of them are worrying about the state of the world? How many of them have any conception, even the smallest conception, of what the hell it's like to fight anything—a war or an idea or just some bastard that's pushing them around?"

As Andy spoke, Pat considered Bill Patrick, civilian. A little over two months before, how much had he cared? Of course, he had wanted the enemy defeated. He had been concerned when the UN forces clung to the tiny perimeter at Pusan, regretted the casualties. But he had thought of it as a useless war. He remembered telling Ann just that. It wasn't a war for practical ends. Now, despite that, he felt his personal stake in the outcome was part of a larger stake. "I don't believe ..." He changed his tack, and started again. "Even if you don't actually put it in words, or even consciously think about it, you still know we stand for something. I mean, it's like ... you don't sit around talking about patriotism or honor or courage or duty ... but that doesn't mean those things don't exist."

"Do they?" Choy said.

Pat ignored the question. "Let's get out of here," he said. "They'll be coming down from the platoons." The others followed him outside, shivering in the first blast of the icy wind. They hunched together against one side of the crater.

"We were talking about the great American public, the home front," Andy said, his voice heavy with sarcasm. "You know what their trouble is? They're soft. Stinking, pudgy, soft. They're looking for an easy way. An easy way to wash their dishes, clean their cars, or fight their wars."

"What do you want them to do?" Allison said, massaging the back of his neck. "Get shot at because we are, freeze because we are ..."

"You don't get the point," Andy said. "I just want them to know and to give a damn. But they don't know and they don't care. Because it doesn't touch them. Hell, do you think there's one in a hundred thousand that understands what this kind of cold is? The coldest thing they can imagine is a walk-in refrigerator in a butcher shop— and I'd be tickled to death to sleep in one tonight! Or they think cold is State Street in Chicago during a January blizzard. Or an ice-cream freezer. Or damp fingers on a windshield. Christ! Twenty below? Means nothing."

"Don't forget, Andy, damn' near everybody has someone over here," Pat said.

"Oh, no, they haven't! And if they've got a kid in service, drafted, of course, then Mama and Daddy'll be pissed off if the Army doesn't make sonny a cook or a radio repairman or a medical technician— anything but a soldier. That's what's wrong with us. Nobody wants to fight. So, the Army gives them lectures on democracy instead of night combat, on how to use a pro instead of scouting and patrolling, on Jap customs instead of how to cut a throat. Those are the kids they sent MacArthur, and expected him to fight a war!"

"That's all a hell of a generalization," Pat said.

"The Army managed pretty well in Normandy, in Italy, in Germany," Allison said.

"Sure, last time around they were given the stuff, and they produced. Last time everybody was involved. Not this Korean clambake. The public murdered those half-trained, confused, helpless kids who were slaughtered last summer, and those who got it across the reservoir the other night. The Corps is lucky. It's small enough to go its own way most of the time. We take the same kind of kid and jam discipline down his throat. We work him until he's dizzy. We knock some of the ego out of him, make him think about something bigger and more important than himself—The Corps, the men around him, Semper Fi."

"Like Cagle said the other day, we brainwash their old ideas, and pour in new ones!" Pat laughed. "That's supposed to be a Communist tactic." Choy came out of the tent. Pat moved to make room for him, but the interpreter sat beside the marine manning the phones.

"What I'm getting at," Andy said, "is that our people will stick and fight. Not because of a bunch of phony idealistic drivel. But because they're marines. They don't care about the rest."

"The Chinese care," Choy said.

"How about you?" Andy asked. "What are you fighting for? Right now. For issues? A cause?"

The Korean leaned toward them. But he spoke so softly that the others strained to hear him over the wind. "Wars are won by determined men." His voice was lost for a moment ... if you have no cause, no cause for which you are willing to lay down your life, you are certain to lose. The fanatics, the beasts will win."

"The question," Pat said, "is which is preferable, Choy. Us with all our faults, or the fanatics?"

"No, Captain. The question is who will prevail?"

A sergeant, followed by a file of marines, entered the command post. "Eighteen men, sir. Horse sent 'em for our reserve. I've briefed em."

Pat got up. "Okay. Have them drop their gear. Might as well use the tent while there's room."

Andy came up beside him. "I don't think much of this idea, Pat. These people ought to be on line where we can use them, not sitting down here..."

"I've thought it all out," Pat said. He was no longer so positive about the plan, not since Andy had criticized it. But he had made his decision in front of the others, and he was determined to follow it. "Keep these people here," he said to the sergeant. "If they're needed, I'll decide where they should be committed, and call for them."

"Nothing you can plan," Andy said. "You ought to have learned that much by now. It's like being a manager in the World Series. Whether you give a man an intentional pass depends on his batting average, on first being open, on the number of outs, who's up next, and the score." He smoothed his beard without taking his eyes from Pat's face. "All the books you've read aren't enough. You've got to play it by ear. If you don't, if you make one mistake, you lose the ball game."

The marine at the phone was suddenly alert. He called Pat. "Post two. Firesteen. Lieutenant Pappas' outfit. They see movement on the right flank."

No sooner had he spoken than two shots sounded. Red and green tracers flashed by on the left, then on the right, marking the flanks of Bad Girl Ridge. Before their light had faded, a shepherd's horn wailed, its tinny voice raucous in the stillness.

Pat was rooted in awful fascination. Allison was up immediately, running toward his position. Choy went to the warming-tent. Andy started across the crater. Pat grabbed his 536 radio, and followed.

"You stay here," Andy said. "Check the listening posts. See that they're withdrawn. Tell the platoons to hold fire until they've got targets. Have the mortars stand by. I'll be in touch with you."

"I'm going forward."

They stood facing each other. Andy put his hand on Pat's shoulder. "This is all new to you. And it's no time for learning," he said, looking up at him. "Now do as I say, huh?" Before Pat could answer, Andy was running toward the crest.

The horn sounded again. Pat instructed the man on phone watch to make his calls. "I'm going to the OP. You can reach me there."

A few scattered shots rang out. Both men looked up. Then, from somewhere out in the night, what sounded like a thousand voices, growing louder, coming closer, screamed, *"Sha! Sha! Shaa-aa!"*

"Means 'kill' in English," the marine said.

21

Moonlight dripped over the rock pillar in the observation post, casting a black finger of shadow across the breast of Bad Girl Ridge. Pat lay there, his long body trembling with cold, his bowels shaken with excitement, his mind acutely aware of sound and range, movement and direction.

The shepherd's horn blew again, closer this time, its tuneless blast eerie in the night. An emerald streak erupted from the darkness and arched toward the defenders. A green flare burst above, rocked gently, and floated back, coating the scene in a ghastly hue, weaving grotesque patterns in the snow. Tracers whipped the flanks once more; and a ragged line emerged from trees and knolls and shellholes and underbrush. Pat turned to The Horse, who was hunched over, sitting with his huge hands between his knees. "Fire your barrage!"

The enemy rushed ahead. Mortars smashed above them. The line was severed. Still the remnants came on. "Walk the fire back to us. Walk it back!"

"Weather's funny with ammo, Captain," The Horse said. "Don't want to clobber our own."

The Chinese had formed again. They were ninety yards away. Eighty. "Keep one tube hot with illuminating," Pat called to the sergeant. A flare burst above them. Seventy. Sixty yards. Christ, only sixty yards! "Fire! Fire!" Pat was standing, screaming to his men below. But the only sound to answer him was *"Sha! Sha!"* All across the valley, for four hundred yards, the advancing line, like a sidewinder, wiggled and whipped forward. To within fifty yards. And coming on. *"Sha-a-a!"* And Pat was screaming with them. "Fire!"

He heard Andy's voice above his own, above the yells of the attackers, above the quavering bugle call. "Semper Fi!"

Able Company replied. On the left, Pat saw Allison's men—black motes on the white face of Bad Girl. Then the breast below him, with Cagle's platoon clinging to its slopes. Pappas's troops were to his right, across the belly and thigh. Together they lashed back at the charging horde, sending interlocking bands of tracers into the night.

The enemy was climbing, scrabbling up, crawling, throwing grenades, firing burp guns. Behind them another chant began: "Sonovabitch marines we kill! Sonovabitch marines you die!"

Pat was struck by the unreality of it. He lay motionless, his radio silent, feeling utterly remote.

The second wave appeared, surging forward, inundating the flat-land. Though mortars scooped at it, and flame and steel hissed above and the tempo of fire increased, the wave rolled on, not slowing at all, and crashed against the battlements. Relentless. Relentless. Pat seized upon the word, repeated it to himself. What purpose, what cause could drive men on like that?

Below him a machine gun chattered viciously. A grenade exploded, and both gunner and assistant slumped forward. The Negro motor-transport man, who had volunteered to remain, pulled the bodies aside, crouched behind the gun, fired. But the enemy was close in now, swarming over the rocks below, working their way toward the weapon. "Swing it free," Pat yelled as the soldier fired it in fixed position. The gun jammed. The soldier began to bang futilely on it, shouting at the man beside him. It was leaving dead space below, and the Chinese were funneling into the free area. Pat pointed the spot to The Horse. "Call it in. Got to take a chance. Only way," he shouted breathlessly. "Hurry!"

"Only six men left down there to handle the mortars, sir."

It took two agonizingly long minutes for The Horse to adjust the fire. "On the way, Captain."

"Take cover!" Pat yelled. Then the shell blasted a geyser of snow and rock and mud and weapons and Chinese bodies. Still the enemy climbed frantically toward the jammed gun. Men on the flanks held them off with grenades while two marines tried to clear the stoppage.

Pat left the shelter of the OP. Sliding, falling, he ran toward the gun. Its crew was clawing the earth as burp guns sprayed the area. Pat shoved the men aside. Then, automatically, calling on skill he had first learned in the sawdust of a hillside gun-shed in Quantico six years before, remembering with uncanny detail the drill he had memorized only weeks ago, he lifted the cover of the heavy gun. Then he extracted a ruptured cartridge, tested the belt feed, slammed the bolt forward again. He freed the weapon, swung it in traverse, and sprayed the climbers below. Within fifty yards, the second wave was charging in to join the first. "Take it!" Pat shouted. The soldier thanked him solemnly, moved beside him, began to swat the enemy like flies on a wall.

"*Sha! Sha!*" Out in the darkness, a third wave was gathering. The shepherd's horn blared its signal. This time a longer wail, a more urgent summons. As they drew closer, Pat saw that most of them were unarmed, that they stopped beside the dead and took up their weapons, that some had reached the base of the ridge, still screaming, determined to wrest a weapon from the defenders. The wave grew, joined the backwash of the others, swept against the battered defenses.

Pat moved toward the observation post to call for mortars again. He saw two men wedged in the same hole, heads down, rifles between their legs. "Get up and fire!" he stormed at them. They did not respond. He pulled them out bodily, shook them and shoved them toward the front. "Fire, damn you!" One got off a shot. Then the other. They began to fire more rapidly, easing forward to seek out better targets. Their moment of panic had passed. Pat got to his knees and crawled toward the rocks.

A wounded man lay there, blood coursing from his shrapnel-torn shoulder, crying, "Corpsman ... Corpsman ..."

Pat took a morphine syrette from his armpit where he had taped it, and injected the drug. The mortars he had called in had been impartial; he had maimed one of his own. The man might die because ... He rejected the idea and called another marine. "Get him to the aid station."

"Lieutenant Anderson said no one was to leave the lines, sir."

"Take him down!"

"Aye, aye, sir."

He climbed to his OP, and fell beside The Horse, panting for breath. The marine he had left in his command post was waiting for him, staring wide-eyed at the carnage below.

"Sir, Sanchez and that doggie. They didn't get in. They're out there someplace."

"Was getting ready to wake you. Not my fault ... Can't see too good ... Wasn't sure..."

Sanchez clapped a hand over Dorn's mouth, and pulled him down beside him. A Chinese officer was walking toward them, leading a column of troops. He stopped a few yards away and yelled at his men, gesturing first toward the ridge, then toward the flank. The Chinese slogged off through the snow.

Woody held his breath. He could hear the chatter of the enemy, the crash of mortars, the frantic stutter of automatic weapons. Everything seemed maddeningly familiar.

Sanchez released him, crawled to the lip of the shell hole, and looked out after the disappearing column. They were sixty yards from the lines, and moving parallel to the position. While the marines were heavily engaged on the front, these Chinese were stealing past them, sweeping wide to envelop the position from the rear! He slipped down beside Dorn and explained the tactic. "C'mon, we've gotta get back."

"Can't now. They're behind us and in front of us. They don't get us, we'll never make it through our lines. Our own people will ..."

"They hit in the rear, our guys'll get slaughtered."

"Sonovabitch marines we kill! Sonovabitch marines you die!" The chant was rising from the front as the third wave rolled against the lines. A marine mortar exploded behind them. Both men pressed themselves to the frozen earth. Shrapnel whined overhead.

"No use," Dorn moaned.

"Gotta try." Sanchez unhooked the sound phone from the mortar-severed wire. "We'll separate. I'm gonna try to get in on the flank. You go in at Lieutenant Cagle's position. That grazin' fire's got the goonies discouraged, so you might slip through there. When you get close enough, just yell out who you are. Tell them the Chinks are movin' around to the rear ..."

But Dorn was shaking his head. "Why can't we go together?"

"This way we got two chances. One of us'll make it for sure. Just keep movin'. You run into Chinks, stay doggo."

"You said we'd stick together. You weren't gonna leave."

"Get goin'," Sanchez said gruffly. Then he rolled out of the shell hole.

Dorn looked after him. He was already a third of the way. Suddenly, he fell in the snow, inert. Boots were sloshing out in the darkness. The Chinese officer was back. Dorn could hear him cursing a man, kicking him to his feet, sending him forward. Then he could see him beside Sanchez, so close that his shadow fell across the marine. Dorn watched, afraid to breathe. He told himself to leave, to go forward. But he could not force himself to move.

He gazed dazedly at the crumpled shadow in the snow. The Chinese officer paced nervously back and forth, yelling at his men as they passed. Sanchez was on his knees behind the officer, moving only under the deafening sound of gunfire. Dorn's muscles reacted to each motion.

Now! Sanchez was up, on the man's back, an arm around his neck to cut off the scream. The two figures rolled in the snow. Dorn watched, horrified, heard the grunts and the scuffling amazingly amplified in the brief silences between the sounds of battle. He had no doubt about the outcome. Sanchez would win. But even as he assured himself, he saw the Chinese pull free, saw the weapon, saw the marine fall under the blow. There was more thrashing, a horrible groan. Dorn flinched in an agony of pain as the enemy stood over Sanchez and kicked him. Once. Twice. Again. Then the officer walked toward Dorn, calling for men to take a prisoner.

Dorn crouched, petrified, as the man approached. Fear expanded in him, filled his chest so that breathing seemed impossible, weighed against his bladder. He wet himself, not knowing it. Then the two men were looking at each other. Dorn in his hole, the officer directly above him. His weapon, a pistol, shone in the moonlight. Driven by instinct, Dorn grabbed the officer's boots, heard the bullet whistle past his ear as the Chinese fell on top of him. Dorn rolled aside and tried to stand, his ears ringing with the explosion. The Chinese kicked with both feet, driving him across the narrow hole. He tasted blood. His face was wet with it. The man was on top of him, pummeling him. Dorn slumped and awaited the inevitable. The man spat on him.

All the humiliations, all the fear and anger he had known in all of his life, rose in Dorn and choked him, impelling him to fight. He lashed out at his adversary, caught him off balance, threw him down, rolled him over, grasped his head by the hair, and smashed it against the rocks. The officer tried to fight back, tried to lift his pistol, but Dorn's hands were on his throat. The Chinese gurgled, pushed desperately at the bleeding face, arched his back, trying to unseat him. Dorn felt the pressure of a scabbard against his knee, grasped it, pulled the knife from the man's belt. Then he drove it again and again into the twitching body beneath him.

When there was no more movement, he leaned back, looking unbelievingly at the contorted face, staring at his weapon and at his bloody hands, grunting with the effort of drawing breath. He felt as if he had murdered his past.

He had known something like this only once before. He was living at the farm, with his father, finishing his school term. Another boy had left the bus with him, taunted him, beat him on the way home, stood on his shoes, held to his collar, while Dorn took one painful step after the other, carrying his tormentor. His father had met them on the road. "Fight him, Woody. Or fight me!" His shame, his despair had been overpowering. The neighbor boy became the symbol of everything that had ever oppressed him. Crying, repeating the single swear word he knew, biting, clawing with his fingernails, he had battered the other boy until he was pulled away, sweating, sobbing, and filthy. His father had walked back to the house with him, his arm around Woody's shoulder.

Now he was astride the mutilated body, his bloody hands clutching the knife. He had been transported for a moment. The scene—so vivid in all the colors of an Iowa autumn—had passed through his mind between the orange flash of a mortar and its crackling explosion. He dropped the knife, retrieved his weapon, and ran to Sanchez.

He was still breathing. He groaned. A bruise puffed one side of his face. Dorn lay beside him, cupped snow in his hand, and washed it over neck and forehead. "Sanchez? Sanchez?" Sanchez opened his eyes and started to speak. But the men summoned by the dead officer had finally come. They were at the hole, looking at the body, talking excitedly, searching the area. Dorn, his mouth to Sanchez's ear, kept whispering, "Quiet. You'll be okay. I'll take care of you."

The Chinese came within ten yards of them, but ignored the mounds in the snow. At last they left, running to the rear. Sanchez spoke painfully. "Watch ... You got ... my watch ..." Dorn returned it. Sanchez's eyes focused on him. "Get back ... not much time ... Get back ..."

"I'm not leaving you."

"They'll send out... for me. Get goin'" He grasped his side where he had been kicked. "Goonie ... licked me." His eyes were closed. "Hurry ..."

The Chinese, varying their attack, struck at points all along the front. With maniacal disregard for death, they hurled themselves against the wall of fire, climbed toward the guns, were smashed, screaming, from the rocks, were corded in grisly piles for four hundred yards across the base of Bad Girl Ridge.

Pat sat in a foxhole with Lieutenant Allison. He was in a fever of anxiety. No message from Battalion. No let-up in the fury of the assault. Less than thirty minutes had elapsed since the first blast of the enemy bugle; and he had run the length of the position in that time, carrying ammunition, helping Huckabee and Choy with wounded, repairing a weapon, rallying the men to close a breach in the line. One incident merged into another in his mind.

Now he waited. There was nothing else to do. Twice, despite the clamor of the wind and the incessant squawk of his radio, he started to doze, only to wake with a start. His body cried out for sleep, but his mind kept nagging him, refusing him any retreat. His units were on their own. He could no longer maneuver them or control their fires. Each was fighting its own pocket war. And each war had its attackers and defenders, its terrain, its generals and heroes, its casualties, tactics, tragedies, honors, and jokes.

Andy, armed with a recaptured Tommy gun, penned four of the enemy in the narrow confines of a rock shelf, and chased them from side to side until, exhausted, they lay in the snow, looking up at him, their hands raised in surrender. He pointed to the farthest Chinese, called his shot, dropped him with his pistol.

"Cease fire! Cease fire!" Chuck Cagle fell beside Andy. "They're trying to surrender."

"No prisoners," Andy said. "Number two!" He pointed to the next Chinese, who was on his knees, waving his arms. Andy leveled his pistol.

Cagle grabbed his hand, held it. "No! Dammit, Andy ..."

"Get back to your job!" Cagle crawled away. "Number two," Andy repeated. One by one, the trapped enemy fell, and lay like rag dolls in the snow.

First Sergeant Goober gathered two wounded men in his arms, holding their heads on his shoulders. "Be still. I'll get you down."

"Well, if it ain't the Grim Reaper," one of them mumbled. "Shut up," Goober said. "Or I'll make you walk, you wedgeass."

"Jesus, I hurt!"

"Don't move. You'll be okay. Think about somethin' else."

"I can see. And I got my balls." A weak chuckle. "All that matters ... Top, you're a mean ole bastard. You gonna give me my purple heart?"

Across the ridge, Corporal Firesteen shouted a warning. A Chinese, explosives on his back, had scrambled over the rocks, worked behind, and was running toward a machine gun.

The crew was alerted too late. The man flung himself across the weapon. There was no explosion. For a stupefying instant, the Chinese, astounded, lay across the water jacket; and the marines gaped at him.

"Get that goonie off there. I don't wanna blow up the gun," Firesteen said. Someone pushed the Chinese. He reeled away. The corporal's BAR fired a burst, and the man pitched backward and fell, his pack exploding among his own troops below. Firesteen dropped to his knees. "Like my ma would say, friends, 'Ken gehaiget vehren'—meaning, roughly—You can get killed around here!"

The gunner, roaring with laughter, swung the gun into a new group of attackers.

Before the warming-tent in the command post, Choy stood over the single prisoner. The ragged, wounded man, dragged back from Pappas' position, was in a delirium, unable to answer questions.

A marine ran up. "Choy, Goober's lookin' for you. Wants you to help with the ammo detail."

"I am coming," Choy said. He shot the Chinese in the head, rolled the body out of his way, and went below.

George Pappas called Pat on his radio. "Have a small penetration in my second squad. About eight or ten Chinks. Can you give me help to counterattack?"

Pat deliberated. His mind was foggy. He forced himself to think, to phrase his answer, to speak. He had held his reserve despite two other requests for them, despite the need for men on the line. They remained his only unit for maneuver, his only chance to cope with the unexpected. Yet they were inactive when every man, every weapon was needed. Andy had pointed that out angrily enough. Pappas repeated his request. "Try to seal it off," Pat said at last. "If you can't, call me again." It was so easy, he reflected, so simple to give the order. As easy as it had been for Skinhead to order him to perform an impossible task. But the reserve had to be held against an extremity, he believed; and he was not yet willing to commit them.

The radio again. "Able Six. Able Two." Cagle's voice. "Can you give us more illumination? Over."

The Horse, who had followed Pat, leaned toward him. "Twelve rounds illuminating, eight rounds H.E. left. Better hold onto it, huh?"

Pat was stunned by the report. Ammunition, medical supplies, food, manpower—all were dwindling away. "Sorry, Able Two. Can't do it. Anything else?"

The voice, amazingly, incongruously gay, answered: "'Send us more Chinks!' 'Retreat, hell, we just got here!' 'We don't wanna live for ever.'" Cagle laughed. "Soon as I get time, I'm gonna come up with something that'll make the history books!"

Pat grinned, then shook with laughter. It seemed inordinately funny. His whole body sagged with the release of it. His eyes clouded. Allison was laughing, too. "Helps to be a little nuts in this lash-up."

The radio sounded again. "Able Six. Able One." Pat acknowledged the call. It was Pappas' platoon sergeant. "Lieutenant's been hit, sir. I'm takin' ..."

There was an interruption. Then Pappas' voice, oddly thick and garbled, came on. "I'm okay. Lost some teeth, got a hole in one cheek. Nothing serious. Busy. Out."

While Pat still felt the upsurge of relief, he was shocked to wakefulness. He held to a rock, his face pressed against its cold, slick surface, listening. Allison had turned, too, was intent. The Horse had crawled a few yards to the rear and was poised, straining for an alien sound amid the din. It was repeated: The sharp snap of rifles and the *pump-pump-pump* of burp guns.

"They're behind us!" Pat shouted.

The Horse was already calling the mortars. Allison started to raise himself from the foxhole. "I'll get some people back to alternate positions in the rear."

A grenade looped over, struck the lieutenant's shoulder, and fell on the parapet in front of their foxhole. There was an instant of terrified indecision. Then Pat screamed, "Down!" The grenade spurted blue, whipped hot fragments of serrated steel.

The Horse heard the groans, the muffled cries. He crawled to the foxhole. "God in Heaven!" he whispered, turning his eyes away. Then, "Corpsman!"

22

Pat stirred. There was a weight on his back. His face was twisted against the broken mouthpiece of his radio, his knees pressed against the bottom of the foxhole. Something warm and wet was soaking his shoulders. He tried to turn, but could not. Then Allison was lifted from him and he could move again.

The Horse and a corpsman were bent over Allison. Pat crawled between them. "Is he—" His voice faltered. Stricken, bewildered eyes peered up at him. Then the torn features relaxed into vacancy. Overcome, Pat turned away and wearily, painfully, stood.

Allison dead. Pappas wounded. The enemy in the rear. Mortars out. Radio destroyed. All in five minutes' time. And on every side the slaughter raged on. The Horse nudged his elbow, prodding him from his stupor. With the dull fixity of a robot, he sent The Horse to alert Cagle, and ordered Allison's platoon sergeant to man alternate positions on the perimeter.

He staggered and fell, wrenching his shoulder, as he made the rocky descent from the position, but was up at once, stumbling through the drifts of snow within Cagle's platoon at the breast, running again up the rising belly toward the command post. The sound of firing behind the ridge was closer now, isolated, intense. He pushed ahead, straining for breath, wheezing with exertion. Did the mortarmen get in? How many enemy? Where was Andy? His thoughts were jumbled, as he tried to clear the cluttered passages of his mind. "Thank God I held onto the reserve," he said aloud.

He was on the point of collapse when he reached the command post. "Have you seen Lieutenant Anderson?"

The marine on phone watch was kneeling with Choy over two bodies. "No, sir."

Pat dropped beside them. Sanchez and Dorn were stretched in the snow. For an instant, he knew an overwhelming sense of relief at their safety. "Couldn't get back in time," Dorn was saying. "Tried ... Chinese workin' 'round flank." He sat up. His face was raw, bruised. "Sanchez is okay. Ribs. I tried, sir."

Dizziness nearly overcame Pat. He dug his gloved fists into his eyes. Recovering, he glanced at the massive form of Sanchez, seeing the puffed, swollen lips, the frozen blood on his cheeks. "You're Dorn, aren't you?"

"Woody Dorn, sir."

"You'll do, Woody."

A surge of pride choked the soldier. "I killed one of them," he whispered, as if it were a secret.

Pat did not hear him. He was no longer aware of Dorn or Sanchez or Choy or the marine on the phone. Frantically, he pulled aside the flap on the warming-tent. Wounded men were packed in a tight, tangled mass inside. They looked at him blankly. He returned to the others. "Where are they? Where's the outfit I had standing by?"

"Gone, Captain," Choy said.

"Where? I told them-"

"Lieutenant Anderson. He sent for them a while ago," the marine said. "Runner from Mr. Cagle's platoon came over."

"He had no right!" Pat shouted, grabbing the man's arms. "Why didn't you call me? Why wasn't I asked?" His whole body shook with fatigue, with anger, with fear. "I need them! I need them now!"

"Sir, I never thought to—"

From below came the high-pitched voice of First Sergeant Goober. "Move out, damn you! Get yourself a hole. Move! Move!" Then the roar of a big gun, firing at close range, and the shattering impact of a shell exploding nearby.

The scream, windborn, urgent, brought Pat back from the edge of panic. "Get on the phone. Locate Lieutenant Anderson. I'm going forward. I want my men sent to me. You tell him that. You tell him I ordered it!" He climbed out of the crater, ran down the path, tripped over a dead man's foot, and sprawled headlong. Clenching his hands, willing the tremor out of his body, he commanded his disordered mind to function. He stood unsteadily and plunged into the wind, toward the other aid station.

Huckabee was dragging a man on a stretcher out of the warming-tent. Several wounded lay in the snow. "Get these people inside," Pat gasped. "They'll freeze to death."

The corpsman put the stretcher down and stumbled toward Pat, trying to recognize him in the darkness. With great effort, as if each word were being torn out of him, he said, "No more room in there." His shoulders sagged. His face was expressionless, drained of emotion. "Have to rotate 'em." He bent over another stretcher. "Like an oven. Put in a loaf. Take out a loaf."

"So many," Pat said hopelessly.

Huckabee stooped to part the flap. He jerked his head toward a group stretched beside the tent, their faces pressed against the canvas. "Made it back from the mortars. Only one hurt. Others too beat to move."

As Huckabee shuffled into the tent, Pat passed him and worked his way down the ridge, guided by the flash of tracers and the cough of gunfire. Twice he slipped, rolled, and clawed his way out of the snow.

Men were crouched among the rocks, firing into the night. Sixty yards away, spurts of light traveled along a wavering line, seeming to trigger the Chinese gun, revealing for an instant the dark shapes of the enemy. *Whirrr-ap ... Shew ... Wham!* The hillside shuddered under the blow. Pat stared as if hypnotized by the tiny dots of flickering blue. *Whirr-ap*—Count one-two-three—*Shew ... Wham!* It was like a spectacular electric sign.

George Pappas and Goober were kneeling behind a boulder, watching the front. Pat slipped down to them. "Oh! Beard fooled me for a minute," Goober said. "Thought you were the skipper."

Again Pat recoiled, as if the phrase were a whip in his face. No matter what, Andy would—by force of will and indifference to danger and invulnerability— retain command. He summoned a curt, level tone of voice: "How many out there?"

A scattering of rifle fire twanged around them. The three men lay flat, their faces against the snow. "Jezoo! Can't even put your head up," Goober said.

"Must be forty, fifty of them," Pappas said. The lieutenant's front teeth had been shot away, and there was a small piece of tape on his cheek. He spoke through his nose, his words flat and garbled. "Still a lot of pressure up front. Couldn't afford to move more than this one squad down here. Got to get some more people..."

Whirrr-ap ... Shew ... Wham!

"Must be a recoilless gun," Pat said.

"Probably a .75 they've captured one place or another," Pappas said.

"We damn' well better put it out of whack," Goober said. "That bastard's got our range and he's liable to hurt somebody."

"Send a bazooka team out?"

"No rockets, Captain. All expended," Goober said.

"Sooner or later they're going to rush us," Pappas said. "They're moving up under cover of the gun."

The men Andy had taken away had been held for just such an emergency. If the enemy succeeded in a breakthrough, they would easily overrun the aid station, threaten the command post, and even roll up the perimeter, away from the commanding belly of the ridge. He had to have enough men to meet the assault. But where could he risk weakening the line? How to knock out that damned gun? He thought of mortars, and remembered the dazed mortarmen at the aid station. "I'm going on up," he said to Pappas.

"If you're lookin' for Lieutenant Anderson," Goober said, "I sent a man for him first thing."

For an instant the two men's eyes locked. Then, "I'll get some men together and be right back," Pat said.

"Yeah. Good idea. You do that, Captain."

Pat turned when he heard the warning Whirr-ap! and ducked behind a boulder as the projectile whooshed in. Shew ... Wham! Somewhere up the feeble line, a man was screaming above the wind and the din of battle, calling for a corpsman. A few feet away, hidden from his view by the rocks, Pat heard Goober.

"I'm givin' it to you straight, Lieutenant. He lost his guts, committed that reserve first time he got rattled instead of sittin' on 'em for the payoff."

"Knock it off," Pappas said.

"Couldn't get him on the radio. Didn't answer. Probably hunkered down in a hole, afraid to expose himself."

The accusation was so unjust that only the *Whirr-ap ... Shew ... Wham!* of the enemy gun restrained Pat from going back and having it out with his accuser.

"Damn!" Goober said. "If we get clobbered now, it's on his head."

"I told you to shut up!" The lieutenant spoke slowly, with thick-tongued pain. "He's CO of this company. And you better damn' well remember it!"

Quietly, Pat got up and began to climb again, back toward the aid station. He stopped to catch his breath, fought the onrush of fatigue, and went on.

The mortarmen were still ringing the warming-tent.

"Get one tube ready," Pat said, after a moment's forgetfulness as to why he had come. "And I want these people on line."

"They're pooped, sir," The Horse said. "Had a hell of a time gettin' in. Chinks all over the place. And ammo and tubes to carry. Had to leave the baseplates."

Pulling one of the men to his knees, Pat roared at him. "Get up!" The marine obeyed, then crumpled. Pat tugged at him again, shook him. "Get up and stay up. You hear?" The Horse steadied the man, and Pat faced the others. The sleepless nights, the bitter cold, the unceasing wind, the freezing, inactive days— all these things had ravaged them. Their recent flight before the enemy had drained their will, and they had been overcome by lethargy. Pat cursed, shoved, and dragged them to their feet. Finally they were all standing, hazily aware of him. One collapsed against the tent. Pat ran to him, furious. "Damn you! Stand up!" He realized that he was screaming, that The Horse was looking at him open-mouthed. He bent down, hauling the man up again. "We need you, all of you," he said, his voice breaking. They took rifles from the stack beside the warming tent. "Can you fire that mortar without the baseplate?"

"I'm no Lou Diamond, Captain, but I'll try." The Horse picked up the tube, and Pat carried the last eight rounds of High Explosive shells. They followed him, sliding, falling, but rising again.

"You came back," Goober said, surprised.

"Get these men in position."

Whirrr-ap ... Shew ... Wham! The gun was in the same place, but the glitter of muzzle blast from the enemy rifles was closer, no more than thirty yards away—well within assault range.

The Horse held the mortar tube between his legs, jammed the steel ball at the base into the packed snow, and braced himself. "Get a round ready, sir." Pat armed the sixty-millimeter shell and held it over the tube. "Now!" The projectile slid, struck the firing pin, arced high above. They watched for its explosion, and saw it flash behind the emplaced gun.

"Higher angle," Pat said.

As if the mortar were their signal, the Chinese charged. This time there was no screaming, only the frantic sloshing of men through snow, the crackling of ice, animal grunts, the clatter of weapons against rocks. Pappas ran by, calling to his men. "Get up! They'll be on top of you."

Pat drew his pistol and joined Firesteen on the line. "Dump your grenades! They're right below us," the corporal yelled to the other three men in his fire team. He propped himself against a boulder, making room for Pat beside him. They waited. Pat drew a deep breath, then released it slowly, trying to expel all the tension in him. Firesteen was listening intently, his BAR at his hip, the birthmark on his cheek twitching.

Whirr-ap ... Shew ... Wham!

The men scrambled. Some started back to seek shelter. "Stay where you are!" Pat shouted.

The enemy appeared. Singly. In groups. Pulling themselves over boulders. Running between the masses of rock. It was no longer a battle of forces. It was one man against another now.

One Chinese jumped at a marine from behind. Firesteen screamed, "Goonie!" and the marine whirled, rifle at the ready. The enemy impaled himself on the marine's bayonet. He fell on the ground, kicking, shrieking. Horrified, the marine began to scream, but held onto his weapon.

Goober pulled him away, placed a foot on the enemy's chest, and tore the bayonet out. Then he lifted the body and heaved it over the side. He yanked the marine erect and returned his rifle to him. "Shoot it, you bastard, or you'll end up where he did!"

Grenades exploded deafeningly. There was the pump-pump-pump of burp guns, the twang of rifles, the mad stutter of BARs. Savage cries and agonized screams as Chinese and marines battled for the same shelters. Pat saw an enemy soldier climbing over the rocks on the flank of Pappas' position. He called a warning, but his voice was a mere whisper in the bedlam. Leaving his niche, he ran toward Pappas, ten yards away. The Chinese was pulling himself over the edge of the boulder. Pappas saw him and fired his carbine, but the weapon jammed. Pat raised his pistol, but was afraid to fire from that distance. As the Chinese got to his feet, Pappas swung the butt of his weapon and clubbed him to the rocks below.

Off on the right, The Horse and two other marines had loosened a boulder. They rocked it free and sent it crashing down the hillside, tearing a great slash in the snow, scattering enemy soldiers like tenpins.

The sound of sliding snow alerted Pat. It was behind him. He crawled toward it and saw the cloudy shape of an approaching enemy. He readied his pistol as the Chinese came on, eyes staring, panting hoarsely. This strange creature wanted to kill him! Pat's lips compressed. He felt cold and sick. He was emptied out. He heard the thud of his heart, felt the beat of his pulses. He licked his cold, dry lips and tasted fear. He squeezed the trigger.

The enemy uttered a cry of astonishment and twitched convulsively. A swath of red spread across the snow. Pat stared at the murder he had done, and gagged. Then he dragged himself back to Pappas' position.

The attack lasted less than five minutes, but in its intensity it seemed endless. When the enemy, still firing, had retreated into the darkness below, Pat sank down beside Pappas. Both struggled for breath, faced each other, smiling weakly.

Goober joined them. "Reamed 'em, didn't we? By God, we reamed 'em!"

Woody Dorn appeared, lugging a case of thirty-caliber ammunition. "Choy sent me, Captain. And some grenades are comin', too. Mr. Anderson called the C.P., says he can't spare the reserve, but he'll come himself in fifteen or twenty minutes."

"Thank God for somethin'," Goober said.

"Get the ammo distributed," Pat said. "And get a corpsman down here. See how many were hurt."

"Got eleven okay," said Goober. "No dead. One wounded who can stay. Others I already sent out."

"Good work, Top."

The first sergeant, oblivious, tore open the box of ammunition and loaded Dorn. "Get this stuff out, doggie. Before we get called on again."

"If we can just hold until it gets light," Pat said, looking at his watch, "we'll be okay. Nearly four now."

Whirr-ap ... Shew ... Wham! The shell exploded in the boulders well above them, erupting in a shower of rock and snow. "Broke their backs before," Pappas said, brushing debris from his parka. "But they'll try again after that gun works us over a while longer."

"Ought to get some people down there, flank it," Goober said, stuffing clips into his pockets.

"Haven't anyone fresh enough for that," Pat said.

"No, Captain, we don't. Now if we had our reserve, sittin' in the C.P., warm and rested—"

"Get the ammo out," Pappas said, cutting him off. Dorn left them. The lieutenant picked up the box and pushed Goober ahead of him. "Better just wait them out," he said. "We've got pretty good cover."

"Well, the skipper'll be comin' ..."

Pat followed them and found The Horse and his mortar. "We've got to try for that gun again," Pat told him.

"I don't think we can do it from up here, sir. Got to get closer, use it like a cannon."

Whirr-ap ... Pat dived for cover, scraping his chin against the ice as he went down. *Shew ... Wham!* A tremendous blow, close by. The Horse hunched over him, offering him a hand. A few yards away, he heard Firesteen screaming for a corpsman.

When they got to him, Firesteen pointed below. "Lieutenant Pappas got it ... in the belly."

Pappas was on his knees, his exposed intestines cupped in his hands. His eyes were tightly closed, his tom mouth was twisted in pain. "Is it bad? Really bad?" he gasped, begging for reassurance, afraid to look.

The Horse made him lie down. Moments later, Huckabee was there. Pat heard Firesteen: "Do something. Help him. Why don't you help him?"

And Huckabee: "Help him? Who do you think I am, God Almighty?"

Pat watched the scene, fixing it forever in his memory. The black night, the white snow, the crimson wound, the glazed blue eyes in the ashen face, the green-clad form, the icy brown strands of hair—and over all, the heartless, pale gold glow of moon. And Pappas dead, his hands still clutched to his ripped belly.

The *whirrr-ap* of another shell sounded. Then the explosion. Earth flew and rock and ice pounded around them. Pat found himself wedged against Firesteen and The Horse. "The bastards!" Firesteen yelled "... bastards!"

Pat scrambled up. "Horse, we're going down. Take the tube. I'll carry the ammo."

They crept down the hillside, between the boulders, sliding over the snow on their stomachs, while the big gun fired overhead and enemy rifles spurted to their front. "Long as they don't see us," The Horse whispered, "long as they don't see us ..."

The gun was fifty yards away. They rested behind a clump of enemy bodies. Using them as a cover, The Horse set the tube in place. Pat moved to the front, readied the shell. "Try to make it good," he whispered. "Once we fire, they'll know we're down here."

The first try was too far to the left, but they could hear excited shouts from the enemy. It had landed in the ranks of the riflemen. "Quick!" The Horse said. "I'll move it 'bout three fingers ..."

Whirr-ap! Pat didn't hear the whistling toward them, only the devastating roar as the shell detonated. It was too high, but they had revealed themselves. Next time ... He thrust a round into the tube. It struck above the enemy gun. "Down!" he rasped. "Get it down!"

"No damn' sight ... I'm tryin'!"

Pat armed another shell, was holding it over the tube when he heard the enemy gun crackle its warning. He dropped the round in the snow and rolled away. An explosion roared beside him, above him, before him. He was tossed on his back and he lay there, staring at a fleecy, sheep-like cloud as it slipped over the moon, struggling for the breath that had been knocked out of him. At last he breathed, convulsively. It seemed to burn. He tried to stand, got to his knees. It took all his strength to speak. "Fire!" The mortar thumped beside him. Its shell blasted into the enemy, and there were cries, far, far off. He saw The Horse's face, his mouth moving, glee spreading over the pocked features. But it was like watching a film when the sound fails. The sense of victory he had expected crumbled before he could grasp it. There was no victory. Only death. If he should die ... Like Allison. Like Pappas ... If he should die ...

He wanted only to survive, to be alive and unhurt and at home once more, to blot all this out, to overcome the odds. All his resolution eroded. I've tried, he thought hazily ... tried and tried and tried ...

He fell forward, knowing that he was falling but powerless to prevent it. He felt the impact of ice on his cheek. He was conscious, but only with the vague awareness of a man succumbing to anesthesia. In that moment he could think of only one thing. It would be good to turn over. It would be good to see the sky.

23

Razor-like, the wind slashed across the command post. Snow foamed up, piling drifts against the inert bodies of the wounded who lay outside the warming tent. Won Kook Choy, numbed by cold and fatigue, moved slowly among them, covering them with ponchos, tom canvas and sleeping bags, molding rude shields of ice to screen their faces from the pummeling of the wind.

Wearily pulling his gloves off, he knelt beside Pat and took his pulse. He held his stiff fingers to the captain's neck, fixed bleary eyes on his watch. Good. Much stronger. Nearly time to carry him inside again. Still asleep. Long time. Choy nodded. His chin dropped to his chest. He, too, slept.

"Freezin' out here. Lay still, Captain. You're okay, sir. Just you lay still."

Through the blur of his senses, Pat fought for consciousness. He was wet, drenched with sweat, racked by a spasm of shivering. He opened his eyes. It was Sanchez speaking to him. And Choy was behind and above him, lifting his end of the stretcher, he and Sanchez carrying him inside the warming-tent.

Reality flooded Pat's torpid mind. The horror of his nightmare slowly dissolved, leaving only a phantasmagoric play of fragmentary images ... *Heaven's morning breaks, and earth's vain shadows flee; in life, in death, O Lord* ... A choir at his father's funeral ... singing *Abide With Me* ... And Walt had been arguing with him ... No, no, it was Andy ... one of them. And a construction shack. Black. With tarpaper ... A place he knew but could not remember ... And he had taken his mother's arm ... with Ann on the other side ... only he hadn't known Ann then ... They'd looked in the coffin ... *View the remains,* a man in white coveralls, with a blue Buick seal on the pocket, had said to ... And it wasn't his father ... but George ... George Pappas ... and he had quarters over his eyes ...

Pat slept again.

Two hours later the dull thunder of distant guns and the crackle of rifles aroused him. He tried to orient himself. The warming tent. Carried inside. Choy. Sanchez. A hazy memory of a nightmare ...

He became aware of the monotonous *rackarackaracka* of an enemy machine gun. Somewhere off on the flank marine rifles answered. Then a shell roared in. He was deafened for an instant. Ice splintered and slid from the top of the tent.

There had been the enemy gun. And the snow ... His face had been in a drift ... There was a tender spot between his shoulder blades, a searing burn beneath the bandage on his chest. With a sudden thought of Pappas, he was afraid to test the wholeness of his body, afraid to know. Cautiously, he moved his arms, his legs. Relief surged through him; he was all right.

"Help me ..." It was a weak groan from beyond the glow of the stove. "Bleedin'. Tourniquet loose."

Pat crawled toward the sound. The man lay with his eyes closed, his fingers wandering feebly up and down his chest, fitful, nervous, as if he waited impatiently for death. Pat stopped the flow of blood. Then, standing shakily, he started for the tent flap. Lightheaded, he felt that his feet were not touching ground. "Choy!" he called.

Sanchez and the interpreter entered with another stretcher. "Captain! You shouldn't be up," Sanchez said.

"Take a look at that man," Pat said.

They put the stretcher down beside the one Pat had left. "Lie down, Captain," Choy said.

"I'm all right."

"You are not to get up," the Korean said, bending over the marine with the tourniquet.

Pat sat down again, warding off dizziness. "Where was I hit?"

Sanchez knelt beside him. He spoke thickly. His face was still swollen, his lips cut, one eye ringed with blue. "You're pretty lucky, sir. Not too bad. Gash on your chest, bruise on your back."

"Must have been out for hours," Pat said.

"Since 'bout this time yesterday."

Pat was shocked by the passage of another day, another night. Four days on Bad Girl. He looked at his watch. "It's 0440! I didn't realize ..." He felt weak, and lay back on the stretcher. "What's been going on?"

Sanchez brought Pat his pistol and holster. "Probing around the perimeter mostly. Not bad. But they beat hell outta us with some artillery a couple hours ago. And the cold wind hits your face like hot grease ... Must be around twenty-five below ..."

Choy crossed the tent and handed Pat the towel he had worn around his neck. "There is a full circle around us now, Captain. They can afford to take their time."

Pat tossed the towel beside the stove and struggled to a sitting position. Then he checked his weapon and adjusted the holster in order to occupy his quivering hands. "Feel a little woozy. Must be from not eating." He grinned, breathed deeply. "I'm hungry. For the first time in a week, I'm really hungry."

Taking a Tootsie Roll from his pocket, Sanchez offered it. "Doggies really did us a favor with these. Only thing you can chew without heatin'. Wish we hadn't left most of 'em in the rear."

"Thanks. And I'd like some water."

Choy began to drag a stretcher toward the tent flap. "Bring the man with the leg wounds," he said to Sanchez. "Time to rotate them again."

Outside the tent, in the command post, people could be heard rushing by. Pat thought he could identify Goober's yell. Someone else was methodically cursing a weapon that would not fire.

Rackarackaracka. The enemy gun was closer. No more than a hundred yards?

When he had eaten half the candy and sipped a cup of warm water, he felt better. "Want Lieutenant Anderson," he told Sanchez. "Get him down here, please."

The new arrival on the stretcher beside him spoke for the first time: "Lieutenant's over on the left flank. Pulled me in when I caught this shrapnel."

"I'll pass the word on the sound phone." Sanchez left the tent, pulling a litter after him.

Pat was trying to place the man beside him. About to give it up, he suddenly remembered the face; it was the sergeant who had been in command of the reserve unit of mortarmen. "What happened to you last night?"

The marine turned toward Pat, careful to favor his crippled hip. "First off ... well, we went up on the lines. Dozen or so Chinks had got into Lieutenant Cagle's position, and were raisin' all kindsa hell. We finally got 'em cornered. Fire fight didn't last long. Twenty, thirty minutes, maybe, and the goonies pulled out. Left three wounded out in front." His voice was hoarse and he spoke hesitantly, as if recalling every detail and telling only part of what he remembered. "The wounded Chinks were screamin' bloody murder ... poor bastards'd had it. We milled around awhile. Then one of 'em started yammerin', like a little kid, you know, sobs and all. Nothin' else goin' on in front, just those three. They'd talk sometimes ... goonie talk ... like they was prayin' or somethin'. And then one would start howlin' again or cryin' ... and another would take it up ... and then the first one again ..."

"Did you stay there?" Pat said. "Did the lieutenant move you someplace else?"

"Not for a while, sir." He cleared his throat, and was silent while he scrubbed his eyes. "Some of the guys were bettin' which of the Chinks would conk out first. And Mr. Anderson said we had to go out to get them. We figured we'd bring them in, you know ... Well, we didn't ... He got each one himself ... and comin' in, we lost a man."

Pat offered him the rest of his candy. The sergeant nodded his thanks and put it in his pocket. "I don't know, Captain. I suppose they woulda croaked anyhow. I mean, they were gonna bleed to death or freeze in their own sweat ... and we couldn't bring 'em in. Can hardly take care of our own." He turned away, his back to Pat.

"You'd better rest." Getting to his feet, Pat began to button his parka. He tightened his hood and pulled his gloves on. "What did you do today?"

"Lieutenant took us on an ambush. Out there two hours, freezin'. Didn't see a single Chink. But they saw us. Clobbered us with mortars.

Finally we went back in. He split us up, a few to each platoon. Had five wounded, two dead by then. Twelve of us left."

Pat looked down at the marine. Silently, he offered his canteen. The sergeant shook his head. "To kill like that ... When they're comin' at you and all, you know, it's different somehow. But ... I think the lieutenant enjoyed it ... I think—it's like—" He swallowed. "I don't know ... I just don't know ..."

Pat understood. He, like the sergeant, just didn't know. He walked to the tent flap, looked back at the men packed side by side across the narrow shelter. When we needed the reserve so desperately, he thought, Andy committed them without permission. No matter how much Cagle needed them, Andy should have asked. If he would have at least brought them back later, instead of holding them for senseless butchery ... This time, he told himself, there'd be no walking away from a confrontation. There'd be no putting off the reckoning. Not this time. He stepped outside. The cold engulfed him and the wind stung his eyes. But the snowstorm was over. For the first time in days the sky was clear, a velvet curtain flecked with stars.

"Huckabee said you are not to get up. You are to rest," Choy said. "Where is he?"

"At the other tent. He was with you much of the night. It was he who made the stitches in your chest."

"I mean Lieutenant Anderson."

"Sent word to him, Captain," Sanchez said.

"Move one of these people into my place inside," Pat said. The volume of fire on the right flank seemed to be increasing. "Platoon radios working?"

"No, sir," Sanchez said. "Froze."

Sitting on a discarded ration box, Pat closed his eyes, breathed deeply, deliberately, trying to slow the rapid thumping of his heart. "Mr. Cagle all right?"

"Yes, sir. He came down to see about you a couple hours ago."

Two officers left besides himself, Pat thought. He'd have to reorganize. Have Andy take over one of the platoons. Check the MLR. Ammunition. Food. "You know the situation on ammo?"

"The Horse's got the ammo detail. Says we're short grenades. Thirty caliber's runnin' low."

"How about medical supplies?"

"There is no more morphine, Captain," Choy said. "Plasma was gone last night. We still have bandages. Little else."

"Any contact with Hagaru or Battalion?"

"No, sir. Woody—that's the doggie, Dorn—he says we need new batteries. Can't get a buzz outta the 300," said Sanchez.

"You look like you need some sleep, Choy."

"Everyone needs sleep, Captain."

The firing on the flank, beyond the aid station, grew in volume and intensity. The *rackarackaracka* now maintained a steady beat; and the reply of marine rifles was ragged. "Who's in charge over there with Mr. Pappas' platoon?"

"Goober," Sanchez said. "Platoon sergeant got it. Artillery this afternoon. There's two corporals runnin' squads." He grinned. "Oughta see Mel Firesteen, sir. With that ripped butt, he can't sit; and he don't let nobody else in his squad sit."

A marine ran into the command post, jumping from the rim above. "Where's Lieutenant Anderson?" he asked, breathless.

"What's wrong?" Pat said.

"Goober sent me. Chinks crept up on the other aid station. Got the tent under fire."

24

"Goonies infiltrated. Must be at least twenty of them." Goober punctuated his words with bursts of fire that chipped the moonlit knoll seventy yards away. "Nobody saw it ... until they started ... shootin' up the tent."

"How many wounded in there?" Pat asked.

"Five. Got the rest moved. Huckabee's still out there. That's why The Horse went out. Jackass. He's tryin' to cover him—with a rifle!" He fed another belt through the light machine gun. "You people keep pourin' it on 'em," he yelled to the squad above, on the rim of the crater. "Firesteen! Your BARs are too high, dammit!"

A grenade, thrown by the attackers, struck the tent. Pat watched it roll down and explode on the ground, ripping the canvas. The Horse was firing again, then yelling to Huckabee. "Take off, Huck. I'll cover you!" The corpsman replied, but his voice was lost in the chatter of the Chinese automatic weapon and the crackle of rifles.

"He's all right, that Huckabee ... Damn fool ... won't leave, though ... He's all right ..."

"Got to get those people out of there," Pat said. He blinked his eyes, shaking off the urge to close them. He had scraped his chest and it throbbed with pain. The enemy gunner stitched a line around the crown of the tent. "Can't just sit here," Pat said to Goober. "Got to flank them, pin them down while we get our people out."

"With what?" Goober asked. "Firesteen, damn your hide, get those BARs on that machine gun out there!" He dropped beside Pat as a burp gun fired wildly into the bank behind them. "Just so they don't rush the tent."

The Horse, a shadow against the snow, fired eight fast rounds. Pat heard the clip ejected, saw the shadow roll aside and move to the right. Then the *rackarackaracka* of the Chinese gun, sweeping the spot The Horse had just left. "If we could pin them down long enough to move the wounded ..."

"Need more people," Goober said. "Soon's Lieutenant Anderson gets here ..." He swung the gun, and tracers lashed the knoll again.

Pat's momentary dizziness had passed and his mind was clear again. He studied the terrain, analyzing the situation, and working out a plan. The same old fear that had clutched him before was lodged in him now, but with a difference. Now it was familiar and expected, as normal as the stutter of gunfire, the sharpness of the wind, the harsh voices of the men around him. The fear was like a piece of shrapnel in his body, and he was used to it, knew how to live with it. But it had to be removed, and he alone could tear it out. "We'll work around the flank," he said to Goober.

"Better wait for the lieutenant."

Pat moved closer to Goober, propelling himself on his elbows. He took three expended cartridges from beneath the gun, and made a U in the snow. "Look, Top. This is the crater. Now we're here at the base, with our people behind and above us. The tent is here, about the center. The Chinks are out there at the open end of the U."

"I know, Captain," Goober said irritably. "I can see."

"Listen!" It was a command; and the first sergeant grunted, fixing his eyes on the diagram in the snow. "We're going to send Firesteen's squad up the left arm of the U to the end. From there they can put plunging fire down on them. When it gets light the Chinks'll have to pull out or be picked off. Meanwhile ..."

Goober fired another burst at the knoll. "Think I clipped one of them that time." He turned to Pat again. "Captain, we move any of the people behind us out, we're the ones'll get pinned. First thing you know, they'll be all over the tent."

Pat swallowed, holding his hand to his chest as if to restrain the pounding there. "No. We take this gun out near where The Horse is, by that cart on the right arm of the U. From there, we could enfilade them. It would hold them while Firesteen gets around on the opposite flank; and then we'll be able to move our wounded to safety."

"Might work," Goober said grudgingly. "But how the hell we gonna get this gun out there?"

Pat felt like a man at the railing of a bridge, determined to jump, but appalled at the depths below. "I'll do it."

"Never make it," Goober said.

Pat got to his knees and cupped a hand around his mouth. "Horse! Take cover. Huck! Can you hear me?"

A muffled, "Yo!" came from the tent.

"Get your people out when I give the word. We'll cover you." To Goober he said: "You crawl back. Get Firesteen started. Send me a man with more ammo."

"Only four belts back there."

"It'll have to do," Pat said, his voice rasping. "Have the rest of the men heave as many grenades as they can on my signal. I'll move under that."

Goober wriggled in the snow, burrowing deeper, his hefty body still an inviting target as the enemy gun fired long bursts. "There's not a dozen grenades left in the whole damn' company."

Pat was brought up short. But what else could he do? Stand, as Andy surely would, and charge the enemy, screaming, "Semper Fi?" No. He was not Andy. "Get back there. After you've sent a man out with ammo, I'll call for grenades. Throw whatever you have. Hold any other fire until we've made it."

"Maybe we oughta wait, Captain. Firesteen's people are beat. Moving in cover, it's gonna take a hell of a while to get them around the left flank while you're firm' on the right."

"They can do it."

"And you're in bad shape yourself. As soon as Lieutenant Anderson ..."

Pat clenched his teeth; fury spurred him on. "Get going. Now!"

Another grenade struck the tent. Pat heard a scream from within, and he saw The Horse fire and roll away, fire and roll again. Goober was still beside Pat. "Move out, Top. Dammit, do as I say!" The first sergeant pushed himself back. Pat waited, rehearsing his plan. When the marine with the ammunition dropped beside him a few minutes later, he was ready. "I'll take the gun. You follow with the ammo and tripod." He turned his head and saw the squad above them on the crater's rim, ready to move, saw, too, the bulky silhouette of the first sergeant kneeling twenty yards away. It was a physical effort for Pat to form the words. "Let 'em go!"

Five men were up; five grenades lofted toward the enemy. One fell short, but the others exploded across the top of the knoll. Pat slipped his arms under his gun, holding it away from his chest, letting it rest on his forearms. Steam rose from his parka as the hot weapon touched it. There was a delicious warmth, then the smell of burning cloth, then searing pain. He was running, weaving forward, past the tent, as the last of the grenades detonated. He fell behind the overturned cart; and the marine at his heels dropped the tripod to receive the gun. "Good boy," Pat gasped. The enemy was firing again, lashing bullets all around them. Pat fumbled with the belt.

"Let me take it, sir." The Horse had hurtled down beside them and before Pat could answer had edged the muzzle around the cart and was enfilading the enemy, sweeping across the long axis of the knoll.

"Huck!" Pat shouted back. "Start sliding them out." He shook the marine who had made the dash with him. "Go help. When you get in, stay there." The man took off.

A shadow only thirty yards away was crawling toward the gun. Pat pointed. The Horse lowered the weapon and battered the enemy to the earth. "How they doin' back there?"

Goober was slogging away from the tent. One man was cradled in his arms, another clung to his back like a child. Huck was dragging a stretcher. The other marine was struggling with a body, falling, standing again, finally dragging his burden to safety. "Last belt," Pat told The Horse. "Fire in short bursts."

Huckabee was darting back to the tent. "One more," he yelled.

When their fire slackened, the enemy grew bolder and The Horse was forced to continue rapid fire. In two minutes, the gun coughed its last. "That's it," he said.

The enemy, unchecked now, directed their fire on the two men with the silent gun. Bullets splintered the old boards of the cart. Pat and The Horse burrowed deeper in the snow. "Huck's gonna make it!" The Horse yelled in Pat's ear. "Pullin' the last man out now."

"Where's Firesteen?" Pat said. "He's had time ..." And then he remembered that The Horse didn't know what he was talking about.

A concussion grenade arched from the Chinese position and fell behind them. The Horse snatched it and tossed it back. It detonated beyond the knoll. Two Chinese charged the gun, their weapons spraying. The wheel above began to spin. Pat fired his pistol. They still came on. It seemed to Pat that they moved across a great distance in slow motion. He fired again. Ten feet away, the first one fell. The next dropped, his hands to his face. "Firesteen," Pat said. "Should be in position by now. Cover us ..."

"All out, Captain!" Pat glanced back and saw Huckabee's shadow, far behind them, on the edge of the crater.

He thought, How stupid of Huck to call out my rank! "Better make a run for it. Go on, Horse. I'll cover you."

A piercing animal sound answered him. The Horse was huddled behind the cart. There was a sash of blood around his waist. Pat threw his arms about him and began to move him back. Surprised by pain, he realized that the hot weapon had burned through his parka and blistered raw welts on his forearms. As he tugged at the sergeant, skin loosened, and he felt as if flames were leaping through his body. The gun. Can't leave the gun, he thought Easing The Horse to the snow again, he crawled back, beneath the stream of enemy fire. The bolt, he told himself. Just take the bolt. Using a cartridge as a tool, he worked furiously. The compressed recoil spring slipped, and he shuddered as it whipped savagely past his face. He removed the bolt, thrust it in his pocket, and returned to The Horse.

Another volley of fire came from the Chinese, ripping the cart before them. Marines were shouting, firing overhead. Goober was yelling. "Come on! Come on!" All the noises became one great roar in Pat's ears. He put his face to The Horse's chest. Heart still beating. Bad wound. He began to move him back. But the searing fire in his arms would not allow him to hold on long. He fastened his teeth into The Horse's parka collar and tugged, sliding on his belly inch by inch across the snow. Get in. Move. Forty more yards. He reset his jaws on the parka, pulled again. And the body followed him, leaving a thin red path in its wake.

"That's it, sir! Keep your butt down!" a voice yelled at him from the line.

Another: "Yer my boy, buddy-buddy. Yer my boy!" Like Justus. Lock Justus. Out of it ... gone.

Then he heard Andy's voice: "Stay there, Pat. I'm coming out for you."

Releasing his burden, Pat twisted his head toward the sound. He could not allow it. The last thirty-five yards stretched endlessly before him, but he knew that he would die before he would willingly be carried over it by Andy. He shouted, his voice strange to him, hoarse but firm. "You stay there. You stay where you are."

"Pat!"

"I'm ordering you!"

A shell burst near the knoll. Throwing artillery at us now, Pat thought dully, as he toiled over his burden, trying to keep his chest clear of the earth. Again the whine of a plummeting shell and its explosion. Again it was off to the rear. He was growing accustomed to the pain in his arms. Or else the cold was numbing it. He grasped The Horse's collar again, pulled him into a shallow dip in the snow, and waited, exhausted, lying across the wounded man to shield him. The Horse moaned, and his lips stretched in a faint smile of apology. Still alive. Pat tried to move again; but each time he inched forward enemy fire creased the snow around him.

"Stay there. Wait 'em out!" Someone shouted.

"Get back! Man, get back!"

Again and again he attempted it, working his protesting body up, his aching jaws taking a fresh grip, his eyes bulging with effort, his head swimming in a red blur of fiery pain. And the enemy guns from behind. And marine rifles before him. And the voices ...

"Oh, you ever lovin' bastard! Don't try it again. Wait fer the flankers."

"Nuts. He's nuts. But look at him, will ya?" a rifleman said to the BARman beside him.

The BARman was yelling, too, calling to the captain, cursing him. "You're gonna kill yourself! Stay there! Wait! Oh, you crazy, sweet Mick sonovabitch ..."

All the voices became a babble, a part of the wind and the bark of weapons. Then, from behind him, he heard wild screams, rifles, and BARs ... and Firesteen's voice. "Thank God," Pat mumbled. The flank unit was above the enemy.

Pat looked at The Horse. Can't last much longer, he thought. He decided to risk it. Taking off his parka, he worked the wounded man on top of it. Holding the empty sleeves, using the coat as a sledge, he stood and bulled his way toward his lines. Another shell came in. Well over Bad Girl. Then arms were reaching for him, dragging him to shelter. In that moment, Pat knew the all but intolerable joy of triumph.

The Horse lay on a stretcher in the warming-tent. He gasped for breath and his torn body fluttered faintly with life.

Pat looked down at Huckabee, who knelt beside his friend. "Is there anything ... can we do anything?"

"No plasma. No morphine. He's hurt awful bad." The corpsman brushed the matted hair from The Horse's forehead. "But he's still alive. I don't know how, but he's"—the broad chest beneath the blanket moved slightly—"he's alive."

Pat held the tent flap for Sanchez and Choy as they carried a frozen, blue body inside. Then he picked his way among the wounded who lay in the snow.

Andy was waiting for him. They walked across the command post side by side. "Well?" Andy said.

"Not much chance."

"Too bad. He's a good man."

Goober rushed up to them. "Jezoo! Rough go for Firesteen's people. Through drifts most of the way, but we got 'em screwed now. Four BARs layin' in on 'em. Chinks can't move!"

"Pass the word to Firesteen, Top. We'll hold up until daylight," Pat said. "Meanwhile, have someone load magazines for his people."

"You're forgetting the machine gun you left out there," Andy said. "I've got to get it in before the goonies start using it on us."

Pat took the bolt from his pocket and showed it to Andy. "If they could get to it—and they can't—they couldn't use it."

Andy seemed surprised. "Well, good. That's thinking. Now the thing to do is to clobber them good before they can exploit the toehold they've got." He put a hand on Pat's shoulder. "You get some rest. I'll go down and handle it."

"No. I'm handling it. We're going to hold where we are. You understand, Top?"

"Yes, sir," Goober said uncertainly.

"See to it."

They watched the first sergeant leave the crater. Perplexed, Andy said, "You're making a mistake, Pat ..."

"Why did you take the reserve without getting my permission?"

"What?"

"You had no right to take those people without asking me."

"What's that got to do with what's going on right now? You're confused. That was yesterday."

"I know damn' well when it was!" He tried to stifle his anger. His arms were burning; he held them away from his sides. "Answer me. Why?"

"They were needed up front."

"That was my decision to make, not yours. They should have been ready to move when they were needed most. God knows how many we lost ..."

"I did what was necessary at the moment," Andy said, his voice also rising. "Wasn't time to find you ..." He shrugged. "You're pooped. Better go back in the tent, get warm, get some rest. I'll go down and look things over. We can talk later."

Two shells struck off on the flank, sending up twin columns of snow. "We'll talk right now."

Andy's lips were set in a tight line. He stroked his bearded cheek with his fist. "Dammit, Pat, I've got to counterattack now, chase them before they get set up on that knoll."

Standing directly before him, Pat blocked his path. "You're not going to counterattack anybody. You know as well as I do that it's going to be light in the next half-hour. Their position will be untenable then. We're above them. And they've got no cover. If they try to stick, we'll go after them in the light, when we know what we're doing."

"I been at this a little longer than you have, you know ..."

"I know all about that," Pat said. He was trying to control himself, but his voice was thick with anger and fatigue.

"I'm going to take a look."

Pat grabbed his arm. "You're going where I want you to go."

"Don't shove me around," Andy said, glowering at him. He pushed Pat's hand away and climbed out of the crater.

The frigid shapes of the dead, their ice-crusted boots outstretched, were outlined before them in the first light of dawn. Pat caught Andy as he started down the ghostly path. "I told you to keep your hands off me!"

"This time you don't turn your back and walk away. This time you listen!" He pulled Andy around.

"You're hurt. You're out of your head. You don't know what you're saying." He tried to push Pat aside, but could not budge him.

"I know what I'm saying," Pat shouted. "You be sure you know it and understand it! I'm saying you're going to take orders the way everyone else does. You're going to stop acting like this company is your own private army. You're going ..."

"I *made* this company," Andy said, raging at him. "I took a bunch of dumb, soft kids and made marines out of them!"

"You made nothing. These men aren't dumb and they aren't soft. And it didn't take you to make marines out of them. There's not one of them who isn't more of a marine than you pretend to be. They know how to take orders!" Pat caught his breath. "You act the part all right. Tough and brave and callous and contemptuous. But your kind of marine retired twenty years ago!"

Andy's face was flushed. His fists were doubled. His lips barely moved as he spoke. "And you're the new version?"

"I'm the one that gives the orders. That's all you have to remember. And, Buster, you'd better damn' well remember it!"

"Or what?" Andy's shoulder jostled him. Pat stumbled over a dead man's boot but caught his balance. "Or what?" Andy yelled, advancing on him. "Or you'll report me to Skinhead for being insubordinate—which I am—or cussing a superior—which I am—or punching one—which I am?" He swung at Pat, and the blow landed on the side of his face, knocking him to the ground. "You won't even do that. You haven't got the guts to be a proper sonovabitch!"

Goober came up the path. He rushed between them. "Hey, knock it off! What's wrong with you?" He helped Pat to his feet. "Skipper," he said to Andy," you don't know what you're doing!"

Pat thrust him aside. "Get the hell out of here, Top!" Goober stared at them. "Get out!" Pat shouted. The first sergeant retreated. "There's only one thing you're capable of understanding," Pat said. He hit Andy squarely, driving his fist into the half-open mouth. The lieutenant was on his knees, wiping a glove across his torn lip, smearing the blood there. Pat let him stand, ducked a roundhouse blow that glanced off his shoulder, and hit him again. This time the fist clubbed Andy's ear. The shock of it sent a shrill pain up Pat's arm and through his body.

Dazed, Andy came at him again, but warily this time. His squat frame was in a half-crouch. He worked his fingers, held his hands before him. "I don't give a damn that they'll court-martial me," he said grimly. He spat blood. "I'm gonna leave some marks on you." He lunged, and the blow caught Pat in the midsection.

The captain staggered back and fell, his face scraping against the ice. Andy was over him, straining to lift his weight, cocking a fist to strike again. Pat blocked it, striking back and hitting him flush on the jaw. As Andy fell, Pat caught him again, on the forehead. His heart pounding, his wounded chest churning with pain, he stepped back and waited for Andy to get up again. "Go back to the C.P.," he said. "When you've cooled off, you can take over Allison's platoon."

Andy got to his knees, staring unbelievingly at him.

An enemy shell came in, falling fifty yards away. Pat ducked instinctively. And Andy was off, down the path, toward the old aid station. "Come back here!" Pat shouted, plunging after him.

Another shell. The overturned cart was destroyed.

Andy was running fast, sure-footed in spite of the treacherous ground. Pat saw him jump from the rim into the evacuated aid station. A blast ripped the snow before him, and the deserted warming-tent disappeared. Andy was down. Pat limped hurriedly forward to help. At the whir of another shell, he threw himself to the ground, struck his bandaged chest, scraped his arms, and cried out in pain. A second round came in, landing in the crater of the first. A moment later he got to his knees, amazed to find that his body still functioned. He crept forward, searching for Andy.

There was only a bloody parka hood and a pink glaze on the snow, and scorched rags. Dazed by the explosion and by the enormity of what his mind refused to accept, Pat crawled down the side of the hole. He was struck by the knowledge that a man had disappeared, was lost, that he himself had narrowly escaped the same fate, that he sat now at the bottom of Andy's grave, untouched.

A piece of metal gleamed dully beside a tom red muffler. He reached for it, could barely make out the letters. Anderson, Joseph M., 063141, USMCR. Now he knew, too, that the pink glaze on the snow was Type "O" and that the scorched fabric and the bloody hood had belonged to a Protestant. And that was all he really knew about Andy. Andy had been erased, smashed into nothingness by a pair of shells which had sought and found him alone. Nothing remained but the basic statistics. Name. Serial number. Service. Blood type. Religion.

"Where is he?" Goober was sliding into the shell hole.

Pat stood without moving, incapable of any action. "Gone."

"We've got to find him!" Goober clambered up, out of the hole again. "Skipper!" he shouted. "It's Wally. Where are you?"

In the growing light, a sniper fired, but Goober was oblivious. Groggily, still dazed, Pat went after him, tugged at his arm. "It was a shell, Top. Two shells. First must have gotten him. And then the second ..."

Goober was stupefied, knowing what he had heard was true, yet unable to accept the fact of it. "No. He's out there somewhere. The Chinks have him. Got to help him." He broke away, ran toward the enemy, slipped and fell.

Pat crawled to him. They lay side by side in the snow. "Got to go in, Top." The sniper fired again and the bullet ricocheted behind them.

Off on the left, Pat heard Firesteen calling. "You mischigunahs! Get back!"

"Getting light," Pat said. "Come on, Top."

Goober was sitting up, his face contorted, his mouth quivering. "I'm not afraid to go out there. Skipper and me, we aren't afraid." He drew back from Pat. "Go on. Get out! We don't need you. Never needed you!"

"He's dead, Top. Dead." He said it softly, but the words sounded ugly and brutal to his ears. Slowly, ponderously, Goober began to cry.

A shepherd's horn sounded, a low and mournful wail in the distance. And soon the sporadic firing from the knoll ceased. BARs were lashing the enemy as they disengaged, withdrawing to the surrounding hills.

"Come on, now," Pat said, as gently as he could.

The two men walked back and climbed the ridge together. Pat limped badly. Goober, staring unseeingly at his boots, trudged clumsily alongside him.

25

The marines huddled in the grotesque wreckage of battle; and the wind, subdued now, hummed a dirge over the scarred body of Bad Girl Ridge.

Pat left Goober at the command post and limped on toward the crest to take over his company. There in the misty dawn he stopped, looked down, and slowly turned in a full circle, awed by the panorama of death that met his gaze. On every side, rooted to pedestals of ice, was the dreadful statuary of the enemy, frozen in their final agonies. Heaped before the guns, spread-eagled across the rocks, crumpled in the valley, were tangled mounds of Chinese bodies, contorted in weird travesties of motion. Around them lay their rifles and burp guns, bayonets, pistols, grenades, flares, Tommy guns.

Within the position, the snow was littered with ration cans, discarded web equipment, ammunition boxes, broken rifles, cartridges, duds, excrement, splintered stretchers, soiled bandages.

Pat moved from hole to hole, listening to his men, talking briefly to each of them. He was struck by their lethargy, by the drunken thickness of their speech.

One wounded man, an arm tied to his side, the other cradling a rifle, insisted he was all right. "Just bushed … that's all … Reckon Chinks are pooped, too?" He pinched his hollow cheeks. "We gonna get us some relief, sir?"

"We'll see."

Farther down the line, he prodded a sentry. "Restin' m' eyes, Cap'n, honest … Wasn't sleepin' … He held both gloved hands before his face. "Any chow left?"

"I'll find out."

A shell roared in, jolting a BARman awake. He stared at Pat, finally recognizing him. Holding out his automatic rifle, he said, "Works now … oiled the bastard …"

He hesitated, began again. "Oiled her with hand—hair—tonic. Need more magazines ... Got some?"

"I'll check."

Their faces, stubbled and gaunt, were expressionless. They reacted sluggishly. Some slept, cushioned by unzipped sleeping bags. Some did their turns as sentries, their heads propped on rock parapets, their heavy-lidded eyes fighting sleep. Some crawled through the rubble, sharing a frozen chunk of food or seeking oil for a weapon or searching for ammunition. All of them ignored the sledgehammer blows of artillery that crunched the earth about them, then fell silent, then began again. The men seemed to sleep or watch or stand or speak or move in a delirium of fatigue.

"Sir, what can we do?" It was the Negro motor-transport man, the soldier who had volunteered to stay behind. Then, when Pat said nothing, "What you think, sir?"

Snipers, somewhere out in the valley, began to fire sporadically. The big guns were suddenly quiet again. Pat slipped down beside the soldier, another man wanting an answer, wanting reassurance, another man surrounded by reality, but needing something to make it seem real. Not the truth. The truth they could see for themselves. A sniper chipped a rock above them. A marine fell on Pat, jolting his arms. The pain was excruciating.

"Sorry." The man spoke, barely moving his cracked lips. "Sure caught hell, huh?" He smiled weakly, with effort. "Ole Able Company ... 'bout had it, huh?"

The hoarse voice of a loudspeaker blared in the stillness of morning, startling them. "Officers and men of the United States Marines!" The enemy spoke in the precise English of the BBC. "We ask you the questions you must ask yourself. So much bitter warfare. How much longer this useless, futile fight?"

The soldier lay on his back beside Pat. "Stupid is readin' from surrender leaflet."

"Will it mean death for you? Will you be crippled for life? Let the warmongers do their own dirty underhanded work. How can you help stop this death and destruction? By surrendering ..."

Surrender. No matter how distasteful, Pat thought, it was something he had to consider. What, after all, would further resistance accomplish? They were only an isolated outpost that had, by now, served its purpose. There could be no victory, only the continuation of a fight against impossible odds, with the result all but foreordained.

"... the Korean Peoples' Army and the Chinese volunteers will guarantee for you safe conduct to a prisoner-of-war camp, full rations of food and tobacco, medical care, suitable housing, clothing and necessities ..."

The Communist cliches grated on him. "Warmongers ... Peoples' Army ... volunteers ... imperialists ... colonial ambitions ... deceitful leaders ..." Disgust welled in him, and hatred. Not for the mangled bodies that lay strewn on every side, not even for the cold and hunger and pain they had inflicted on his men. It was hatred for that voice, that calm and confident voice inviting surrender, a voice that proclaimed the victory of tenor. In a sense, Pat thought, Choy had won his point. To be right was desirable, but to prevail— ah, that was the thing. To prevail.

There was an alternative to surrendering. And that was to fight on, no matter what the outcome. It was not the same as winning, but it was something. As long as you could raise a hand against it, as long as you could hold on, you were denying that voice. His gaze wandered over his men, his exhausted, battered company. He wondered how he could explain it to them. If only he could phrase the fragments of his thought in communicable language, if only he could make them understand, would they have anything left to give?

"... thousands of your buddies"—the word sounded alien and false out of that mouth—"have already made this decision. Join them now. Live to see your homeland again. Lay down your arms, marines ..."

Pat saw Sanchez standing above him, looking rough and immovable and dependable. He was gazing fixedly in the direction of the enemy, a scowl on his face. Very deliberately, he spat.

Another man pushed himself from his foxhole, was silhouetted against the light of morning, and cupped his hands to his mouth. "Tell your troubles to Stalin, you slant-eyed, limey-talkin', chop-suey-eating laundry-washin', nose-pickin' sonovabitch!"

The motor-transport soldier yelled, "Surrender yourself, you yellow bastard!"

The marine who had stumbled on Pat got up. "That's tellin' 'em, huh? What say, Cap'n?"

Pat held out his hand, and was helped to his feet. Excitement, anger, an overwhelming desire to lead these beleaguered men, all stimulated him. "We're going to hold this ridge," he said.

"Hurray fer us an' screwyoo!" the marine yelled.

Men emerged from craters and foxholes, from behind rocks and snowbanks, a band of ragged, tottering ruffians, swearing, shouting their hatred and contempt. Watching them, Pat rediscovered something about the fiber of the human will. It was something that he and the others had all learned amid the sand fleas of Parris Island, in the swamps of Camp Lejeune, on the power-line trail in Quantico, on the rugged hills of Camp Pendleton. Will can conquer weakness. The mechanism of the body continues to operate beyond the demands of the mind.

Though some men held to one another, all were standing. "Semper Fi!" Sanchez shouted. Woody Dorn, beside him, took it up. The men were chanting now, drowning out the voice of the enemy. "Semper Fi! Semper goddamn' Fi!"

Six hours later, Chuck Cagle limped into the command post. His trousers were ripped, his face black; there was a bloody gash on one hand. "Huck, I'm hurting like a neuralgia ad. When you finish with the captain, how about fixing this hero?"

Goober was carrying a limp body from the warming-tent. "Skipper's gone, Mr. Cagle."

"I know, Top." He dropped beside Pat as the first sergeant lumbered away to stack his burden among the dead. "So many. And you forget so damn' fast," he said, half to himself.

Pat winced as Huckabee coated his arms with ointment. It was true, he thought. Sorrow was short-lived here. It vanished like smoke. You were too concerned with other things, commonplace and personal things. Dawn and darkness. The strength of the wind, the light of the moon, the warmth of the sun, the renewal of sleep, the consistency of food, the taste of water, the mechanics of evacuation, the security of shelter, the pleasure of dry clothes, the comfort of cleanliness, the luxury of speaking aloud and laughing at bad jokes, the precious miracle of life. Perhaps it was because death, too, was commonplace. Another death and another and another reduced the importance of death in the abstract.

"How's The Horse?" Cagle asked.

"Doesn't seem like it's possible," Huckabee said, his mouth twitching nervously. "But he goes on breathin', one breath after the other." He wrapped gauze around Pat's arm. "One breath after another."

"Were you able to sedate him?" Pat asked.

"Yes, sir. Dorn, the doggie, he went clear around Bad Girl, checked every NCO. Found me three syrettes. Gone now." He got up. "Be back to you, Mr. Cagle. Got to see about him."

Cagle rubbed snow over his face, washing the dirt and smoke away. "You got yourself a company again, Captain. For a while this morning, I figured you were off your rocker." He laughed, smacked Pat's knee. "But damn if it didn't do something to jazz 'em up. They're back to bitching again, complaining like mad. And for a marine, that's the best sign of all." He stopped suddenly and stared in mock amazement. Then, getting to his knees, he held out his hands, framing Pat's freshly shaved face. "He's lovely! He's engaged! He uses a razor!"

"I'll 'lovely' you!" Pat grinned. "But I damn' well feel like a new man."

"Wait a minute!" Cagle pounded his fist on his leg. "What a piece of copy! Get this ... off the top of the head, of course, but here's the general idea: Half-tone of a sad-looking, whiskery guy who can't get a date or a raise or a screen test. And an animated tube of shaving cream, dressed like a magician, is standing over him ... And then the clincher, the slogan squeezed out of the tube, Tresto-Chango-Alacazan! The Magic Shave Makes You a New Man!' What a campaign! It's worth

..." He waved his arms wildly. "Who knows? A fortune. Batton, Barton, Durstine, Osborn, and Cagle—just a matter of time!"

Pat laughed. He had a feeling of well-being, of pride, sensing for the first time a bond between himself and Cagle, between himself and his men. That morning, acting swiftly to sustain the momentary fervor brought about by the Chinese, he had forgotten fear and indecision.

Work and responsibility had been safety valves that expended the pressure of tension built up within him. To lift the men from their lassitude, he had changed their routine, given them direction, occupied their minds and bodies. He had Goober organize police details to salvage equipment and bury refuse on the slopes. He had Cagle redistribute ammunition, allocating percentages for machine guns, automatic rifles, and riflemen. Choy collected all food and rationed it man by man. Sanchez prepared a weak brew of hot coffee; and the men were relieved in fire-team groups to drink it and to massage one another's arms and legs. Automatic weapons were moved to different positions to mislead the enemy. Foxholes were deepened by stacking rocks, mortared by snow. And in the hours Pat had walked the slopes, he reflected now, he had seen his men begin to show interest in their tasks, begin to revive.

"Tried to count the bodies out front, Captain." Cagle's voice recalled Pat from his musings. "Can't be done. There were so many before the heavy guns, we had to push them aside to clear lanes of fire. Must be over a thousand. We licked them. We licked the bastards, didn't we?"

Goober had returned for another body. He bent over, his face close to Cagle's. "We licked them? This lash-up had five officers and two hundred and fifty men when we jumped off on this deal!" He began to count on his thick, blunt fingers. "Now we got two officers and maybe a hundred and fifty fit to squeeze a trigger. Not a bite of chow. Not even a unit of fire left. If they hit us during the day, we'll have to fight with knives and bayonets tonight. All our radios are out. Thirty-seven wounded we can't even give morphine and twenty-one more who're rotten with frostbite ..." His shrill voice wavered. "Can't even hear them now. They don't have the strength to groan." Coughing, he straightened up, still glaring at Cagle. "You figure because we got some faces washed and some garbage dumped things have changed? We're sittin' here on our butts circled like a wagon train. And they're out there gettin' ready to come after our scalps!"

The others in the aid station had turned to look and listen. They waited for the lieutenant's answer. "Buck up, Top," Cagle said. "Next thing you know the U.S. cavalry comes charging to the rescue!" But Goober didn't hear him. He was already in the warming-tent, removing a body, making room for one more.

A steady drone could be heard in the distance, swiftly increasing in intensity. The men looked skyward, not daring to hope. Then Sanchez was up, pointing to the distant hills. "Planes!"

Every man who could stand was on his feet, waving as the aircraft appeared, four of them in formation, dipping over the surrounding hills and circling. "Aussies!" Cagle yelled as the planes banked and roared overhead.

"They spotted us," Dorn shouted, slapping Pat's arm and then in horror apologizing for his thoughtlessness.

One plane peeled away from the others, leveled off, and came in, rocking its wings. They could see the pilot. Then a yellow streamer fluttered down and fell on the head of Bad Girl. Before the flight had disappeared, a runner brought the dropped message to the command post. Inside a canister, Pat found the note. "Hold on. Relief coming. Cheers!"

That single sweep over the ridge by friendly planes, that brief message, kindled hope. It was proof they were not forgotten, that they were still linked to the outside world. Pat had the note passed among the men. It was memorized, quoted, described for hours. The men elaborated on the meaning of those few words, embroidered them. Rumors were started that promised a helicopter airlift of the whole company, that the division was attacking toward them, that planes were coming loaded with supplies, that paratroopers would join them.

In the warming tent, Huckabee dressed the gaping wound in The Horse's side. "He was conscious," he told Choy. "Didn't say anythin'," but he knew me. Then he went off again."

"You rest now," Choy said. "I will watch him."

"Later." Huckabee pulled the clothing over the bandage. "You think we'll get supplies?"

"I do not know."

"It would be somethin' if he made it, wouldn't it? I mean ... it's a miracle he's alive now." He blinked and swallowed drily. "He's got a chance. Don't you think," he said hopefully, "if we get supplies ..."

"Expect nothing," Choy said. "It avoids disappointment."

Above them, on the belly of the ridge, Sanchez and Dorn sat behind a boulder with Mel Firesteen, cursing the weather, massaging their arms and legs. "If they'd just get us some chow," Sanchez said. "Man, I could eat it on a shingle!"

Firesteen wriggled his toes in his boots. "You know what today is?"

"Thursday," Dorn said.

"Friday." Firesteen beat his arms against his sides. "On Friday, me and Ruth and my mom go to my sister's place ..."

"I bet you got letters waitin' at Battalion," Sanchez said. "Got a feelin' you're gonna have that kid."

"Your wife expectin'?" Dorn asked.

"Don't know." He smiled. "Haven't thought about it since I got this shrapnel in my butt. That's somethin', huh?"

He closed his eyes, seeing himself at the door of his sister's apartment. He went in. The smell of cleanliness greeted him—of waxed floors and polished silver and gleaming surfaces, of sun-washed rooms and scrubbed woodwork and crisp linen and fresh-cut flowers. And there were the kitchen smells: The heady ambrosia of prunes and apricots and raisins bubbling beneath a lid, and the rich, hefty scent of chicken soup, and the pungent wafting of crisp bits of chicken skin and onions as golden fat was rendered, and the good comfortable smell of *chala* and the sweet aroma of crusty pastry and the peppery fume of *gefilte* fish, and the piquant savor of dill and garlic and the delicate fragrance of cinnamon and nutmeg. For a moment, his nostrils held all the odors of Friday. "You know, like Lock used to say, I'm so hungry I could eat the ass-end out of a skunk!"

The Chinese attacked boldly in midafternoon. They formed on the surrounding hills and moved down to the valley. The marines watched helplessly, unable to call on mortars or artillery to reach out for the enemy. The big guns began their deadly pounding again. Air bursts crackled above, splattering the ridge with shrapnel. Mortars skipped their fire from flank to flank, traversing again and again. The ground rocked as the fury of the attack mounted. And the din was like that of a thousand piledrivers battering frantically, ceaselessly, toward bedrock.

But no waves of infantry were launched. Instead, the attackers struck in small groups at points all along the perimeter, hitting alternately at the head and breast and belly of Bad Girl, probing for a soft spot on the lightly manned line, a line depleted by wounds and frostbite and death. Pat went from one position to the next, sent Sanchez and Dorn with messages to control weak points, moved guns to meet each new thrust, drove his men from one silent flank to a threatened break a hundred yards away.

Able Company held. Hope is the last thing to die, and they clung to that. It was dim, but it sustained them.

In late afternoon the whir of planes sounded overhead. Men gazed skyward again. Four Marine Corsairs came winging in.

"Get out the panels!" Pat shouted to Goober.

"They been placed since the Aussies came over this morning Captain. The Book says ..."

Pat grinned at him. He called out over the roar of the planes. "The Book says you need a first sergeant who knows the score!"

Goober frowned, uncertain if he was being praised or ridiculed. "Come on, you buzzboys!" he shouted as the Corsairs circled like sleek eagles over their brood.

One after the other they dove, lashing out at the enemy emplacements. The Chinese broke and ran, scrambling across the valley. The planes chased them, striking within fifty yards of their own troops, diving so low that the prop wash forced the enemy to the snow, continuing to strafe until it seemed they could never pull up.

The men stood in their holes, cheering, crying openly, unashamed. "Come on, you gyrenes. Give 'em hell!"

"Oh, you sweet, easy-livin' zoomies, pour it on, pour it on!"

"Don't let one of them goonies get up!"

"Bet you a pack of smokes that guy in the second plane's a second looie, and no brown-bagger."

"Where you gonna get smokes? Look at 'em! They get any lower, they'll ram the Chinks."

"Hey, you doggies! That's the way it's supposed to be done. Them's marines up there!"

Within twenty minutes the planes had cleared the valley. They worked over the surrounding hills, finding their own targets, scattering bombs, skidding napalm tanks of jellied flame against the slopes, and melting great patches of brown out of the white. They laced rockets into machine-gun positions, blasted artillery that had fired unmolested for four days. Finally, they climbed, orbiting above.

An Air Force transport was guided in. It made a pass, climbed again, circled, leveled off, lost altitude. This time five huge orange chutes blossomed below her. A sixth failed to open and plummeted to earth. The rest floated down, rocked gently by the wind. "They're goin' back to warm sacks and good chow," Goober said, watching the plane climb again. "And them flyboys figure they do the fightin'!"

Sanchez was following the chutes as they drifted in. "I'm prayin', sir," he said. "Just let the rest of 'em be on. Just let 'em be where we can get 'em."

The first three landed with incredible accuracy, well within the perimeter. Men were collecting them before the fourth dropped within twenty yards of Cagle's lines. The last one carried farther, wafted toward the enemy. In the confusion men left their holes, and followed the canvas containers to the command post. Goober drove them back.

The first bundle was opened. Stretchers. Blankets. Morphine. Plasma. Gauze. Adhesive. Two complete corpsmen's kits. Choy took charge of it. Huckabee was overcome and could not speak coherently at first.

Choy pulled him aside. "Plasma is all right. We will keep it between the legs of the wounded so it will not freeze."

Huckabee laughed. "Remember Monk Nelson, the radioman?" His whole body shook. "Claimed he had the hottest crotch in this outfit."

Another bundle was opened. Extra batteries for the 536s. Sound phones. Communications wire. A 300 radio had been damaged in the drop. "Ought to be able to get her going, though," Dorn said. "I'll switch some parts."

"Get a move on, doggie. Wanna hear stateside music," one of the wounded mumbled. He reached for Huckabee's parka and jerked it irritably. "Hell of a clapshack. Too much fresh air. Ugly chancre mechanic for a nurse. No bedpans ... no radio ..." The effort of speaking exhausted him. His hand dropped. There was a wan smile on his face as he drifted off to sleep.

The third container held illuminating shells. "We'll light up that valley like a drivin' range," one of the mortarmen promised.

When the fourth package was brought in and opened, the men stared silently at its contents: barbed wire, metal stakes, and a quantity of mosquito repellent. "Where the hell do they think we are, Iwo?" Goober cursed. "We need ammo. Jezoo, we got a night ahead of us, and not a hundred rounds to fight with. What's wrong with them?"

"No chow. No chow," Sanchez mourned.

"Packaged drop," Cagle said. "Stuff was on hand, I guess."

"And two were lost," Pat said. "That's where the ammo and chow went."

They climbed to the crest. From there they could see the orange cloud on the slopes of the enemy hill. They watched the Chinese clustering around it. The Corsairs swept down again and the enemy scattered, but not before the planes had littered the hillside with more dead. "If they could just blow the stuff so the Chinks don't get it," Cagle said. But the Corsairs, bombs and rockets expended, returned, rocked their wings in salute, and headed back to their carrier.

Pat called Cagle aside. He saw Goober watching them, and motioned for him. "You too, Top. You're part of this brain trust."

The first sergeant shambled toward them. "Gettin' late. Dark in another hour. They'll never get another drop in here ..."

"We got two choices," Cagle said. "We stick until there's nothing left, and try to take them on with bayonets. Or we leave without orders and try to slip out under cover of darkness."

"We couldn't carry our wounded out of here, move through a whole Chink army practically unarmed," Goober said.

"I agree." Pat sat beside him. "We've got no choice but to stick as long as we can. If we can make it till morning ..."

"There's always choice number three," Cagle said. "We can do like the man said. We can quit."

"Is that what you want to do, Chuck?"

Cagle grinned. "I'm a sucker for tradition, Captain. You know, 'Marines never say die,' and all that jazz."

The voice of the enemy sounded again as dusk fell over the valley. "Marines! You are beaten. Lay down your weapons ..."

It was silent on the ridge except for the droning, metallic voice: "Your numbers have been reduced to half ... your ammunition is exhausted. We do not wish to destroy you all, for we know that you have been forced to your crimes against the Korean people by the unprincipled reactionary leadership of your country. We wish to end the suffering. You may consider for one half-hour. You may bring in your dead and wounded. We will not fire upon you. We remind you that we have received from your airmen a gift of grenades and mortar shells and bullets ..."

The men unsheathed their knives, fixed their bayonets, and lay back in their holes to await the enemy.

26

From the observation post, Pat looked down on the circle of his lines and beyond. The surrounding hills were wrapped in the violet of the darkening sky. The wind that had died with morning was gaining strength again, whipping fresh snow across the valley.

"Sky's like that this time of year in my part of the country, too," Dorn said.

"You ever stand in Central Park, looking toward Columbus Circle, about dusk?" Cagle asked. "All that granite jutting up ... and the last of the sun sparkling like an auction-house diamond ..."

Goober slumped against a boulder. "Not likely we'll be admirin' nature tomorrow this time."

"Lived on Ninety-second near Central Park West," Sanchez said. "You're right, Mr. Cagle. City's different, clean-like when it starts gettin' dark." He stood beside Pat. "Kills me, Captain. All them souvenirs out there, and no way to get at 'em."

"You countin' on tradin' where you're headin'?" Goober shrugged. "I'm goin' back down. Huckabee and Choy got their hands full."

"Hold it!" An idea was taking shape in Pat's mind. He gestured for them all to be quiet while he thought it out. Then: "Sanchez, you've got more sense than any of us!" He laughed at their expressions. "We're going to take them up on it. We're going out to bring in our dead and wounded."

"We don't have anybody out there," Goober said.

"The Chinese don't know that. And they're too far away to tell their dead from ours."

"Then what's the angle? I don't—" Cagle slapped his forehead. "Damn! What's wrong with my high-priced intellect?"

Pat crouched, and the others knelt around him. "There's ammo down there. And weapons. And chow. I can see an arsenal from here. Chuck, you cover your sector. Top, you set up a supply point at the C.P. where they can't see what we're up to. Sanchez, you and Dorn pass the word to the platoons. We'll have the men work in pairs, with a poncho. Have them load a body and all the ammo and weapons they can haul, and bring them in."

The others were caught up in his excitement. "It just might work. Got to move fast," Goober said. "We'll stay out as long as they let us. Captain, don't forget that wire we got. We can use it soon as it gets a little darker."

For Pat it was a fresh start; his plan, his idea. He was part of the show now; and though the stakes were forbiddingly high, the challenge was irresistible. It was the ancient, time-honored challenge of two leaders dueling by tactic, skill, and guile.

Within minutes the ridge was alive with activity. Within minutes the men were piling the enemy arms within the position, out of sight of the Chinese, and then hurrying back to carry in still another body and another load. Stiff hands were pried from Japanese, Russian, and American weapons; bandoleers were chipped from frozen shoulders. Enemy bodies were stacked like sandbags around foxholes. Containers of rice were sent to the command post where Choy poured them into helmets and cooked the company's first hot meal in five days. By the time the deadline had expired, they were only half finished, but the Chinese did not open fire on them. When darkness closed in, men with rag-wrapped hands held circlets of wire, and walked huge barbed concertinas to positions blocking the most vulnerable areas on the perimeter.

When the Chinese spoke again over the loudspeaker, the men were settled in their holes, sorting their ammunition, working the bolts of their strange new weapons. "... We have seen how great are your losses," the voice called out. Laughter rippled over the ridge. "We have kept our word not to molest you."

"Sucker!" someone shouted in reply.

"We are prepared to give you the treatment we have promised. We keep our word. Fire five times to indicate you are ready to lay down your arms. We repeat: Fire five times ..."

Pat signaled the mortarman. Holding the tube between his legs, he nodded to the man beside him. The last high-explosive round was dropped in. It shuttled out, arcing over the valley and falling in the vicinity of the loudspeaker. The marines heard no more. They settled down, with hope again, to await the night and its developments—and the morning and planes and relief.

The soft glow of the wood stove illumined the warming-tent. A helmetful of rice was boiling, adding its odor to the stench of vomit and gangrene and unwashed bodies.

Sanchez held a flashlight while Dorn spread the parts of the 300 radio on a poncho and scrutinized each. "Well, we've got enough to get one set workin — I hope."

"You gotta make it work, Woody." Sanchez's clothes were steaming, and he stepped back from the stove. "You gonna be a 'lectrician? You're pretty good at it."

Dorn checked the contacts on the wiring. "Didn't know a condenser from a rectifier until I got in the service. Anyway, no, I've had a notion a long time to buy me a farm. Got it all worked out. Some money comin' to me ..."

"They grow corn out where you live, huh?"

"Not there." He stripped the insulation from a wire. "Don't want to go back there. Thinkin' about South America. Colombia." He hesitated, as if he were afraid Sanchez might laugh at him. "I knew a guy once, heard about him really. He went there. Did real well. Wheat. Rice. Cattle." He moved the batteries closer to the stove to thaw. "You ever want somethin' real bad, bad enough to do anything for it? And you feel ... like you're all alone, and you're scared, deep down, you haven't really got what it takes ..."

"I know what you mean." Sanchez lowered his voice and switched the flashlight to his other hand. "Not like wantin' a woman either. Different. It's like when somebody does somethin' for you, and you wanna make it up to 'em, and you wish—I dunno ..." His swarthy face was corrugated in a frown of utter concentration. "Like some guy is kickin' hell outta a friend of yours, and you can't do nothin' about it ... or like some guys you read in the paper had it tough one time, they get to be champeen or a big-time ballplayer, and they go back to the old neighborhood and teach boxin' to the kids or give them autograph baseballs ... and you wanna do somethin' big like that ... only, you know ..."

Huckabee brushed past them and squatted beside one of the wounded. He shifted the stretcher, pulled back the blanket. The feet were black with frostbite. Already the ankles were swollen twice their normal size and the greenish flesh was darkening. "How's it look?" the marine whispered.

Huckabee lifted one foot tenderly. "Hurt bad?"

"Not too bad."

"Okay, crap out."

"Know somethin'?" The marine grinned, his voice cracked. "Wouldn't believe it ... Fell asleep a while ago ... yesterday, I think ... damnedest thing ... had a wet dream." He tittered, his chest heaving. "Damnedest thing ..."

In the corner of the tent, The Horse lay motionless, swaddled in blankets. Huckabee removed the dressing and examined his wound. The lacerations extended from below the ribs to the pelvis. His mind was so dull with weariness that he was no longer sure of treatment. He did not know the extent of the injury, and was afraid to explore it. Binding the wound again, he pulled up the blankets. When he glanced at The Horse's face he was startled to see he was awake.

"Huck?"

"Save your strength," Huckabee whispered.

"... tell you somethin' ..." The Horse wet his lips. His fingers tightened on Huckabee's hand for an instant, and then relaxed. He closed his eyes again.

Huckabee sat beside him. He pushed the straggling brown hair back from the pocked forehead. If we could get him out, to a hospital and a doctor. There was so little he could do for him here. His drowsy mind could not even recall enough elemental anatomy to know what vital organs lay beneath the torn flesh. And what about nourishment? Water? Sedatives? He had sutured the wound after inserting a piece of tubing for drainage. Was that right? Had the tube been sterile? He tried to remember where he had got the idea of using the tubing. In the hospital in Mobile when he was an orderly? Great Lakes? Maybe

I made it up, he thought. Maybe it's all wrong—a mistake. If he were a doctor, he would know. The Horse would live. A doctor would make him live. And yet, despite his ignorance, despite the lack of drugs and equipment and competent care, this man was alive—alive because of him. In spite of him? Sitting there, one hand on the stretcher, Huckabee fell asleep.

Choy found him that way. For a moment, he hesitated uncertainly. Then he eased Huckabee to the ground beside The Horse and spread the blanket to cover them both. Taking a spoon from his pocket, he stirred the rice on the stove. "Sanchez, you will feed those who are awake?" Sanchez nodded and put his flashlight on the poncho with the radio parts.

At the far end of the command post, Pat and Goober were bent over a new casualty, giving him morphine. Choy crossed to them. The wounded marine had been carrying rice to the foxholes, and someone had mistaken him for the enemy. They had fired a burst from a burp gun, nearly severing his leg. He was writhing now; his breathing was labored and his tongue worked over his lips. "Huckabee is asleep," Choy said. "The first time I have seen him asleep."

Goober stood. "Well, wake him, dammit. Somebody's gotta take that leg off."

The marine's eyes were wide with anguish. "No-oo! Please. No-oo! Sew it ... fix it up." Then as if to reinforce his plea, "It's my birthday ... my birthday ..."

"There is little alternative," Choy said.

Pat had removed his web belt and slipped it above the dangling leg at the thigh. He was twisting a bayonet to tighten it, cutting off the flow of blood. "All right, Choy. You do it."

"Please! Oh, God, please. No-oo! Captain ... don't ... sir ... sir ..."

Choy returned to the warming-tent. A few minutes later he came back with a combat knife that glowed white-hot. Pat held the boy's shoulders and talked to him gently. "You want to be all right, don't you? You've got to let us help you." The words sounded inane, even as he spoke them; he didn't try to say any more.

The wounded marine was losing consciousness, but he clung to Pat's hand, speaking feebly, pleading. "Promise ... promise ... not my leg ... Promise ..."

Choy held the knife out to Pat. "I can not," he said. "I do not know how."

Pat looked at Goober. "Well, Top ... I'll hold him. Go ahead. Take it off."

"I'm gonna wake Huckabee. Chrisakes, he can go back to sleep afterward! What difference does it make?"

"We have lost five corpsmen already," Choy said. "Three dead. Two wounded. There is only Huckabee and that man on the lines."

"Let him sleep," Pat said, "or he won't be any good to any of us."

"Oh, God Almighty, please ... promise me ... birthday ... birthday ..."

"It is no use. Why do it?" Choy said.

"There's a chance. Always a chance," Pat said. He took the knife from Choy. Goober was watching him, eyes narrowed. "Hold him," Pat said. Then he placed the blade on the ragged wound, heard the sickening hiss, tasted the cloying odor in his throat, and began a rhythmic sawing. He cut through tendons and ligaments, and after an eternity felt muscle resisting the knife. Sweat streamed down his face and body. He pressed harder against the blade.

"He's dead," Choy said. But Pat did not hear him. "Captain!"

"Yes?" Pat said, as if awakening from hypnotic sleep. "What?" Choy put his hands over Pat's, stopping the motion of the blade. "He's dead."

Pat got unsteadily to his feet. He felt lightheaded, cold and giddy. "There was a chance ..." He swallowed and looked away. "I'm going to the OP. See what I can do with that heavy gun. When you finish, Top, I can use you up there."

The first sergeant stared after him. "I'll be up." He watched the captain climb out of the crater and move off into the darkness.

Once out of sight, Pat dropped to his knees and buried his face in the cleansing snow. His bruised back, his sore chest, his burning arms were all subordinated to the turmoil of his mind and the convulsive heaving of his stomach.

Back at the command post at that moment, Goober was saying to Choy: "He was cold as a witch's tit. Sawed on that thing like it was a T-bone steak. Ain't he got feelin's?"

Choy was wrapping a poncho around the dead man. "He has feelings."

"That's the kind of thing the skipper woulda done."

Choy nodded. "Anderson was the most fearless man I have ever known. Most men walk a chalk line ... between cowardice and heroism. In responding to the moment, they fall one way or the other. But he responded to something else— something that had no relation to either fear or bravery. You could see it in his eyes." He lifted one end of the stretcher. "But for Captain Patrick such things do not come easy. He does feel, you see. He is human. He is even typical of his kind. But his kind do not make the best soldiers."

They carried the body to the long line of dead, and Goober returned to the warming tent. "How you comin' on that radio, Dogface?" he asked.

"Pretty soon," Sanchez said. "He's puttin' it together now."

"Jezoo! That's all I get. Pretty soon ... pretty soon.' Pretty soon, my ass!"

In the back of the tent, two men lay side by side, one with a broken back, the other with a severe neck wound. Neither could move his head. They whispered to the tent top.

"Funny, the way things go. Coupla months ago, I'm runnin' a loom in Passaic, makin' reserve meetin's once a week ... had a slot lined up as forward on the plant team. Ever play basketball?"

"Naw. Never did." The corpsman, the same man who had argued with Huckabee a few days before, tried to clear his throat, grunting, straining with the effort. "First game I seen was in New Orleans when I come in to enlist in the Navy. Lord, I seen some things since! Was seventeen. Three years ago. Just a kid. Never been out from home. Seen the whole country now ... damn' near the whole world. France. North Africa. Italy. Blessed by the Pope ..."

"If I wasn't married, think I'd stay in. Peacetime, must be a good life." The drug was wearing off, and the pain was stealing up from the small of his back. "Wife wouldn't go for it. You know how it is with women. Same friends to play cards with, in the Altar Guild with her ma, priest confirmed her ..."

"Didn't think you was Catholic. That 'ski' on your name, and you're kinda dark, and your nose, and from up North. Guess I had you down for a Jew."

The man smiled. "Polack. Me and my wife both. My folks was born Americans, though. Sent me a rosary last mail. From the old country."

"Lost mine," The corpsman tried to ignore the tremors in his neck. He did not want his companion to stop talking. "Musta took it offa me when I got hit. Huckabee. Gotta ask him. I was seein' after a fella got hit with Mr. Anderson's reserve bunch. Sniper got me. Huckabee come out. Couldn't move me till they got the Chink. And he stayed there with me. Musta been an hour ... more. Kept tellin' me 'You're gonna be fine ... gonna be fine.' And I cussed him 'cause I knew he was lyin' ..."

The marine from Passaic held on to consciousness by trying to speak. His voice was weak, lost. "What's the date?" he asked after they had both been silent for several minutes.

"Lost track. December somethin'."

"Been here how many days—six, seven?"

"Tomorrow, I think, is five."

"Tomorrow. Heard somebody say eleven-fifteen a bit ago. Be light, another six hours."

"I ain't fixin' to sleep."

"Me neither. My turn to go out soon. Wanna be awake. Don't wanna go to sleep out there."

"Yeah. That could be bad."

"Keep thinkin' I'll freeze to death, I sleep out there."

"That's funny."

"What?"

"A fella gets the idea he's the only one thinks somethin' ... I keep dreamin' the same thing. They put me out for my turn ... and I ... die out there."

The marine worked his hand under the blankets, felt the edge of the stretcher, reached across the inches separating him from the corpsman. He slipped the crucifix on his rosary into the other man's hand, held the beads himself.

"They're out there, Captain. I can hear 'em." Goober was peering into the darkness. "Coulda used a moon tonight."

"Here. Screw the barrel in. We're going to need this gun." Pat had salvaged a belt-feed pawl from another weapon. He was reassembling the bolt now, feeling his way, visualizing the part in his hand. His fingers trembled. The tension of waiting was beginning to tell on him.

"Not gonna be able to get this thing together in the dark, not in time, anyway," Goober said. But Pat had his grudging admiration. The captain knew his weapons. Getting the bolt together in the pitch black was no snap. He tightened the barrel, fixed his eyes on the front again. "Listen! Can't you hear them sloshin' out there?"

Pat didn't look up. "With all those tin cans on the wire, and the trip flares and booby traps, we'll know when they get close. No use wasting illumination." He busied himself with the weapon, finally sliding the bolt in place. "Never was any good with this spring. How about you, Top?"

Goober's head was bent over, eyes closed, straining to hear. Slowly he moved his heavy body behind the gun. Using a cartridge, he compressed the long spring and turned it in place, locking it. "Never thought we'd make it in time," he whispered.

"I'd still be at it tomorrow morning if I'd have had to set that spring." On the sound phone beside him, Pat called Chuck Cagle and had him send men to take the gun to its position where it could fire along the barbed wire.

A marine brought a large can of hot rice. "Go on," Goober told Pat. "Just leave me some."

The mush was watery and flat; it smelled rancid and looked like laundry starch. But it was steaming. Pat felt the warmth of each mouthful travel through his body, and for a moment he felt comforted.

It was two forty-five. By five-thirty it would be light enough to see a little. Examining the level of rice between spoonfuls, to be sure it would be divided evenly, he considered the time. Two hours and forty-five minutes to go. He wondered if the ammunition would last when the attack came ... as it would surely come, as surely as the sun would rise.

The machine gunners came for the weapon. "Glad you fixed her, sir," one of them whispered. Then, smiling, "Gotta admit, though, I was sorta hopin' we could drink the vodka in the water jacket."

"Top and I held off, too," Pat said. He passed the rice to Goober. "When we get back with the rest of the battalion, we're going to have a party with the vodka we left."

"Yes sir, when we get back."

Goober motioned them to be quiet and beckoned Pat forward. "Captain, I ain't hearin' things. They're out there."

Ten minutes later, they heard the cans clanking on the wire. It started below the observation post, and was taken up before Cagle's platoon. The whole wire vibrated with noise. "I'll call for flares," Pat said.

"Here they come!" Goober grabbed the sound phone, shouted into it. "Open fire!" Leaning over the rocks, he yelled to the men below. "Open fire!"

"Wait!" Pat cried. But it was too late. A machine gun began to chatter, then some rifles, then another gun, and another, until every workable weapon on that side of the ridge was sweeping the length of the barbed concertina.

The assault was completely uncharacteristic of the enemy. No blasts on the shepherd's horn. No flares to mark boundaries. No probing. No attempt to cut the wire or breach it with explosives. "They're not out there," Pat shouted at Goober. "It's a trick!"

"I heard the wire. They were hittin' all along the line."

Pat called the lone mortar and asked for illumination. When the flare burst, the front was deserted. The Chinese had crawled forward, tied strings to the wire, moved back, and shaken it. "Cease fire!" Pat called. He repeated the order by phone. But it took five full minutes to quiet the ridge again. "That cost us. We wasted a lot of ammo. And they watched our tracers, marked the automatic weapons for sure." Sanchez joined them. "Thought I'd better come up."

"Any luck with the radio?"

"He's still workin' on it, sir."

"Get on the phone. Have the platoons move their BARs and machine guns wherever it's possible. Quickly."

The calls made, Sanchez said, "The Horse, sir. He was awake for a couple minutes. Wouldn'ta give him a chance ..."

Before Pat could reply, the enemy mortars, silenced since the Corsairs struck during the afternoon, began to burst across the ridge. Their fire might have been called by the defenders themselves, for each shell was predictable. First the machine guns on the flank were tried for. Next the light guns that tied in the platoons. Then the automatic rifles. Most of the weapons had been moved in time to alternate positions, but the machine gun Goober and Pat had repaired was knocked out and the gunner killed. Two BARmen were wounded. A light gun was damaged. Pat listened grimly to the reports relayed to him by Sanchez. "They're smart," he said. "No denying that."

"Damn! I coulda swore they were comin' in!" Goober said.

Chuck Cagle, breathless, clambered up to them. "What the hell gives? Why did you pass the order to fire? Gave away our positions, got clobbered ..." His voice was harsh, and he made no attempt to control his anger. "First round they got my heavy. First damn' round! The kid had the tripod, was just moving ..."

"Sorry, Chuck. Everybody's edgy."

"The ammo we threw away!"

"It's over. Forget it."

"Forget it?" Cagle raised his voice again.

Pat walked him toward the path. "Get back to your platoon, Chuck." He spoke softly, but his tone was firm. "I need you down there ..."

When Pat returned, Goober sat across from him, no longer studying the front, looking instead at the captain. First, he had expected to be berated for his stupidity, for behaving like a boot replacement. Then he had thought Pat would defend himself against the lieutenant's accusations and fix the blame for what had happened. As usual, he thought, can't figure this bird. "Got to be more careful about ammo now, sir," he said.

"Sanchez, have the platoons pass the word about conserving ammo."

The shepherd's horn. The colored flares to mark the flanks. The screams of *Sha! Sha!* They could hear men running through the snow as the enemy approached the wire, hear the sharp commands of the officers above the tumult. A trip flare was set off. Another. In the glare, Pat saw men rush the wire, throw themselves face down across it, pressing the barbs into their bodies, but pinning the barrier to the snow. Then silhouettes emerged behind them and other men rushed across their backs. Pat called for more illumination from his mortar. The three men watched marine gunners blast the breach in the wire. As the enemy approached, trampled their comrades underfoot, rushed across in single file, they were knocked down until there was a great mound weighted on the wire.

"Sonovabitch marine we kill! Sonovabitch marines you die!" The chant came from the left flank, then from the right. The entire company was engaged as the Chinese tightened the great circle around them, drove in against the wire, slowed, were battered down.

"Can't manage for long at this rate," Pat said to Goober. "BARs must be about through now." A phone check proved him right. The machine guns were still in ammunition. The rest of Able Company fought with enemy weapons. The shepherd's horn sounded in the rear, a longer, more insistent wail. Firing ceased as the enemy withdrew. The call was repeated in the front. Again the enemy pulled back. "They're going to lick their wounds and try again," Pat said.

"Or they're gonna bull through at one spot," Goober said. "Maybe we better get ready to move some people if they do."

"You do this for me, sir?" It was Huckabee.

"Do what?"

"Goat's chicken. Choy says you're okay at this sorta business." He held out his hand. There was a long, deep cut on his thumb. A needle hung from the wound. "Grenade. I was sewin' myself when I had to quit ..."

"The captain could do it all right," Goober said. He chewed at his lip. "Never tried it ... but, hell, I guess I can ... Captain's busy."

Pat watched them. While Huckabee lay there, Goober followed his directions, sewed a ragged stitch, drew the ripped flesh together, finally knotting the suture.

The shepherd's horn alerted them once more. Sanchez, who had been holding Huckabee's arm, put it down carefully. "They're comin' in again."

"They've got to practice to blow that bad," Huckabee said.

"Sir!" Sanchez crawled up to Pat. "Supposin' Huck sat up here and imitated their calls. Blow that withdraw one, where they wail real long, that kind of thing."

"It'd confuse hell outta them," Goober said. "Wouldn't know what was goin' on."

The bugle was brought up from Huckabee's gear in the command post. Twice he mimicked the withdrawal call on the captured bugle. Twice the Chinese disengaged. On their third assault, he attempted it again, but this time the enemy ignored it and began to signal with flares instead.

"Reckon they finally smarted up," Huckabee said.

"You saved us an hour at least," Pat told him.

"All right if I go below, sir? I'm gonna try The Horse on some chow."

The sergeant who had led the ill-fated reserve appeared. Following him were four of the frostbite cases being carried by men with superficial wounds. "We come to help," the sergeant said.

"The Chinks are working in too close," Pat said. "If they break into the perimeter, you men wouldn't have a chance."

One of the Army volunteers sat up on his stretcher. "Hellfire, Captain! It's better than layin' flat on your back down there with nothin' to do but wait for some goonie to come and slit your throat."

Pat shrugged. He had them propped in holes below five minutes later.

Now Able Company's front was extended in every direction. Bad Girl was entirely surrounded; and the Chinese were concentrating on the belly where only one machine gun was still in action. Pat switched every available automatic weapon to stem the advance. But the wire was finally breached by bangalore torpedoes and mortar fire. The enemy poured through, heading for the rocks. The platoon on the head of Bad Girl was already out of ammunition. Cagle's men on the breast could manage only a feeble line of fire. And dawn was an hour away.

The marines fought on, scavenging for weapons and ammunition in the brief lulls, rolling boulders down on the climbing enemy, swinging their rifles like clubs as the Chinese struck within platoon positions, using combat knives as daggers. Pat went to the belly where the pressure threatened to sever the final lines. With bayonets fixed, the men stood in their holes, met the enemy, and twice drove them back. Somehow, when the first light began to give shape to the forms in the darkness, the line still held.

Pat heard a wild cheer coming from somewhere on the ridge near the command post. It was taken up until it encircled him. He looked up, expecting to see planes. But there were none. Climbing to the crest, he saw that the enemy was disengaging all along the line; and within the position marines had slumped back in their holes, as if they had given their last breath in a curse, and could say or do no more.

"Captain!" It was Chuck Cagle, running, waving his arms. "The radio! The radio ... They want you down there ..."

27

"Able Six. This is Chancellor Six... How do you read me? Over." Skinhead's froggy voice croaked between long, weighted pauses.

Pat's lips worked to form words as his mind groped blindly for a proper reply. He found he could not speak. After all he and his company had suffered—the subzero weather, the unyielding terrain, the relentless enemy—at last relief had come. And yet there was no gladness in him; only unspeakable weariness.

"Able Six? Able Six?" Hidden in the rising mist of morning, only five hundred yards away, the battalion commander stood at the crest of another rocky ridge, the remnants of two companies sprawled below him. A chill shook his body. Able Company had held. His battalion had come to midpoint in its ordeal. "Able Six ... I say again, how do you read me?"

"Chan—Chancellor Six. I read you..." Pat had to pause to summon breath enough to finish. "I read you ... five by five."

"Tell him about Lieutenant Anderson," Goober said.

"Pat, it's good to hear your voice." Skinhead bit his lips, struggling to subdue a wave of strong emotion. "Wait, one," he said. He sat down. Since first plunging through the Chinese lines, he had rammed his battalion across-country, over eight tortuous miles. When dead and wounded multiplied, when they were forced to claw their way at night over a two-thousand-foot mountain range, when the surrounding enemy threatened to entrap them, his men had been pushed to the limits of their endurance—and gone beyond them. He had concealed his dreadful certainty that Able Company had been destroyed. But the men had never doubted. They had not considered the odds, the weather, the uncertain leadership, the dearth of food or ammunition, as he had. It was so much simpler for them. Somewhere before them, they had known, other marines—surrounded, outnumbered, alone-awaited them. Able Company had to hold; and they had to relieve them. It was as clear-cut as that.

Skinhead rubbed his glove unobtrusively across his temple and the corner of his eye. "Pat. How many casualties do you have?" He wanted to say more, but could not. So he clenched his teeth, and made noises in his throat, and shielded his eyes. "Over."

Pat pictured Skinhead as he had seen him last; that image did not correspond at all with this trembling voice. "Wait one, sir." He tried to recall the casualty figures, but could not clear his mind. "Top, you have a strength report?" Dizziness assailed him and he had to lean on Dorn's shoulder. When the soldier looked up, Pat said, "Good work ... the radio." Dorn smiled.

The first sergeant was searching his pockets for a scrap of paper, but his hands worked clumsily, and he had to take off his gloves. "Tell him we lost"—he coughed furiously—"we lost Lieutenant Anderson; tell him that first."

Looking at Goober, Pat noticed that the jowls were gone, and the rolls of fat beneath the chin as well. "I'll tell him ... about all we lost," he said. Goober handed him the slip of paper. The figures had no immediate meaning for Pat as he labored over the writing. He might have been reading a grocery list or a livestock inventory. They were not names, not people. "Ninety-eight men, two officers, counting slightly wounded, still effectives. Thirty-two evacuated. Thirty-four K.I.A. Eighty-three wounded or frostbite, forty of those stretcher cases. Over."

There was a long silence. Six miles to Hagaru, Skinhead was thinking. The regiment was still fighting its way down the road from Yudam-ni. With luck, he might get his battalion through before the enemy closed the escape route. "We'll talk ... later," he told Pat. "Sending Charlie Company to carry you out of there. We'll cover withdrawal with planes. Have a radio relay through Hagaru. Over."

Carry you out of there. Pat had missed the rest of the transmission. He studied his men, sitting around him in the snow, listening intently, watching him with hollow eyes, mouths slack. They had expended themselves in false hope so often; and now they, too, were unable to feel anything but numbness. But carry us out? Of course. To do otherwise would be ... theatrical. Still ... only the helpless should be carried. The danger was not that they would fail to cross those five hundred yards to Battalion's position. The danger was that, believing themselves helpless, they would never reach Hagaru. When Pat spoke, he was not entirely sure of his motive; but his voice was firm as he committed himself and his men by saying, "Send us some 30-caliber ammo. Able Company will come out on its own, sir. Over."

"Pat, are you sure ..." The battalion commander changed his mind. There would be air cover, supporting fires. Able Company need move alone for only five hundred yards. "Roger. Coordinate with me on requests for support. See you soon. Out."

"Tell him," Goober said. "Tell him about-"

"Not now." He could not single out any one man. Tightening his hood against the rising blast of the wind, he forced a note of command into his voice. "All right. Let's get squared away. I want you people ready to move in an hour."

The icy wind spilled across the hills like an invisible river, driving black clouds before it.

In the command post, everything that could not be carried was thrown on a huge bonfire. The stretchers of the wounded surrounded the inferno and marines stood behind them, soaking in the warmth as flames licked at tent canvas and broken stocks and web equipment. "Huck?"

"You been talkin' too much, Horse. We got a long haul ahead. You rest."

"Y'think I'll make it ... don't you?"

He did not. The wound in his friend's side was full of pus and badly distended. Drainage had stopped. Only constant sedation could hold the pain in check. He had been hit two days before. And a doctor was ... how many days away? "Sure you will," Huckabee said. "There'll be a hospital and doctors ..."

"Thought a awful lot ... 'bout you bein' pissed off at me ... before I got hit, I mean. Even when the captain was draggin' me in, was thinkin' how I never meant ... it was just ..."

"Try to sleep, Horse."

"Wanna tell you." Against his will, he trembled and winced. "All right to laugh at yourself ... let people laugh at you ... sometimes. But you ... wanna be doctor, don'tcha?"

Huckabee nodded, knowing all the while that it was impossible, that it was unattainable, a hollow promise he had lulled himself with, a boast he had made, deceiving everyone but himself. "You sleep, hear?"

"... People got to respect you, take you serious, but they won't if you don't ... respect yourself." His face twitched. "Never been good sayin' things ... but I know, Huck, really. Miserable when nobody ever knows you for real ..."

Huckabee fumbled with the blankets, not knowing how to reply, no longer knowing even how to react.

The Horse had closed his eyes, but he did not sleep. His mind was full of the past, full of old memories. Eddie Gleason was thirty-three years old. At twenty-eight he had been a washed-up boxer. He had made up his mind to quit. He was getting hurt more often, and there were long jumps between fights. And no future. For a year he framed the arguments he would use with Morrie. But something always happened. He had three wins in a row. Decisions. Close. But maybe ... Morrie gave him a toy terrier for Christmas, a tiny thing that licked his face and slept in his lap. He bought a quack's course of treatments for acne, and went into debt. He substituted in a main bout that was televised. Outpointed, but he made it a good fight. Then his father needed money, so Eddie waited.

After a preliminary with a tough kid, in which he'd been mauled badly for four rounds before being tagged for the count by a wild left, he blurted his decision to Morrie.

The good-natured old man heard him out. "All right," he said at last, his cadaverous face serious. "So you don't want to fight no more. So what's for you to do? You got no education, no trade. What kinda job you gonna get?"

"There's lots of things ..."

Morrie knocked the bowl of his pipe into his dry, wrinkled hand. He sat on the rubdown table while Eddie dressed. "You're no dummy, but what can you do to make a buck? Be a dishwasher? Be a elevator boy with a Philip Morris uniform? Be a hackie making change with dimes and nickels so maybe you'll get a tip? Or you wanna be like your old man, herding a bunch of tourists around on sightseeing trips, breaking your neck to get a cut from the souvenir stores? What's the matter with you?" His false teeth rattled on the pipe stem. "Listen to me, Eddie. I been thinking about you plenty. I always liked you. I promised your mother I'd treat you decent. You got clean habits. You play fair. We get along. Right? Ain't I always did what's right for you?" Eddie had to agree. "You been straight with me, Morrie." Combing his hair carefully, he turned from the mirror. "You know I'd do anythin' for you."

Morrie laughed. "Don't do for me. Do for yourself. I been thinking. Tell me this now, what's that blonde broad in the movies got—you know, the one we seen in Tampa last week?" He didn't wait for an answer. "She's got tits, that's what. Tits! So she makes a mint. Durante. Tell me what Durante's got? A nose! And Cantor, he's got pop eyes. And Joe E. Brown's got a big mouth!" He slid off the table, and walked across the room. "So what's this got to do with you? You wanna know?"

Eddie tied a neat Windsor knot, dimpled it. He was used to Morrie's thinking processes. "Sure I wanna know."

"Okay. What do you have? I tell you honest. You got a mug only a mother could love. So you use it. I thought it all out. And you can go to work as soon as you learn a few simple gimmicks. You'll wrassle." The fighter looked at the concrete floor, counted the cracked lines, noted the discarded tape by the table leg, his black trunks with the shamrock his mother had stitched for him, the bottle of liniment on the chair. Morrie meant well, he told himself. But he sometimes forgot that people have feelings. "I don't know how ..."

"What's to know? All you got to know is how to put on a good act. The promoters don't give a damn about anything else. I got four boys wrasslin' right now. And they're doing good. They don't get hurt and every guy gets his share." Eddie was shaking his head. "I ever give you a bum steer? I treat you right or don't I?"

"I don't think I wanna do it, Morrie. I decided I'm gonna find me a decent job. Settle down. Get married maybe."

"Married?" The old man curled his lip. "You got somebody in mind?"

"You work. You meet a girl."

"Listen to me. Okay, you wanna get married. So you gotta have dough. Listen. I got it figured, the whole business. This ain't just on the spur of the minute." He helped Eddie into his coat. "We shave your head. You grow yourself a black, bushy mustache, a big one. We fix you up with one of them big fur hats." He put both hands on Eddie's shoulders. "And we get rid of the pooch. We get you a big dog, a wolfhound, something we can put a muzzle on, some kind of mean-looking, bastard, see? Then we call you The Terrible Cossack!" He beamed, his enthusiasm mounting.

"Morrie, I ain't no wrassler."

"When you get in the ring, you dance a kazatskey or say a Russian prayer or something. We'll get one of them jewel-handled swords, a watchacallit, a smithereen. We'll find somebody can give you some Russian words. You'll make dough like you never dreamed. It'll catch on. Everybody hates the Russians. The Terrible Cossack! We'll bill you as The Ugliest Man in the World!"

As it turned out, The Terrible Cossack did make money. He danced and prayed before large crowds. He agonized, grimaced horribly, screamed at referees, threatened spectators, fought golden-haired, muscle-bound heroes, posed for pictures with a mastiff he hated and waved a jeweled scimitar in his Russian Dance of Victory.

On his thirtieth birthday, he rammed his shaved head into a ring pole and was carried from the arena while the crowd booed. Morrie paid the hospital and the doctors. Morrie promised he'd be as good as new. But as soon as he was up and about again, Eddie Gleason walked into the Federal Building, stopped before the first recruiting sign he saw, and volunteered for the United States Marine Corps.

Snow crystals brushed his face as Pat watched the steel-gray sky. Corsairs were circling again after foiling the enemy's attempt to shell the position. Slinging his pack over one shoulder, Pat left the command post for the last time and strode down to the base of the ridge. He had ordered the dead moved there. The virgin snow lay on that slope and the scars of battle were all but blotted out. A wide, sheltered crater offered some semblance of a grave.

The bodies were laid side by side, rigid and alike as toy soldiers, forming an unbroken supine rank. Someone had carved an uneven Cross and a Star of David in a shattered tree trunk. Pat stood looking down at the poncho-draped men. Not men, he thought. There seemed to be nothing of man in the frozen forms of the dead. Above him he saw his company moving through the curtain of snow toward the crypt. Slowly they wound down until they bunched below him, before the open pit. Only the rear guard remained above to secure the withdrawal. The stretcher bearers still held their burdens, afraid that if they put them down they wouldn't have the strength to lift them again.

One of the wounded was speaking, but Pat could not make out the words. The bearer relayed the message. "Sir, couldn't we at least cover them over? Like this, it's ..." his voice trailed off.

"No way. No tools. You know that."

Firesteen climbed up beside him. "Sir, shouldn't somebody say somethin'?" There was no answer in the captain's eyes; and the corporal turned to the group below. "Mr. Cagle? You're a good talker."

The lieutenant was tightening a splint for one of his men. "Huh? Oh." He shook his head. "What's there to say?"

"It's not right," Firesteen said. "Sir, it's just not right, leavin' 'em without a decent buryin', without even a word."

To make a speech, to use the usual trite phrases about dying for country or giving their all, to mouth the words "courage," "honor," "sacrifice," would profane the dead. And when Pat tried to recall a single prayer, he could not. "Suppose we just ... everybody is just quiet for a minute."

Sanchez knelt. Dorn dropped beside him. Stretchers were put down. Other men dropped to their knees. Pat slipped down between Firesteen and Huckabee. "Take off your helmets!" Goober shouted.

Pat closed his eyes. It was not sorrow, or even resignation he felt. It was pity, and anger. Pity for the dead that the frozen earth would not receive, pity for the living, pity for himself. Anger because they had—all of them—lived so little, known so little about the world that had brought them to this place. And yet, he had seen in all of them, no matter how they suffered, no matter how cruel the pain, a deeply rooted love of life and a fierce tenacity in clinging to the last parting strand of it. He knew a nearly overpowering need to weep, to purge himself, but he remained dry-eyed. After a moment, he stood. "Saddle up. We're moving out."

The men gave no sign that they had heard him. "Captain, it don't seem right to leave our people like this." The soldier, the motor-transport man who had become a machine gunner, came forward. "We're not leavin' the goonies no gear ... so why leave—"

"Can't help it," Pat said, cutting him off, trying to explain to him, to all of them. "We just don't have enough hands. We've got wounded to carry. And our weapons. There's still a fight ahead. We've got to make the road before we're cut off. Nothing we can do about these men anyway. They're dead."

One marine, his head swathed in bandages, rolled off his stretcher and pulled himself to his feet. Then another, and another. All along the path the wounded who could move were trying to leave their litters, pushing themselves off into the snow. The others stood watching Pat, waiting.

Exerting all his will, he held himself in check, afraid to give himself over to the wonder that welled within him. What made such men? What drove them? "All right," he said at last. "All right." And as they began to gather the bodies, stacking them like corded wood, three to a stretcher, he moved past them to the assembly point below.

The crater was soon emptied. Goober stood where the dead had lain. He took off his burned red muffler, hesitated, then folded it and placed it beneath the tree trunk. Walking a few steps, he stopped and looked back. Then he returned, grabbed the tattered rag, shook the snowflakes from it, and lumbered away.

Sanchez, slinging his newly gathered souvenirs, had been watching him. "Go on with the captain," he told Dorn. "I'll be along." Neglected in the crisis of the night before, two of the wounded—linked by a rosary—had frozen to death outside the warming tent. One held the crucifix, the other the beads. Sanchez had separated them, and kept the cross to be turned in. Taking a Chinese rifle from his back, he plunged it into the snow at the center of the crater. He didn't believe, he told himself. But that couldn't matter. In the trigger guard of the enemy weapon, he placed the crucifix.

"Better come now," Dorn said, lifting the radio.

"I told you to go on! Got to be hangin' around me all the time?" At that, Dorn turned and shuffled down the trail, past the stretchers. But he stopped again to wait for his friend.

"Must keep moving, no matter what they throw at us," Pat told Cagle. "Should join the rest of the battalion when we clear the valley. Then six long miles ..."

Cagel was looking back at the ridge. "What good did it do?" he asked. "What in the name of God did we prove?"

Pat shrugged. The snow was whirling about them now, settling over the scabrous mountain, already piecing together a white shroud for Bad Girl Ridge.

28

They fought the enemy. They fought the brutal hills. They fought the blizzard that swept down upon them, buffeting their ranks, driving them to the earth. Prodded and cursed, they stood again, and trudged on.

The three companies of the battalion plodded across the mountains, rescuer and rescued intermingled. New dead joined the old as the badly wounded weakened and died, as small bands of Chinese ambushed segments of the column, as hidden mortars dropped death among them. There were no more stretchers, no more men to carry them. Sleds were made by lashing saplings together, and the living were harnessed to them.

In the bleak light of noon and in the darkening hours the Corsairs kept vigil. Defying visibility, the capricious wind, and enemy fire, they were guides, artillery, and scouts. With nightfall, they made one last run along the length of the battalion as it wound up another mountain; then they streaked away. Crawling, sliding, falling, the infantrymen staggered through the dark, storm-swept night.

"Take five ... Take five ..." The message was passed four hundred yards along the line. Men dropped in the snow where they stood.

Skinhead conferred with his officers. "Got to rest them, sir," the Baker Company commander said. "They just don't have anything left. If we got hit in force now—"

The captain who led Charlie Company choked on the force of the wind, turned his back to it. "Think so, sir."

The battalion commander looked at Pat. "Well?"

"We can't feed them. We can't build fires to get them warm... "Can't hear you."

Pat shouted above the wind. "Wounded can't last much longer. Got to get them in." His back was stiff, aching with the old bruise. The blisters on his arms had broken again and were rubbing raw against his sleeves. "If we wait for light, we'll have a hell of a time getting them up again."

"I got fifteen, twenty men sick as dogs," the Baker Company officer said. "They're weak..."

Skinhead fingered his cold pipe. The wind was battering at him and his face itched. "Hagaru says both regiments are still beating their way down from Yudam-ni. Road must be about two miles from here. If we reach it by early tomorrow, we can probably intercept them. If we don't, we'll have to fight our way in alone. By then the Chinks'll own that real estate. So, we've got to go. It's a gamble; but it's one we'll have to take."

"You all right, Woody?" The column was moving again, but Dorn still lay in the snow. "I'll carry that radio," Sanchez said. "Got to get up to the captain." The soldier, his eyes lost in his bony face, looked up at him. "You're not gonna crap out, Woody."

"Get your ass in gear!" Goober roared. He carried a body across one shoulder, holding it there like a plank. "What's wrong, doggie? You waitin' for a bus?" He grabbed his arm, pulled him erect. "C'mon, damn you. You wanna end up on my other shoulder?"

Dorn refused help with the radio. He righted it, adjusted the straps, tugged at the harness, slipped his arms through. Each operation required careful thought and agonized movement of each freezing, clumsy finger. "I'm ... comin'."

Sanchez walked in step with him. "Not much longer, Woody. We got it made." His lips moved, but his words were lost in the wind.

They climbed without speaking, watching the dark shapes of the captain and Lieutenant Cagle a few feet above them. When the march was stalled by a lone sniper hidden in the rocks above, they lay facing each other. "Goat, remember we talked ... about the farm I wanna get ... in Colombia?" Dorn said suddenly.

"South America, yeah."

"Been givin' it lotsa thought."

"Want me t'carry that radio a while?"

Dorn shook his head, leaned closer. "Couldn't do it alone—run a place like that. I'd need help." The sniper was flushed. They climbed again. Dorn shifted the load on his back as if it were an anvil. "You speak Spanish, don'tcha?" Sanchez nodded. Gripping his arm, Dorn shouted, "Goat, why couldn't you go down there with me?"

"Don't know nothin' 'bout farmin'."

"We'd be partners," Dorn said.

Sanchez indicated that he could not hear. Lifting the soldier's hood, he yelled, "Talk later."

They crouched on the trail, waiting while still another marine was transferred from a stretcher to a sled.

"You could boss the men," Dorn yelled. "And you could do the talkin' when we buy land. And when we buy seed and stock. Couldn't do any of that without you. You'd teach me. And I'd teach you about farmin'." He panted with the effort of shouting. "Everything fifty-fifty."

The path grew steeper as they climbed again. They helped lift a sled over the rocks. A litter fell and they piled the wounded man back onto it. "You don't need me," Sanchez said, as if their conversation had not been interrupted by a hundred yards and half an hour of grueling labor. "I wouldn't be any good to you. Not for me, Woody."

"Somethin' else you wanna do?" He repeated the question in Sanchez's ear. "Your family? We could take turns goin' back." He rushed on, insistent. "You got a girl, you could get married, come down to live. Few years, we could do swell, Goat ..."

Sanchez had no plans. He had even talked with Lock Justus about staying in The Corps. He had no family, no girl, no home. "We'll talk about it sometime. No good jawin' about what you wanna do, not when you're up the creek without a paddle, like us."

"Nothin' wrong in havin' somethin' you're aimin' for, is there?"

"Too hard to talk," Sanchez shouted. "Later."

"Life's not worth a damn if you don't have somethin' you want."

Sanchez hunched his shoulders, pointed to his ears as if he could not understand. But he had heard, and in that instant he thought of his sister. ("You and me, Jesus. We know what we want. Together, we'll get out of this. We'll be somebody.") His head ached with cold, and he didn't want to talk any longer.

"What about it? Rice. Wheat. Cattle. Really pioneer ..."

"Later!" Sanchez formed the word, but made no attempt to yell it.

"Think about it. Huh?" Dorn was pleading, his face beside Sanchez's. "Don't have to say definite right now. But think about it." He rolled his head on his shoulders, flexed his arms. He had never discussed his plan with anyone else. Now the talk gave substance to his dream. He slogged forward, breathing deep of the cold night air. In his imagination, he could see himself milking in his father's barn in the early morning, and he could smell the steaming dew on the cow's sleek flanks.

The *rackarackaracka* of an enemy gun sounded on the trail above them. Though every muscle rebelled, and his chest threatened to burst with the effort, Pat jogged past Choy, Huckabee, The Horse, and Firesteen. "Have them face outboard," he yelled to Goober. "Watch both flanks."

A soldier dropped to his knees. "Where's that guy get the piss and vinegar?"

"Pretty tough bastard." Goober put down the body he carried on his shoulder. "Don't let me forget him," he said, nodding at the frigid form. He started after the captain, shouting orders to the men along the path.

Pat had Dorn call for Baker Company's mortars. With Sanchez at his side and a fire team from Cagle's platoon, he moved under cover of the concentration from the 60's. When they charged the Chinese gun, the one surviving enemy soldier did not fire on them. He sat beside his loaded weapon and his three dead comrades. Staring vacantly, he held monstrously swollen hands behind his head. His feet, clad in canvas shoes, were caked with ice.

Goober appeared. "Finish him off," he told Sanchez.

Sanchez looked questioningly at Pat.

"Disarm him," Pat said. "Leave him alone."

"Are you nuts?" Goober blurted angrily.

"He's nearly dead," Pat said wearily. "Can't hurt us. We can't take him along. We can't kill him."

"The hell we can't!"

Pat stepped in front of his first sergeant. "Don't raise your voice to me! Get the company up. I want every unit to count their people each time we stop, and again when we move."

They left the Chinese sitting there in the darkness, his hands still behind his head, his face immobile, his eyes fixed glassily ahead of him. Goober, cursing under his breath, retraced his steps and checked the platoons. Then, slinging his pack, he looked for the body he had been carrying. He grabbed the soldier who had been sitting beside the frozen corpse. "Where is he?" he demanded.

"Who?"

"The guy I was totin'. Left him here. Next to you!" He shook the man roughly. "Why didn't you keep your eyes open? What did they do with him?"

The soldier pulled away. "I put him on a sled," he said, staring at the first sergeant. "He was dead, and I put him with the others ..."

Running up the path, Goober checked two sleds before finding the body on the third. For the first time, the thought struck him that there was no need for him to carry the dead man. He had packed the burden for so long that he had thought of it only as part of his gear, like his weapon or his helmet. For a moment he looked at the pinched little face. "Don't even know him," he muttered. He got to his feet, and hurried forward to be within hailing distance of the captain.

The column had moved only a few yards farther when it was stopped. The rear guard was hit. Again the men of Able Company dropped to the snow and watched the flanks, half hearing the sounds of the fire fight below.

Goober puzzled over the sudden protest of his body, its craving for rest. He felt sluggish, as if he had eaten a big meal, and then lay in the sun. He felt like yawning, but could not. Sitting down, he rested his head on his knees, closed his eyes, and immersed himself in the soothing warmth of a recurrent daydream.

The Girl was crippled (or blind). And in need of help. And he was her friend. When she got to know him, she'd have the operation. Later they would take off the cast (or the bandages from her eyes) in a hospital room with a fan and a potted plant, with the blinds drawn, and him and the doctor waiting. She'd say, all of a sudden, "I can walk!" (or, "I can see!") And even the doctor, a man with horn-rimmed glasses and white hair and a friendly kind of smile, would have to swallow hard. For a while, none of them would be able to talk. Then the girl would look at him and say, holding his face in her soft little hands, "I owe everything to you, Wally." And he'd say, "You don't need me any more." And she'd put her arms around him—after the doctor left—and she'd tell him, "I need you more than ever now ..."

He had played out this scene many times. Only the girl's face changed. Once it had been a waitress in a roadside diner near his home in Matoon. Then, at seventeen, he would sit on the porch of his parents' rooming house, his mother beside him in the green wicker rocker, his father across the table, teaching him to play chess. His brother would watch over his shoulder, then sidle off. "Take him? It's a dance, Pa. And he doesn't like dances. Do you, Tubby?"

Later, the face was that of a cashier in a Norfolk movie theater. At Little Creek, he had been taunted: "What's with you, Lardbucket? Ain't you human? Don't you need a woman?" He went only once, and then no farther than the parlor. There he spent three hours sitting with the madam, playing with an infant, hearing the egg timer on the mantel ring every five minutes, signaling the allotted time for romance. "Catch somethin'? Hellfire, Fatso, what they got pro stations for?"

The Girl also had the varying faces of a woman marine in the Navy Annex in Washington, an Apple Queen whose picture had appeared in the Richmond paper, the wife of a mess sergeant he knew and an elevator operator in a Los Angeles store. But the plot, vaguely that of a movie he had seen and long since forgotten, never varied.

On duty after the war in Shanghai, he had met Grace. She had deep, dark eyes with large pupils; her hair was black and her skin was creamy white and she spoke English. More remarkable, she loved him. She sat at his feet, encouraging him to talk. She told him how desolate her life had been, how lonely she was, how she had suffered under the Japanese occupation, how she missed her sister who had married an UNRRA man and lived in Atlanta. She cooked his meals in her apartment. She smothered him with affection for the smallest gift. For him, it was all unbelievable, a fantasy. He dared hope for nothing more than her friendship. After three weeks, when he was due to ship out, she asked him to marry her.

His commanding officer said, "I'm sorry, Goober, but I can't condone it." The chaplain said, "Perhaps, if you knew one another longer ..." Barracks talk: "You're out of your head, Gunny. All those White Russian broads are lookin' for is a ticket to the States..."

But he persisted. Two years later she joined him at Oceanside, in California.

There was no more firing in the valley. Goober got heavily to his feet. Thinking of Grace had sickened him; and still, standing there, waiting for the company to move out, he tortured himself by reviewing the hopelessness of their life together.

So often, she had cruelly itemized his inadequacies: He wanted to stay home all the time. He would not consider leaving the service. He made noises when he ate. He left his shirt cardboard on the dresser. His friends were bums, and their wives talked about her. And when they were in bed, she gave directions, urgently, cursing his ineptness. It was like her counting for him when they tried to dance together.

He could visualize her, magazines scattered beside her bed, talking when he wanted to sleep. She'd tell him about the characters in the stories she read as if they were personal acquaintances. Men in slacks and sport coats called Rip and Jay and Rock, who never worked and had girls named Cindy and Penny and Candy, and came into inheritances and went on honeymoons to Bimini, where there were palm trees and natives and nobody knew how rich they were. Or she would insist he read a letter from Atlanta, and she would compare her lot with the luckier sister who had a husband who could tell a joke and danced so well and traded his Chrysler every year and was a professional man.

She had promised to live with her sister when he left for overseas. But her infrequent letters enumerated her excuses for staying on alone in Oceanside. Then, in Osaka, a sergeant just in from the States had told him: "Maybe it ain't none of my business, but I hate to see a guy gettin' the shaft. And, hell, you're gonna find out yourself sooner or later ..."

He grunted and reached for his weapon. God, let me get out of here, he prayed. Just let me get back to the States. I'll gladly roast in hell to see her dead ...

As hour followed hour, step followed step, and death followed death, the violence of the wind abated to a murmur. The marines stumped along through the swirling snow, groping their way toward dawn.

They floundered through the drifts, trying to put their snow-weighted boots in the footprints of the man ahead. Pat waited where the path turned back on itself, watching his men pass by. All were anonymous automatons, with one face, posture, and gait. Like being in a barber chair, he thought, with a mirror before and one behind, and seeing yourself forever bibbed and covered, repeated in the same detail into infinity.

He called to Chuck Cagle. "I'm going up front. Want you to push the stragglers, switch the litter bearers where you can."

Cagle worked his way back through the company, rotating men from carrying stretchers to dragging sleds, walking awhile with those who fell behind, making them talk, making them laugh at his foolish jokes, keeping them a degree above the stupor of fatigue. Two men fell with a stretcher, and he threw himself beside the wounded man to protect him. It was The Horse.

They lifted him on again, began to move. "How's he doing?" Cagle asked Firesteen.

"Alive, sir."

"Keep talkin'," The Horse whispered.

Firesteen shrugged. "He don't know what he's sayin' or where he is," he told the lieutenant.

"Keep talkin'," The Horse repeated. He groaned and turned his head from side to side. "Talk to me."

They stopped again as mortars fell somewhere above them, in the ranks of Charlie Company. Firesteen rubbed The Horse's face; Choy and Cagle massaged his legs. "How can he live?" Firesteen asked.

"I don't know," Huckabee said.

"It's Mel," The Horse said. "I know you. Tell me ... 'bout your family, and ... 'bout tryin' to have a baby ..."

It was like telling a bedtime story to a sick child. Gently, Firesteen stroked The Horse's hair, spoke slowly, restraining the quaver in his voice. "Well, you got to do all kinds of things ... My wife, she's got a chart. And there's a whole scorecard business we kept ..."

The Horse licked his lips. "Temper ... ature," he managed to say. "Take temper ..."

"He does understand," Firesteen whispered to Cagle. "He remembers ..."

"Talk," The Horse said.

"Well, she takes her temperature. And on this chart, she's got to make an Y when ... whenever we ... you know. And then there's a place to make dots. She keeps it right by the bed ... and when the temperature goes up ..."

Cagle stood. "Must make you feel funny, keeping book on it."

Firesteen grinned. "Gotta be scientific, this day and age, Lieutenant."

Cagle moved forward with Huckabee. "How have you kept him alive, Huck?"

The corpsman shivered and hugged himself. "Not my doin'. Suppose if I knew more, I'd give up. He's hurt bad inside." He coughed. "But he doesn't know he's supposed to die. So he holds on. There's some of us—Firesteen, Dorn, another doggie, and Goat—we been prayin' for him. I don't know. Maybe that's the answer."

At the head of the column again, Cagle reflected how open and revealing and unaffected men are when they stand so close to death. They are themselves, he thought, without pretense or sham. They are the self they want to be and feel in need of being. For that reason, he decided, few men died cursing their friends or denying God. No pretense. It was more than he could say about himself. He was still masquerading. What had begun as a harmless lie about his salary had grown into a whole web of idiotic deceit. When would he stop playacting?

For Charles Brandon Cagle, self-styled advertising executive, had been in the business for less than three months, and not even with an agency, but with Macy's. His salary was eighty-five dollars a week, less social security, withholding, and insurance. He and Ellen went up on the roof of his brother's apartment that night after he got the job. The sky was clear, and heat lightning flashed on the horizon. It was humid, sticky weather. Another couple, with an infant, were stretched on a mattress beside the skylight. Across the court formed by surrounding buildings, a man in swim shorts was standing on his fire escape, his back to them. Cigarettes glowed in the darkness.

He put his arm around her waist. "Did you take me up here, hoping I'd propose again?"

She laughed. "No more. You're going to have to beg me." Pulling him behind a chimney, she kissed him. "Go on. Beg me."

He took her head in his hands. "I will. I'll beg you. Soon." She walked to the wall and he followed her. "As soon as I can … Darling, I don't want us to be trapped, like Gert and Joe, living three blocks from where I was born, in an apartment always smelling of diapers, having you look for bargains in Klein's, taking vacations in the Rockaways, spending a lifetime in a world bounded by two rivers, and never getting any farther south than Trenton or any farther north than Peekskill."

"They're happy."

"In spite of everything, yes." He tried to make her listen. "Ellen, there's so much we haven't seen and places we haven't been, foods we haven't tasted and wines we haven't drunk …"

"But we're on our way now. We can do those things for the first time together." They looked out over the bleak court below, seeing the tangle of pulleys and clotheslines and television antennas, the crooked maze of garbage cans and a rusting bicycle frame. "There's nothing we can't do. Nothing," she said.

I'm a damn' fool, Cagle said to himself, getting stiffly to his feet. If I ever get out of this, I'll beg her … I'll get on my knees and propose in Macy's window at high noon… He stretched, rubbed the tip of his nose, and went ahead to find the captain.

The long night faded into first light, then into dawn and a dull gray morning. Pat stood beside a frozen waterfall that formed icy steps down the mountain. It seemed that he could remember no other life, no brace of hours that was not compounded of agony and snow, blood and death. Now, waiting while his men carried their wounded and dead to the trucks below, he gazed at the caravan stalled along the twisted ribbon of road.

What Able Company and the First Battalion had endured on the march was but a scratch compared with the terrible wound inflicted on the two regiments. Ten thousand men, besieged on all sides for every foot of the twelve miles from Yudam-ni, had pried open the jaws of a massive trap. The convoy stretched beyond the limits of his sight. But as far as he could see, in either direction, from the point where an artillery piece fired at an enemy roadblock to the curve where planes strafed and rocketed a Chinese emplacement, there was the clear imprint of suffering and the mark of death.

Choy came up beside him. For a time they watched the road in silence. Then, "A terrible price has been paid already because their country traded a great idea for political expediency," Choy said.

"It's hard to believe any of us made it," Pat said. "Only a few miles to go now. We'll regroup, get reinforcements, get in shape again..."

"No," Choy said. "What we see is only the beginning, Captain. We might have won an enduring victory. We might have been the first to stop the Communists. But from now on, there will be only the degrading aftermath of folly. From now on, they will push us back, into the sea."

Pat walked away from him. He did not want to think about it, about why they had been caught or why they were withdrawing, or about any of the issues or their meaning, or about where the blame should be placed. He called to his men, urging them to hurry as they lifted their dead from the sleds on the ridge and began the descent to the road. "Move out! Don't dawdle!" He thought: Is this a man's death? Feet frozen black, bowels open and running, to be thrown like rubbish in a heap? He said sharply: "Some goldbricks in your squad, Firesteen. Get 'em going." He thought: Don't let up; don't give in. Keep moving. Got to keep moving.

The men did not increase their pace. They could not. Each step was a major accomplishment. Their backs ached, their muscles cramped, sweat poured from their limbs in spite of the dry, crushing cold. They lifted the rigid forms of the dead in their arms, carried them to the road, stopped behind the tail gate of a truck, and stacked them aboard. Then they turned, retraced their steps and shouldered another load. At last, like mechanized toys, the springs wound down, they fell to the earth, expressionless.

The convoy moved again. There was no rest. There was no time when, somewhere along its length, men were not under fire from the encircling enemy.

The planes shepherded them, flying low on either flank, darting into valleys, skimming ridgetops to reconnoiter ahead, pulling up in steep climbs that barely grazed the rocks, strafing, bombing, rocketing.

"Gotta get me the names of those pilots," Cagle said wistfully. "Gonna buy them each a bottle of scotch. I love you, you zoomies," he yelled. "I know what that makes me, but I love every last one of you!" A faint ripple of laughter rewarded him. And again the men pulled one another to their feet, rose from the snow and walked. They put one boot ahead of the other. They slipped on the icy surface. They stamped their feet to keep the blood moving. They readjusted the loads on their backs. They worked the bolts of their rifles. They rubbed their legs and hands. The road, the cold, the men and guns firing from either flank, before them, behind them—all were The Enemy.

Pat felt as if he tenanted a strange body, a body wholly lacking in spirit and grace. His seared arms twitched. A pervading ache throbbed through him. His feet seemed encased in concrete. And still he moved from one end of his company to the other, allowing himself no rest, afraid that if he stopped he would be unable to move again. Over and over, he made the circuit, talking to his men, lying to them, threatening, promising. "On your feet. Planes'll help us ... Keep going ... You can do it ... Only another mile to Hagaru ..."

He used the phrases until they skipped, unbidden, through his consciousness, repeating themselves until they lost their meaning and became a ritualistic chant, part of the dogged rhythm of his stride. "Onyourfeet ... Planes'llhelpus ... Keepgoing ... Youcandoit ...

Anothermile ... Anothermile ...

29

Pat turned on the pallet, pressed his cheek to it. In his dream, it was a silky thigh. And he was being lulled by the motion of a boat. Ann stroked the back of his neck; her fingers were cool. She whispered something to him, but he could not make out what. He grunted, burrowed deeper, slept on.

Later he flung an arm to one side and the pain awakened him. He groaned. There were hands on his forehead, soft hands. He opened his eyes. A young girl, no more than eighteen, with black hair and the delicate features of a figurine, was poised beside him, on her knees. She was looking away, toward the two high windows on the mud brick wall. It was like a continuation of his dream.

He closed his eyes again. Baffled, he tried to orient himself. He remembered leaving the hospital after checking his wounded. That was soon after they had reached Hagaru in midafternoon. Then there had been a report to make while the company was billeted. It was dark when he had left Skinhead's command post. A short, barrel-chested man with a ridiculous mustache had been waiting for him. He brought a note from Chuck Cagle: "Captain Patrick: Just follow Mustaches. Ask no questions." And it was signed, "Cagle, V-P in charge of big deals." Pat had been led to a brick-and-thatch house, and shown into this room.

Now he opened his eyes again and looked at his watch. Eight o'clock. He had slept for one or thirteen or twenty-five hours! The Korean girl—the only attractive woman he had seen since leaving Japan—and the warm room and the soft pallet and the foreign courier were all unexplained mysteries.

Satisfied that he was at last awake, the girl offered him a cup. The liquid was hot and faintly sweet. He sipped it, pausing while she washed his face with a warm cloth. She began to unbutton his jacket and he insisted on sitting up. Smiling, she bowed herself out of the room.

Pat stretched, and was suddenly aware of shocking pain in both arms. There was a stack of clothing behind his pallet. It was all new issue. Skivvies. Socks. Fatigues. Parka. Alpaca vest. Sweater. While he fumbled through it, the girl returned. She carried pitchers of steaming water and emptied them into a wooden tub beside a glowing brazier in the center of the room. Again she bowed and backed out. Taking off his shirt, he eased the sleeves over his arms. Then he checked the bandage on his chest. Two stitches had pulled out, but the doctors had pronounced it an amazingly good suture job. Must remember to tell Huck that, he thought. The bruise on his back would heal in time. It was his blistered, torn arms, aggravated by cold and abrasion, that concerned them most. He had to report to the battalion surgeon later in the day. Taking off his socks, he worked his grimy toes against the warm tile.

The girl came in again and poured more water into the tub. Then she began to circle him, obviously curious. She ran her hand over his chest and between his shoulder blades. She laughed delightedly. Then she unhooked his belt and attempted to pull down his trousers. Pat balked. "No!"

"No!" she said, mimicking him. She attacked the buttons again.

"I know it's boorish to refuse a lady," he said, holding her hands. "And I appreciate your generosity, but I'm not in the mood. Too tired. Too sleepy."

"Slee-pee?" She pulled away.

Amused by her quizzical expression, he pantomimed sleep, putting his hands together and resting his cheek on them. "Sleepy." She shook her head vehemently, and reached for the buttons again. He backed off. "You're just a child," he said. "But damn if you're not a persistent one!" Holding her shoulders, he started to turn her toward the door.

"No slee-pee! No chile! Hope to die, Gyrene!" And she darted past the curtain into the next room.

Pat laughed. "The language barrier," he explained to the empty room. He removed his clothes. Standing nude before a large mirror, he soaped his face, used the razor he found in his fresh gear, and began to shave. The face that looked back at him had changed. It was leaner, nearly gaunt, stark white, the eyes deeper set. And his hair was thick and matted, growing over his ears and long down the back of his neck. Looking into the mirror, he saw the girl behind him. He grabbed the new parka and whipped it around his waist. This time she had a chaperone, a craggy-faced, wrinkled old woman who cornered Pat and stood before him while he clutched the coat, waving a finger in his face. "No push-push," she said severely.

The girl tugged at the parka; and when he refused to let go the old woman pulled on it, too. They hauled him around the room, scolding, dragging on the coat while he argued. With one last triumphant yank, they snatched it from him and tossed it on the floor. He stood cowering, half turned, covering himself ineffectively with his hands and one raised knee. He heard wild laughter from the doorway.

"September Morn!" gasped Chuck Cagle.

"Get these women out of here. Get me my parka," Pat roared.

"Carry on, sir, for the glory of The Corps. I leave you to a fate worse than death."

"Chuck!" But the lieutenant, still convulsed, left him. The women stalked him as he backed away, until he was forced against the steaming tub. Then the utter absurdity of the situation struck him, and he too began to laugh. "What the hell! No secrets among allies." The girl took his hand and urged him into the tub. He tested it with a toe and complained it was too hot, but the old woman took his other hand, and forced him, protesting, into the water.

Gently, careful not to injure his arms, chest or back, the girl rubbed him down. His legs were kneaded, his hair scrubbed, his toenails, fingernails and ears cleaned. Every few minutes the old woman would bend over him, inspect a neglected area, sniff suspiciously, and order another sudsing. Luxuriating in the warmth, in the sensation of cleanliness, he forgot his embarrassment. He was alive. Rested. Hungry. He could smell the savory odor of coffee and fried meat wafting from an adjoining room.

When the girl had dried him with a rough towel, combed his hair and run her fingers through the black mat on his chest once more, she helped him dress. Although the throbbing pain in his arms was constant, he felt refreshed, buoyant. Bowing to each of them, he patted the girl's cheek, turned in front of the old woman to be inspected. She nodded her approval. "No push-push," he said, smiling. "But I'll give you a kiss, Grandma." He brushed his lips over her forehead.

She smiled. "Kiss? Kiss?" Then, searching her marine vocabulary, she struggled for the correct response. "Kiss ... me ... took-us!"

Pat hooted with laughter. Here was the answer to the whole mystery. She could have learned that phrase from only one man. Impossible, he thought. But, then, everything was impossible. He parted the curtain and followed his nose down the narrow hall toward the odor of cooking food.

Bending his head to get through another doorway, he entered a low, long, and narrow room dimly lighted by small windows and Coleman lanterns. He saw two men seated before the fireplace. His head bumped one of the hanging lights. Someone called, "Ten ... hut!" It was part of the ridiculous scheme of things, and that order, bred of a discipline he had all but forgotten, seemed hilarious. Automatically, he responded, "As you were!"

"How was the sack drill and the beauty treatment, Cap'n?"

He had been right : There was Lock Justus, bowlegged and smiling, standing before him. "Well, I'll be damned!" Pat said. "Where in hell did you come from?"

"Better have some chow before he gives you the scoop, Captain. When I got in, I thought I was in heaven, but then that didn't make sense 'cause Justus showed up." Cagle was eating eggs. Fried eggs. Sunny side up. And crisp strips of meat. And there were rolls, brown and crusted. And canned milk for the rich, black coffee. And sugar.

Pat pointed at Cagle. "Haven't decided if I'm talking to you, Judas! Feed me, Lock. Don't tell me anything yet." The old Korean woman brought his breakfast. "We're old friends," Pat said. "She invited me to kiss her took-us!"

The others laughed. "I went through the whole bit first," Cagle said. "So I knew you'd survive with your virginity intact." He stuffed another roll in his mouth. "She brought me a potty! Stood there, refusing to budge, like a boot corpsman demanding a specimen. I had to break the damn' thing to get her to leave me alone."

Pat would have gorged himself, but after two eggs, a roll, and two cups of coffee, he could find room for no more. "Yer stomach's shrunk up," Lock said, flipping a half-smoked cigarette into the fire. He noticed Pat's glance, and offered him a pack of Luckies. "Or would you rather have Camels or Chesterfields?" Reaching into a box, he produced the other brands.

Pat accepted one, lighted it on a faggot from the fire, inhaled, and choked on the smoke. "I'll have to learn all over again." He propped a cushion against the wall and leaned against it. "Now, tell me how and why and where all this," he said, gesturing to the room at large.

"Sure," Cagle said. "Tell him. He can't do more than toss you in the brig. And that'd be a hell of a way to repay your hospitality."

"Wal," Lock drawled, "when I got back here, the medics looked me over and decided I was dopin' off. Said there was fellers fightin' had more wrong with 'em …"

"Don't bother with the details." Cagle sipped his coffee.

"When they tole me I was gonna be stuck here, I snuck around and seen how the rear-echelon pogues was livin'. High off n the hog. Tents. Stoves. Plenty of chow. Nobody hardly gettin' shot at. And talk? Man, they think they're as good as us footsloggers. Really got me p.o.'d. So, I started tradin' Goat's souvenirs to the zoomies flyin' in from Tokyo. Got enough together to make a deal fer this here house."

"And who are the women?"

"Old gal and her daughter was livin' off garbage in a shack. So I let 'em stay here. Usta be a cathouse, I think, till the gals took off to the hills." He paused to light Cagle's cigarette. "Soon's I paid off the gooks that was in here, I was in business. Me and some limey marines from the hospital is good buddies. They come over lots. We're gonna have us a party tonight, and you'll meet 'em. They's good joes. Bigger thieves than us! And then the Turk come over to cook and handle the dice."

"You mean you've been running a crap game?" Pat tried another cigarette.

"Craps is jest nothin', Cap'n," Lock said proudly. "Why, we had us a sweepstakes on how much runway they'd get down each day on the strip. And we had us a real raggedy-ass cockfight till some thievin' limey ate my best rooster. And then there's been poker and blackjack. Even got us some cloth and made gen-u-wine Chink flags to sell the zoomies!"

"But how've you been able to get away with it?"

"It ain't gamblin' if'n you don't use money. And what good's money? Use cigarettes, clothes, pogie bait, flour—anythin' you can smoke, wear, or chew. By the way, I got all our Tootsie Rolls stowed away. Figgered they wasn't really mine." He poked the fire. "Sickbay never give me no trouble. Let 'em have all our vodka."

"No!" Cagle groaned.

"Wasn't exactly gonna give it to 'em. But MPs picked me up whilst I was haulin' it here. And I had to tell 'em it was fer sickbay. Damn' if they didn't stay with me till I delivered it. Wal, can't win 'em all." The Turk, a hairy barrel of a man, came in wrapped in a towel and nothing else. "You met him last night, didn't you, sir?" Pat nodded. The Turk grinned and extended a small, horny hand. "He's the best damn' crapshooter ever spit on dice, and the best cook in Korea. You'll see tonight. We're gonna have us a ball."

"Tell him the rolls were terrific," Pat said. Lock communicated in sign language, and the cook smiled happily, then left to take his bath. "Where did he come from?"

"Hospital. Don't know how he got there. But ever'body says they's fierce as all get out, them Turks. Say they fight with swords four feet long."

The two officers listened incredulously while Lock revealed the extent of his wholesale, retail, manufacturing, and gambling interests. "Like they say t' home, you gotta get up early of a mornin' to fox a hill-country man!"

"Getting late," Pat said finally. "Want to see our wounded before they fly out. And I've got a meeting, too. Chuck, I got the word last night that a provisional platoon of artillerymen will check in our area. And a lieutenant from the Eleventh Marines is coming with them to join us. How about getting them squared away?"

"Sure. Anything else?"

"Where are the men now?"

"First sergeant took them out," Cagle said. "They've been drawing fresh gear and sleeping it off. Goober came by to leave you your stuff and to make sure nobody got you up."

"Can't figger where he dug them duds up," said Lock. "Hard to come by. Even I can't get no new stuff."

"Where's Goober now?"

"Gone to pick up some replacements," Cagle said.

'They been flyin' 'em in here for days now. More than five hun-nert," Lock said. "Marines from hospital in Japan, some from the islands, some from the States. Hope to die, Cap'n, we're gonna hold Hagara. We can set here till we all die of old age."

On the way to the landing strip, Pat and Lock saw some of Able Company's men in a nearby field, and cut across to the center of the working party. The men were clearing potato cellars, hollow mounds of earth that looked like sunken brick kilns. Firesteen was in charge.

"Any spuds you find," Lock said, "how 'bout savin' 'em fer the party tonight?"

Two replacements, who had joined the company that morning, carried a frozen body between them. "Hey, Corporal," one of them called. "You wanna save out all the coons and put 'em separate?" Jesus Sanchez grabbed the man by the front of his parka and shook him hard. "You stupid bastard!" The marine tried to defend himself, but Sanchez tripped him and threw him to the snow. "You open your trap again, I'll stick you in one of them holes!"

"What did I say?"

Pat took Sanchez by the arm and led him away. Together they carried the body and put it down beside Firesteen. Woody Dorn checked the dogtag and made an entry for Graves Registration. Then they gently pushed the dead man inside. Firesteen straightened up. "Sir, we been at this a couple hours now, ever since the chaplains left. It's an awful cruddy detail ..."

"Send a runner to Mr. Cagle at the C.P. Tell him I want a relief for you." Pat started across the field. For a few hours, he thought, he had escaped the terrible reality of their situation. He had been eager to laugh for the slightest reason, eager to talk, to soak up warmth and rest, eager to forget. But you could not forget. Death and misery were still his inseparable companions.

Behind him, he heard Lock. "Be sure you get them spuds."

One plane was taking off, another following it onto the short runway as they arrived. They stood by while replacements disembarked and watched them as they lined up in ranks alongside the stretchers. They seemed incredibly robust beside the haggard marines who were being evacuated.

Pat spotted The Horse. Huckabee was with him. "Good luck, Horse"

The Horse's eyes were dull with drugs, but he recognized Pat. He tried to speak. Mist rose from his lips, and Pat had to put his ear to the man's mouth to catch the words. All he could make out was 'Thanks."

"It's December fourth," Pat said. "You'll be back in the States in a few days, maybe home for Christmas." It was difficult to think of anything to say. A miracle lay revealed before him. The man had endured unimaginable exposure and pain for four days with only rudimentary care. What had kept him alive?

Huckabee helped the stretcher bearers raise the litter. The Horse held to the corpsman's hand. "Huck ... gonna ..." He swallowed painfully. "Gonna make out ... HI make out ..." He labored to say more, but could not.

Huck said, "Write me."

They lifted Sergeant Eddie Gleason, The Horse, The Terrible Cossack, The Ugliest Man in the World, and carried him inside the plane.

"You ought to be proud, Huck," Pat said. There was no reaction. "There are so many people alive right now, who wouldn't be if it hadn't been for you ..."

Huckabee said expressionlessly, "Thank you, Captain." He turned away, walked through the crowd and crossed the field alone.

Pat watched the men pass by, some asleep, some smoking, some with tears of joy, some drugged. He went through the plane, talking to those he had missed. As he stepped down, the last of them came up. It was the soldier who had been with him that morning when the Chinese called for surrender. The man's hands and legs were swollen with frostbite. "How're you doing?" Pat asked, appalled at the gangrenous odor.

"I got it made." The soldier grinned. "Good knowin' you, sir."

"You'll be okay."

"Sure."

"I won't forget you."

"Me neither, sir." The soldier smiled. "Once a marine, always a marine!"

Somewhere above Pat a marine was calling down to his friend: "Good luck, ponyo. I got mine; now you get yours ..."

The port was closed. The engines revved up. The plane taxied to the end of the runway. There was the long, thunderous pull up, up, until it cleared the rim of the hills and swept off into the leaden sky.

Goober found Pat. "You look better. Thought you'd about had it last night."

"Thanks for the clothes, Top."

"Thought you'd need the stuff. No strain, no pain. Plenty of gear around if you know who to ask."

A marine brushed past, jolting Pat's arm. He recoiled, grinding his teeth. "You could use some clothes yourself," he managed to say.

"You all right, sir?"

"Yeah. Dopey from sleep, I guess."

Goober was squinting at him, frowning. "You wanna wait for our people? We got ten replacements out of this lot. It'll be an hour or so before they assign the warm bodies; and I wanna see a marine gunner I know who might survey our radios."

"I've got a meeting at battalion C.P."

"I'll take 'em over." It was Lock who had come up beside them.

"Okay," Goober said. "And while I'm thinkin' 'bout it, Justus, we got you back on the rolls. Don't be wanderin' around like you don't belong anyplace, understand?"

"Sure." He started toward the straggling group of replacements, then turned again. "Top, we're havin' us a little shindig tonight at my place. Expect you."

Goober growled something, and then, to Pat, "I'll show you the way."

When they parted before Skinhead's tent, Pat took the first sergeant's arm. "In case you don't know it, Wally, you're ..." He broke off. He wanted to tell him that he had done a good job, that he was a damn' good marine. But now that he was facing him, it all seemed a little corny. "... you're a big help to me ... You're okay."

Goober stood looking after him as he went inside to report.

Lock carefully chose the man who would get the benefit of his unique protection. Putting his arm around him, he walked with him at the head of the column while the other replacements followed.

They crossed the strip, cut between decaying buildings, toward the checkerboard of tents. "Anythin' you want to know, buddy-roe, you ask me. We're gonna stick together."

"That's white of you."

"I'm gonna cut you in on all the hot poop, gonna learn you how to keep yer M-1 firin', gonna show you how to take a dump in this here twenty-five-below weather."

"I didn't realize you had to ... never thought about things like that."

"I see." Lock shook his head sadly. "Didn't brief you. Too bad. But don't worry about it none. I'm takin' care of you."

The replacement was pathetically grateful. "Thanks. Cripes, guess I'll need all the help I can get till I catch on."

"Fergit the thanks, buddy-buddy. We're all marines, ain't we? We're all in this together, ain't we?"

The youngster offered his hand. "Sure we are," he said fervently. "Side by side, all the way," Lock said, pumping his hand.

"I'll try not to be too much trouble."

"Your problems are my problems," Lock said in ringing tones. "I learn fast."

"Share and share alike," Lock assured him, guiding him down the road. "C'mon, friendo, I've got a box of Tootsie Rolls fer you. It's the only food that ain't froze."

"Why ... Why, thanks, pal."

"Share and share alike," Lock said, reminding him. They crossed the road and walked toward the line of tents that housed Able Company, the other men straggling along behind. Pat was crossing the field toward them. "That's the ole man."

"Big guy. What kind is he? Tough? By the Book? Chicken?"

"Rough as a cob," Lock said. "But I know how to handle him." By way of demonstration, he called, "Cap'n! Cap'n Patrick!" Pat didn't look up. "Can't hear me," Lock said. Then, remembering his mission, "By the way, ponyo," he said, smiling pleasantly, "I better hide them three bottles of booze you got under your parka."

The replacement flushed, chagrined that his hoard had been discovered. "Why?"

"Buddy-roe," Lock said earnestly, "there's fellers in our company that'd do damn' near anythin' fer a drink of real likker!"

Pat had not heard his name called. He had just left the meeting at Skinhead's C.P. and he was stunned by what he had learned. The division would not hold at Hagaru. Though more than a hundred thousand of the enemy encircled them, though more than sixty miles of contested mountain road lay between them and escape, the division was going to fight its way across the jagged hills, was going to break through six encircling enemy divisions and battle its way to the sea.

But Pat would not be with it.

30

"We're colder than a witch's tit.
We're colder than dry ice.
We're colder than a tombstone.
We're colder than dead mice.
We're colder than a frozen fish.
We're colder than a sword.
Dugout Doug can have the glory.
We'd all like a nice hot broad!"

Americans and Englishmen, sailors, soldiers, and marines, leaned against the walls, beating with spoons on the tile floor. They lay on their stomachs, propped on their elbows. They sat cross-legged, plates in their laps, keeping time with cups and glasses. Chuck Cagle led the singing. Pat, Sanchez, and Dorn sang harmony. A burly Royal marine coaxed weird sounds from a Japanese shamisen, playing it as if it were a guitar. Lock Justus pulled Huckabee from a back room, half-asleep, and talked him into adding his bugle to the uproar as they sailed into the chorus:

"For marines all stand together,
And shout their battle cry:
Semper Fi! Semper Fi! Semper Fi!"

They couldn't have named the things they had eaten. Mustaches appeared at regular intervals, announced a dish in Turkish, and retreated to his kitchen. There were steak, ham on toasted buns with an egg sauce, candied carrots, potato pudding, shishkabob served flaming on bayonets, cutlets, a steaming sauce of GI hot dogs and beans that had been mysteriously flavored and emerged a delicacy. There was pilaf—rice, onion, garlic, and meat. There were a thick, sweet coffee with froth on the top, and a confection made of jelly, sugar, and flat pastry. Their shrunken stomachs could not consume it all. Even so, they heaped their plates high and picked at them long after the food was cold.

The meal was served at the beginning by the old Korean and her daughter. But after the steaks, the woman complained through Choy. The girl had been approached in the universal language of troops: "Push-push, baby? Pom-pom, honey? You-me, beddy-bye, doll?" By the time the shishkabob came out, the old woman was protesting again. Some charitable and tipsy celebrants had pinched her, too. After the cutlets were served, the two women retired, refusing to run the gauntlet of friendly and suggestive pats and pinches, and—in the case of one uninhibited sailor—bites.

Volunteers were sent for from the replacements. Five of twenty applicants were accepted. They moved in and out with dishes and glasses, eager to be near these veterans of the wars, stimulated and shocked by them and sure they would never be one of them. They wanted to believe all the fabulous lies and asked questions only to keep them talking. They were alive. And they had been through it. That, for the time, was proof to the newly arrived that it was possible to fight and survive.

Unnaturally keyed up, seeking forgetfulness of their harrowing experiences, the men drank jungle juice—an underfermented three-day old mixture of raisins, prunes, white rice, yeast, and sickbay alcohol— and convinced themselves that it was the best of all possible drinks, that their friends were the best of all possible comrades, that there had never been allies so firm, friendships so enduring, liquor so soothing, voices so beautiful as were gathered in glorious conclave that night.

"I tell you, chaps, give me ten lorries full of marines and Turks, I could take Peiping in two weeks," one of the Englishmen said.

"Yer right, cobber," Lock said. "They's got six divisions surroundin' us, but hell, if'n ever' coolie in China worked at nooky 'round the clock they couldn't make enough Chinks to whup us!"

Cagle stood unsteadily, leaning on Pat's shoulder. "Gentlemen!"

"How about us enlisted peons?" Firesteen yelled. Other voices shouted him down.

"We're all peons," Cagle said. "And all gentlemen." He waved for silence. "It has come to my attention that we have yet to raise a glass of this superb libation to the diligent and talented hands that fashioned the sumptuous repast which lies skeletonized before us."

"Listen to them words! Sir, you buckin' for the Royal Marines?" Cagle stared Lock into silence. "Gentlemen, fourscore and twenty-odd minutes ago, our benefactor brought forth upon this table great delicacies, conceived in genius, and dedicated to the proposition that all men should die happy. Therefore, having surfeited myself, I raise my glass to our able ally, our Lucullan compatriot, our mustachioed maestro, the chef!"

Sanchez brought the Turk from the kitchen. He came out, his face flushed crimson, laughing and tugging at his mustaches in a welter of embarrassment. "Knock it off, you guys," Sanchez said. "Let him talk."

"Hope to die," the Turk said. He slapped Sanchez on the back, nearly toppling him.

"Gentlemen, please rise for the Turkish National Anthem!" The English marine went through an elaborate pantomime. The Turk, after listening to hummed strains of the British and American anthems, understood. He began to sing in a soft, pleasant voice. There were apparently interminable verses, and Mustaches sang every one of them. By the time he reached the fourth, all the men were humming the tune with him and he was swinging a bayonet, leading them, the tears streaming down his ruddy cheeks and nesting in his magnificent mustache. Wiping his eyes on his apron, he retreated to the kitchen.

"He looks like a Turk, don't he?" Lock said. "Now Jack, here, he don't look like no limey."

"I defy you to explain the facial conformation and characteristics you attribute to limeys, Yank."

"I tole you I fer damn' sure ain't no Yank."

"And," Jack said haughtily, "I am no bloody limey!"

"Ain't it somethin', the way he talks?" Lock said, admiringly. "Jack, if'n you'd stick around, I might learn you some English."

"Lochran, we have been as Jonathan and David, as Castor and Pollux; and you have made it possible for us to live as befits warriors among peasants, but the noises you utter bear no relationship whatsoever to English!"

Pat interrupted in time to stop a clash. "A toast to His Majesty, the King of England!"

Then the Royal Marines toasted the President of the United States. There were toasts to Friendship, and toasts to Victory, and toasts to liberty ports, to six different states of the Union, to Scotland, Ireland, and Wales, to Generals Cates, Shepherd, and Smith, to Colonels Murray and Puller and Litzenberg, to Skinhead and the Royal Marine commander, Lieutenant Colonel Drysdale, to the Air Force and the Army, to the Australians for their women and the New Zealanders for their hospitality, to a Fetus for Firesteen, to the next man who died, and to a tongue-tied prostitute in Liverpool.

Goober, who had been waging a quick-drink battle with a British sergeant, rocked to his feet. "Gimme quiet!" he yelled. "This is yer first sergeant, goddammit!" The noise gradually dissolved. "Nobody's drunk a toast yet to the man who ..." His voice broke. He held his glass up. "To Lieutenant Andy Anderson, one good marine!"

It was quiet for a few seconds, as if the men felt chastened for forgetting so quickly. Then Woody Dorn got up. "I'd like to propose—"

"Let's drink to the doggies!" Goober shouted. "We're keepin' ours hid so they won't have to go back to the Army." He began to sing, and a few joined him.

" 'Thirty thousand Chinamen,
Runnin' down the pass.
Playin' burp-gun boogie,
On a doggie's ass.
They're movin' on—' "

"Shut yer holes!" Sanchez yelled. He rubbed Dorn's balding head. "Let my buddy have his say."

"We haven't heard from Captain Patrick," Dorn said.

"Speech! Speech!"

Pat's head ached. His back was damp with perspiration and he could no longer clench his fists without feeling the bite of pain in his arms. He had lied to the doctors in order to stay out of the hospital for the night, if only to put off the inescapable until morning. Though he had joined in the spirit of the party, one fact constantly intruded to unsettle his peace of mind. None of them yet knew it, but they would all know soon. They were leaving, to fight their way over sixty harrowing miles. And he was flying out.

He stood. "Before you give us a pep talk," Cagle said, "Lock's got another job for you."

Justus brought out a cardboard mortar container. It was decorated with strips torn from an aircraft panel and tied with a bow made of marking tape. "Remember? Yer supposed t' give it to Huck," he whispered.

Pat was grateful for the reprieve. He took the package. "Everybody knows that marines hate swabbies. And particularly chancre mechanics. Everybody knows that sailors never fire their weapons, not even to clean them. Everybody knows that they're shiftless and lazy, that they never work and they're not good enough to be marines. So, with that in mind, all of us ran over to the best liquor store in Hagaru this afternoon, and had this gift-wrapped for our own particular swab-jockey. And though we all insist that everything we've ever said about gobs still goes, we want him to know that no man who ever wore our uniform ever rated it more. Huck, come on up here!"

The corpsman was standing in the doorway of the kitchen. Justus and Sanchez pulled him forward. Pat handed him the package. "Thank you," he said mumbling. "Don't know why you went and did this."

"Give us a speech, Huck. Went to lots of trouble to get that," Lock said. "There's a replacement in Charlie Company right now wonderin' how come I took him to Able by mistake this mornin'!" There were more shouts of encouragement. Huckabee stood uneasily, his bloodshot eyes squinting at them, his white teeth nibbling at his lip. "My friend Choy rates bein' called a swabbie, too." Cheers. Applause. "You bellhops ... you ..." Again he tried to speak; conscious of the men, fumbling with the gift. "We swabbies," he said, and cleared his throat, "... We swabbies can't stand you either ..." And then he turned and walked quickly into the kitchen.

One of the Englishmen led the men in "three ruddy cheers" for Huckabee and Choy. Pat joined in, watching the interpreter, who sipped his drink, smiling thinly. The faces all around him were animated, shouting, laughing. Pat saw them at that moment as they had looked on Bad Girl Ridge, saw the men in the potato cellars and those with shrapnel piercing them and those on the laden sleds on the mountain trails, and the soldier being lifted to the airplane, and The Horse. When they called for him to speak again, he could think only that he was leaving them; and that they did not know it.

"You characters don't need a pep talk," he said. "And what most of you need, even Lock can't provide!" They cheered him on. "We've come a long way together ... all of us. I know, for myself, even if I could forget these past weeks, I wouldn't want to ..." The silence, the suddenly serious mood his words evoked, oppressed him. "To all of you," he said, and raised his glass.

"And to Motherhood and the Marines!" Firesteen shouted.

There was a disturbance at the door. Two MPs pushed their way inside. One of them saluted. "Sir," he said to Pat, "we got orders to pick up a man in here. Complaint from Engineer Battalion." The other MP passed through to the kitchen and came out again with Mustaches submissively in tow.

"What's the charge?" Pat asked.

"Engineers were usin' him to haul stuff in deep snow, sir ..."

"The Turk?"

"No, sir. A horse. This character stole him this mornin'. He was spotted this afternoon, tradin' steaks to some galley for rice and garlic." He saluted again, did an about-face, and left, pushing Mustaches before him.

The door slammed. The men all examined their plates, then looked at one another. "Couldn't have been better if it was Man O' War," Pat said. And the meal was forgotten in the laughter.

" 'Oh, here's to Goober!
He's true-blue!
He's a Gyrene thru-an'-thru!
He's a boozehound,

So they say!
He won't go to heaven.
Naw, he'll go the other way!
So drink, chug-alug-chug-alug.
So drink, chug-alug-chug-alug!' "

The first sergeant turned up the pitcher and gulped the jungle juice. The crowd around him parted. The other groups looked up from their card game, their bull session, their crap-shooting as Goober was led to the line of ration cans that ran down the center of the room. He pushed his helpers aside, gave a heroic belch, and mounted the first can, balancing on one foot like a baby elephant. "Stan' back," he said imperiously, stepping from one can to the next, teetering down the line. "I can do this blin'fol'ed. I'll show these limeys!"

His rival, the Royal Marine sergeant, stood at the end of the obstacle, perfectly composed. "You're a great hairy ape," he said. "I shall be cold sober when you are flat as a carpet!"

"Don't let him get your goat, Gunny. We got our money on you!"

"I'll show ya," Goober said, tottering, but miraculously regaining his balance. "I can lick a limey any time, any place, doin' anythin', or I'm a ... a bastid!"

"You happen to be a liar of the second rank, an unimaginative gorilla who can not even curse with style. That I know. About your parentage, I'm not prepared to offer an opinion."

"That's it, Harry-boy. You'll give the bloke a blasted go! We're with you, Harry-boy!"

Goober, aided by the encouragement and shouted directions from the marines who lined his path, finally made it. The English marine was led back to the jungle juice. "We're even, Goober," he said. "This one should do you in." He raised his third pitcher.

Partisans of both sides began to sing again:

" 'Oh, here's to Harry:
He's true-blue! ...' "

In a far corner of the room, four of the privileged replacements surrounded a group of veterans. Huckabee had just told the story of the Tootsie Roll raid, and the men were laughing.

"There was that time we swiped the bread from the Army bakery, too," Lock said. He swatted one of the new men on the back; and the boy sank to his knees, smiling happily. "Ole Goat dropped a hunk of C-2 in the officers' head ..."

"Latrine," a soldier said.

"Wal, when that stuff exploded, there wasn't a square foot fer miles wasn't covered with paper, splinters, mud, and manure. Trees. Trucks. Jeeps. Tents. Streets. And a coupla majors!" He swung at the newcomer again, but the youngster ducked in time. "They thought it was a air raid, and while they was hittin' the shelters we scooted off with sixty loaves of bread, four trays of sweet buns ..."

"Ten loaves an' two trays," Sanchez said.

"... enough yeast to make jungle juice fer the whole damn' division."

"That over near Yongdong-po?" Dorn asked.

"That's the place," Huckabee said. "I remember."

Dorn laughed. "It was my old outfit! You'd have thought the Chinese had bombed the White House. Officers had to use the enlisted latrine for a week."

"Ain't that a pity," Lock said. "Hope none of the troops caught anythin'."

Before the fireplace, the floor was covered with sleeping men. Mel Firesteen and a soldier had cleared out a space and were bent over a hefty replacement who had been commandeered for the occasion. "Never learn," Firesteen said, ceding the contest by default. "I'm jus' never gonna learn, buddy."

The soldier patted his back. "Try 'nother time, pal. I got four kids; and there's nothin' to puttin' on a diaper. Nothin.'" He nudged Firesteen. "Lessee ya do it this time. Middle of the night, and the kid cries, and the wife gives ya the elbow, and ya gotta change the seat covers on Junior. Go on!"

The replacement, six feet tall and weighing two hundred and fifty pounds, tried to sit up. "Hey, you fellas, I had about enough ..." Firesteen pushed him down. "Didn't they teach you a damn' thing at PI?" Turning to the soldier, he said, "Wasn't like this in the ole Corps. Boots respected an NCO!" He made the young man raise his legs, shoved the towel beneath him again, straightened the corners. "I'm only a li'l' stewed," he told the soldier. "Can't see where I get messed up." Lacking a safety pin, he used one of Huckabee's needles. The marine screamed and shot upright, holding his rear. The soldier shoved him down again. "Stop hollerin,'" Firesteen said. "I gotta learn, don't I? Trial and error."

The soldier held up his hand. "Okay. One more time. Push the pin to ya, not at the baby." He watched as Firesteen bent to his task again. "Not too close, a bit to the side," he cautioned. 'Thing about diaperin' a boy baby, you gotta be outta the line a' fire. Three clicks too much windage, and you're a drowned daddy..."

Wandering around the room, Pat had cheered Goober on his fourth quart of jungle juice and another successful walk down the ration cans. He had been taught five verses of "My Alma Mater, Pusan-U," had agreed not to turn in the two soldiers still with the company, had moderated three arguments, answered dozens of questions, and listened to jokes, stories, scuttlebutt, and fanciful exploits:

"It was Maggie Higgins, I tell you. Right there in the chow line today. And I got up to her real close, and she's got a smell, oh, man, she's the sweetest smellin' thing ... like grass and soap, kinda. All covered up in coat and trousers, but underneath all that stuff there's a woman. They say Chesty blew his top when she showed up ..."

"When we gonna get some mail? Bet the pogues in the rear been gettin' theirs regular. I know for a fact, my girl writes me every day. Must have thirty-five, forty letters..."

"Mail's down the road at Koto-ri. And there's mucho Chinks between us and it ..."

"Come on, Limey, roll 'em ..."

"Lad, I didn't finish the tale. Like I said, I kissed the old girl's arse for eight years—her sixty, and me bloomin' with youth and vigor-waiting for her to give up the ghost. Three bloody weeks after I got in uniform, she departed this life. Left me her portrait and twenty pounds. Left her estate to her maid, her butler, and her four cats!"

"Your dice. Roll ... roll ..."

"The winners tell stories and the losers say, 'roll'!"

"Seven, baby. Be there. Come on, you seven. Seven and I'm in heaven." The dice were spat upon, shaken, kissed, rattled at the ear, and tossed.

"Ah-hh! Uncommonly rotten luck you blokes are having ..."

"So the guy says to her, 'Honey, how about it? We're gettin' married in the mornin' anyway.' And she says, 'Sorry, sweetie. When I walk down that aisle tomorrow, I wanna know I'm a virgin. Besides, it gives me a headache!' "

Lock called Pat away from the joke-swappers. "Sir, we want you to hold the money. Ever'body's puttin' up five clams in IOUs. Fer that, we give 'em a number. When Firesteen gets his mail, we cover up the postmarks, scramble 'em up, and number 'em. Now, the letter that tells him is he or ain't he a daddy, that's the one collects. We're callin' it the Firesteen Sweepstakes! Good, huh? Now, don't you say nothin' to Mel 'bout it."

Before Pat could reply he heard Chuck Cagle shouting: "Captain! Captain Pat! Come a runnin'! Captain Pat!"

Chuck Cagle, lolling in a tub of steaming water, greeted him: "Captain Pat, ole buddy, come take a bath with me!" The lieutenant was unaccountably happy, and eager to share his joy.

Choy sat in another tub alongside. The bottle of bourbon Lock had pressed on Pat earlier in the evening was on the floor between the two, and an empty floated in Cagle's tub. "He is defeated in argument," the interpreter said. "And he has sent for reinforcements." He jerked a thumb at the lieutenant. "He is well-meaning, but not intelligent."

"And he," Cagle said, leveling a finger at Choy, "is a good interpreter and a pretty fair corpsman. But he's a creep!"

"You're tight!" Pat laughed, sitting on the floor between the two. "Both of you!"

"Begging your pardon, sir. I am not tight or plastered, polluted, greased, blind, sozzled, ossified, or atomized. I am only a very little bit oiled. I have been drunker at two in the afternoon." He winked at Pat. "In the advertising game, we do lots of business over martinis," he said confidentially. "Where was I? Oh, yes." He frowned and leaned toward Choy, who was being scrubbed by the old woman. "Won Hook Choy-boy, Captain Pat's here to back me up!"

"We are discussing, Mr. Cagle," Choy said. He held up a hand, motioning for silence while his stomach rumbled ominously. "There is no need for you to become acrimonious."

"Well, I am, by God, I am!"

Pat was surprised and pleased to see Choy so out of character; drink had not robbed him of his habitual sullen dignity, but it was distinctly frayed around the edges.

Choy spoke sharply in Korean to the old woman and raised his spindly legs to the rim of the tub. "He is intolerable of another opinion."

"You're intolerable. I'm intolerant!"

"This is typical," Choy said, speaking with the extreme deliberation of the mildly drunk. "You will not see the truth about yourselves, you Americans. All is black or white. You live by a code of impossible truisms. America is good. Russia and all its works are bad. Britain is dying. France is decadent. Germany is industrious, ergo, moral, honest, and decent. Desirable women have long legs and firm breasts ..."

Pat was amused. He started to speak, but Cagle cut him off. "He's doing just what he's been doing since I first saw him!" He slapped the water and sent suds foaming over the top, wetting Pat's legs. "He's orating on how damn' awful we are, how we've done every damn' thing but de-testicle-ize Rhee!"

"When you scream," Choy said, "there is no argument. You abandon logic for hiss—histri—histrionics."

Laughing, Pat picked up the bottle and took a drink. "Chuck's right. I've heard you accuse us of innocence, of lacking culture, of a Coca-Cola mentality, of stifling free speech, of having too many bathtubs, radios, and automobiles."

"Out of context," Choy said, protesting. His stomach gurgled again; and he listened to it, smiling wistfully. "I can forgive America for her materialism, but not for her compromises, her self-deception, her complacency."

"You can forgive! Who the hell are you to forgive or not to forgive?" Cagle stormed at him. "He can forgive," he said to Pat. "You get that? *He can forgive!*"

"What have we ever done to you, Choy?" Pat lit a cigarette and took another drink. "Why are you so down on us?"

"Forgive!" Cagle said, wresting the bottle from Pat. "Forgive!"

"Yes. Yes." Choy had not raised his voice. He stood in the tub, his bony frame covered with soap suds. The woman scrubbed him with a long handled brush as he declaimed, one hand raised in a ludicrous attitude. "Yes. Yes. Yes." he repeated. "Because I had a dream of America—a dream from books and from the words of great men. America was young and strong. It was not sick and torn as Europe was. It had not become diseased and festered with ancient sores," he said, growing more impassioned. "It was a nation of ideals." He flopped back into the tub, and the water flooded over. "But no longer. America no longer believes in ideals."

"And what have we done to destroy your dream?" Pat asked.

Cagle spat the word, repeated it. "Your dreamy-dream-dream-dream?"

"Have you even been to the States?" Pat said.

"No."

"So you formed all your ideas from books."

"I formed my ideas from observation, Captain. My ... my mis— mis—" He tapped his forehead, seeking the word. Finally, "My misconceptions," he said, looking pleased with himself, "I got from books."

"He reads! A regular Clifton Fadiman!" Cagle stared open-mouthed, as if he were tremendously impressed. He put the soap in the girl's hand, and rubbed his chest.

Choy had the old woman scratch his back. "Your strength was based on your ... legacy of history ... on ingenuity, the hunger for equality and liberty, the willingness to take a risk, the belief—even foolhardy at times—in principles." He paused, suddenly contemplative, smiling wryly. "Now you have lost those qualities, and your greed won't let you return to them." He rapped his knuckles against the tub, emphasizing each word. "This—will—destroy—you!"

"Cassandra!" Cagle shouted.

"Not Cassandra," Pat said. "She turned out to be right."

"You in America have poisoned the wells that once sustained your thirst, Captain, the things that gave you birth, and then strength and power ..."

"Pretty phrase," Cagle said, and was drowned out, sputtering, as the girl poured a pitcher of water over him.

Pat sensed the depths of Choy's despair. That it was now distorted by bourbon made it none the less poignant. "Nietzsche said all this long before you, Choy. He, too, thought the good and the heroic were dead, that there were no more great leaders and that mediocrity was glorified. And, you know, Nietzsche died a madman."

"Irrelevant," Choy said. "I do not speak as Nietzsche." The old woman began to scrub the soles of his feet, and he grunted with pleasure. "I speak as your own Franklin did when he warned that you could be impoverished by luxury. It has happened."

"Dammit! Let me get back to what I started!" Cagle scratched himself. "Before you came, Captain, Choy was saying that Russia's the prophet of the future. Now he's backtrackin.'"

"Be exact!" Choy said. "We have talked of many things. I have followed you back and forth over the same ground as you discovered another minor point you had forgotten ..."

"That's the way I think," Cagle said.

"Yes. That is the way your mind works," Choy said. "It is interesting in itself that America must depend on such as you for her defense." He frowned. "Now, what I said of Russia: I said that since America has abdicated the moral leadership of the world, Russia is *passing herself off* as the prophet of the future. She is offering the world, particularly the East, not only guns and bread, but a religion—the religion of Communism."

"Democracy's a religion, too," Pat said. He rubbed the tip of his cigarette in a puddle of water. 'You think Communism, which denies God and the individual, is a workable faith? And that democracy, which affirms God and upholds the common man and liberty and truth ... you think democracy's not a workable faith?"

Choy stood in the tub, hands on his hips, while the woman dried him. "Why not argue logically, Captain, instead of giving vent to the unreasoning jingoism of a schoolboy? Who is the common man? And what is liberty? And what is truth? And how perfect are they in your country?"

"From what I know of history," Pat said, "there's never been a Utopia."

As the argument raged on, Pat felt a depressing sense of frustration. Choy talked about imperialism, about inequality, about the failures of America, and Pat was unable to frame a cogent rebuttal. But the intricacies of the problem, the interplay of politics, diplomacy, and economics, the temper of the people, the great complex of the America he knew and had thought he understood—all these things had to be made clear. It was like being carried back in time to an age that knew nothing of electricity, automobiles, television—all the machinery of civilization which you had taken for granted all your life. And in trying to explain these phenomena you found that you had never really given them much thought. You turned a switch, and a light flashed on. But now you had to explain the origin of the energy, its conversion into electric power, the way it traveled by wire, how it was activated by the switch, and what made the bulb glow. In the same way, how could he explain America without explaining the divergencies of its origin? The condition of the minorities? The peoples' dislike of involvement? The geographical factors? The distribution of wealth? For the first time, all these questions had a personal importance to him.

"... the truth is on our side," Cagle was saying.

Choy had stepped from the tub and sat on the edge while the old woman dried the stubble on his head. "It is not what is true," he said. "It is what the East believes is true that must matter to you. Russia is winning the East by convincing them that she is one of them, not looking down on their condition or their color, giving them hope as well as food."

"Let's talk about one thing at a time!" Cagle shouted.

"But we have covered everything, gentlemen. We have talked of your opportunism which backfires, of your flagging culture, of your intolerance, of your naivete ..."

"I insist you shut up for a change!" Cagle leaned back as the Korean girl scrubbed his milk-white legs. "I have the floor. I will not 'linquish it. I'm a big talker, an accomplished talker, and I'm gonna talk." He leered at Choy. "See?"

Pat wanted to see Choy humbled, wanted to share in Cagle's fervent denial, despite its simplicity. He spoke angrily now, seeking to reassure himself. "We're so materialistic," he said, "that we've given away billions in the most generous act in human history. We're—"

"Back to that!" Choy said, shrugging.

The women were chattering again. Cagle yelled at them. "Shut up, please, ladies. When my buddy talks, ever'body shuts up. Even me! Proceed, Captain."

"We're so opportunistic we've done our share of dying in two wars, and fought this one practically alone. We're so dead culturally that we've produced great art, and changed the lives of men the world over with our science. We're so intolerant that we've made a nation out of every race and color and religion!" He jabbed a finger at Choy. "We're so damn naive that we've made democracy work, shown that it can be shared ..."

"Let me tell him," Cagle said. He stood, stepped from the tub, and bent over the interpreter. "Believe what you want about us. Cuss us. Belittle us. Talk in fancy phrases you got from some jerk's book. Quote and prophesy." He held onto the rim of the tub, steadying himself. "I don't pretend to have all the answers. But I know you're wrong. Wrong!" He stepped into his underwear. "And now, I am going to hit the sack. I leave you with the weighty problems of the world."

Pat and Choy shared the last drink. Before they had downed it, Cagle was blissfully asleep. Pat pulled a cover over him. Time to leave, he thought. Get back to the hospital.

"This has been interesting," Choy said, lying on another pallet beside Cagle. "But even if you had overcome me with logic—which you surely have not done—one monumental fact remains. That is, you are running. The greatest nation in the world?" He shook his head. "Then why run when this battle could save all Asia for you?"

Pat recognized that, as usual, there was some truth in much of what Choy had said. "We've made mistakes," he said impatiently. "But that's the nature of democracy. It's our weakness that we can't always act decisively, but it's our strength, too. You can't ignore—"

"Captain, you must face up to it," Choy said, sitting up, leaning on his hands. "You, even you, do not know why you are here. And those men in the other room, making believe they are drunk on a few glasses of punch, do you think they know why they are here? Do you think they are concerned with anything more than getting out of here? Do you think there is one among them who wouldn't join the rush to leave if he thought he could accomplish it?"

"I'm not sure," Pat said, knowing all the while that he was doing just that. He was getting out. And he was glad to be going. And Korea be damned. And the issues be damned. Still, if it was wrong, even degrading for America to retreat, why wasn't it just as wrong, as degrading for him ...

Choy's voice droned on. "I have listened as you tried to defend an America which has not existed for a long time. As you tried to defend it without understanding its sickness, explaining it away with slogans and dogmatism." He yawned. "You do not know what really constitutes America." ,

"And I suppose you, in your omniscience, do?"

"Yes. Even drunk—and I am only a very little drunk—I, in my rational, unemotional, and impartial approach, understand." He lay down again. "It is a tragedy for all mankind, for you are doomed to follow the relentless parabola of history: the rise, the peak, the fall. You will atrophy and you will die."

Pat felt angry and ashamed. He knew he had been bested in argument, even as Cagle had been. Pounding the floor with his fist, he said, "You can't see us as we really are ..." He stood, crossed the room, turned on Choy again. "You're wrong!" But his anger was really directed against himself, for he realized that he knew too little, understood too little, and so was a poor champion for his country. He could not credit Choy's prediction of America's doom. There were valid reasons why Choy was wrong. But it was something he felt, rather than knew. He had neither the knowledge nor the understanding to produce the incontrovertible reply.

Choy had turned his face to the wall. Pat picked up his pack, his pistol, and slowly left the room.

The party had subsided. In the center of the floor, Goober and his Royal Marine opponent were stretched out side by side. Lighted candles were at their heads and feet. Around them men were squatting, humming solemnly, passing a jug along the circle. Sanchez was sprinkling the prostrate figures. Firesteen stood above them, intoning, *"Yisgadal vyiskadash shmay Tabor ..."*

"God have mercy on their souls," Sanchez said.

"... mercy on their souls," the men chanted.

"For they are disciples of the Devil."

"... disciples of the Devil," the assembly moaned m chorus.

"But we all got to go sometime," Huckabee said.

"Amen, brother," Lock said.

"Amen," the congregation sang. "Amen."

Pat stood at the door, watching them for a moment. Then, slipping his tender arms into the sleeves, he buttoned his parka and went out into the bleak, cold night.

31

Pat lay on the hospital cot, the green issue blanket pulled up under his chin. The stove glowed red, and shadows played across the canvas above him. Carefully, he slipped an arm from beneath the cover, felt for the cardboard label on his pack, and examined it in the flickering light: *Patrick, William A., Capt., 041521, USMCR. Evac: Flight Charlie. 6 December 1950. Sec Deg. Bums. Infection.* Then there were some medical symbols he could not make out. He would be on the plane, the last from Hagaru, when the division began its attack.

Sixty miles to the sea, to Hungnam.

With luck he would be home in a month, maybe less.

He had taken medication, been inoculated, had his arms coated with unguents and wrapped in bandages, been examined and reassured and ticketed. Only an hour left to wait. Instead of elation, he experienced a restless unhappiness which had driven him to his tent and kept him there for hours. It was against all logic, against sanity itself to feel so guilty. And in any case, how could he ignore the doctors, rebuff authority? He had not asked to be evacuated; he had not sought a way out. He was being ordered. He had done all that had been expected of him.

He heard the grating sounds of canvas being folded down, of tents being struck and trucks grunting through the rutted streets. He could hear in the distance the boom and echo of artillery. A sentry passed by the tent flap, stamping his boots in the snow. Someone cursed, called for a winch. Across the tent another officer lay sprawled on a cot, groaning in his sleep from time to time. Out on the perimeter, a machine gun fired rapidly. Across the airfield a bulldozer was laboring. Able Company would be awake, getting ready to take the road.

Pushing the blanket aside, Pat reached for his cigarettes. The first inhalation made him dizzy and he snubbed it out on the mud floor. Who would hesitate to leave if he could do so honorably? Who would choose to stay on? Andy had said a man was always impelled by fear. He had disagreed, believing that some compulsion lay dormant in all men, unspoken, unphrased, holding them accountable to their country and their own consciences. Yet he had no thought of country now. If anything, he felt a bitterness toward his fellow citizens at home, so comfortable, so unaware, so uncaring, so safe. And he had no inclination to stay on in this frozen hell for the sake of any abstract idea. Then what was it that was goading him? Fear of what others would think? He would probably never see any of them again. What was it, then? Why had he kept his leaving a secret from them? Right now they would probably be making wisecracks about it. But he would be forgotten as quickly as Andy or Allison or Pappas or The Horse had been forgotten.

Months before, at home, he had wrestled with another decision. For days he had worried over it, debated it, unable to make up his mind.

"It's cut and dried," Walt had said. "What's the big decision? Your mother's a dependent. And you're working on a housing project for the Army. Christ, that's excuse enough. I got somebody up at the Navy Annex who'll handle it for me. All you got to do is sign this piece of paper. Now stop screwin' around, Pat. With the bids in on the Miami job, you've got a chance to do something big, really big, for yourself. One guy less in Korea won't mean doodly-squat to the marines. But it'll make a hell of a difference to you—and to me!"

Pat had talked to his mother about it. And she had her usual advice: Seek guidance in prayer and be sure what you do is right. "Right for whom?" he had asked angrily. "I've done my turn. Plenty who haven't aren't going this time either ..."

That night he had found her Bible propped on his pillow, with a marker referring him to the chapter in Proverbs: "Trust in the Lord with all thy heart, And lean not upon thine own understanding. In all thy ways acknowledge Him, and He will direct thy paths."

Later, Ann had only said, "If your mother can't get along without you, and the Army project is really so important, and you feel you have no obligation, that settles it. Doesn't it?"

No. It settled nothing. He had known, as she did, that his mother would be perfectly all right. And the Army project—already under construction—could be handled by any other man in the office. An obligation? Why? Why? He had let the days go by without deciding. In the end, time had made the decision for him.

His mind wandered. He wrenched himself back, thought of that afternoon, recalled his leave-taking of Skinhead.

"We're marines. We're not stragglers," the battalion commander had said. "And we'll go out of here fighting." It was the final briefing. Pat had turned over his command to a first lieutenant from the artillery battalion. "The enemy'll dog us all the way to keep us from joining the First Marines at Koto-ri. We'll keep our trucks on the road, and patrols in the hills. Everybody walks but drivers and radio operators ... Perimeter around each vehicle on stops ... Destroy nothing that can move ... We'll leave no equipment ... There'll be artillery support toward us, from Koto, and behind us from the rear echelon here in Hagaru ..." Finally, Skinhead had shaken hands with him. "Good luck, Pat."

"I feel funny about pulling out like this."

"Can't argue with chaplains or doctors."

"No."

"You've done a good job, Pat."

"Thank you, sir."

A truck outside the tent in which he lay was stuck in the slush. Its wheels were spinning, and Pat could smell burning rubber. He closed his eyes. They'll have to fight for every ridge, he thought—every road junction, every mile. He lit another cigarette. The artillery rolled out again, began a constant barrage off in the north.

A corpsman came in, holding a flashlight. He stopped for a moment to warm his hands before the stove, looked at the wounded man across the tent, and walked over to Pat. "Captain Patrick?"

"Yes?"

"Suppose to give you a shot, take your temperature before you board the plane."

He sat up as the sailor peeled the blankets away. "I've been feeling better."

The corpsman eased him over, checked the hypodermic. "Better take it in the butt, sir." He pulled down the trousers, the heavy drawers, plunged the needle and swabbed with an alcohol patch.

"You flying out?" Pat said.

"Taking the road."

"Good luck."

The sailor shook down a thermometer. "Looks like we'll need it."

"Any outfits on the move yet?"

After putting the thermometer in Pat's mouth, the corpsman lit a cigarette. "Guess they're waiting for daylight. Seventh Marines and some doggies goin' out. Limeys and the Fifth'll be rear guard. Give us time to get the last of you off and pack our gear."

Pat swung his legs off the cot, making room for the corpsman to sit. "Going to be rough, fighting down that mountain," he said, his speech garbled by the thermometer beneath his tongue.

"Better not talk till we get the temperature, sir. See how much good that penicillin did." The officer on the other cot groaned, and the corpsman glanced at him. "Still knocked out. Poor guy. It'd turn your stomach to look at his foot." He field stripped his cigarette and took the thermometer.

"Well?"

Making a notation on his pad, the corpsman said, "Okay. Barely any fever. It's 0400 now. You're to report to the main building in thirty minutes for transportation to the strip." He began to put his things in his pack. "Say, you hear what General Twining in the States said?" He grinned. "Somebody told him there was six Chink divisions surroundin' us up here. And he says, 'Sure do feel sorry for those Chinamen!' "

"You believe it?" Pat asked, smiling.

"Makes a good story. But it's not the goonies I'm worried about." He hunched his shoulders. "I'd give my left nut to have a million-dollar wound like you got." He waved cheerily, and left.

Pat threw the blanket around his shoulders, leaving his arms free, and followed him out. The snow was blowing again. The stars were dissolving one by one. The guns to the north boomed in steady rhythm, hammering on his nerves. "No reason," he said aloud. No reason to walk when he might fly, to freeze when he might be warm, to suffer when he might heal, to die when he might live ... Against logic, against sanity, he told himself again. But should logic and sanity always be obeyed? You could not foresee how any man would respond to any situation. A man was prompted more by the need of the moment than by the cautions he had learned in the past. A man acted more often on the wild promptings of his heart than on the calm judgment of his mind.

He went back inside, sat on his cot, the blanket still draped around his shoulders. The cigarette burned his fingers. He dropped it and watched the glow of the ash.

Pat took his place in line before the dark silhouette of the plane, watching the men ahead of him clamber up the ladder and disappear into the blacked-out fuselage.

"Sir?"

He looked up. Goober was standing beside him. "What the ... What are you doing here, Wally?"

"Wasn't feelin' too good after last night. Had to get somethin' for my gut. So I thought I'd come by, leave you this gear you forgot." He gave Pat his dirty sweater and his map case. "Told me at the hospital where I could find you."

"Well ... thanks."

"Just made it."

"Yeah." The line moved up and Pat followed it toward the plane.

Goober shifted uncomfortably. "Arms pretty bad?"

"Doctors think so." Watching the first sergeant, Pat noted a new and stately dignity to his bulk. "Company all squared away, I guess."

Goober nodded. "They—all of them—Sanchez and Justus, the doggie, Huckabee—they been askin' about you, sir."

"Wally, I'm sorry I didn't... have a chance to ..." He floundered to a halt. Then: "Tell them I wish them good luck."

A lieutenant stepped behind Pat, and checked the evacuation tag on his pack. "Seat from the rear, please, Captain. Stretcher cases forward." Pat nodded, and took another step toward the plane.

"Probably, you'll be in Tokyo in a coupla hours," Goober said.

"Doesn't take long."

"I caught a hop with MATS once," Goober said, moving up as the line moved. "Only took eight hours from D.C. to Frisco."

The marine in front of Pat slipped on the ice, and Pat helped him to his feet. "Wally, it's ... getting late. Guess you ought to get back." He held out his hand.

The first sergeant took it, shook it solemnly. "I'll see you again some time, sir." He dropped the hand. "I mean, sometimes you run into people." Forcing his fingers deep into his gloves, he concentrated on tucking the parka cuff over his hands. "Well ..."

"So long, Wally."

Goober stood there a moment, looking at him, as if there was more to be said. Then he turned and walked away.

Pat climbed up the ladder, felt his way into the dark cavern of the plane, and found a bucket seat at the rear.

The company would be standing-by now. Ought to put Cagle up front. His outfit's beefed up with replacements. Chuck's a good man to have at the point. The new company commander's an artilleryman. Of course, like all marines, he was an infantryman first. He'd had training. But no matter how competent, he would be handicapped. And the company could not help but suffer.

"Hey! Move it over, will ya, Mac?"

Without looking up, Pat shifted to the next seat. He could see out the hatch now. Goober was still standing there, on the edge of the crowd, watching the plane. What the hell is he waiting for? he thought angrily. The new CO would need him now ... Should pace the men, tighten control when they're on the mountains as flank patrol. Weapons ought to be checked. Mingle replacements with old men ... Surely the lieutenant would realize ... and if he didn't Wally would damn' well tell him.

He could hear the artillery again, sounding like a thousand bowling alleys... C.P. ought to be somewhere near the center when in column so you could move to front or rear when anything developed. Ought to switch experienced NCOs to platoons with new officers ... The artilleryman was no fool. He seemed conscientious. He'd know all those things. Of course, it would all be new to him ... Well, it was someone else's worry now. After all, Pat thought, I'm not the only marine who can run a company.

Someone was retching up forward. And another man, on the stretcher below, was cursing the sick marine. A corpsman started to go to him, and tripped on Pat's outstretched feet. "Christ! Why the hell don't you— Pardon, sir!"

"Sorry," Pat said ... They'll get to Koto-ri without me ... and then to Hungnam, he was thinking. And yet ... And yet, he knew his men, knew how much he could demand and get from them. They had given him their best, blindly, without question. Even when he had doubted their strength, even when he had toyed briefly with the idea of surrender, they had transfused him with their own dogged will and defiance. And now, he knew, though he alone could not save them, he might ... "shorten the odds," he mumbled aloud. That was what he might do. He had to admit that. No more. But that much he might do. Shorten the odds. And that's why they need me, he thought. That's why.

I'm not going to do it, not going to be a damned fool, he told himself. It'll be that march from Bad Girl all over again, but ten times worse. But he had learned that nothing is so terrible it can not be endured. Nothing but guilt.

Andy had accused him of thinking too much, of always searching for an answer when there was no answer. Walt had accused him of hair-splitting, of making a moral issue out of practical decisions. Pat knew he could never explain what he was going to do to anyone, not to his mother, not to Ann. He could not fully explain it to himself.

Standing, he pushed past the line coming through the hatch, and descended the ladder.

"Hold it! Where you think you're going?"

"Forgot something," Pat muttered, and hurried away. Goober had not moved. He was still standing where Pat had seen him last.

Neither spoke as they followed the road in the gathering light, toward the battalion area. The wind was rising and they walked with their heads down, their hoods drawn about their faces, picking their way past the waiting trucks, tanks, and guns, climbing the banks to avoid the traffic.

"Over there," Goober said, pointing to the cluster of men behind a radio jeep.

"You'd better wait here," Pat told him. Skinhead was bent over behind the communications jeep, warming his hands on the exhaust.

He straightened up as Pat approached. "I'm off the sick list," Pat said. "They released me."

The battalion commander squinted at him suspiciously. "Let you out, huh?"

"Yes, sir." This compounded the felony, Pat thought. To lie to a superior, to be absent without leave from the hospital. "Feel great," he said, flexing his arms.

Skinhead stepped back to make room for the men before the exhaust pipe. "It's going to be tough. Able Company'll be climbing for hours. Got them on the left flank."

"I'm okay."

"Sure." Reaching behind him into the jeep, Skinhead pulled out two radio batteries. "Take these with you." He swung them unexpectedly fast. One of them hit Pat's arm. The pain was immediate and intense. His temples pounded with it, as if they were seared, too.

He picked up the cartons and put one under each armpit. When he looked up, Skinhead was watching him. "I'll shove off now, sir."

"You wouldn't crap an old marine, would you, Pat?"

Pat said, "It never was as bad as they thought."

Skinhead nodded. "All right. Take over. Send that artilleryman back to me. I can use him here. I'll be in touch with you."

"My people up ahead?" Pat forced his voice to be steady, but his stomach was knotting convulsively. He had to get away, had to sit down or risk fainting.

"About two hundred yards from here. Just ahead of Charlie Company." Pat started off. "Glad to have you aboard, Pat."

He turned, answered the ritual. "Glad to be aboard, sir."

Skinhead watched him go. Then he spoke to his sergeant major. "Get the surgeon over here. We're going to get a blast from upstairs, and I want someone to shortstop it."

Pat found Goober. "It's fixed." He rested against a snowbank.

"Let me take those batteries."

Sweat was pouring down Pat's sides and he trembled uncontrollably. He gave up the cartons, sighed in relief. Then, holding his arms lightly away from his sides, he bent into the wind, and went to find his company.

32

Pat held up his hand and turned wearily as the column behind collapsed in broken fragments. "Deploy!" he whispered. "Face outboard."

Goober mouthed the words. "Face outboard. Pass it on."

Alone, Pat worked his way forward through the crusty drifts, pulling himself across an overhanging slab of ice and granite. For a moment he lay there, resting. "Face outboard … Pass it on …" The phrase receded behind him like an echo. "… Pass … Pass … it … on."

They had cleared Hagaru at eight in the morning. By eight-thirty they were engaged by an enemy that struck from the hills, from roadblocks and from frozen paddies, an enemy that possessed and used a full complement of mortars, artillery, machine guns, and rifles. Fifty men were allowed to pass so five hundred could be ambushed. At the end of the first mile, Able Company had two dead, five wounded.

Those numbers were multiplied by every mile they wrested from the enemy.

Able Company had held off the Chinese while engineers swept mines. Then they moved on to blast a roadblock. Three dead. Five wounded.

Able Company had left the road to burn every hut and shack along the route, depriving the enemy of sanctuary from the cold. No losses.

Able Company had found the machine guns that sprayed the column. Planes destroyed the position with rockets. One dead. One wounded. Two with frostbite sent to the trucks.

Able Company had called for artillery fire on a hillside emplacement. The first shell started a landslide. Snow and rock roared off the slopes, crashing to the road. They searched desperately, but could not find two of their dead. Two missing. Two dead. Three wounded. Another frostbite case.

Able Company had struggled up a mountain again, manhandling a recoilless .75, straining for footholds, feeling their sweat freeze a husk about their bodies. Reconnoitering aircraft had reported a Chinese field piece in the area in position to rake the column below. Planes failed to dislodge it. Able Company was detailed to knock it out. Chuck Cagle's platoon moved to flank it while Pat waited to support his attack.

He glanced at his watch. Seven hours had passed. Hagaru was three miles behind them. Koto-ri, a magic name, a haven of warmth, rest, and safety, lay in the distance, all but inaccessible, six miles away. He felt hands on his boots. Goober was boosting him. Sliding forward to the rim of the slab, he grasped it. The first sergeant, puffing clouds of white, wriggled up alongside.

They could see the Chinese clearly. Six of them were gathered around a small fire. Behind them, its snout projecting from a cave, was the field piece. "Wonder how the hell they got that big job up there," Goober murmured in his ear.

"Can't see Cagle's people yet," Pat whispered. The enemy was too far away to hear conversation, but every sound seemed amplified in the vastness of the mountains. He signaled to the replacement lieutenant who had taken Pappas' place. He had forgotten his name, remembering only that it sounded French and that he was six weeks out of Basic School at Quantico. The young man prodded Firesteen, who sat at his feet. The corporal called a squad forward. They slushed through the snow, weapons clanking. One fell and cursed. Goober waved a fist at them, motioning for silence. They took up firing positions below, sighting in on the unsuspecting enemy.

Pat gazed down at the familiar panorama, now in miniature, a thousand feet below. The trucks, spewing lazy fumes, were halted. The regiment, spread across three miles of coiling road, was being hit only at its center. At the head of the column, tiny figures in green lay inert along the road. Two curves away the same scene was repeated at the rear. Those men were isolated for a moment. In the center, dwarfs waved their arms. Others wriggled mole-like through the snow, crawling toward the hollow croup of enemy guns. And then the Chinese were silenced and the regiment rolled once more.

Seventy-five yards across the ridge, the gun crew under Pat's surveillance ignored the approaching column. They were seated, passing a bowl around the circle of their fire, taking turns eating. The last man drained the food. Another man grabbed the bowl and placed it on a soldier's head. Pat imagined he could hear their laughter. The man with the bowl chased his tormenter, who threw snowballs at him. "Bastards!" Goober swore. "They're warm."

"Cagle ought to be moving faster. The regiment'll be passing under that gun in another few minutes."

"Damn 536s! Dorn can't keep 'em workin.'"

Pat touched his sleeve. They could see Cagle at last. He was just above the enemy, moving silently through the drifts. Thirty yards below, the Chinese had gone unhurriedly to their weapon. One was watching the progress of the column on the road. One held a shell. One was urinating. The gunner was at his sight. The man who had thrown snowballs was lying on his back while the man with the bowl rubbed his legs.

"That's right, fellas, play grabass while you can." Goober's expression was one of grim satisfaction.

Watching Cagle's movement, then the road, then the swinging of the enemy gun, Pat poised himself to give the signal. Below his vantage point, riflemen, fascinated, watched the enemy through their sights.

The Chinese began to push their field piece forward as the regiment moved into their view. Then Cagle's .75 fired. It was a close miss. Pat called to his riflemen. They swept the shelf. The enemy, caught simultaneously from front and flank, unable to move back, unable to use their weapon, darted back and forth in panic, stumbling over one another, seeking cover behind the gun, the shells. They were like frantic chickens, penned and doomed. Their leader was shouting at them, standing alone in face of the fire. They began to push their big gun back into the cave. They made it, but the snowball thrower was hit, and fell. His friend ran from the shelter of the cave, and began to drag him toward it when he went down across the body of his comrade and lay with his feet kicking. The .75 blasted again, whooshing snow behind it, making a direct hit on the mouth of the cave, sealing it. Another round. Tons of debris covered the shelf.

"Jezoo!" Goober brushed ice from Pat's shoulders. "Think they can live in there?"

"They're dead," Pat said, still whispering. "I hope they're dead." He slid down and found the new lieutenant.

The other men had gotten up, but the young officer still lay in the snow. Firesteen tapped his back, and he rose hurriedly. "I ... didn't fire." He was brushing his parka, not looking at Pat. "It was over before I thought to fire!"

Pat allowed himself the luxury of a secret smile. "Saddle up," he said kindly. "We'll meet Cagle on the road." He walked across the spine of the ridge. Bent over like old men, easing the pack straps that ate into their shoulders, stamping their feet, his marines looked worn, haggard. They spoke, but in a soft, dull monotone, without animation. It seemed impossible that—only a day before— they had been laughing, boasting, arguing, gambling, drinking, complaining. The hours of dragging snow-anchored boots, the nerve-racking proximity of danger, the glacial cold had numbed and drained them. Pat forced himself to keep his shoulders back, to step deliberately, to conceal his weariness. *Could have been warm ... could have been safe ... could have been in Tokyo by now...* He taunted himself with the thought. Only once— when he had first reassumed his command and the survivors of Bad Girl Ridge had gathered silently around him—only then had he been glad of his decision. Now he knew he had set himself a task, and had become its prisoner. He slipped. Goober caught him. Pat noticed that there was no pain in his arms. They were numb. He began to work them, trying to restore circulation. Goober was scowling. "They botherin' you?"

Pat grunted noncommittally and walked past him. Sanchez and Dorn fell into step behind. As he started down the hillside, Pat began to knead his upper arms. There'll be a strip at Koto-ri, he was thinking, and a hospital. If he could just make it to there ... when they made it, he could turn in. He glanced over his shoulder, saw his men following behind, clinging to the scrub growth. He crossed a field and reached the road again. The march had halted. There was firing somewhere in the rear. A mile away another company took over the battle.

Night came, intensifying the cold, concealing the enemy, forcing the men to grope their way as they guided the trucks over the twisting road.

Another halt. Five hundred yards ahead, in another cosmos, mortars were falling unerringly. There were shouts of command, shattering flashes.

The men of Able Company, spared for the moment, crawled behind trucks and into snowbanks. Pat slogged up the road, calling to the shadows on either side. "Get to work on one another's legs. Plenty of massage. I don't want to catch anyone doping off ..." Stopping before one group, he pulled a whimpering man to his feet. He didn't recognize him; he was a replacement flown into Hagaru from some torrid Pacific island. "Don't you understand English? I said 'massage'!"

"Just did, 'bout an hour ago," the boy complained.

Pat shook him. "Now! You hear me? Now!" The marine slumped back into the snow, lifted his foot and took his friend's leg in his lap. "The rest of you get to it! You want to lose your legs?" Pat went on up the line. "Massage, dammit! You've got three miles to go yet ..."

When he returned to the point where he had left Dorn with his company radio, he listened for a moment to the crackle of orders on the net. Crossing the road, he sat down, easing himself into the snow. His arms felt lifeless. He found it difficult to clench his fists. There was a persistent throbbing in his neck and shoulders. He took a morphine syrette from his pocket and loosened his clothing.

"I will do that for you, Captain."

Pat was startled. He tried to hide the syrette. Choy took it from his hand, pulled aside the clothing, and jabbed below the hip. "Thanks."

"You walked willingly into this trap. That surprised me." It was the first time anyone had mentioned his return to the company.

"I was released," Pat said.

The interpreter was shivering. "Goober has told it differently." He stood there, looking down at Pat for a moment, then padded off up the road toward the truck where the wounded lay.

Goober appeared. "Been lookin' for you," he said, dropping to his knees. He picked up Pat's boot and began to unlace it.

"I can do that, Wally." The first sergeant ignored the protest. "All right," Pat said. "Let me do yours."

Goober thrust out his huge boot. Pat fumbled with the laces. "Arms pretty bad?"

"Cold fingers." The lace came undone at last. Pulling off the heavy boot, he began rubbing the first sergeant's feet.

Far above them, in their own world of luminous dials, pilots were listening to the calm voice of an air-controller and watching for a spurt of light that might guide them to a target.

Woody Dorn propped the radio behind him and sank down beside Sanchez. His head nodded and he closed his eyes. "So awful damn' tired ..."

Sanchez squeezed the water from his sock, and then slipped it back on and laced his boots. His teeth were chattering. "We're close now."

They could hear the planes. The mortars still pounded. Flames leaped up around the next curve. "I been figurin', Goat. Oughta take us two years, three at the most, to get a place cleared, start gettin' on our feet."

"I wouldn't know, Woody. One thing I decided though; I wanna pay my way."

Dorn leaned toward him. "Sure. A little at a time ... outta your half."

"You still tryin't' con my ponyo inter bein' a dirt farmer?" Lock hollowed out a spot beside them, and stretched out. "Lissen to a feller who knows, buddy-buddy," he said, pulling at Sanchez's arm. "Scratch-in' fer a livin's fer the birds. You stay in The Corps with ole Lock."

"Love The Corps," Sanchez said, grinning.

"Three squares a day. A sack. Good liberty. Twenny years of it, and you can be a dirt dauber if you wanna—an' in the good ole U.S.A."

"We're gonna do it," Dorn insisted. "In a few years—you'll see, won't take us more than a few years—we'll have cattle and rice and wheat. Right, Goat?"

"It'd be somethin'," Sanchez said. "No bosses but ourselves. A chance to ... y'know, well ... there'd be somethin' to show for your work."

"Hope to die, I know'd this weather could dry up a feller's love muscle, but the cold's workin' on y'alls' heads!" Lock laughed weakly, and called across the road, "Hey, Huck! Get on the ball, buddy-roe. Where's the chow?"

"How's the captain doin'?" Woody asked, yawning.

"Okay. Huck's keepin' an eye on him."

"Why you figure he jumped hospital?" Sanchez said.

"Got me."

Huckabee brought them two ration cans. "Thawed 'em on the engine block, but they didn't get hot."

"They's loose, ain't they?" Lock gave the chicken and vegetables to Dorn and Sanchez, and shared the limas and ham with Huckabee. "Mel's got a box of Tootsie Rolls hid. Huck, how 'bout goin' back and findin' him so's we can have dessert?"

Huckabee pushed Lock's helmet over his face. "I've done my share. I cooked. You go find Mel."

"Yer a hell of a buddy," Lock grumbled. "Miserable as I am, you're gonna have me doin' all that walkin' ..."

Three planes suddenly swooped into the black valley. The men could see the vague outline of their wings, the flash of their exhausts. The night fighters banked in turn, rocked for an instant and dropped their bombs. There were three explosions, bursting high on the distant hillside. The mortars were silenced.

"Them flyboys got more nerve than brains," Lock said. "They'll be chewin' steak and sleepin' in a warm sack in an hour, but I wouldn't swap jobs with 'em."

"Lock, you oughta rent yourself out to psychiatrists' conventions," Huckabee said.

Justus slapped his back. "Soon's yer doctorin', you let me know. I'll let you book me."

Huckabee got up. "We'll make a pile," he said, shivering. "I'm goin' to see after some of my people. When I get back, you have me some pogie-bait."

Goober was yelling, "Saddle up!"

"Off and on," Lock sang out. Sanchez and Dorn were dozing. He pulled them up. "This minds me of the time we was goin' frog-giggin' —'course it wasn't no twenty-five below, but honest to Aunt Bessie, hope to die, I tell you true, buddy-roe ..."

The trucks were rolling. Huddled figures returned to the road and began the shuffle again. They passed the flaming wreckage of a jeep, were briefly bathed in its light and slowed to savor its warmth.

"I tell you I can ride a horse?" Sanchez asked Dorn.

He put the 300 radio in the company jeep and lurched drunkenly alongside. "Huh?"

"Used to work part time in a ridin' academy near Central Park, New York. Stable boy. You ride?" He rubbed his nose until the feeling began to come back to it. "Horses. You ride?"

"A little. My dad had an old mare on the farm."

"We get a big place, got to have horses."

"Stay in The Corps," Lock said. "We always ride."

A man ahead of them limped to the side of the road and collapsed. They went to him. "What's wrong?" Sanchez asked.

"Legs. Can't make it." The voice was muffled beneath the hood. "Been botherin' me bad."

Pat broke through to them. "Get on your feet."

"Looks like he's had it," Lock said.

"Get up!" Pat tore the man's hood aside.

"Let me be. I can't."

"Try!" He wrestled the marine to his feet, and pain increased his rage. "Don't you think everybody'd like to crap out? That's what they want us to do. Now you walk, mister. Walk!"

The marine stumbled forward again. Justus and Sanchez took his arms, helping him. "Bastard," the man said, without malice. "Real first-class ... bastard ..."

"Shut up!" Sanchez said.

Pat swayed on his feet. There seemed to be a massive pressure in his shoulders. He watched his company straggle by. "Not much farther," he kept repeating. "Not much farther ..."

At seven o'clock, with Hagaru twenty-three hours and nine miles behind them, they entered Koto-ri, a weaving line of exhausted men, still on their feet, but hardly aware of it.

They were given coffee. Hot, pungent, black, searing the gullet, bringing beads of sweat to chalk-white foreheads. And then their helmets were stacked with steamy pancakes. Most of the food was left untouched as the men sat there with eyes closed, mouths ajar.

"All squared away," Goober said, when the last of the men had been billeted.

Cagle fell on his cot. Choy slept across the tent. Pat sat down. Goober fed the fire. "Go sleep, Top."

"At least we're together again, sir."

"Hm-mm?"

"The division, Captain. Practically all together again."

Pat's eyes were shut. Goober eased him down, lifted the injured arms gently, slipped off his boots, covered him. He walked to the tent flap, turned back as the captain seemed to speak to him.

"Dear God ..." he was mumbling. "Dear God ... forty-five miles more."

Goober waited until he was sure he was asleep. Then he took the muffler from his neck, wadded it, and approached Pat. He stood there uncertainly, then tossed the dirty red cloth on an empty field cot, and left the tent.

33

"Mail call!" Lock stood in the center of the company bivouac, shading his eyes from the glare of the snow.

Huckabee blew a wavering blast on his bugle. "I'll get killed for wakin' 'em." He blew again.

"Mail call!" Lock yelled again. "Drop the rocks and grab yer socks!" Able Company, still bleary-eyed and stiff from exhausted sleep, staggered past the tent flaps, buttoning parkas, pulling on gloves, tripping on unlaced boots—a shaggy, unkempt procession of sleepwalkers.

"Gotta be Christmas packages."

"They don't come till Easter."

"I'd give a month's pay for a fur-lined jockstrap!"

They gathered around Lock. "You people knock off the chatter, and I'll get started."

There was a horrifying shriek from the far end of the row of tents. Mel Firesteen careened toward them as if jet-propelled. "I'm comin'!" He sprawled on the ice, scrambled to his feet again, and charged down on them. "Be there! Be there, baby."

"Baby'll be there if'n you put him there," Lock said.

"Gimme. Gimme." Firesteen held out his arms. "Just pile 'em on." Lock reached into the mail bag. "Abernathy. We got a Abernathy?" One of the replacements ran forward for his letter.

"C'mon, Lock, gimme my mail," Firesteen said.

Huckabee yawned. "Hold it down, Mel. You'll wake these fellas up."

"But I been waitin' ..."

"We all been waitin'," Lock said. "No priv'leged characters."

"They don't mind," Firesteen said, turning to the men around him. Some were leaning on one another. Some had their eyes closed. A few sat back to back in the snow, chins on their chests, already dozing.

"Let him have it."

"Give it to him. Curiosity's killin' me," Huckabee said.

Sanchez, rubbing snow in his face, shivered, slowly coming awake. "Think you did some good, Mel?"

"Naw, he was just snappin' in," Lock said. "Gotta wait till he gets home t' fire fer record."

"I got ten bucks says Firesteen shot blanks," Goober said.

"I'll take that!" The corporal reached for the first sergeant's hand. Both realized, even as their gloves touched, that it was the first time more than orders had passed between them since Thanksgiving. "What the hell! No hard feelin's, Top. I'll invite you to the bris."

"Okay, Firesteen. What's a *bris?*"

"That's what's wrong with Mel," Lock said. "When he was a baby, he lost that little extry that does the trick!" Someone began to giggle; and the others, as if cued, laughed.

"Get the mail out, for God's sake!"

"Adler ... Arnold ... Asten ..." He flipped through a stack of envelopes, putting some of the letters aside. "Those guys were KIA around Inchon."

"Please!" Firesteen shouted.

"Keep your shirt on, ponyo. If'n you got mail, you'll get it."

"Whatta ya mean, 'if?' I oughta have fifty letters..."

"Dammit, Justus, get on the ball," Goober said. "These crudheads been sleepin' all day. This place gotta be policed, everybody shaved, weapons cleaned for inspection before the captain gets back from battalion."

"Bellini... Braznell... Burton ... You fellers sing out, you want yer mail." The men began to file past, then drift to the back of the crowd to read. "Carney ... Carter ... Casey ... Cavelli ..."

"Hospital."

"Back in the States."

"... Cerewski ... Chalmers ... Chaney ..."

"Got it at Kimpo."

"Got it at Seoul."

"... Earnhardt ... Eason ... Ebert ... Emmons ... Evans ..."

"Got it on Bad Girl."

The roll call was answered by less than half of the men. But there was always someone who recalled a face, a gesture, a voice, a piece of ground, a town, a ship that went with a name.

"... Faircloth ... Farber... Feagin ... Finn ... Flynn ... Freeman ..."

"You skipped me," Firesteen said. "Gimme my mail, damn your hide!"

"Fullerton ... Furst ... Gaffney ... Gleason ..."

"That's The Horse," Huckabee said. He took the letter, postmarked Chicago. "Morrie Schiff. His manager."

"You been through the 'Fs.' You let me have my mail, Lock, before I cream you!"

"I'm just passin' it out, Mel. I don't have nothin' t' do with writin' it." Lock dropped more letters in the bag. "Glazener ... Goober ..." He saw the first sergeant's expression of surprise. It was the first time he could remember Goober getting mail ... Granger ... Gross ... Gudger ... Gowalski ..."

"You're hidin' my letters!"

"Top, will you tell this here smuck to shove?"

"It's sh-*muck*," Firesteen said, "and you're beggin' for a bruise!" Goober had drifted off with his letter. The other men, apparently sharing a joke with Lock, dragged Firesteen back. "C'mon, Mel. Clear out, now. We feel for you, but it's just toughsky titsky."

"... Haggerman ... Hartford ... Huckabee ..." Lock shuffled through some letters and dropped them in the bag.

"What were those?" Firesteen demanded.

"I got to explain it to you?"

"I'm gonna cold-cock you, Lock!"

"Write a letter through channels to the Commandant, you got any gripes 'bout the way I handle mail call. Ireland ... Isenberg ... Ivey ... Jones, B ... Jones, C. W ..."

"This may be funny to you guys, but it's not a damn' bit funny to me!" Firesteen was on the verge of tears.

"Quesane ... Raphael ... Roth ... Sanchez ..."

Men wandered back to their tents, reading as they walked, transported for a time to a distant, hazily recalled world, magically warm and comfortable.

Huckabee studied his mother's painfully exact lettering. The street at home was being paved. ("Your daddy says it's about time, but leastways we didn't have to pay for it.") His brother Simon was working at the hotel. ("Mostly, they use light-skinned boys, but Mrs. Mack got him in 'cause the manager is her brother-in-law or some such kinfolk. He likes the job fine and they like him. You know Simon never met a stranger and can make anybody like him, just by knowing how to jolly them and cut the fool. So it is fine except your daddy wants him to go stay in Detroit with Uncle Albert, but Simon wants to marry and Billie May says she don't want to go, so it looks like he'll stay and I'm real glad ...") She had gotten a raise. ("Me and Mrs. Mack always watch the *Life of Romance* program on her television there in the parlor. Eat our lunch right together except when she is out and then she is always reminding me to see it so I can tell her and keep her up with it. And this noon we was waiting for it to come on, and drinking tea, and she told me she's raising me to thirty dollars next week. She's a awful good woman, a real Christian. And she wants to help you when you get back, always asking about you and I know worries about you. Mentioned two times now how Mr. Mack can get you something here in Mobile, maybe even with the city. They pay real good, so if you change your mind ...") They had been planning for his return. ("Your daddy and me talked on it and with his retirement and what we got saved and the government, and all, we'll be able to help you right smart if you really got your heart set on it. But it sure takes lots of money with college and all, and a mighty long time. But if you're sure you want something bad enough, and you're well and the Lord helps you, you can do it. Loreen is in bed now taking shots and feels better. She says to tell you she could save money if her little brother was a doctor. Ha! Your father says you will do better in one year doctoring than he could do in ten years in a dining car. And be home with us, too. We all pray for you...")

He folded the letter carefully, and put it in his pack, imagining his mother's small-featured, anxious face, hearing her gentle voice. No dining car for me, he thought. No serving in a hotel either. No laundry work or truck driving or portering or bellhopping. And he wouldn't shine shoes or work on the docks or be a chauffeur. He wouldn't run an elevator or tend furnace or take care of someone else's yard. He had said all those things before. Urged on by his father, he had argued with his mother, bragged to his brother and sister. But he had never convinced them—or himself.

Now, he realized, he had at last decided on his course. Now he really meant it. Without reservation. Without seeking assurance from anyone. Why was he so sure? He could not fix the reason. But somewhere along the way he had found the thing he had been seeking. He was no longer clinging wistfully to a dream. It was a certainty.

Wally Goober waited until he was in his tent to open the envelope. His palms were wet as he took out the letter and began to read:

"Dear Wally, I rite this tho I am knowing you will say she has got some nerve. I guess you will be rite at that. But you know I never wished harm to you. I am bad in need of some helping rite now. And you cood do it all rite. Don't say no you won't rite off and tare up this. After all we were two years together and you can't wipe off that from the book. I was sick and taking treatments and am better now but it eats up every cent. Anyway I can't work. Tried in a five-and-dime place, you know there on 101 near La Jolla where we went once you wanted something to put on gold buttons. But I coodn't stand it on my feet so much hours. If I cood get to Atlanta I wood be all rite. I don't want that my sister shood know about us or anything. It is fonny me riting you like this. But no matter we did not all the time get along, you allways were kind and of good nature and wood help a person ..."

He could summon no hatred, only revulsion and pity. She was sick, reduced to asking him for help, begging, crawling for train fare. Ripping the letter to pieces, he lay back on his cot, reliving the scenes that had once left him weeping, that had once stirred him to livid rage and promises of vengeance. But now they were only sordid memories, incapable of hurting any more. He was free. She deserved nothing, he thought. Nothing.

He reached to the ground, pieced together her address on the envelope, and put it in his pocket.

Three tents away, down the company street, Jesus Sanchez tossed his letter on his cot, and sat down. "Aren't you gonna read it?" Dorn asked. Without answering, Sanchez tore it open. Father Saracino:

"My dear Jesus, I have just left our little church, and come home. There was a boy on the street outside, carrying bottles to the grocery; and I helped him as I once helped you. I remember you got thirty-four cents, or maybe a little less. And you dropped a dime in a grating, and we tried to get it out with chewing gum and a stick, but couldn't. And you gave all your pennies for the poor box.

"Well, I thought about all that once more. Now at my desk, I've questioned myself again as to whether I lacked understanding, whether I've failed you. So many times, Jesus, I've prayed God to give me strength and wisdom to help you, and to give you the desire to help yourself.

"I've tried to explain to you; and I've failed. I ask you only to remember that bitterness is an acid which eats into our beings and cripples us. Surely you can find room to forgive, if you can't find the understanding to accept. All of us need God in our lives..."

He put the letter in the stove, watched the flames for a moment, and clanged the door shut. "Your sister lived away from the Church," the priest had told him. "She died out of the Church." But Jesus thought only that his sister's sin against God and man had been dramatized. She had been branded in death. This was the unforgivable thing to him, for he saw it as cruel, senseless.

It had all happened in the space of a single day. He had skipped school, and gone to see her in the morning to get money to enroll in a manual-arts course. And he had found The Greaser, a reptilian little tough who worked as a presser for a neighborhood dry cleaner. They were on the bed in her dark, shuttered room. His sister had grasped his legs, holding him, while The Greaser made his escape. Then she had sworn that the man had forced his way in, but that she was untouched, that calling the police would only make trouble for her.

He had waited until The Greaser left work that evening. Then he had slugged him, beaten him until he lay bleeding in the gutter. He had tom the pleated lavender shirt, made one stroke to carve BASTARD on the heaving chest. Through his rage, he heard the frantic protests: "I wasn't the only one ... lotsa guys ... paid her!" Sanchez, eyes wild with horror, had grabbed his victim's throat. Terrified, The Greaser had clawed at the hands, babbled on. "I give her that watch ... last time ... honestagod, I give her ... the watch ... you got on ..."

Sanchez had released him. The man was whining with pain and fear. Jesus had pulled off his watch, thrown it down, and walked away. Sitting in the shadows across the street, he had watched the inert form beside the fence, heard the faint moans like echos of his own deep-rooted sobs. ("You and me, Jesus. We're not animals ...")

Afraid when the sounds stopped, he had put the unconscious man in a cab and told the driver to take the limp body to a hospital. Then he had run. Later, he remembered the watch and hurried back to get it before it was found. He had it in his pocket when he was picked up. ('The policeman is your friend ...")

Although The Greaser said he did not know who had attacked him, the taxi driver remembered. Sanchez spent the night in jail. The next morning he was taken to his sister's flat. He identified her frail body on the floor beside the open gas oven. And later, because Father Saracino refused his plea, there were only four mourners at the burial—Jesus, his guard, his uncle, and an Italian lady who smelled from babies and gave him a cake wrapped in a paper napkin and pressed a crumpled dollar bill in his hand.

When the priest came, Sanchez refused to see him. But the padre was at his side when he went to the judge's chambers. And though Sanchez ignored him, the priest spoke to the young judge. When it was all over, he was freed on condition that he join the service. For two days—by court direction—he lived with Father Saracino, awaiting the results of his physical examination. And in that time, he did not once speak to the priest.

All this churned in his mind as he lay on his bunk. From outside, he could hear Lock still calling out names. He examined his watch. The glass on the cheap Elgin was smoky, but he could read the time. "Four-fifteen," he said to Dorn. "That right?"

Woody opened his eyes. "I don't know. Some Chinaman got my watch."

"You're supposed to get out of the Army two months before my hitch is up. You goin' down to Colombia right off?"

Surprised by the question, Dorn sat up. "Why ... I'll wait for you," he said. "We'll go together."

Outside, one man after the other walked off with a stack of letters. Then packages. Lock slung the mail bag. Firesteen grabbed his arm. "You're pullin' a gag, huh? You're hidin' my letters? That's okay. I can take a joke." He laughed mirthlessly. "How 'bout it, Lock? Gimme my mail now."

"Sorry, Mel. Truly I am. Rest of this is fer the cap'n, Mr. Cagle ..."

"Can't understand it."

Lock's sorrowful glance made it clear he was deeply sympathetic. "I could maybe mosey down and check with them mail clerks. They's always gettin' things fouled up."

"Will you do that for me, Lock?"

Justus patted Firesteen's shoulder in tender reassurance. "Buddy-buddy, you know how it is with us. I'd do anythin' fer you. And you'd do anythin' fer me if'n I asked you."

"Sure."

"Hope to die?"

"What is it?" he asked, resigned.

"Hope to die," Lock insisted.

"Okay. Hope to die."

Lock was smiling. "Okay. Now all you gotta do—if'n I happen to dig up some mail fer you—is t' let me have it fer an hour..."

"But—"

"In case I find it, Mel, I'd like fer ever'body in the company to get in on it, sorta. We're all hopin' you scored. Ever'body's a-pullin' fer you. And I bet they'd like to get together and fix up a present fer the little fella ..."

"Lock, what did you do with it?" Certain that he was being tricked, Firesteen collared him, backed him up the narrow company street, through a laughing crowd.

"Now you wait a minute. You listen! My idea is we're gonna have us some fun ... the Firesteen Sweepstakes!"

34

The earth shook. There was a dull rumble, and the walls of the tent puffed out feebly. Snow began to slide over the limp canvas. The battalion commander paused, then faced his officers again. "One way out. One bridge. And it's been destroyed."

Another explosion. This time the adjutant stepped outside. "Burial detail," he said. "They're blasting a trench."

Pat stood by the stove, warming his back. "Isn't there any way to detour?"

"There's a sheer drop. And the Chinese are around us in a tight band, squeezing down on Koto-ri. That bridge site is the funnel; and they'll try to plug it." Skinhead held the bowl of his pipe against his cheek while the roar of another blast died. "The regiment's going to seize the high ground and hold it until a bridge is up and the vehicles can pass across."

The new Baker Company commander, a first lieutenant, sat on a folded field desk. "Sir, I heard some scuttlebutt. You know the Air Force dropped some Army bridge sections in this morning by chute. But one drop was lost. Some of the stuff got beat up. They need special trucks to haul it. On top of that, the engineers would have to put up a hell of a lot of bridge under fire—"

Skinhead broke in. "Our job, Lieutenant, is to take the ground and cover the engineers. It's their business to get it up. We'll do ours. They'll do theirs." He spoke softly, but it was clear that the subject was closed. "Final briefing at 0500. You can shove now." They began to move toward the entrance. "Want to see you, Pat."

They were left alone. Skinhead put his helmet on his shiny dome, buttoned the parka that was now several sizes too big for him, and steered Pat outside. Dusk was coming, and heavy black clouds hung over the hills. The battalion commander led the way through crowds of traffic. The greater part of the division was collected in a small area; the roads were jammed with transport and equipment. "How are those arms, Pat?" Skinhead said, speaking for the first time. "How do you feel?"

"Not bad. Really."

"You look like hell."

"I'm okay."

Skinhead began to walk toward the open field where bulldozers were clearing the rubble left by the dynamiting. Pat followed. Long hours of sleep, warmth, and hot food had not replenished his strength. The surgeon had sedated him, treated his arms, given him woolen sleeves to wear. But, though Pat was not conscious of pain, he felt depleted, as if his body had been drained of blood. He recognized the same exhaustion in the dazed movement of the men around him. Even Skinhead seemed not quite himself, but slower, more deliberate.

"Should have ordered you out at Hagaru. Can't get enough planes on this little strip to move all our wounded. We'll have to carry a lot of them down with us." They walked in silence for a while. "Not really the same outfit, is it, Pat? All these new people. You're the only one left of the company commanders..." Two weeks before, Pat thought, he had been an outsider. Skinhead had been the austere voice of authority, a distant and knowledgeable man, seemingly inaccessible and remote. He looked at him now, at the long, skinny frame, slightly stooped, at the deepening lines beneath the bloodshot eyes, the grim slash of mouth. "You learn and keep learning," he was saying. "Only it seems you never learn the right things."

They found the field where a great crevice had been torn from the frozen earth. Marines were standing around the fringe, watching the trucks disgorge their awful burdens. The bodies that were carried out had stiffened in the grotesque attitudes of death. They were put side by side, sitting, face down, stretched out. Then, while the living watched, the dead were bent and fitted into their common grave.

Bulldozers thrust great mounds of earth into the trench. Across the cut, protesting hands and feet and knees rose above the chunks of dirty gray ice. More rock was brought. More gravel and snow. Before long, the dead—marines and soldiers, Englishmen and South Koreans —were covered and their grave was smoothed and hidden.

Chaplains spoke. The flag was lowered to half-mast. Taps. A rifle volley rang out. The watchers stood in a ragged circle, stamping their feet, huddling together for warmth. Then the brief ceremony was over. But no one walked away. Pat brushed his eyes with a glove. Bad Girl Ridge, at least, had been cheated of its bodies. "You feel ... so ... so impotent," he said.

"Kills you," Skinhead said. The trucks moved off, racing their motors, puffing white gusts from their exhausts. "To come to that, to be shoveled under ..." He shook his head. "If we had won, if we were holding ..." The words trailed away and he was silent. After a moment he said, "And no one will ever know ... never really know, what it was like."

"The papers will be full of it."

Skinhead nodded. "And the Secretary of the Navy will send telegrams. And you'll write letters to their wives and their parents. And I will. But no one who wasn't here will ever really know."

They walked back to the battalion C.P. without speaking, dodging the prime movers, the tanks, two trucks loaded with bridge sections, clambering through drifts and across the frozen streets. "Those letters," Pat said. "A hard thing to do."

Skinhead stopped before his tent. "No, Pat. Easy. Just write what they want. They want a lie, a nice fat lie. He died saving his platoon or a buddy. He died in the highest traditions of the service. He died gallantly, courageously. And always, he died painlessly."

Pat kicked one boot against the other, loosening the caked snow. "What good would it do for them to know the truth?"

"What good does it do for you to know? For me to know?" He spoke more in perplexity than in anger. "Hell, for once, I'd like to tell them the truth. With all the blood and gore and stink and hunger and fear the truth involves."

"But you won't."

Skinhead shuffled his boots in the snow, his head down, gazing at the pattern he had shaped. "Better get back to your people, Pat. We've got to clear the way for that bridge tomorrow ..."

It was dark when Pat finished his inspection and returned to his tent.

Cagle was asleep. Firesteen, brought to the neutral ground of officers' country, sat on a poncho engrossed in his mail. Two marines, like poll watchers, stood above him to prevent collusion. The rest of Able Company awaited the news as each letter was read, and the list of possible winners of the Firesteen Sweepstakes narrowed from fifty-two to twenty-one.

"Anything yet, Mel?" Pat asked.

"No, sir." The other marines dropped to their knees and tried to look as Firesteen picked up a sealed pink envelope with "19" scrawled on it, and the postmark obscured. The corporal held the letter behind him. "Dammit! She's entitled to some privacy!"

Pat arranged his mail before him on his cot. Puzzling over the delicate handwriting, he read the last of his mother's brief notes. Like the fourteen he had already opened, it was a schedule of her day, a clipping of the "Daily Chuckle" from the Washington Post, and a short biblical quotation. "... the Lord your God is He that goeth with you..." he read, and put the note aside.

Taking the most recent of the ten letters from Ann, he read it again. It had been written on Thanksgiving. She had spent the day with his mother.

"I never really knew her until you went away," she wrote. "I used to think that she was quaint, a little forbidding and inflexible. And I thought you were so unlike her. I began seeing her often for your sake, hoping she might lean on me through these months. Instead, I find myself leaning on her. She is stronger than I. And she is quaint only in that there are too few like her. My other judgments were just as wrong. I see that your sense of humor, your sense of right—which you won't recognize and which you battle—might well be a reflection of her. Or am I just looking for things? I don't know, my darling. I want so to discover everything I haven't learned about you..."

She described the new shopping center near Georgetown, writing, "I went out prepared to detest it, because the sketches you submitted weren't accepted. But I liked it. The architect's probably ten years older than you, and a foot shorter and hasn't got a hair on his head, and surely isn't going to be my husband, but the way he used the central plaza ..."

He skipped to the final paragraph: "'When you come home'— that's what all the days revolve about. That's when I'm going to buy a slinky black negligee and change to your brand of toothpaste and read Dr. Spock and save on grocery money so I can buy you undershorts for your birthday. That's when I'll count hours instead of days and months, when the nights will be short, when I'll clip recipes from magazines and read Thursday's grocery ads and watch you shave as Victoria watched Albert and leave notes for the milkman and take your suits to the cleaners. Do I sound like a schoolgirl with her first mad crush? No wonder. I'm in love. And so that's all I can think of— 'when you come home ...'"

"Oi vay!" Firesteen groaned in torment. "She says here that the rabbit dropped dead!" He ripped another envelope. "Only twelve more left. Suppose ..."

"Dry up," one of his guards said. "Read the stuff, Mel. The guys are waitin.'"

Pat flipped through his unopened mail. One was from the golf pro at his club: "Hope you're not practicing too much, duffer. And take care. I wouldn't want to lose a meal ticket!" Another was from a dealer in foreign cars notifying him that his Porsche had been sold, and a credit was being held for him. A thick letter from Walt. He held it aside. Another from a coed at College Park, a girl with a preposterous bust and an amazon's grip who had agreed to a week end in New York with him a year ago. After lunch at Twenty-One, dinner at Pavilion, the theater, and Sardi's, they had returned to the luxury of a Waldorf suite. And there, with deftness and tenacity, ignoring pleas and subterfuge, she had held stubbornly to her virtue. Pat smiled, recalling his losing battle.

He opened Walt's letter, and lay back to read it. His long-time friend might have been in the tent with him, for he wrote as he spoke, and Pat could imagine his gravel-throated rasp, dictating to Miss Anson, one of the legacy employees Walt's father had insisted be retained in the company. The young tycoon, sitting on his desk, would talk at a rapid pace, delighting in shocking his virginal secretary.

"Dear Tough Guy," the letter began, "While you're out there, fighting for mom's apple pie, your A-hole buddy"—and Miss Anson would ask primly, "Will you spell that, please?"—"is raking in the old mazooma. If I only had my Number One! These hermaphroditic draftsmen who call themselves architects and have an AIA membership to prove it, know less than I do. And, since you oiled my way through school, you know I can't draw a straight line with a T-square. They hock me all day about something called artistic integrity. They antagonize clients. They bitch about the dough. They scare contractors. They think specifications are a bible they wrote personally.—All this crap they've got plenty of."—"Crap, Miss Anson, I said 'CRAP' " —"Ideas are something else. There they're big blanks.

"And still we've got more work than we can handle. A California mortuary in Evisceration Modern and Bastard Gothic. A dress shop— chain operation that could be big, except there's a pay-off to the comptroller. Offices for a baking company—the president of the outfit's a redheaded widow with a zillion bucks and hair on her chest. But what the hell, you know I always give my all for the company!

"And there you are, you loafing S.O.B. Trouble is, I got charm, personality, a fantastic intellect, a line of hooey that gets them on the dotted line, but nobody around this joint can produce without stealing from some shnook who designs privies for Siamese twins ..." (At this point, Miss Anson would threaten to quit again. And Walt would kiss her cheek and promise to reform.)

Pat read on. Walt had remembered Pat's mother's birthday, sent her flowers with a card from Pat enclosed. He had seen Ann twice, thought it "a shame such a rich, well-stacked dame should be so brainy." And, finally, he wrote about the Miami Beach hotel job.

"... There are some minor changes in landscaping, and he's got some peculiar ideas of his own on exterior painting. Only big thing is in the main lobby. He says it's too empty ..." Pat cursed. "What you call 'a feeling of space,' our client has decided is a 'big barn like you're in Pennsylvania Station.' Some fruity interior decorator with adenoids and a red Jaguar has talked him into an African motif. You know, tiger-skin sofas—so, all right, there ain't no tigers in Africa, but who knows that?—and zebra-hide footstools and probably giraffe-scrotum lampshades. Of course, there's grass-green carpeting and bamboo up the rectum. So your shaft is out. Instead, there's a goddamn' cage. Fifty feet high and loaded with monkeys, African foliage, fresh bananas daily—and possibly tsetse flies.

What the hell, kiddo! Maybe he'll call it the *Ubangi Arms* and the maitre d' will wear a loincloth! Even if he doesn't get anybody to register, he can always make a fortune on monkey manure ..."

Pat's first reaction was anger. The hotel was to be his first real accomplishment, the first significant product of his brain and talent and training. It was his. Not Walt's. Not the client's. One thing was certain: there had been no defense of the original plan, no argument against the idiot's dream that would transform his creation into something vulgar and pretentious. "Satisfy the guy with the mazooma"— that was Walt's creed. He had heard it when a restaurant façade was defaced with garish borders of neon, when adequate insulation was dropped from the specs for a housing project, when he had demanded that lath work be tom out and rebuilt. Of course, you had to satisfy the client. But there was also the question of honesty—an honest evaluation of the client's ideas, an honest presentation of your own, an honest brick, an honest girder, an honest day's work. If only I'd been there, he thought. But he knew that would have made little difference in the outcome. He would have raged and threatened and gone along in the end. Well, his "tower in the sky" would be a monkey palace, would rival a dozen other resort spots in bad taste and flashiness. Other architects would make jokes about it, but until another monstrosity took its place a month or a year later, it would be a show-place. And there would be more commissions for the firm. And Walt would raise his percentage. And he would buy a Mercedes Benz. He grinned. The whole situation was funny. Bill Patrick, Shining Knight of the American Institute of Architects, leading the crusade against the infidel, and filling his pockets with Saracen gold. The idea amused him.

Firesteen screamed, jumped up, waving a letter. "I did it! I did it!" He danced wildly around the other marines. "Come May, I'm a daddy!" He grabbed Pat's hand, shook it. "I did it!" He jerked Chuck Cagle awake, and while the lieutenant stared at him, mouth agape, he yelled, "I did it!" Followed by the others, he ran from the tent, screaming the news.

Cagle was sitting up on the far bunk, rubbing his eyes. "Big day," he said dryly. "Firesteen's got proof he's a man; and I've been served an ultimatum." He slipped off the cot and stretched. "I been laying here with the stirrings of a gut ache, doing exercises to keep a tight sphincter, and my girl comes through with an either-or. That's really hitting a guy when he's down."

"Marry the gal, Chuck."

"I want to! Dammit, I'm going to! But isn't it something the way they play you on a loose line, and then, Whammo! the hook's in your mouth and she gets that let's-shop-for-a-refrigerator look in her eye?" He was silent for a few minutes, occupied with his thoughts. "Pat, I've done some thinking ... I'm in the mood for confession." He laughed uneasily. "You wanna listen?"

Pat folded his letter and put it aside. Cagle sat at the foot of the cot. "Well, padre, it's this way ... He hesitated, tugged nervously at his belt. "I've been putting off getting married ... His voice dropped, and he began again with new resolution. "I know you're going to think I'm a jackass, but ..." Again he deliberated, then plunged ahead. "All that crap about my making big money, working for a big outfit—that's all it was, plain, unadulterated crap. I work for a big outfit all right, the biggest—Macy's. And I'm in advertising all right—writing copy for direct mail." He looked at Pat, awaiting some comment.

Not quite knowing what reaction was expected of him, Pat said nothing. He had been amused by Chuck, had discounted part of his glib story of affluence and influence. But the lieutenant's obvious embarrassment was touching. "That's a hell of an excuse to keep a gal waiting. She's right." He walked to the tent flap, held it open. "Who gives a damn if it's BBD & O or Macy's? Who cares if you're making fifteen thousand a year or ten?"

"Not even five," Cagle said gloomily.

"Or not even five then," Pat said. "Marry her." Then, either out of compassion for the incongruously shame-faced Cagle, or because the idea leaped into his mind, and he had a sudden impulse to commit himself to an irrevocable position, he said, "Hell, I'm going to get married myself. And the first thing I do when I come back from my honeymoon is go out and look for a job!"

He stepped outside, breathed deep of the piercing air, watched the first flutter of snow ride across the capped peaks of the tents. Off in the distance, like summer thunder, he heard guns. There was a sharp stab of sound from the perimeter, and then machine guns in prolonged conversation. There was laughter, and voices were raised down the company street. He could hear Firesteen and Lock Justus arguing.

Goober stomped out of his tent and began to curse. The group disbanded, and Justus, propelled by the first sergeant, went back to his bunk. Goober found Pat. "Damned knuckleheads. Dead on their feet, and they gotta grabass. Seems Justus won that Firesteen Sweepstakes, and the others figure he pulled a snow job." He dug a hairy knuckle in his eye. "Cost me ten bucks myself." Yawning, he said, "Better get some sack time, sir. You look bushed."

"Okay. Good night, Wally."

"Your arms okay? You wanna take care of 'em."

He had grown used to the feeling in his arms, used to the tingle of pain that returned when the medication or drug wore off. "They're four-O," he said.

"That's good." Goober walked away, plodding through the thickening flumes of snow. Again Pat noticed the startling physical change in Goober; even his voice seemed deeper, less shrill.

But all the men had changed. He had gone from tent to tent with Goober that afternoon, checking weapons, studying the faces of his men, trying to fix their names in his mind. Shoulders had braced, eyes had stared straight ahead, rifles had snapped to inspection arms. But there was something intangible that distinguished the veterans of Bad Girl Ridge from the new troops, something more revealing than the baggy, loose fit of their uniforms, the haggard eyes, the drawn skin over the cheekbones.

Choy came up to him. He, too, looked spent. His narrow shoulders slumped, his gaunt face had a tallowy cast; and he spoke in a monotone. "They sent me back."

"What did they have you doing?"

"There are refugees. Hundreds. Maybe a thousand. They have been trying to come into the town. They are starving and sick and—" He broke off. "I am going to sleep. Good night, Captain." He went into the tent.

In the south there was a sudden flash of light, outlining the rim of the mountains. The snow swirled around him, and Pat searched the black sky for a single star. He saw none.

He followed Choy inside, pulled off his boots and lay down. In the silence, he thought again of Walt, of his aborted hotel, of Ann. He was just on the edge of sleep when Chuck Cagle said, "Pat?"

"Yes?"

"Think they'll manage that bridge?"

"I think so"

Choy struck a match, lit a cigarette, his face glowing in the darkness. When he spoke it was with sorrow, not bitterness. "Aristotle said young men are easily deceived, for they are quick to hope ..."

35

Snow obscured their vision, camouflaged the enemy, hid obstacles, encased swollen feet, froze their bodies, dulled their senses, denied them the aid of planes or artillery. But Able Company fought doggedly up the mountain and wrested it from the Chinese dug in high above the road.

Below, at the lip of the great ravine, engineers worked with maddening calm, bolting massive steel sections together, backing equipment to precarious angles around the rim of the gorge.

"How long you think it'll take them?" Cagle asked Pat.

"Five, six hours maybe. I don't know." He was caught up in a spasm of chills, and dropped to his knees, hugging his aching arms to his body.

"Be a miracle if they do."

"Was a miracle they could drop those sections—more than a ton apiece. A miracle the only gear that could handle them happened to be in Koto—" A mortar shell exploded within the lines, only sixty yards away. Pat hesitated, waiting for the cries of wounded. But quiet followed instead. In the moment of anticipation, he closed his eyes and wavered uncertainly as his torpid body relaxed. The worst is still before us, he thought, and I'm already about finished. He gritted his teeth and stood erect. "... miracle when they lost a truck and it had only spare parts aboard. All a miracle."

"Could use a couple miracles right here." It was Goober. Although he was only ten feet away, they could barely identify him through the cascading snow. "Goonies push us off here, they'll cream those engineers, stop work on the bridge."

"They won't push us off," Pat said.

Another mortar round dropped in, striking in the same barren area. *Rackarackaracka.* A Chinese gun opened up against the company on the left flank. Two others began to fire into Able Company. "There's your answer," Cagle said. "They're going to give it the old college try. Well, got to get back to my people."

"Your gut still actin' up, Lieutenant?"

"Yeah. And my can's burning. And I'm cold as a first sergeant's heart. And my mouth tastes like a Chink division marched through it barefoot. You want to carry me the forty miles to Hungnam?"

Pat grabbed at the sleeve of his snow-creased parka as he started off. "Remember, Chuck, we can't move. No place to go. If they boot us off, if that bridge doesn't get up, no one gets out. The division's backed up behind. We get across that gorge or we're all dead."

"I'm dead right now," Cagle said. "Must be around twenty-five below. My head's still working, but the rest of me's deceased." He started off toward the sound of the increasing enemy fire, tripped, and fell.

Goober helped him up. He had fallen over Sanchez, Dorn, and Justus, who were bunched together, keeping one another warm. Uncharacteristically, Cagle had nothing to say. He brushed himself off mechanically and strode away.

"Up, you pogues!" Goober yelled. "Move around. Keep the circulation goin'."

"Top, I'm tuckered as—as—a sow with a litter. What's the Book say to do fer a frozen took-us?"

"Don't sit on it," Goober said, and dragged Lock to his feet.

For two endless hours, the enemy swooped down on every side, like impatient birds of prey, and were battered away. They darted to safety, returned to peck and claw, were beaten off, flung themselves upon their quarry and were driven back again.

Pat fought the rebellion of his body. He was furious that it should fail him, that it should falter when his mind ordered it to plunge ahead. It was as if brain and body were separate entities refusing to act in concert. And on every side he saw his condition reflected in the men.

He loaded BAR magazines for Mel Firesteen. Clumsy fingers fumbled with each round. The corporal lifted a single bullet, concentrated on placing it, pushed his thumb into position, depressed the spring, tried to engage the lip of the cartridge, failed, dropped the round in the snow, searched for it, grasped it again, moved the thumb, pushed down the spring ... Normally he would have loaded a magazine in twenty seconds or less. Pat watched him as he sighed, cursed, and finally snorted in triumph. It had taken him ten minutes to complete the simple task. And the other men in the squad were no more effective. They were rolling grenades down on the attacking enemy. They held the grenades awkwardly in both hands, slowly pulled the safety pin with their teeth, opened their palms, let the bombs roll away, and fell back, burying their bodies in the snow as the explosion sounded below.

Later, Pat knelt in an icy trench next to the lieutenant with the French name who had replaced Pappas. The lieutenant was directing fire on four crazed Chinese who were crawling into the face of a machine gun. His voice betrayed no excitement, no fear, only appalling lassitude. "Range one hundred ... got one that time ... man in front going to break ... standing ... coming in ... get him ... get him..." The lifeless tone suggested the synthetic voice of a robot, contrived at a distant keyboard.

With Huckabee and Choy, Pat helped move three wounded and five frostbite cases to the rear. Choy bruised his knee on a needle of rock. One of the frostbitten men rolled from the litter into a crevice and had to be dragged out. A wounded man sucked on a tube of morphine, trying desperately to thaw it so he might get relief. Huckabee cleaned the face and hands of a marine who had vomited over himself. And through it all, not a groan, not a curse was uttered.

Sanchez, Dorn, and Justus were disarming six enemy soldiers when Pat returned to the command post. The Chinese, staring dumbly, held their rifles before them. The marines had to rip their frozen fingers from the weapons.

"Yer safe no matter where you shoot," Lock said, crawling behind a boulder. "Goonies ever'where."

Dorn was protecting the 300 radio by sheltering it under a poncho. "Quiet!" His teeth were chattering; he clenched them before going on. "Captain, I thought somebody ... tryin' to raise us ..."

Two and a half hours after the first bridge section was moved into position by the engineers, Skinhead messaged Able Company in the prepared code: "God helps those who help themselves. Well done."

Night. The road again. Biting wind and cold, ice and frostbite and the enemy. Weapons, rations, plasma, morphine and men—all froze again. And the division—stretching for ten miles—wound down the mountains, inched toward the sea, pausing only to fight and load its dead and wounded. Thirty-five miles to go ... thirty ... Twenty-seven ...

A hazy moon. The deadly flight of tracers. The flames of gutted vehicles. The muzzle blast of opposing guns. The crunch of boots in snow. Cries of pain. Curses. The whine of stalled motors. The shattering impact of a shell. The sharp crackle of distant rifles. The wintry desolation of the wind, moaning through the passes.

The raucous shriek of a tank's high velocity shell sounded above the wind. Somewhere toward the front, an ambush cut the column. The sky was alight with orange flame. Movement stopped. Pat looked back at his men. They had already dropped in place, and lay where they fell. "Get to work on those weapons," he ordered. "Check your buddy's feet and face." He wanted to sit with them, if only to ease the needles of pain in his arms and legs. But to rest was to surrender. He could not risk it. "Nobody sleeps," he said, trying to put authority into his tone. But his voice was too weak to carry far. "Sit up. Dammit, you NCOs keep your people alert!" After checking security on every side, he returned to the jeep. "Woody, see if you can find out what's happening up front." The radioman batted his eyes stupidly. There was a lacing of snow on his lashes. He nodded, went to his radio.

"Captain!" Goober was puffing, trying to jog ahead. He gave up, plodded the rest of the way toward Pat. "Don't like the looks of them civilians in the rear. Too damn' many. More all the time. And we can't keep 'em back."

"Choy!" The interpreter was working over a marine in the center of the road. He motioned for them to join him. "What's your trouble?" Pat asked the prostrate marine.

"Huckabee told him to get on a truck," Choy said. "He will not ride. His legs ..."

Pat pulled up the trousers. The marine said nothing. From knee to ankle, the legs were green-black and distended. "Get on the truck."

"I'm okay, sir. Okay now," he said, gasping.

"You ride for a while." He helped him to his feet. "You need a little rest."

"Don't wanna get in with them dead guys." As they neared the truck, he hung back, whining. "Chrisake, sir, don't make me! Not with them stiffs!" His voice was rising, shrill, hysterical. "I won't do it!"

Goober lifted him around his waist and pushed him over the tail gate. The marine screamed and thrashed. He tumbled out, fell four feet to the frozen road. His face was contorted, his eyes glowering and wild. He rolled in the snow, squirming and kicking, his arms lashing out, foam flecking the comers of his mouth.

"A little while ago he was guiding a truck. A dead man's legs, hanging over the fender, struck him, knocked him down," Choy told them, as if that were explanation enough. He held the man's head in his lap as Justus and Sanchez restrained the struggling arms. "We will not make you ride," he said, crooning to him. Wiping his sleeves over the froth on the purple lips, he repeated his promise. "You can walk. You can walk."

"Get Huck," Pat said. Dorn walked slowly up the road. "Move!" The soldier hurried for a few paces, then lapsed back into a shuffle. "Wally, stay with him until Huck gets here. Choy, come on. We'll see about those people in the rear."

When they reached the end of the company, they saw a mass of civilians, all of them dressed in white, mingling with the rear elements. Firesteen, brandishing his BAR, flanked by two other marines, was cursing, trying to drive the Koreans back. "*Move out, you shtik fleish mit aigen, before I cram this in your pipik!*"

But those that were forced back soon pushed forward again. There were hundreds of them crowding together in the darkness: women holding babies in their arms. Girls with mountainous bundles on their heads. Wailing infants sucking hungrily at shriveled breasts while their mothers tried to shield them from the wind. An old crone carrying a wooden ladle and a splotched mirror. Dwarflike children with mucus frozen on their faces, with bulging eyes and running sores, with potbellies and stick-thin legs. A crippled man, his feet swaddled in rags, his crooked back loaded with a porcelain tub and a rocking chair. Younger men hung back, watching sullenly.

"How in hell did they get between us and Charlie Company?" Pat asked of no one in particular. "Tell them to move back or they'll be in the middle of it when we get hit again."

Choy spoke to an old man whose upturned white goatee had been frozen by the wind at a pitifully jaunty angle. Haunted eyes stared at him, but there was no answer. "They are frightened, cold, hungry," Choy told Pat. He added, almost apologetically, "They want to be protected."

Sickened by their misery, yet unable to assist them, Pat turned his back. From up front he heard the thunder of a rocket striking home. "Tell them again. They must stay back."

Choy repeated the warning to the old man. Again there was no answer, nothing but mute terror in his eyes. "He is afraid to speak."

"Fire over their heads," Pat told Firesteen.

"Captain, sir, there's a load of little kids there. These poor gooks are already bad shook, scared silly ..."

"Over their heads! Don't argue with me," Pat shouted into Firesteen's face. "You think I don't know? Think I can't see?" He caught himself. "Go on, Mel," he said softly.

They sent a volley above the milling crowd. A few children scattered. The others stood their ground. "No use," Pat said. "Choy, you stay here for a while with Mel. I'll send word back to Charlie Company. And I'll tell the lieutenant this squad'll be fifty yards behind the rest of us." He paused, slowly thinking out a plan. "These people move any closer and we get hit ... they'll be ..." He fumbled for the word he wanted. "... be ... be massacred."

"I'll try, sir," Firesteen said uncertainly. "But seems like every time you turn around there's more of 'em."

The column was moving again. Pat talked to the young lieutenant and to Cagle, called the Charlie Company commander, sent three cases of rock-hard rations to the civilians. Then he slogged ahead to overtake the point of his company.

In the rear, behind Firesteen's squad, more men slipped down from the hills above and fell in with the white-robed procession. Under their cloaks they carried rifles, ammunition, and grenades. The Koreans made way before them, were cursed, ordered to bunch around them in the darkness. The Chinese infiltrators moved with the terrified civilians, tracking the marines.

Another mountain. Another roadblock. Another body to stack among the dead, to lash across a hood, to prop upon a fender. Another two hours gone by. Another mile behind. And, finally, another dawn.

The snowstorm blew itself out. The Corsairs returned, heralded by their comforting drone over the ten-mile column. Two. Six. Ten. Eighteen. Twenty-four. They ranged themselves above, diving over the flanks, rocketing a tank position, bombing a string of emplacements. Then they rose to circle and come in again.

Inside the rattling ambulance, the battalion surgeon, a pediatrician from Montpelier, worked over his patients. Now his children were bearded giants—torn, mangled, ragamuffins. Most could not see him, but they felt his hands, heard his voice. He soothed them. He bound their wounds. He amputated a limb. Steadying himself with one hand against the wall, he peered down at a ravaged face, now curiously empty. "Gone," he said. Hand and voice were steady.

The chaplain assisting him caught himself as the ambulance jolted to a stop. He accompanied the body to the truck, helped place the man among the rigid forms. More wounded were waiting. He returned to the ambulance. "Wash your hands," the surgeon said. "How many times do I have to remind you?"

The chaplain, a Methodist minister from Ohio, said irrelevantly, "Give them strength." Then, "Give me strength."

"Now!" the surgeon said impatiently. The scalpel descended once more.

There was no respite from the encircling enemy. Each regiment, battalion, company, and platoon shared the ordeal. But every man is the axis of his own universe; and it seemed to Pat's men that it was Able Company against the Chinese, Able Company against the cold, against the road, against everything under the frozen sky.

Mel Firesteen walked backward, keeping an eye on the civilians. They were not pressing any longer. A few at a time were straggling off, crossing the road to the railroad track that ran alongside. Aimlessly, he wondered why. He felt giddy, and caught himself just before losing his balance. Ordering another fire team to take up the task, he turned and began to slog forward. A cramp seized his leg; he limped on, rubbing it. The unhealed wound on his buttocks ached. His stomach was knotted with hunger. His eyelids were heavy, rough. Help me, God, help me, he prayed.

On Yom Kippur, the Day of Atonement, he had landed at Inchon. Less than ten weeks before. September twenty-first. He had been too occupied to attend the brief shipboard services; and he had decided that to fast would be unnecessary, even dangerous. That was a mistake, he thought now. Here he was, asking God for help, and he had not even observed Yom Kippur, had been unwilling to deprive himself of food and drink for a single day. As he hobbled down the icy road, one prayer kept running through his mind, the Oonsaneh Toekehf. In years past, he had said it in reverence and awe. Now, conscious of his debt, conscious of his failure, conscious of the child God would give him, conscious of the weakness of his own body, he trembled at the import of the words as he fitted them together:

" 'On the Erst day of the year it is inscribed, and on the Fast Day of Atonement it is sealed and determined, how many shall pass by, and how many be born; who shall live and who die, who shall finish his allotted time, and who not; who is to perish by Ere, who by water; who by the sword, and who by wild beast; who by hunger, or who by thirst; who by earthquake, or who by the plague; who by strangling or who by lapidation; who shall be at rest and who shall be wandering; who to remain tranquil, and who be disturbed; who shall reap enjoyment, and who be painfully afflicted; who shall grow rich, and who become poor; who shall be cast down, and who exalted. Ooshoovor, Oosfeelor, Ootsdorkor,' " Firesteen said under his breath. " 'But penitence, prayer, and charity can avert the evil decree.' "*

Lock Justus put his hand on the corporal's shoulder and shook him gently. "Mel? You taken to talkin' to yerself?"

"Thinkin'," Firesteen said.

"Cap'n wants to know how yer doin' with the gooks."

The corporal glanced over his shoulder. The crowd behind was thinning out. More men were collecting on the railroad tracks. He could not see the weapons they carried beneath their cloaks, nor the machine gun shielded from view by those closest to him. "Okay," he said. "No strain, no pain."

The old Korean with the curled goatee was brought back by a marine. "He's talkin' a mile a minute, Corporal. Can't make no sense out of it."

"*Chung-Kuk!*" the old man said, screeching. "*ChuMo-uee Chung-Kuk byoung-joung!*" He pointed to the white-robed figures on the tracks.

Firesteen nodded. "Okay, Grampa," he said, "long as you stay behind us. Behind-us-okay."

"*Suman-un fwa-po!*"

"Lock, you better send Choy back. Can't make out what the old geezer's crabbin' about."

"Okay. 'Fore I go, Huck said ask you fer some Tootsie Rolls—somethin' the wounded can chew on."

Firesteen cleaned his pockets. "Gave the rest to those gook kids." He scrubbed his eyes. "Pooped. I'm ever more pooped, buddy."

Lock took the candy. "Don't be a *smuck*, Mel. Stay loose. We got these Chinks beat ..." He started back toward the head of the company, swinging his arms, taking long bowlegged strides. When he could no longer hear the old Korean's fitful wailing, *"Chung-Kuk! Chung-Kuk!"* his pace slowed. His neck was stiff and he took off his gloves to rub it. Before he could get them on again, his fingertips were puckered and numb. His throat felt choked, as if plugged with phlegm, and he coughed furiously but could not dislodge it.

It was not the pain or discomfort or hunger that bothered Lock. Those things he could stand up to by fighting back, by seeing them in others and assuring himself he could go on as long as they. It was the premonition of death that worried him, invading his thoughts, plaguing him when he was left alone with no one to laugh with, no one to listen to him. He firmly believed he was going to die. It had started with the letter he had gotten in Koto-ri. His parents had moved to town. His father was working in a feed store, his mother in the mill. They had bought a cemetery plot. That night he had dreamed of the cemetery. Just a dream, he told himself.

He saw Huckabee taking a bottle of plasma from beneath a truck's hood. "Here's all the pogie-bait Mel had left."

"Thanks." The corpsman stuffed his pocket, began to walk alongside the vehicle, shaking the bottle in his hand.

"Huck, you don't believe in dreams, do you?"

"I don't know." He sighed deeply, releasing his breath like pent-up steam. "Some pretty smart people say they got meaning. All to do with symbols and stuff ... like you dream 'bout climbin' ladders, means you want a woman ..."

Lock frowned. "Buncha stuff, huh?"

"Course, Joseph in the Bible read Pharaoh's dream ..."

"There's this feller—a replacement in ... Mr. Cagle's platoon— he been tellin' me 'bout a dream he had. Thinks it means he's gonna die."

"Everybody's gonna die."

"I mean, right soon."

"He's just shook up and worried." They walked in silence for a few minutes. Huckabee stepped gingerly, as if he were walking barefooted on broken glass, for he had strapped a bottle of plasma between his legs, and morphine syrettes were taped in his armpits. Dragging along awkwardly, he relived a precious moment with the battalion surgeon: "You've got good hands. Damn' fine suture job. Neat. Quick. If I can get you a relief, I'll pull you in to help me." Those were the doctor's words. Huckabee knew he would find reasons for not leaving Able Company, but he treasured the praise. Good hands. Neat. Quick. For a moment he had a vision of the tiled amphitheater, of Dr. Huckabee, hands upraised while a nurse slipped on the rubber gloves, assistants waiting beside the patient on the table, interns and doctors watching from the glass above—watching to learn. He was a doctor, a skilled one, who could save lives, whose knowledge and nerve and technique were unsurpassed. He would treat anyone who needed him. And they would all come—white and black—because he had good hands ... and he was neat ... and quick ...

Lock was speaking to him, and Huckabee strained to hear him. "This dream this feller had ... well, seems like there's a grave in his hometown cemetery, sorta like a tomb. And this woman with T.B., she died and wanted a winder in it fer to see the sun. And people said you could look inside, and see her, with long black hair. Well, this feller, this replacement, he tole me he looked in one time and never could see nothin'—either gone to rot or her folks didn't want nobody lookin'—so they painted the winder ... or somethin.'"

Huckabee took the syrette from his mouth. "Been workin' in his subconscious," he said.

"I don't know where it's been workin', but he dreamed 'bout that tomb t'other night. Tole me he looked in the winder, and saw hisself laid out inside!"

Huckabee studied his friend. "He's just scared, Lock. Sees other fellas gettin' it. Thought about the tomb ..."

"That's what I tole him," Lock said. "Damn' foolishness. Hell, I don't hold with superstitions ... But folks at home—and they ain't scared of nothin' livin', and just a mite afeared of God—they's still awful careful 'bout hants and things ..."

Huckabee boosted himself over the tail gate of a truck, careful of the bottles he carried. "It's a lot of bunk, Lock. Doesn't mean a thing. You tell that replacement to keep his butt down and his eyes open and stop thinkin' about that kind of mess."

Lock found First Sergeant Goober crawling out of a tank. "Where's the cap'n? Firesteen says everythin's okay in the rear. And he wants Choy to talk to some old gook who's yackin' at him."

Goober balanced a canteen cup in one hand; he slipped over the side of the tank as it moved on. "Choy's feedin' some frostbite people. You relieve him, send him back. I'll pass the word to the captain." Steam was rising from the cup. "What you got there, Top?"

"Tankers gave me some hot joe. It's for the captain."

Lock sniffed at it. "Hope to die, I want a transfer to the tanks. Put my papers through."

Turning away, Goober took a few steps. He looked behind him and saw Lock still standing there. "Come here! Have a sip, you damn' wedgeass—but just one. Then get your butt back and find Choy." Justus took off his gloves, held his bare hands around the lukewarm cup. "Man! Fer as I'm concerned, nooky is now the secon' best thing in the world!" He took one gulp while Goober laughed at him. "Yer okay, Top. I'm gonna talk to Gen'ral Shepherd 'bout gettin' you a warrant."

"Get outta here!" Holding the coffee before him, Goober went down the road to find the captain. That Justus doesn't give a damn about anything, he thought. Nothing bothers him. A good marine. And a CO like Patrick who could outmarch any of them, who rarely raised his voice but took no guff, who let a man know he was human, too, and could get more out of his people with a pat on the back than most men got by ranting and threatening. A skipper like that and men like Justus. Bastard Chinks can't beat that combination. No marine outfit's ever been licked. Nowhere. Never. And this one, made up of snotty-nosed kids, half of them Reserves, and one-hitch NCOs and damn' few old pros, this one wasn't any different from the others. Everything else might change. But not The Corps. It was the one thing he could believe in, the one thing that needed him, the one thing he loved.

Beyond the next truck, he saw the captain, Sanchez, and Dorn helping another man into the still-rolling jeep. "Got some hot joe for you, sir," he said as he caught up with them.

Pat nodded his thanks. "Don't know how you find time," he said thickly. His lips were puffed and cracking. He licked them, gulped the coffee. "Good. Thanks, Wally." He passed it to Sanchez, who drank and gave it to Dorn.

"Justus says everything's secure in the rear." Goober took the cup from Dorn and swallowed the remaining liquid. "Damn! It was hot when I started back ..."

"Tasted good anyway," Pat said.

He was obviously lying, Goober thought. The coffee was cold and rank. Unaccountably, his eyes filled and a surge of affection choked him. He turned away abruptly.

Rackarackaracka. Rackarackaracka. For an instant they were rooted by the clatter of the enemy weapon. Then a truck halfway up the column swung wildly and smashed into the wreckage of a deserted British weapons' carrier. Men scattered. Pat studied the sound. It came from the railroad tracks that ran parallel to the road toward the rear of his company! The Chinese were traversing, shooting high, riddling the canvas-topped trucks.

"Wally, get these people in position to protect the wounded. Goat, you and Woody come with me." He wanted to run, but it was impossible. His legs were too heavy. After a few steps he could not catch his breath. "Follow the blind side of the trucks," he panted to Sanchez and Dorn.

"Captain, for God's sakes!" Hands tore at Pat's legs, pulling him to the earth. It was Chuck Cagle. "What you standing like that for?"

"They might try to move in on us," Pat said, ignoring the question.

"Chinks got in with the civilians," Cagle said. "Word passed back. They got our people pinned. Killed some gooks."

"Move some men above the road, others where they can fire over the trucks." He focused on each word, trying to hear himself above the noise and the throbbing in his ears. Cagle rolled over on his back, drew up his legs in agony. "What is it, Chuck?"

"Gut again. My damn' ... lousy ... gut." He writhed in pain and disgust, clenching his teeth, as he soiled himself. "I stink," he said. "I'm filthy and I stink ..."

Pat turned his head away and gulped a lungful of fresh air. "I'll find your platoon sergeant. You've got to get in a truck."

When he looked at the lieutenant again, there were tears in Cagle's eyes. "No! I'll be okay ... in a minute ... It passes." He was crying and laughing at the same time. "Just that I stink ... so." He got to his knees and crawled away.

Pat moved on, running a few feet between trucks, then waiting and running again. "Return fire!" he called to the men behind the vehicles. "Move out where you can see, and fire!"

The enemy machine gun slashed the canvas on the end truck. Someone inside screamed. Dorn put down his radio and pulled himself into the crowded truck bed. "Don't panic," he said, his voice hoarse and trembling. "Get down as far as you can, fellas. I'll help you ..." Those wounded who could move began to burrow under the bodies of the dead.

Standing above the marines who had taken refuge behind the truck, Pat ordered them across the road. No one moved. "You hear?" Sanchez shouted at them. "You hear what he told you?"

One man got up, then another, and more followed. They ran, weaving across the open area, and dropped in the ditch on the far side of the road. A Pfc., an artilleryman who had joined the company at Hagaru, assumed command. He knelt in full view of the enemy, calling out fire orders like an actor in a training film.

Pat looked out across a no-man's land of fifty yards. At the end of it, to his front, he could see Firesteen's squad. Three marines lay in the road. He could not tell whether or not they were alive. Five more had sought cover in a shallow crater and were pinned there. Firesteen and the lieutenant with the French name were behind a 105 artillery piece that had been placed at the end of Able Company. Its gunner was tugging at the heavy trails. Beyond them, Choy stood in the center of the road, dragging a wounded civilian out of the line of fire. Now the corporal, the lieutenant, and the gunner were trying to manhandle the big gun, to move it into firing position against the enemy.

The Chinese, to Pat's left and sixty yards away, had formed a skirmish line on the railroad tracks. He estimated forty of them.

All this he registered within seconds. "If they can turn that 105," he said to Sanchez, "we could ..."

Goober had joined them. "Watch it out front!" he shouted. The men behind the gun turned in time to see three Chinese drop from the tracks, break into the open and head for them. The enemy had recognized the threat and were determined to keep the weapon out of action. Sanchez fired his rifle from off-hand position and the first Chinese fell. The second went down before Firesteen's BAR. The lieutenant got the third with his carbine. Working frantically, the marines pulled at the gun trails. They had been buried in the snow when they dropped from the prime mover, and had to be worked free.

"Need help," Pat groaned.

Four more of the enemy moved from the tracks, bent on destroying gun and crew. Goober fired his Tommy gun but the range was too great and the shots went wild. Firesteen crouched over one of the tires, resting his BAR there, shooting carefully. Two of the enemy went down, but five more appeared in their places. Now the men with Pat behind the truck, those with the artillery Pfc. across the road, and the three men caught behind the big gun all concentrated their fire on the attackers. Only one reached the gun. He was killed as he fired his burp gun. The lieutenant fell back, wounded.

The two remaining marines made vain efforts to swing the gun. Choy rushed to help them, but left again when an old woman walked unconcernedly toward them. He pushed her down, pulled her by one foot back up the road.

The Chinese launched yet another assault on the gun. This time there were two men, working together, making short dashes. "I'm going out there," Pat said. He checked the magazines in his belt. "Try to cover me ..."

Goober caught his wrist. "Sir, you can't."

"Let go, Wally."

"You won't have a prayer, dammit!"

"How much longer you think Firesteen and that gunner can hold the Chinks off?" He didn't raise his voice; he didn't have the strength to do it. Goober held him fast. He spun around. "Sergeant!"

"Jezoo, let's get Charlie Company to hit them from the other side ... and we'll move up then ..."

"No time!" Without thinking further, without weighing his chances, Pat thrust Goober away, broke free and ran toward the gun. He was alone, in the open; and the Chinese turned their weapons on him even as the marines fired at the two enemy soldiers who were trying to reach the same gun. Pat's chest was bursting. He had no feeling in his feet. He stumbled and pitched forward, smashing his face on the frozen road and scraping his arms. Bullets flew around him. Cursing, he rolled into a ditch. Ten yards away, he saw the two Chinese rush the gun. Neither reached it.

"Stay there!" Goober shouted.

The artillery Pfc. raised up from his position and called to him. "We'll cover you. Soon as—" A burst of enemy fire cut him off. He was hit in the leg. "Soon as y'give us ... signal." He fainted, and fell over in the road.

"C'mon in!" Firesteen shouted. He began to spray the front wildly, firing from the hip. Pat staggered the last ten yards, and fell exhausted behind the gun. The gunner and the corporal worked at the trails again. The lieutenant, clawing at his face as pain overcame him, tried to sit up, actually got on his hands and knees and approached the gun, as if to help. But he could not make it; and he lay sprawled on the ice. Pat braced himself and pushed. Imperceptibly, the weapon moved. Then the wheels caught. All strained, grunting. Suddenly it came free. Firesteen was giggling hysterically. He touched Pat's shoulder. "Did it, huh? Huh?"

Enemy fire increased around them as the gunner lowered the barrel and opened the breech. Then a wave of Chinese came lunging toward the gun, throwing grenades and screaming as they charged. Pat fired his pistol. Firesteen, out of BAR ammunition, used the lieutenant's carbine. The gunner worked over the 105 round, trying with furious concentration to prepare the fuse. "Short. No more than three-tenths of a second," Pat called over his shoulder.

The enemy assault closed in. Forty yards. Thirty. Only two of ten were down. The others had slowed, were moving more carefully, firing, dropping to the snow, standing again to gain a yard. "Hurry!" Firesteen called to the gunner, his voice barely audible over the interchange of fire. "They'll be all over us ..."

Goober had been shouting instructions to the marines around him, forcing more of them on line, setting up a light gun. It seemed to him that the men behind the artillery piece were certainly doomed. Some of the Chinese were sure to reach them. The enemy automatic weapons were all fixed on the spot. He could see Firesteen flat on the ground, Pat beside him. The gunner, too, had been forced to the earth. The captain was getting to his knees, moving back to the wounded lieutenant, then dragging him to cover. The oncoming Chinese were only twenty yards away from them. The enemy fire began to shift to allow the assault. "They're goners," Sanchez wailed.

"No-oo." It was a deep-throated sound of horror and anguish; and before it had died away Goober bolted from cover. "Skipper!" He ran up the road toward Pat, holding his Tommy gun at his waist, screaming, firing from the hip. "Stay down, Skipper! I'm coming!" The enemy soldiers started their final dash for the big gun, ignoring the huge marine who bore down on them. "You bastards!" Goober howled. "You goddamn' slimy, sonovabitchin' bastards!" His weapon raked the leading Chinese, knocked the next two down. He stood in the open, facing them, and fitted another magazine. It was impossible, but he was untouched; and for a crucial moment he had stopped the enemy.

The gunner pulled the lanyard, firing the 105. The shell detonated an instant later, blasting the Chinese emplacement. Men on either side were shaken by the concussion. But Goober, oblivious, plunged on, spraying two Chinese who stood up in his path. "Fight, you dirty stinkin' bastards! Stand up and fight!"

Sanchez crossed himself. "Top! Get down!" He raced into the open, running after the first sergeant.

Pat screamed, "Wally!"

"I got 'em, Skipper!" He waded on toward the enemy, all caution and sanity submerged by the murderous intensity of his hatred. "You can't lick us!" he shouted. He was hit. But he kept moving and shooting. He was hit again. And again.

"Wally! Oh, my God, Wally, get down! Don't! Don't!"

36

Pat knelt beside Goober, cradling the shaggy head in his arms. The bone-white face, drawn now, twitched. One sunken eye pulled down, quivering as the lips puffed and sucked for breath.

Dorn squatted beside them, and Skinhead's voice croaked profanely over the radio. The 105 fired again. Cagle's machine guns went into action. Sanchez led twenty men across the road and fell upon the surviving enemy, killing with a calm, methodical efficiency that was not quite human. Huckabee brought a dogtag from the dead officer— the lieutenant with the French name—and the name was Murphy. Pat wondered where he had got the idea ...

The first sergeant mumbled unintelligibly. Then, clearly: "Bastard Chinks ... crap on 'em," he said. And died.

Pat wept.

They searched the vehicles for places to fit five more bodies. They carried their nine wounded to an ambulance. They pushed the disabled truck over the side of the road, listened as it crashed far below. They loaded their weapons. They faced the south; and pushed forward again.

In the hours that followed, Pat walked beside the jeep that held the crumpled bulk of Goober's body. Nothing was clear-cut any more, but all run together in a swimming montage. Fragments of sights and sounds fixed upon his mind but had no coherent meaning. In time to come, he would remember Choy feeding a Tootsie Roll to a wounded chaplain ... the blind-staring visage of a man whose clothes had been burned off ... Sanchez, bent with exhaustion but collecting discarded souvenirs and adding them to the growing hoard he carried ... the stripped bodies of two long-dead Royal Marines ... Cagle, still sick from melted snow and frozen rations, enduring the torment of cramps, but refusing to ride ... a Korean woman who put her dead infant on a rock, and walked on, not looking back ... the uncanny drop of four cargo chutes that fell along the winding road while enemy machine guns fired from the hills at the low-flying planes ... and the air-controller, whose mangled hand would keep him on the ground, calling the pilots above by nicknames ... Dorn searching for a bandsman-rifleman's friend and falling asleep atop a mound of bodies ... Justus, rubbing his black, frostbitten nose and reciting his Jewish vocabulary to Mel Firesteen ...

Just twelve more miles to Hungnam and safety. Three frozen Chinese, rheumy eyes set in gaunt faces, tennis shoes encased in ice, gave themselves up. Unguarded, they lurched along, frantically trying to keep pace. Someone gave them a can of rations. They could not open it and begged for help but they were unheeded. They fell back, straggled at the rear. One dropped out. The last Chinese, still clutching the unopened can, fell asleep in the road ...

And always the halts. Always more casualties to the weather and the enemy. Since the trucks could hold no more, the dead were strapped to the tubes and trails of artillery pieces, on jeeps, across radiators, on fenders, on bumpers, along the sides of tanks. Dead were stacked beneath the wounded on the steel-cold beds of weapons carriers, were tied to tail gates, to trailers. Frostbitten men by the thousands held to the doors of vehicles or were carried by friends. Somehow, the division managed to keep moving.

"Watch yer buddy's face."

"You lay there, you'll freeze."

"Shoulda stood in Koto."

"Wait and see, cobber. We'll have to take all this real estate over again."

Pat listened without comprehension to the radio as orders were relayed to destroy a tank that had thrown a tread. In the distance he saw a monstrous sweep of snow and rock that rose like a glacier beside the road. He tried to focus on it, to use it as a goal. But his eyes blurred, and he had to look away. The wild, unformed beauty of the mountains, the jagged spires of ice, the bite of wind, the vapor hanging in the valleys below, the darting, circling planes in the tallowy sky, the curious rhythm of the enemy guns—these things were palpable. What was unreal, what outraged his senses, was the maddening repetition of incident and the numb listlessness of his men. They performed the same tasks in the same manner until desperation crystallized into routine. Walk. Halt while someone else fights. Sleep a moment. Massage legs, arms, fingers, faces. Repair weapons. Return fire. Load the dead. Patch the wounded. Move on. Walk. Halt. Sleep. Fire. Load. Patch. Move ...

He had been prepared for confusion and exhaustion, prepared for the bitterness of the cold and the full-circle attacks of the enemy. He had been through it all before. He had expected his men to react as they always had, to summon strength from some hidden source. But this time they had no reserves on which to draw. They had used themselves up on Bad Girl, on the march to Hagaru, on the frantic journey to Koto-ri. He watched as the cold and the Chinese hammered at them, leaving them groggy, apathetic, stunned.

Still, he drove them. If they dozed in the snow, waiting for the column to move again, he would shake them, order them to check their weapons, load belts and magazines, rub their faces, massage their legs. If they staggered and fell he would be on top of them, dragging them, kicking them to their feet, shoving them forward again. If they dropped in a ditch, their rifles in their laps, heads down, while the enemy fired from above, he would crawl beside them, thrust the weapon before them, place their hands on the trigger guard and force them to fire.

A plume of breath followed him as he swayed drunkenly down the road. He was racked by fatigue; his arms throbbed; his chest wound ached. His neck was stiff; and when he moved it, pain spread over his shoulders and back. The cold was a knife that stabbed at the ganglia, sending piercing impulses through him until he shook in a convulsion of trembling. Sweat poured from his dry and frozen body, scalding his eyes, obscuring the totality of misery around him. His mind, disembodied, was a turning prism with a different sharp color on every side. He fought delirium, not by holding on to reality, but by pushing it aside. He could escape only by exploring the vaults of his memory.

He moved, not on the icy road, but in remembered places, detailing them with fanatic concentration. There was the classroom in Somerset, Kentucky, with the pull-string lights and the fold-up seats and the map where England was red and the United States was yellow instead of the usual pink and green. There was the rich, traditional entrance foyer of Ann's home in Alexandria, with the curving staircase and the thick burgundy carpet and the mahogany clock stopped at ten after nine, and the high, corniced windows with the wrong-color drapes ... And ... and ... His mind, checked by drowsiness, balked. It took him twenty minutes to conjure up a picture of the green dining room of the hotel in the Adirondacks, with the stippled walls and the cream-colored woodwork and the worn kitchen door panel where generations of student waiters had bumped oval metal trays. Now. His own bathroom. He started on that, set himself in its doorway, fumbled with color and placement ... Maroon and gray tile, gleaming stainless steel fixtures, the glass stall with five shower heads—four, one didn't work. And the tufted-pile towels, monogrammed WP. The sliding mirror before the medicine chest, and the orderly rows of unguents and creams, soaps, powders, talcum, lotions. And there was the bookstore in Lexington with the flystreaked window and the islands of floor showing through blue linoleum, the dirt hugging the cracks, and the signs ... He fought to recall the lettering, their positions over the cash register. "Let's Stay Friends—Don't Ask for Credit," and "Jesus Saves," and "Anybody Who Loves Work Will Have a Hell of a Time Around Here." And there was ... the Miami Beach project, the luminous panels that floored an under-the-sky ballroom, and roofed a poolside cocktail bar below ... What else? What else? ... The spiral shaft that opened the lobby to light, and set off the panorama of ocean, sand, and horizon ... a monkey cage now.

"Mr. Cagle's in bad shape. Can't keep him clean. But he won't quit. Wanna talk to him?"

"Leave him be, Huck."

Not think of Cagle's pitiful stench. Instead ... the lush scent of Magnolia Gardens in Charleston. And the barbershop in Memphis where he waited for his father ... Tonics and disinfectants and cologne, steaming towels, and shoe polish and dye. And ... and ... With a sense of triumph, he added the musky odor of the shine boy. If your mind can keep going, keep going, he promised himself, you'll be all right ... mind keep going ... Smells. The crisp smell of paper and India ink and blueprints and salted crackers and a starched shirt. And the clean fragrance of Ann's neck and her nail polish and her lipstick ... And the shaving lotion of a long-forgotten lieutenant who supervised the butts at Parris Island ... Oh, you know a million smells ... What? The exciting smells of the oily pocket of a fielder's glove, of a woman making love, of a new car ... of a lathered horse. And there are working odors ... of sweaty overhauls and sawdust, of wet cement, and there's the chalky fume of fresh plaster. And the smells of ... of a new telephone book. Of a hot electric bulb. Of a Chinese restaurant in San Francisco. Now ... outdoors ... the scents of hickory logs and wood chips and resin and pine bark and the loamy earth and damp underleaves and moss and the smell of the hidden, vine-covered creek where he caught crawfish and tadpoles ... and they had a smell ...

"Sir, can ... carry ... my own pack."

"Help you awhile."

"Know what? Swear to God, gonna name kid after you. Pat it's boy, Patricia it's girl. Honest, Skipper. Be somethin', huh? Patrick Firesteen ... imagine!" He dropped back, laughing, and Pat heard him say to Lock Justus, "Swear I will, Lock. How you like that? Me with a Mick in the family ..."

What's there to laugh about? Not Firesteen's notion, which would be forgotten the day he got home. Jokes. Think. Can't remember. Never could ...

There was scattered fire behind them—the first enemy action in over an hour—and the trucks stopped. Men dropped to the road, automatically taking up firing positions. "Check weapons," Pat said. No one seemed to hear him.

Leaning against the side of a tank, Pat closed his eyes. They felt gritty, as if coated with sand. The pulsating tremor in his arms was now as steady as his breathing, the pain constant and undiminished, forever beating on the anvil of his mind. Morphine would relieve him, but it might also force him to sleep. Must not. Stay up. Don't sit. Keep mind working.

They rolled on. Two men were asleep in the road. Dorn and Choy were prodding them. Pat hauled at one man. "Come on." No reaction. "We're moving." The head slumped. "Get up!" Pat slapped him viciously. The marine opened his eyes with sudden fury. Choy got behind him, hoisting him erect. Dorn lifted the other man. Pat lurched ahead.

"Sonovabitch!" He heard the curse behind him. "Hit me ... put the bastard on report ... stay up long as he can ... be standin' when that sonovabitch craps out..."

"Sir, rifle's froze," Sanchez said, catching up with Pat.

Taking it, he tried to force the receiver open, but could not. He rested the butt on the ground, tried to kick the bolt to the rear, missing every time. "Kick it. Heat chamber. Coat with oil ..."

"How am I gonna ..."

"Do it," Pat said irritably. How to ... How to ... clear a stoppage. How to double-clutch a car. How to use a slide rule. How to figure stress. How to cantilever a roof. How to measure tension. While the caravan moved still another mile, he busied himself with each process, reciting formulas, intent on maintaining the discipline of his mind, pausing only to answer a question or give an order, resenting even those intrusions ... How to drive a golf ball ... head down, "imagine the club head's on the end of a string. Swing the club head and follow through. Examine the line between your two feet ... and you slice because ... And that'll be ten dollars ..."

He was weaving across the road. Justus caught him from behind as he nearly veered into the side of a truck. Neither spoke. Pat forced his eyes open. Think! he ordered his addled brain. Fix on something. Anything. Think! Not about Justus or Huckabee or Dorn or Sanchez or Firesteen or Cagle or Choy. Not about Nelson or Allison or Pappas or Andy or The Horse or Goober. None of them. Stay awake! Think about ... others ...

About the deaf couple at the newsstand on Fourteenth Street, happily working their fingers, their mouths half forming words, their eyes, lips, arms, alive with secret meanings. And ... he wore an aluminum watch band ... and she, a charm bracelet of silver coins ... About the client with the parrot face, the one who tried to hire him on a retainer as architect for his theater chain, and who contrived in a ten-minute conversation to mention his butler, his accountant, his lawyer, his chauffeur, his masseur, his banker, his gardener, his broker ... About the methodical schoolteacher from Quincy ... name? ... Belle? ... Bertha ... Betty ...

Beulah ... hell with it ... but she had broad hips and fingernails like stilettos. And she made him send the bellboy on an errand, explaining, "I propose to let you use my body, but not my toothbrush." More. More ... About the friend of his father, a brick mason, a swarthy, frenetic little man who tried to comfort him at the funeral. "Nobody's fault. The winch broke. Wished I hadn't of saw him, Billy. Smashed up the way he was ... But the undertaker sure fixed him up so's you'd hardly notice. Looks real natural. Sure does ..." About the woman he had seen on the street in San Diego, across from the U.S. Grant. An aging whore, pale and faded, one cheek puffed from a beating. Their eyes had met for an instant that night. Someone had dropped a bottle of milk on the sidewalk. And they both had to walk around it. And she had offered a hopeless little smile of invitation ...

The pinnacle of ice and rock was closer. Gaining on it. How far? Mile away. Mile is 5,280 feet. Two feet to a pace. He counted. One ... two ... three ... There was a terrible pressure in his head, a vise at his temples, squeezing them together. He took off his helmet; and was stunned by the bleak embrace of the wind. Still the weight persisted. Every muscle screamed weariness. He felt he had no joints, that all his bones were working raw, one against another. Forty-five ... forty-six ... forty-seven ...

"Pat?" Skinhead, his drawn face a tight mask of parchment, was waiting for him at the bend of the road.

Pat didn't answer. His eyes were fixed on the rising mountain of ice. It was a first goal. And he counted as one foot fell and then the other. "Closer," he muttered. "Fifty-nine ... sixty ... sixty-one ..."

"Pat!" The battalion commander stared with bleary, bloodshot eyes. He shook him. "Pat!"

"Huh?"

"Not much farther." Skinhead licked his puffed, chapped lips. "Navy's shelling perimeter to keep Chinks off us. Army set up to let us come through. Only one thing ..."

"Eighty-nine ... ninety ... ninety-one ..."

"You hear me?" Spittle had frozen in the creases at the corners of his mouth. "Pat!"

"All right," Pat said, whining in annoyance. He had to keep counting, and he strained to hold the last number in his mind while he answered. It seemed all-important that he not lose count. "Ninety-two ... ninety-three ..."

"That big hill"—Skinhead pointed to the landmark Pat had been watching for more than two hours—"Few Chinks, maybe a dozen holding it." He spoke in brief rushes, sucking his breath between phrases. "Planes can't catch 'em in open. Whole division tries to run the gauntlet, and maybe there are mortar observers up there ... Those few'll give us ... trouble ... bad trouble. Have to—Pat! Dammit, listen to me!"

"Listening." He was still counting. "One nineteen," he whispered. "One twenty ... one twenty-one ..."

"Have to send someone up there, clean out Chinks."

"Yes." He could hear Skinhead, and wondered what he was talking about. But it was merely noise in his ear, an interruption. "One thirty-three ... thirty ... thirty-four ..."

"Baker and Charlie ... in pretty bad shape."

"Everybody ..." He rolled his neck on his shoulders, biting his lips to still the gasp of pain. "Damn! Lost count."

"What? Count what?"

"Paces."

Skinhead stopped him, turned him around, reaching up to grasp his shoulders. "We've got to send ... people up there. And Baker and Charlie ..."

Now Pat caught the sense for the first time, and was shocked awake. It could not be. Out of the whole division, surely some other company ... He's not going to ask ... He's not! His mind, like a frantic spider, spun out filaments of hope too weak to support reality. Impossible. You might beat the men, curse them, threaten them, shoot them like animals. You might leave them to freeze or drag them by their heels. But you could ask no more of them. They had gone for days without sleep, without warmth or shelter or hot food or decent water, without rest. To climb a mountain, to assault the enemy—sheer lunacy. Why us? he thought. "God in heaven ..." he said at last.

They looked at each other. And in that instant, each saw deep into the other's mind. Each knew the other's thoughts. "Somebody's got to do it," Skinhead said, answering the question Pat had yet to ask.

He nodded, feebly, like a sick old man. "Signals ... we'll need signals ..."

Pat ordered each platoon to send fifteen of its best men. They reported. Forty-five marines—muffled in rags and tatters, wasted, pinched and worn—stood on the opposite side of the road, shivering, stamping their feet, leaning, half-asleep, on their weapons.

He cleared his throat. He wanted his voice to give no hint of his own doubt or fear or fatigue. "Need volunteers. Thirty men. While division moves the long way on road, we'll short-cut, straight to that hill over there. By time column winds around under it, we'll be on top, holding it"—he paused to catch his breath, scratched violently at the stubble on his frozen cheeks—"holding it so our people can pass under. Then we'll come down the other side ... join rear guard. Those of you want to go, fall out behind me."

No one moved. Chuck Cagle, holding himself erect by grasping the tail gate of a truck, made a noise in his throat, as if he were struck dumb. It could not be done, he thought. Just to climb it ... He wanted to protest, but he had no strength even for anger. Besides, he knew Pat needed him, and he would be unable to respond. Pain riddled the pit of his stomach; and he ground his teeth together, enduring the cramp, praying for it to pass.

Sanchez leaned on his rifle, swayed, his eyes closed. Too near now. Too near to take a chance. He had plans. A fresh start, away from everything he hated, away from all the mistakes he had made. More than luck had kept him going, he knew. More, even, than the captain's firm, strong hand and his calm voice amid chaos. It was God who had sustained him. Despite his blasphemy, despite his sins against Him. Soon's I get to a padre, he thought, going to confession. Get absolution. Do my penance. Start fresh. And Colombia is warm ...

Beside him, Woody Dorn, the 300 radio propped at his feet, watched his friend's face, then looked at the captain and read the utter despair in his apparently steady voice. He felt an allegiance to both men. But he could identify more closely with the captain. So often, in a stark moment of decision, he had glimpsed that haggard face and seen the suffering there when men lay dying ... I'd go with him, he assured himself. But not gonna leave Goat. Got plans. Gonna make it out. It's gonna be, after all ... He had never really believed he would have a farm, would go to South America, would have a friend beside him. But now ... now it was possible. It could happen ...

Justus and Firesteen had their backs turned. "Oughta go," the corporal whispered. "He's askin' us ... could order us if he wanted.

... He's askin' ... Must be beat worse than any of us ... never sits down ... not off his feet since we left Koto ... and carryin' my pack ... and the way he came out to that gun when they had us ...

"Be a *smuck!*" Lock said fiercely. "Y'gotta wife t' think 'bout, kid in the oven... He drew his crusty tongue over his teeth and spat, but nothing came. "Hope to die, Mel, I'd go ... I'd give an eye to that feller if'n he needed it ... but I got a awful feelin' ... they'll kill me up there ..."

Huckabee scraped at the caked blood on his gloves. His mind was speeding. He tried to slow it. It was the same sensation a man has after driving for hours on a highway, the feeling that he's still moving though he's really standing still. No sense my going, he thought. Don't need me. Couldn't help if a man got hit up there. But without being able to define it, he believed he owed a debt to the captain. Long after The Horse had argued with him weeks before, long after he had forgotten his words, he remembered that the captain had given him responsibility, not to prove something, but given it naturally, because it was his right. Perhaps it had all been inadvertent, but it had opened a door for him.

Cagle stamped across the road, swinging his arms. "Captain, you get these— these knuckleheads in uniform of the day, make them shine their shoes, I'll—I'll run them up that hill." There was no laughter. He turned on the men. "You characters get a whiff of me, you'll keep moving!" Still no response.

"I'm taking them," Pat said. "Leaving you in command on the road."

It had only been a gesture; everyone knew it. Cagle did not protest. "Aye, aye, sir."

Getting up from the snowbank where he had been resting, Choy trudged over toward the group of men. Pat stood there, immobile, waiting for his volunteers. It was not like Anderson, Choy mused. Anderson would have had them on the move already. Yet, it was strange, although he would have admired Anderson, he would have remained an observer, divorced from it all. It was not so with the captain. For some reason he could not understand, it mattered to him that this man should succeed. He is all that is weak and soft and empty-headed in Americans, he thought. And still ... Still he is all that distinguishes them from the enemy. He has decency and honor and an implausible strength in crisis and childlike gentleness and the capacity ... the capacity to love. The interpreter dropped his pack, picked up his weapon, and crossed the road to stand beside the captain.

A long moment passed, and Choy was still the only man who had responded. "Not you," Pat said. "Thanks. But ... there's no reason for you to go."

Choy slung his carbine. "You cannot go alone."

Sanchez was pounding the butt of his rifle against the packed snow. He looked up. "Able Company's always gettin' the crap end of the stick," he said angrily. "Always gettin' the shaft. They got it in for us?"

"Somebody's got to do it," Pat said.

"But all the goddamn' time!"

"Somebody ... Somebody's got to do it," Pat repeated. He had no other answer for him. He could not pretend there was justice or equity ... or even sanity in what he was asking of them. "I need you," he said to his men.

"Here goes nothin'," Lock said disgustedly, and joined Pat and Choy.

Firesteen followed.

Two more. Four more.

"What the hell," Sanchez said, grumbling. He entrusted his souvenirs to Cagle and shuffled over to stand with the others.

Dorn was at his heels.

Huckabee was next.

"You're needed here," Pat told him.

"I want to go, sir."

"All right." When he turned to the others again, all forty-five of them had crossed the road and shouldered their weapons. He selected thirty men, organized them into three squads, gave a brief order. They trailed behind him as he started down the road, past the stalled column.

"Take it easy, you wedgeass pogues," Lock said, taunting the marines who watched them. "Like usual, Able Company's doin' yer fightin' fer you."

It's my penance, Sanchez told himself. Climbing that damn thing's my penance. "Tell ya somethin'," he said to Dorn. "There better not be one damn' mountain in Colombia ... Better be flat ... like a—a—"

"Like a table?"

"Yeah, like a table."

They left the road and struggled across a frozen paddy until the steep slope of the pinnacle rose only a hundred yards away. The valley was shaped like a football stadium, with the platoon advancing from the goal line, and the enemy waiting high in the end-zone stands. "I got a horrible feelin'," Lock told Firesteen. "Like I'll never come off'n that hill," he whispered. His eyes were cloudy with fear.

"That's crazy."

"I jus' know it."

"Only God knows when you're gonna get it. Only God." *Who will live,* he thought. *And who will die ... who by fire ... and who by the sword ...* Had to come. I had to, he told himself. It's all decided anyway. If it's today ... was it the eleventh? ... *eleventh of December* ... or if it's on the road or on that hill ... or if it's in bed when I'm seventy ... all decided.

Huckabee worked his way up the line. "Anybody gets hit, stay put. Don't yell or anythin'. I'll get to you. Remember that," he said, cautioning them. "Anybody get's hit ..."

They began the climb, dragging themselves up the dizzy steepness of a narrow path, clinging to hand holds in the thick-ribbed ice, pulling, boosting one another over outcropping rock, through powdery snow, over razor-sharp shale that left knees bloody. They wallowed in drifts. No one spoke. A grunt, a cough, a gasp, the crumbling of ice underfoot—these were the only sounds. Each man, moving in a ghastly ballet of follow-the-leader, fought his own battle with fatigue. Pat gave no orders. He took a step; and every man behind him parroted the movement. He stopped to gauge distance and direction. They stopped, looking blankly at him. He sat, allowing himself a timed minute of rest. They too sat. He crawled as their goal neared. They crawled after him. He waited, eyes closed, head canted forward, straining for the sound of the enemy. They too stood and listened. But the only enemy confronting them was the great mount of snow and rock on the crest of the hill. It had to be conquered. A yard at a time.

Pat looked at his watch. The glass was coated with ice; and he breathed on it and rubbed it clear. Only an hour had passed, an unbelievably long hour. And no sign of the Chinese. The advance guard of the division would be following the long, winding course, drawing closer to the opposite side of this last barrier, expecting the signal that would send them by to safety. Must hurry, he thought. His throat was burning, and when he breathed there was a deep rattle in his chest. He stood outside himself, watching his own body fumble and start, fail and try again. And then his mind revolted. Each motion and plan and thought came slowly, and was examined while other thoughts crowded in on it.

They had reached the place for assault. Thirty feet above was a shelf of rock where the enemy, with infinite patience, must be waiting. Glistering above it was the forbidding needle. Like a candle in a saucer. But no flame from the candle. Enemy. Maybe no enemy. Maybe planes killed them. How far to go? Yards ... depth-perception test and you pull two sticks, line up with strings ... Assault, that's it. Grenades. Then run up. My God! Run. Can dead men run? We are dead and in a frozen hell, damned to climb forever, to see nothing and feel nothing and hear nothing ... *to walk for a ... certain time upon the earth ...* Read that. Where? What the hell's the difference? Go on. If they're up there, would have picked us off long ago ... For an instant, Pat clung to that hope. Then it melted away, and his muddled brain fumbled with something else. Chinks freezing. Cold. Like us. As cold as we are. Scared. Sitting up there scared. Know we're coming to get them. And scared. Of us. He laughed. But it was voiceless.

Think one-two-three. One: Take grenade. Two: No, one still. One: Move lead squad on line for assault. (But if Chinks are up there ...) Keep mind on one thing at time! Think one-two-three. One: On line for assault. Two: Two ... two ... Grenades ready. Throw. Three: Up. Stand, move when grenades go. Every gun blazing. Rapid fire. (Weapons work?)

Exerting himself over each detail, he motioned for Firesteen, mumbled the order, one-two-three, made the corporal repeat it until, on the fourth try, he got it right. Pat got to his knees, tightened his fist about the handle of his grenade, pulled the pin, saw every other man in the assault squad was ready. Then, on his feet, he lobbed the grenade. The others tossed theirs. He was up and going forward, holding Goober's Tommy gun before him, firing blindly. No reply from the enemy. "Keep going," he called, "keep moving!" They reached the embankment, the last bit of cover. Now! Surely now we'll run into them. They'll hit us now. He clambered over, still sweeping with his weapon, still expecting to be struck down at any moment. He crawled onto the flat saucer of snow and ice. There before him were three dead men, stretched behind a Chinese gun. And that was all.

The marines collapsed in the snow. Pat lay with his face pressed against his hands, shaking with cold and with relief, fighting for breath. He looked up at the lone needle of rock, rising sixty feet above. Then he glanced around him. Choy was a few yards away, sprawled on his back, his mouth open, panting. Huckabee was crawling the thirty yards to the far side of the saucer where he could look down on the road. Firesteen was on his knees, bent over, holding his stomach, retching. Sanchez and Justus were behind him. When Pat tried to move his leg, he found that Dorn was holding his boot as if his hands were frozen fast to it.

For nothing, he thought. All for nothing. Chinks dead. Planes did get them. And we climbed ... Now to signal. And then the road again. God! Will we ever get down? To move ... even to move! He had a wild desire to laugh, to hear his voice. But only a muffled gasp came out, and then his body was racked as he sobbed out his tension.

Sanchez was on his knees. " '... but deliver us from evil, for ...' "

The rest of the men dragged themselves over the rocks behind them. Pat turned and saw their fleeting expressions of disbelief before they, too, fell to the snow. No enemy. Safe. Prodded by habit, he spoke to his squad leaders. "All-round security ..." But they did not hear, or could not act if they did. They lay where they had dropped. And since he could not bring himself to stand, he could not order them to.

Huckabee called to him from across the clearing. "Can see division now. Comin' to this side. 'Bout four hundred yards ..."

Pat crawled to Justus on his hands and knees and reached for the smoke grenade he carried. Lock glanced at him, but did not help him get it, allowing himself to be turned over and the grenade taken from his belt.

"I do it, Skipper?" Sanchez, blinking at him, was still on his knees. "Let me." Pat nodded. Taking the grenade, Sanchez went toward Huckabee, to give the signal that the area was clear. He stopped beside one of the Chinese bodies, bent down. "Hot damn. Officer." He pulled a black notebook from the man's pocket, held it for the others to see. "Diary. Bet you." He put it in his parka and walked to the ledge where Huckabee was waiting. Pat made it over to him. They looked down at the road, a thousand feet below. Sanchez dropped the grenade. The handle pinged away. A red cloud billowed over the white mantle of the hill, signaling the division to safe passage.

There was a clattering, like pebbles on glass from above. Then a sharp spurt of blue light, and a cacophony of explosions. Pat fell, with Huckabee and Sanchez, behind a boulder. From the needle point of rock above, hidden guns swept the flat area. The marines searched frantically for what little cover there was. The enemy, watching from their vantage point, had them all under fire. They had watched them make the ascent, waited for them to signal. They had invited them into the trap. And now the division was moving into the avenue below, where mortars and artillery would pummel them at will.

Across the clearing, Pat saw one marine hit, saw him begin to roll back, clawing at the air. Choy dived for him, caught him as he hung precariously over the ledge.

Another man was hit. Another. There were no screams. Only the whimper of wounded. He felt he must go to his men. Isolated by thirty yards and the comparative safety of the boulder, he felt like an observer at an execution. So now it was all over. This was how it ended. Just like the Chinese they had cornered, he thought. Where was it? ... Cornered, and sealed in a cave ... and Wally had cursed them because they were warm ...

His men were going down on every side. One was fully exposed, unmindful of the scene around him. He held his bloody hands to his face and stood there, wobbling. Huckabee climbed over Pat and Sanchez. Then, moving with painful precision, in what seemed like slow motion, he crossed the area, tackled the marine and dragged him to the flimsy cover of a snowbank.

No chance. No chance. Another marine went down. They were not even returning the fire. They had no target. The enemy was lodged above, protected by the pinnacle of rock. Another hail of grenades rolled down from the heights and exploded among his men. Nowhere to go. No place to hide, no concealment at all. Fish in a barrel. To fall back was impossible; the flanks were closed to them. They rushed from one embankment, from one meager pile of rock to the next, all around the circle of the saucer; and fire from above followed them. *Rackarackaracka!* The sound was so familiar it seemed almost friendly.

"Skipper!" Sanchez rolled toward Pat. He held his torn and bleeding shoulder. "Hit. Holy Mary, Mother of God, I'm hit!"

Pat crouched over him, began to fumble with the wound, trying to stanch the flow of crimson that spurted over his hands, drenching the snow. But his eyes were fixed on the carnage all about him. "Lie still, Goat. Lie still. Lie still ... still ..." It was all he could think of to say. Only two minutes had elapsed since the enemy unleashed its first grenades, but the time seemed even longer than the agonizing climb up the mountain. Do something. Take charge. Help them. He tried to shout, but his voice was lost in the rattle of enemy fire. Only one thing to do. Get up. Go up the pinnacle. Take the path. But at least sixty yards ... and into the face of their guns ... Try. Try! He pushed up on his elbows, exposing his head and shoulders.

Sanchez lifted his rifle. "I'm with you," he muttered, already knowing what Pat intended. "Let's ... go." He rolled over the rock, was on his feet, bent over his weapon, blood streaming down his arm. He turned toward the pinnacle path, and was cut down.

Pat screamed. Anger surged in him, and lust and hatred such as he had never known. He felt the throb of his pulses. Blood rushed through him, filling him, choking him with savage rage and fury, endowing his weak and trembling body with immeasurable strength and courage. He was up, running for the steep path that lead to the needle above. And he was yelling, a shrill bellow of vengeance that rose above the noises of battle. His body hurtled forward; his feet were on the narrow pathway. He saw it through the tears that clouded his vision. Kill. Kill. No caution. No fear. No plan. No weakness. No cold. No pain. No future. Only the need of the moment, the need to fight back, the obsession to do murder. He had a swift vision of Andy: "Semper Fi! Semper Fi!" He was alone, but still moving. Then, behind him, he heard the others charging.

Dorn was suddenly firing beside him as they tumbled up the winding path. And then Justus, heaving grenades. Firesteen's roar as he yelled to his men. The top. One Chinese stood in the path, firing steadily. Pat dropped him with two shots. And then they were in the bowl at the pinnacle's summit. Nine Chinese and five marines. No room for more. Pat swung his empty Tommy gun, knocked an enemy soldier to the ground, shot him with his pistol. In his dying agony, the man clutched his legs. Quivering with fury, Pat kicked him savagely away. He killed a third man, firing directly into his face. Another jumped on his back from behind. Pat went down, throwing the enemy over his shoulders. He smashed the face over and over and over again with the butt of the Tommy gun.

Then it was over; utterly silent. Sanity and a sensation of sickness engulfed him. He leaned against a rock and looked about him. Firesteen, Dorn, Justus, and Choy lay on their backs among the enemy, covered with enemy blood. He slipped down beside them, going from one to another, assuring himself that they were alive. They stared at the sky, or groaned, or coughed, too exhausted to speak or move. He found another marine. Dead. A boy's face, serene, untroubled, unmarked by suffering. Pat's shaking hand caressed the face, and found the tiny puncture behind the ear.

He stood, remembering Sanchez. He started down the path, tripped and careened down the ice, not even attempting to arrest his fall. At the bottom, on the saucer again, he righted himself. Huckabee sat beside Jesus Sanchez. "You okay, fella?" Pat whispered, bending over him. "You got us going," he said. "Thanks. You got us going ..."

Huckabee was tugging at Pat's collar, talking to him. "He's dead. Sir, he's dead. Nothing I could do." Through all the horror and brutality of the past weeks, the corpsman had been calm, efficient, ruthlessly concerned only with the living. Now he could contain himself no longer. His head fell on Pat's knees and his whole body heaved.

Below them the ten-mile train of the division passed unmolested. The advance guard was already out of sight. The rear guard was still coming down from the foothills.

They lifted Jesus Sanchez's body; and Chuck Cagle and Huckabee bound him with parachute cord to the barrel of a 155 gun. He was frozen in the spread-eagled position in which he had fallen. Miles away, the forward elements of the division were entering Hungnam. The rear guard moved again.

Woody Dorn, bewildered, silent, stumbled along beside Sanchez's body. He had gathered his friend's souvenirs and he refused to part with them. The fabric of his life was so woven with defeat that he had voiced no protest, shed no tears. It was as if he had expected what had taken place. He took the diary Sanchez had found, held it clutched to his chest mile after mile. At last, he handed it to Choy. "Read it, please."

"Another time."

"Now."

"Doctor's callin' me," Huckabee said. "Do like he wants, Choy."

"Captain? Tell him to. Want him to read for me."

Pat had dropped off the truck ahead after examining his wounded. It took him a long time to catch his breath, to understand what Dorn wanted. "Choy? How about it?"

The Korean opened the diary. " 'The wind is cold this day ...' " He nodded. "And then there is something I cannot read." His brows lifted. " '... enemy is colder than we. And have no will to fight. Want only to escape. Run before us.' And then more I do not understand."

'Read it," Dorn begged.

Choy glanced at Pat, then turned to the diary again. He read in a hoarse monotone, as if the words were meaningless... they do not believe in their cause. We are ready to die for ours. They are weak amidst plenty. We are strong amidst want. Our bravery ... and our will ... have triumphed over their machines and their gold. They have spent themselves in living, and do not know how to die.' " He sighed. Here was the gist of all he had said in argument with the Americans. "I have told you all this," he said to Pat.

Dorn, lost in a stupor, said, "Don't understand." Then, with the passionate intensity of grief and youth, he grasped the stiff, clawing fingers of his friend.

The interpreter flipped through the pages to the last entry. " 'It is said by our leader that our people will take courage from our glory and our feats. Then, renewed, they will know greatness. But who among the people knows the soldier's war? Who among the people draws strength or wisdom from the soldier's sacrifice? Perhaps it will be so. And in my time. For death waits patiently. It can shatter plan and purpose, deny hope ... The days of youth are brief.' " Putting the diary in Dorn's pocket, Choy said, mumbling, " 'Who among the people ...'" He had spun out his bitterness for so long. And now the threads were used up. His confused mind could not reassess the men around him. He knew only that nearly sixty frozen miles were behind them, that they had fought an epic battle, a battle more lonely and dreadful than the retreat from Moscow, bloodier than Chickamauga, more intense than Belleau Wood, more futile than The Bulge, more furious than Tarawa. Already the legend was written on their faces. What was it that had changed? The men? Or his understanding of them? They are beaten, he reminded himself, as I knew they would be. Beaten. But why was he not convinced? "It has happened, Captain," he said, almost wistfully. "I told you. It is the enemy who has prevailed."

Pat did not bother to answer. Even his dazed and sluggish mind could reason that Choy was wrong, had always been wrong, and that the Korean knew he was wrong. Because the qualities that had made America strong were not lost. Submerged, perhaps. The need brought them to the surface. They had only to be recognized, encouraged, appreciated ... Was that the only meaning, the only hope he could wring from the tragedy of defeat and suffering?

They could hear the Navy's guns firing off in the distance. And they smelled the sea. They saw the level road before them, watched placidly while hundreds of the enemy surrendered and joined the column, begging for food.

A jeep moved toward them, hugging the shoulder of the road. An aging, red-faced man got out. He wore a correspondent's insignia. He walked back among the men, offering oranges, talking to them. He spoke to Lock Justus. "Where are you from, marine?" No answer. "You're the last ones in, son. Pretty bad up there?" He held out a piece of fruit.

"Bad enough."

"Lose some buddies?" Lock did not reply. He frowned, held out his hand for the orange. The correspondent gave it to him. "Haven't had a hot meal in how long?" Lock shook his head. "Terrible experience, wasn't it?" Lock was trying to bite into the fruit, but lacked the strength. The correspondent took it from him, bit away the peeling and squeezed it so the juice bubbled up. Lock seized it, sucked thirstily. "Think you were going to make it, son?"

Lock sighed, and his whole body shivered. "Yeah."

"Why?"

Lock stared at him, as if seeing him for the first time. Again, he shook his head dumbly.

"I've been talking to the men since the division started coming in," the correspondent said gently. "All of them say they knew they'd make it. Some because of the planes, some because of their officers, some because"—he smiled, touched Lock's arm in a comradely gesture—"because marines are never licked." Still getting no answer, he urged, "What about you? Why do you think you made it?"

Tearing the orange in half, Lock chewed, spat seeds as he shuffled slowly along. "I dunno," he said at last.

"Sure you do. Tell me, what do you think of this lousy war, anyway?"

Lock rubbed his eyes. "Huh?"

"I said, 'What do you think of this war?' "

Lock considered the question gravely. "Better than no war at all, I reckon."

The correspondent walked beside Pat. "You hear that guy? Where n hell do you marines dig up guys like that?"

It was a question Pat had asked himself so many times during the past weeks. Where did they come from? What made them the way hey were? Even now, he knew, they did not believe they had been defeated. What chemistry had worked the miracle of their survival? The elements could not be broken down, isolated, catalogued. Only one thing ... one thing. They believed. They believed in the invincibility of their Corps ... and in one another.

The correspondent was speaking again, watching Pat's face for a flicker of animation, some hint that he was listening. "All this," he aid, his arms outstretched as if he could encompass the whole wretched procession, "all this ... and for what, Captain?"

Pat glanced at him, feeling sorry for the man. He seemed like a stranger at a funeral. Even his obvious sincerity and warmth were out of place, alien. Pat could think of nothing to say to him.

"A hell of an end for a crusade, huh?" His eyes caught Pat's gaze and held it. "The crusade ... to stop the Reds," he said bitterly. "You're up to your neck in it, huh, Captain?"

"Somebody's got to do it," Pat heard his own strange voice saying.

Surprised to hear him speak, the correspondent leaned closer to him. "What? Didn't get that. Somebody's got to do what?"

Pat did not answer; his numbed mind was wrestling with the words he had spoken without thought. Then: "Somebody's got to do it," he repeated. It seemed to him that the whole scene had been lived through long before, that he had heard those words long before, even said them long before ... Skinhead had told him that ... And he had used the same words to answer Sanchez before they scaled that last terrifying mountain. Standing there on the road, half-frozen, only half-conscious, Pat grappled with a profound discovery. Not simple. Not a cliché. But something that had to be learned, part of becoming a whole man ... *Somebody's got to do it.* Always, somewhere, somebody has to take the ridge, has to struggle and fight and maybe die for all the rest, for the weak and the fearful and the selfish and the ignorant and the unaware.

The correspondent was staring at him; and Pat looked away. Raised before him he saw Jesus Sanchez's body, pinioned to the upturned gun barrel, canted against the sky. And Woody Dorn walking alongside. And there were Firesteen ... and Justus ... and Huckabee ... and Cagle. Their arms were raised, beckoning him. "Skipper!" The single word came back over thirty yards as if from a great distance.

"Here!" Pat said, straining to lift his voice. Then, clearly: "I'm coming!" He went forward, down the straightening road, to join his men.